5/18
D0595302
BOARDWALK
SUMMER

INCLUDES

FIFTEENTH SUMMER AND *SIXTEENTH SUMMER*

SIMON PULSE

NEW YORK LONDON TORONTO SYDNEY NEW DELHI

This book is a work of fiction. Any references to historical events, real people, or real places are used fictitiously. Other names, characters, places, and events are products of the author's imagination, and any resemblance to actual events or places or persons, living or dead, is entirely coincidental.

SIMON PULSE
An imprint of Simon & Schuster Children's Publishing Division
1230 Avenue of the Americas, New York, New York 10020
This Simon Pulse paperback edition May 2018

Cover designed by Nina Simoneaux
Interior designed by Karina Granda and Nina Simoneaux
The text of this book was set in Berling.
Manufactured in the United States of America
2 4 6 8 10 9 7 5 3 1
Library of Congress Control Number 2017949967
ISBN 978-1-5344-1432-7 (pbk)
ISBN 978-1-4424-7268-6 (*Fifteenth Summer* eBook)
ISBN 978-1-4424-2345-9 (*Sixteenth Summer* eBook)
These titles were previously published individually.

Fifteenth Summer

For Paul, Mira, and Tali, for all seasons

With special thanks to Elizabeth Lenhard

June

When you're stuck in the backseat of your parents' car—on hour twenty-five of the drive from Los Angeles to Bluepointe, Michigan—the last thing you're thinking about is love.

But somehow that's what my two sisters were discussing. They chatted over my head as if I was no more than an armrest between them.

Actually, it's a stretch to say they were talking about *love.* They were really talking about boys. The boys of Bluepointe. Two of them in particular.

"Liam," Hannah breathed. She propped her feet on the hump in the middle of the backseat, even though that was clearly *my* personal space. "That was my guy's name, remember? We saw him at the beach at least four times, and the last two, he definitely noticed me. Now, which one was yours?"

"You know," Abbie said impatiently. She did most things impatiently. "The guy who worked at the market. That boy could *shelve.*"

I snorted while Hannah said, "Well, did you ever talk to him? Was he interested? What was his name?"

Hannah always liked to have all her facts straight.

"John," Abbie answered, nodding firmly as she stared out the car window. Then she frowned and clicked one of her short, unpainted fingernails against her front teeth. "Or . . . James? It was definitely John or James or . . . Jason? Ugh, I can't remember."

"If you were a boy," my dad chimed from the front seat, where he had the car on cruise control at exactly sixty-five miles per hour, "we were going to name you Horatio. No one *ever* forgets the name Horatio."

My dad thinks he's hilarious. And because he works from home, doing other people's taxes, he's around a *lot* to subject us to all his one-liners. My mom is the only one who doesn't roll her eyes at every joke. She even laughs at some of them. Dad always says that's why they're still married. That and the fact that my mom is super-practical with money, which is very romantic to an accountant. All it meant to me was that I had to babysit to earn every paltry dollar of my spending money.

I sighed and glanced at the novel in my lap. That book—the latest dystopian bestseller—was torturing me. I was dying to read it, but every time I did, I got carsick. I was still feeling a little green after reading two irresistible pages (two words: "prison break") twenty minutes earlier.

Texting with my best friend, Emma, made me feel slightly less queasy.

Ugh. Today is the shortest drive of our trip but it's the most soul-killing. I feel like it will NEVER. END. And why do I always get the middle seat?

BECAUSE YOU'RE THE YOUNGEST. BE GLAD THEY DIDN'T PUT YOU IN THE TRUNK.

Don't gloat cuz you're an only child.

. . .

Are you texting with Ethan right now?!?

HOW'D YOU KNOW?

I can tell your palms are sweaty. Plus there are the long delays.

HAR-HAR. YOU KNOW BALLERINAS DON'T SWEAT.

Uh-huh. Even when they're sending mash notes to their boyfriends?

. . .

Hello?

GOT TO GO TO CLASS. LUV U! AND ETHAN SAYS HI. ;-)

Ethan was Emma's boyfriend of two weeks. And class was at "the Intensive," which is this hard-core, fast-track-to-prima-ballerina summer program at the LA Ballet. All spring Emma had talked about nothing else. She'd angsted about her floppy fouettés and worried that she'd be too tall for the boys to partner. She'd wondered if the *mesdames* would be harsh and beautiful, like the ballet teachers on *Fame*, and she'd considered cutting off all her hair to make herself stand out.

But then Ethan Mack asked Emma to fast dance at our spring semiformal, and everything changed.

When it happened, I was already out on the dance floor (which was just our school gym floor covered with a puckery layer of black vinyl) with Dave Sugarman.

Dave was nice enough. He had a round, smooth face and one of those nondescript bodies that always seemed to be hidden inside clothes a size or two too big. He was in a couple of honors classes with me, so he was smart. I guessed. He never really spoke much in class.

He was, I thought, a tennis player. Either that or he did track and field.

Dave was perfectly nice.

But here's what Dave wasn't. He wasn't Mr. Darcy. Or Peeta Mellark. He wasn't even Michael Moscovitz.

And *they* were the boys I was searching for.

I don't mean I wanted an actual revolutionary hero or a guy with an English accent and ascot. (Okay, I wouldn't turn down the English accent.)

I didn't want the perfect boy either. We all know Mr. Darcy could be a total grump.

What I wanted was to *feel* like Lizzy and Katniss and Mia felt. And not because my boy was tall and broad-shouldered and blue-eyed. That wasn't how I pictured him. He wouldn't be everybody else's version of gorgeous. He would have a funny extra bounce in his walk or a cowlick in his hair. He would be super-shy. Or he'd have a too-loud laugh.

He would make me swoon for reasons that were mine alone. I just didn't know what those reasons were yet.

Dave Sugarman?

There was no swoon there. The most I could manage for him was an uncomfortable smile while we raised our arms over our heads and swished our hips around, throwing in the occasional clap or semi-grindy deep knee bend. When I glanced at the other couples nearby, I took comfort in the fact that they almost all looked as awkward and goofy as I felt.

There was one exception, though. Emma and Ethan. They seemed to fit together as neatly as their names.

Ethan was definitely tall enough to partner Emma. He put his hands on her waist and swung her around in graceful circles.

He held her hand over her head, and she improvised a triple pirouette before landing lightly on his chest. She turned and leaned back against him, and they shimmied from side to side as if they'd rehearsed it.

Do you even have to ask if their dance ended in a dip?

After the song ended, Dave gave me a little pat on the arm, then hustled back to his friends, who were pelting each other with M&M's.

But Ethan left the dance floor with Emma.

They headed directly outside, where, according to Emma, they leaned against the school and kissed for a full twenty minutes without coming up for air. That twenty minutes was all she needed to fall deeply, *deeply* in love.

Dancers are like that. One good dip, and they are *yours.*

After that, Emma stopped obsessing about the Intensive and started obsessing about her new boyfriend.

"Kissing Ethan," she told me one night after a long make-out session on Ethan's patio, "it's like ballet. My head disappears and I'm just a body."

"Wow," I said. I couldn't relate at all. Most of the time I felt like I was just the opposite—no body, all head.

"I mean, he kisses me and I just *melt,*" Emma went on. "It's like our bodies *fuse.*"

"Whoa," I said this time.

"Oh my God, not like *that,*" Emma said, reading my mind. "I'm just saying there's something about being mouth to mouth with someone for forty minutes . . ."

"You beat your record," I muttered.

"Yeah," Emma giggled. She hadn't caught the tiny touch of weariness in my voice. "Anyway, it's almost like you're touching each other's souls."

"Really?" I said. "Your souls? *Really?*"

"Really," she said with the utmost confidence.

I knew nothing of this soul-touching kind of kiss. The few kisses I'd had had been brief. And awkward. And, to tell the truth, kind of gross. I'd clearly been doing it wrong.

I was happy for Emma. But it felt weird to watch her join this club that I was *so* not a member of.

Before you became a member of this been-in-love club, life was murky, mysterious, and, most of all, small.

Post-love, I imagined, your world expanded with all the things you suddenly knew. You knew what it felt like to see a boy's name on your caller ID and suddenly feel like you were floating. You knew a boy's dreams and fears and memories. You knew what it was like to open the front door and feel a burst of elation because your boy was standing there.

You'd kissed that boy and felt like you were touching his soul.

I didn't know if Abbie had ever felt that way. She had a string of two-month relationships behind her. Almost every time, she'd been the one to break things off when the boy had gotten too attached.

But Hannah had definitely been there. She'd dated an older boy, Elias, for a year. Then he'd enrolled at UC Berkeley and had broken up with her to "focus on studying." Which Hannah had sort of understood, being a studious type herself. It was when Elias immediately hooked up with a girl from his dorm that he'd broken her heart.

She seemed to be completely recovered now, though.

"When's that sailboat race they have every year?" she was asking Abbie. She grabbed her sleek, white smart phone out of her bag. She'd gotten it for her eighteenth birthday in March. Abbie and I were bitterly jealous of it.

"It's probably sometime next week, right?" Hannah muttered, tapping away at the phone screen. "I'm sure we'll see them there. . . ."

"Hannah, honey," my mom said a little too brightly, "don't completely fill up your schedule. You know we want to spend some quality time with you this summer. I know you. Once you start classes in the fall, you'll work so hard, we'll never hear from you!"

"I know, Mom," Hannah said with the tiniest of sighs.

"I think my guy is a runner," Abbie said. "I could tell by his legs. So maybe he'll just *happen* to go running on the beach while *I* just happen to do my two miles in the lake, and one thing'll lead to another—"

"Abbie," I broke in, "do you really think hauling yourself out of Lake Michigan after swimming two miles is the best way to meet a boy? Who knows what you'll look like. You could have dune grass or seagull feathers in your hair. Yuck."

"Plus, there's the issue of your Speedo," Hannah pointed out. Like all competitive swimmers, Abbie snapped herself into a high-necked, long-legged black bodysuit for her distance swims. It made her look like a slick-skinned seal. A cute little bikini it was not.

Abbie put on her cocky Supergirl face.

"You know I look hot in my Speedo," she said.

Hannah and I glanced at each other, silently agreeing. Abbie's arms and legs were long and lean. She had a perma-tan that made her limbs almost glow. Her waist had been whittled down by eight million strokes of the Australian crawl. And while pool chlorine turned some swimmers' hair into yellow straw, Abbie's long, straight hair was dark brown and silky.

Clearly just the thought of swimming made Abbie antsy. She flung her perfect legs over mine and planted her feet in Hannah's lap.

"Hey!" Hannah and I protested together.

"I can't help it. I've gotta stretch. I'm dying in here!" Abbie groaned. She flopped her arm into the front seat and tapped my dad on the shoulder. "You guys, remind me why we got rid of the minivan again?"

"Other than the fact that it was a giant, ugly egg, you mean?" I asked. I had a dream of someday having a vintage car with giant tail fins, a pastel paint job, and wide, white leather seats.

Mom twisted in her seat to look at us with wistful eyes that she quickly whitewashed with one of her forcefully perky smiles.

"Abbie and Hannah, you're both driving now, and Chelsea will be next year too," she said, her voice sounding tinny and cheerful. "You girls don't need us to carpool you anymore. It was time for a grown-up car."

"Plus, this little guy gets fifty-one miles to the gallon," Dad said, giving the putty-colored dashboard a pat.

"'Little' is the operative word," I grumbled. "There's barely room for us, not to mention certain essential items."

"Are you still pouting that you couldn't bring that ridiculous box of books?" Abbie sighed.

"No," I said defensively.

By which, of course, I meant *yes.* Ever since my e-reader had been tragically destroyed, I'd had to revert to paper books. I'd spent *weeks* collecting enough of them to last me through the long Bluepointe summer, but at the last minute my mom had nixed my entire stash.

"We just don't have room in the car," she'd said as we were packing up. "Pick a few to throw into your backpack."

"A few? A *few* won't get me through Colorado," I'd complained.

"Well, maybe next time you try to prop your e-reader on the soap dish while you're showering," Mom had responded, "you'll think twice about it."

Which had caused Abbie to laugh so hard, she'd dropped a suitcase on her foot.

Hannah had been slightly more sympathetic. Probably because *she* got to bring all her books with her. She was starting her freshman year at the University of Chicago in September and had given herself a huge stack of summer reading to prepare.

Even now, as she gazed out the car window, Hannah was being scholarly.

"Dad, don't forget," she warned, "we've got to get off at exit forty-eight if we're going to the Ojibwa history museum."

"Ooh, arrowheads and pottery bowls," Abbie said. "Thrilling."

"Well, if you know how to look at them," Hannah said haughtily, "they are."

Now it was Abbie and I who sent each other a silent message in a glance: *Our sister is a super-nerd*. She'd already mapped out her future of a BA in biology and anthropology, followed by an MD-PhD. Then she was going to get the CDC to send her to some third world country where she'd cure malaria. Simple, right?

It didn't seem fair that, in addition to being ridiculously smart, Hannah was just as pretty as Abbie. She had the same coloring and same long willowy limbs, though her skin was less tan, her figure softer, and her shiny hair chopped into a chin-length bob.

Whenever anybody saw the three of us together, they assumed I was some distant cousin, because my skin was freckled and anything but golden, and my hair was red. *Bright* red. It was also very thick and *very* curly, just like my grandmother's. Until I was born, she was the only member of the family who had this crazy hair. . . .

As I thought about this now, with endless, flat Iowa skimming by outside the car window, I inhaled sharply. Something had just occurred to me for the first time.

Now *I* was the only one in the family with this crazy red hair.

My grandmother had a stroke early one morning in January.

I'd just woken up and had been walking down the hall to the bathroom. My dad had blocked my way to tell me the news.

"Granly's in a coma, sweetie," he told me. His eyes were red-rimmed, and his face looked pale and clammy beneath his early-morning scruff. "Her friend, Mrs. Berke, went to the cottage after she didn't show up for their breakfast date. You know Granly never locks the door. Mrs. Berke found her still in bed and called 911."

There was no sit-down, no soften-the-blow discussion about the circle of life. Dad just blurted it out.

I stared at him, completely baffled.

Through the open door of my parents' bedroom, I could see my mom frantically packing a suitcase. Hannah was in the bathroom, issuing updates: "Mom, I'm packing your toothbrush and your moisturizer, okay?"

And Abbie was curled up in my parents' bed, hugging a pillow.

"But she's gonna be okay, right?" Abbie cried. "She'll wake up, *right*?"

So that was why my poor dad had broken the news to me so bluntly. He'd already had to tell Hannah and Abbie.

My brain refused to register what had happened. The only thing I remember thinking at that moment was that I really had to pee.

After that I remember thinking I should call Granly to clear up this ridiculous rumor.

"I'm *fine*, Chelsea," she'd say with a laugh. "You know Mrs. Berke. She's an alarmist. She's the one who always used to wake her husband up in the middle of the night because she was sure that he was dead. And of course, he never *was*. Well, except for that last time . . ."

Then she'd laugh wickedly, and I'd say, "Granly!" and pretend to be shocked.

But of course that phone call never happened.

After Mrs. Berke called the ambulance, Granly was taken from Bluepointe to South Bend, Indiana, which was the closest city with a big hospital. My mom took the first flight out and spent an entire day and night at Granly's bedside, holding her hand. Then Granly's doctor told my mom that Granly *wasn't* going to wake up. My mom had followed Granly's living will and allowed her to die, which she did "peacefully" two days later.

Through it all, none of it felt real to me. Granly's number was still in my phone. I still had e-mails from her in my inbox. She was in at least half of the Silver family portraits that hung on our dining room wall. And in all those photos she was surrounded by the still-living. The irony was, she looked more alive than any of us in the pictures. She always seemed to be laughing, while the rest of us merely smiled.

Depending on the year the photo was taken, Granly's hair was either closely cropped or sproinging out wildly, but it was always the exact same glinting-penny red as mine. That's because when I was little, Granly snipped a lock of my hair and took it to her hairdresser.

"*Nobody* could get the color right until you came along," she told me after one of her triumphant trips to her salon. "Now I have the same hair I had when *I* was a girl. You should save some of your hair for you to use when you're old and gray like me. Red hair is really difficult, Chels."

"It *is* difficult," I agreed with a sigh. Of course, I'd meant it in a different way. I hated that my hair was as bright as a stoplight. I cringed when people assumed I had a fiery temper or was as hilarious as an *I Love Lucy* episode. And I resented Granly's *Anne of Green Gables* law (that law being that a redhead in pink was an abomination and completely undeserving of gentleman suitors).

So I kept my hair long, the better to pull it back into a tight, low ponytail or bun. And if I fell for a coral shift dress or peppermint-colored circle skirt at one of my favorite vintage shops, I bought it—Anne Shirley be damned.

Before Granly died, my hair had felt simply like an inconvenience, like being short or needing glasses. But now it seemed like this precious legacy, one I wasn't worthy of.

Thinking about this in the backseat of the car made me feel short of breath—not from carsickness but from panic.

To put it as bluntly as my dad had that morning in January, Granly's death had freaked me out. I knew that she was gone. I knew she was never again going to call me just to tell me some random, funny three-minute story. I knew that we'd never again pick her and her enormous, bright green suitcase up at the airport.

I *knew* this, but I couldn't quite bring myself to *believe* it. It just didn't feel possible that someone could exist and then—poof—not.

That was why I hadn't wanted to look at Granly in her casket before her graveside funeral service.

And it was why I really didn't want to spend this summer in Bluepointe.

We'd never stayed at Granly's cottage without her. The cottage *was* Granly.

When I was little, Granly had also had an apartment in Chicago.

That's where my mother grew up, spending weekends and summers at the cottage.

Granly's apartment had been filled with masculine mementos of my grandfather, who'd died before I was born. There'd been a big leather desk chair and serious Persian rugs and a half-empty armoire that had smelled like wood and citrus, like men's aftershave.

But Granly had decorated the cottage all for herself, and eventually she'd decided to live there full-time. The walls were butter yellow and pale blue, and the floorboards were bleached and pickled, as if they'd been made of driftwood. Every wall was a gallery of picture frames. She'd hung the same family portraits that we had in our house in LA, plus oil paintings, nudes drawn with breathy wisps of red Conté crayon, arty black-and-white photos, and, in the breakfast room, paint-blobbed kindergarten artwork by Hannah, Abbie, and me. She'd picked the fanciest frames of all for our "masterpieces." It was a gesture that had seemed kind of goofy when Granly was alive. Now that she wasn't, I cried every time I thought about her framing those sloppy paintings.

But apparently I was the only one who felt that way. My parents spent most of the drive through Nebraska debating whether to keep or sell the cottage, as if the decision should be made purely on the basis of property taxes and the cost of a new roof.

And when we were deep in Iowa, Hannah gazed out at the wall of cornstalks that edged the highway, and laughed suddenly.

"Remember Granly's garden?" she said.

"You mean the petting zoo?" Abbie replied with a laugh of her own. "Oh my God, it was like Granly sent engraved invitations to every deer and rabbit within a five-mile radius. 'Come eat my heirloom radishes!' They loved it."

"Well, it was her own fault," my dad said from the front seat. "She refused to build a fence or use any of those deer deterrents."

"Coyote pee!" Abbie snorted. "I mean, can you imagine Granly out there in her Audrey Hepburn sunglasses, spraying the stepping stones with coyote pee?"

"She wouldn't admit it, but you know she loved watching those deer walk by her window every morning. They were so pretty," Hannah said. "She didn't even *like* radishes. She just liked the idea of pulling them up and putting them in a pretty basket."

My mom shook her head and laughed a little. "That was *so* Granly."

"Wait a minute," I said quietly. "I didn't know Granly hated radishes. How did I not know that?"

Hannah shrugged lightly, then closed her eyes and flopped her head back. Clearly the subject of Granly's radishes didn't make her the slightest bit sad.

Meanwhile I was biting my lip to keep myself from bursting into tears.

I knew this was what we were supposed to do. We were supposed to talk about Granly and "keep her memory alive." Mrs. Berke had said that to me after Granly's funeral, before giving me an uncomfortable, hairspray-scented hug.

I didn't want to forget Granly, but I didn't really want to think about her either. Every time I did, I felt claustrophobic, the same way I feel every time I get on an elevator.

It's a well-known fact in my family that I'm a mess on an

elevator. My ears fill with static. I clench my fists, take shallow breaths, and stare intently at the doors until they open. When they do, I'm always the first one off. Then I have to inhale deeply for a few seconds before resuming normal human functioning.

I wondered if this whole summer in Bluepointe would feel like that. Without Granly there, would I ever be able to take that deep breath and move on?

We spent most of Illinois in silence because we were so hot. And cranky. And completely sick of each other. Hannah had even consented to skipping the Ojibwa museum in favor of just getting to Bluepointe—and out of the car—as soon as possible.

Just when I started contemplating something seriously drastic—like borrowing my mother's needlepoint—we began to follow the long, lazy curve around Lake Michigan. We couldn't see the lake from the expressway, but we could *feel* it there, waiting to welcome us back.

I'd always preferred Lake Michigan to the ocean. I liked that it was a moody, murky green. I liked that it was so big that the moon mistook it for an ocean, which meant it had waves. But not loud, show-offy Pacific Ocean–type waves. Just steady, soothing, unassuming undulations that you could float in for hours without feeling oversalted and beaten. Lake Michigan was like the ocean's underdog.

As we drove through Gary, Indiana, which was riddled with paper mills that spewed sulfurous plumes of smoke, I daydreamed about jumping into the lake. It would wash away the ickiness of too many fast-food french fries and too many gas station restrooms.

I pulled a pen and a little notepad out of my backpack. Lethargically I flipped past page after scribbled-on page until I found a blank one.

Gary, Indiana, I wrote in green ballpoint. *Our motto is, "The Smell of Rotten Eggs Is Character-Building!"*

What's it like to live with that smell in your pores, your tears, your breath? What's it like to smell a smell so much that you don't smell it anymore? But then you take a trip. You go to Chicago for the weekend. You go camping in the woods. You go to summer camp in Iowa, where the air smells like fresh corn. And you come back and realize that your hair, your clothes, the sheets on your bed, you, *smell like Gary, Indiana.*

I flipped my notebook closed and tossed it back into my pack. Then I breathed through my mouth until we reached Michigan.

Finally we pulled up in front of Granly's squat, shingled house on Sparrow Road and all limped out of the car. As my sisters groaned and stretched, I was stunned by the sudden wave of happiness that washed over me. The air smelled distinctly Bluepointe-ish—heavy and sweet with flowers, and pine needles, and the clean aftertaste of the two-blocks-away lake.

I tromped up the pea gravel drive to the screened-in front porch, where everything looked just the same as it always had. It was neatly furnished with deep-seated wicker rockers and a couch, lots of glass lanterns, and a big bowl full of shells from the lake.

My mom, already in to-do mode, bounced a big roller suitcase up the steps and joined me in the screened porch. She gave me a big grin before turning the knob of the front door.

It didn't turn.

It was locked.

Of course it was. My parents had probably locked the house up after the funeral. It made sense.

Mom shook her head and grinned at me again, but this time her smile was tight and her eyes looked a little shiny. She fumbled with her key chain for a moment before finding the right key.

Even though part of me didn't want to go into the cottage, I took a deep breath and went to stand next to my mom at the door. I pressed the side of my arm lightly against hers as she unlocked it.

Maybe it's mean to say, but it kind of helped me to realize that my mom might be in even more agony than I was at that moment, that she needed my support as much as I needed hers.

Mom opened the door, and I followed her in.

The air in the cottage felt still and stale, so my mom briskly started opening windows. I rolled her suitcase to the tiny bedroom my parents always used, then wandered back to the living room up front. I let my eyes skim over the framed watercolors of beach scenes and cozy cabins. I peered at the crowd of family photos on the mantel. I kicked off my flip-flops and padded across the nubbly braided rag rug and . . . continued to feel surprisingly okay!

Outside, Hannah was struggling to pull a big bag of shoes out of the back of the car, while Abbie lurched toward the house, dragging another suitcase behind her.

She spotted me through the open door and scowled.

"Why are *we* doing all the unpacking while you just stand there?" she said. "You're not allowed to crack one book until you've helped us unload."

I stomped to the screen door and said, "You're not the boss of me." Which made me feel about ten years old. But it was true! I couldn't *not* say it.

I also couldn't get away without helping, so I shuffled my feet back into my flip-flops and began hauling stuff from the car to the cottage.

I think we were all glad for the distracting bustle of unpacking. While Mom organized dry goods in the kitchen and Dad lined our beach shoes up on the screened porch, Abbie, Hannah, and I crammed into our room. Abbie and I were in the bunk beds, and Hannah had the twin bed near the window, with the slightly faded flower curtains Granly had bought at a local antiques shop.

"It's nice to be here," Hannah said, sounding as surprised as I felt.

"Well, yeah!" Abbie said. "*Thirty* hours in that car plus two nights in icky motels. It's cruel and inhumane, if you ask me."

"That's not what she meant," I said, frowning at Abbie.

Abbie looked down at her feet.

"I know what she meant," she said quietly.

That also made me feel better. So I *hadn't* been the only one freaking out about coming to the cottage. And I wasn't the only one feeling half-guilty, half-happy to be here.

I headed to the kitchen to see if Mom had unpacked the

bread and peanut butter yet. As I passed through the breakfast room, my gaze fell on the shelves holding Granly's egg cup collection.

Some people collect silver spoons or snow globes. Granly collected egg cups. Egg cups in graduated sizes painted like Matryoshka dolls. Egg cups shaped like rabbits, guinea pigs, and a mama kangaroo. (The egg sat in her pouch.) Egg cups made out of jade-colored glass and crackle-glazed ceramic and whittled wood.

Granly and I had had a breakfast ritual. She would boil water and put white bread in the toaster while I pondered the hundred or so egg cups. I would agonize over the choices. Did I want the shiny blue striped cup or the minimalist white one with the funny mustache? The cup bedazzled with pink jewels (always a popular choice, especially during my tween years) or the one made of hammered pewter?

By the time I'd made my decision, Granly would have fished our eggs out of the water and cut our buttered toast into narrow strips.

Then, pretending we were in a Jane Austen novel, we'd carefully *tap, tap, tap* the caps off our shells with tiny teaspoons and scoop the egg out in tiny bites, occasionally dipping our buttery toast strips into the yolk.

The secret I never told anyone was this: I did not like soft-boiled eggs. They were jiggly and runny in a way that made my stomach turn just a little bit. But I ate them with Granly (and with lots and lots of toast) because I loved the ritual of it. And I loved the just-us-ness of it. (Abbie and Hannah had made no secret of their loathing for soft-boiled eggs, so they never joined us.)

And, of course, I loved those egg cups, just as much as Granly did.

Looking at them now, I tried to remember which one Granly had bought on her trip to Moscow, and which was from Norway. Had Grandpa given her the *Make Way for Ducklings* cups for their anniversary or her birthday? Which had been her favorite?

My answer to each of these questions was, *I don't know.*

And now, I realized as tears began to roll down my cheeks, I never would.

I turned abruptly and headed for the back door. I slammed through it, swiping the tears from my face.

Out of the corner of my eye, I saw Granly's vegetable garden. It looked awful—so overgrown with weeds that I could barely see the neat brick border. The laminated signs Granly had made—TOMATOES, CUKES, SQUASH—had faded and tipped over.

I quickly turned away from the garden. That put me on the stepping stones, which led me to the road. A left turn would take me to the lake—a right, to town. And even though diving into the lake might have felt delicious, at that moment there was something else I needed even more.

I turned to the right.

"Uh, Chels?" my dad called from the screened porch. "Going somewhere?"

"I'm going to the library," I announced, hoping he couldn't hear the choke in my voice. "You didn't let me bring my books, and . . . and I need some."

My dad cocked his head and gave me a long look. I saw him lean toward the front steps, on the verge of coming over. If he did, he'd be close enough to see my pink-rimmed eyes and to say those dreaded words: "Want to talk about it?"

But here's the thing about my dad.

He may not get that his bad puns are really, *really* bad.

He may not understand that showing up somewhere in the right outfit is much more important than showing up on time.

But the guy lives with four women, and he knows when one of them needs to be left alone.

So he waved me off and said, "Be back before six. I'm cooking tonight."

I felt myself choke up again, partly because I was grateful to my dad and partly because I'd just pictured Granly's chair in the dining room.

How could I possibly eat next to Granly's empty chair?

At the moment it didn't seem to be an important question. Thinking about those soft-boiled eggs had killed my appetite.

A mile later I stood in front of the Bluepointe Public Library, sighing wearily.

I'd been coming to this library since I was a kid, but every summer it was freshly disappointing.

I wanted all libraries to be made of ivy-covered stone bricks, with tall, arched windows and creaky wooden floorboards. I wanted quiet, romantic staircases and window seats where you could read all day.

Bluepointe's library had none of these things. It was a squat single story, and it was made of sand-colored concrete that left scratches on your skin if you brushed up against it. The floors were covered in forest-green carpeting.

But the worst part about this library was its hours, in that there were hardly any of them. The place seemed to be open about four hours each morning. This being the afternoon, it was locked up tight.

I shoved my hands into the pockets of my cutoffs and found a couple scraps of paper I'd scribbled on in the car, as well as a wad of crumpled dollar bills that I'd forgotten about. I'd stuffed the money into my pocket that morning, thinking I'd want it for snacks on the road. But there are only so many stale corn nuts a girl can take, so I'd never used it.

I decided that if I couldn't get myself a book, at least I could get something cold to drink. The wooded road that led from the cottage to town had been shady and breezy, but now the sun felt scorchingly strong.

I headed for Main Street.

This was the one part of Bluepointe that looked just like it should. The storefronts all had big plate-glass windows and striped awnings, and above them were loft apartments owned by artists who hung burlap curtains in the windows and made sure everyone had a good view of their easels.

The first shop I passed was Ben Franklin, a this-and-that store that sold dusty stuff that wasn't supposed to exist anymore, like quilting supplies and shower caps and rainbow-colored glue that you could blow into balloons with a little red straw.

I smiled at the inflatable rafts, buckets, and shovels in the window. The store had the exact same display every summer. Each year it just grew more yellowed and saggy.

I also loved Estelle's, the art gallery a few doors down.

All the artists in town sold their stuff at Estelle's, *except* for the rotating roster of people that Estelle had decided to feud with. That was her thing. She loved to throw people out of the gallery, shaking her fist at them and making a big scene.

Today on the sidewalk in front of Estelle's, I spotted the Pop Guy and his gleaming silver freezer on wheels, complete with a rainbow-striped beach umbrella.

Unlike the Bluepointe librarians, the Pop Guy was *always* around. His frozen pops were famous for sounding weird but turning out to be delicious.

Perfect. By then I was parched.

But when I alighted in front of the Pop Guy's chalkboard menu, my heart sank a little bit.

BALSAMIC STRAWBERRY, GRAPEFRUIT MINT, AND LEMON ROSEMARY.

What was with all the herbs? I'm sure my parents would have swooned over these flavors, but to me they sounded like the names on bars of soap. I steeled myself for another bummer, until I came to the last item on the menu. Then I grinned.

"Raspberry Limeade," I said with relief. I handed him a few bills and said, "I'll have one of those, please."

"Nice safe choice there," the Pop Guy muttered as he dug into his steamy freezer. I would have been stung, but the Pop Guy was also famous for being a cranky food snob, so I just ducked my head to pull off the cellophane wrapper, and headed off.

Before I could get very far, though, the Pop Guy called after me, completely ignoring a cozy-looking couple who looked like they'd been just about to order.

"Hey, I've seen you here before, yeah?" he said. "I recognize that hair of yours. Been a while."

I nodded.

"Been a year," I said.

I thought back to the fourteen-year-old me the Pop Guy remembered.

That version of myself wouldn't have even caught the Pop Guy's dis. The insult would have skimmed over her head—most stuff that adults said did. The fourteen-year-old me had also been wearing her first underwire bra. She'd worn way too much frosty lip gloss, and she'd wanted nothing more than to have a sleepover with Emma every Saturday night.

And it had never occurred to her that her grandmother wouldn't be around forever, or at least until she was very old herself.

To the fifteen-year-old me, that fourteen-year-old seemed really, really young.

I did still like her taste in frozen treats, though. My herb-free pop was fabulous—almost as good as a dunk in Lake Michigan.

I strolled slowly up the sidewalk, pausing to peek into each familiar shop.

But then, on the corner of Main and Althorp, I spotted something that almost made me drop my pop in the gutter. Across the street, next door to Mel & Mel's Coffee Shop, where I'd been eating pie since I was a toddler, was something *new*.

There was *never* anything new in Bluepointe.

The sign over the door said DOG EAR in a funky typewriter font. Next to the name was a cartoon of a floppy-eared Labrador retriever. The dog was resting its chin on its front paws while it gazed at—

This was the part where I really did drop my pop, right onto my flip-flopped toes.

The dog was reading a book.

Which meant not only was there a new shop in Bluepointe, but it was my favorite kind of shop ever—the kind that sold books.

As I race-walked across the street, pausing only to shake the sticky raspberry juice from my feet, I tried to lower my expectations.

It could be a new age bookstore, I told myself. *All crystals and tarot cards and self-help books.*

Or worse, *I bet it's a pet store, with an entire* Dog Whisperer *book section and toy poodle outfits and liver-flavored cupcakes.*

I arrived at the bookstore and plunged through the door with so much breathless drama that the little bell on the door *clanged.* I could feel a dozen heads turn toward me.

"Welcome to Dog Ear!" said a woman behind the counter. She had long, gray-streaked hair that looked soft and pretty instead of scraggly and old. She looked small behind the stacks of books on the corner of the L-shaped counter. Propped against these stacks were little cards with paragraphs written in pink, orange, and lime-green ink.

"Grab something to read and a cookie," the woman told me with a warm, deeply dimpled smile. "We've got vanilla wafers today."

She gestured toward a lounge in the back corner of the shop.

Two people were already there, tucked into a faded blue couch, absorbed in books. At their feet was a huge black Labrador retriever. It must have been the dog on the sign. One of the readers, a woman in cuffed denim cutoffs just like mine, had her bare feet propped on the dog's ample back as if he were no more than a furry ottoman. She popped one vanilla wafer into her mouth and tossed another to the dog, who gulped it down with a loud smack.

On the lemon-yellow wall overlooking this little lounge was a gallery of amazingly detailed posters, each advertising a book signing and featuring a mash note from the author.

To the best little bookstore in town! And I'm not just saying that because you're the only bookstore in town. . . .

Tell E.B. he owes me my sandwich back. XOXO . . .

On the opposite side of the store, tucked behind a few rows of turquoise bookshelves, was a children's area enclosed by a tiny white picket fence. It had a fluffy green shag rug and beanbag chairs, plus a bright-red train engine, the perfect size for a toddler to climb into.

String after string of fairy lights swagged from the ceiling. Between the light strands dangled random stuff like a cardboard moon, a Chinese lantern, and a disco ball.

Normally I would have fallen on the bookshelves like a bear just out of hibernation. But I found that I couldn't quite move. Because when you walk into the bookstore you've always fantasized about but never thought could exist in real life, it kind of throws you. Some irrational part of me thought if I went any farther, or touched anything, it would all vaporize and I'd wake up from a dream.

When the woman at the counter started to look concerned, I did take a few stumbling steps forward.

I picked up one of the index cards propped against the books on the counter. Next to the book's title, someone had written: *A-minus. As you know, I rarely give out such a high grade. I read this book when I was recovering from a breakup. Yes, I know all of you were rooting for the breakup. Don't gloat, people. Anyway, next time somebody stomps on your heart, you should read this book. You'll hate the lead character for being much prettier than you, but you'll forgive her when she fails to make tenure at her hoity-toity liberal arts college.*

"Everyone who works here writes up little book reviews," the woman at the counter said, interrupting me. "That one's by Isobel. She's not here right now, so I can tell you . . ."

She shifted to a stage whisper.

"She's a bit of an oversharer."

I laughed.

"Good books will do that to you," I said.

"Oh, honey," the woman said, "Isobel doesn't need a good book to tell us the most appalling things about her personal life. She'll read the *weather report* and start spilling her guts."

This woman was talking to me in that frank way that middle-aged people only talked to other middle-aged people. Which made me feel both proud and paranoid. This couldn't all be for real, could it?

"Who *are* you?" I blurted. "I mean, um, when did this store open? It wasn't here the last time I was in Bluepointe."

"Do you like it?" the woman said with a conspiratorial grin.

"Good, 'cause it's mine! Well, my husband's and mine, but I do more of the day-to-day because he's a professor in Chicago. We're nearing our one-year birthday."

"I like it," I said as I continued to take it all in. Outside the kids' picket fence was a tall refrigerator box painted purple and labeled THE PHANTOM TOLLBOOTH. And next to the couch, where you'd think there'd be an end table or something, there was a basket of yo-yos. Not shrink-wrapped yo-yos for sale. Just loose, mismatched yo-yos, their strings trailing over the basket's edge. Clearly the Dog Ear owners believed that shopping for books just naturally led to the urge to yo-yo.

"I like it a lot," I breathed.

"Well, go get you some cookies, then, before E.B. eats them all," the woman said. "Yesterday we had Fig Newtons, and he did not like *those* at all, so he's playing catch-up."

She craned her neck to address the dog, who was still sprawled beneath the feet of the reader.

"Aren't you, ya big fatty?" the owner cooed.

The reader with her feet on E.B. gasped.

"Don't you listen to Stella," she told the dog, feeding him another cookie. "There's just more of you to love."

Stella rolled her eyes and said to me, "He looks more like Wilbur the pig than a dog. That's why we named him after E. B. White."

While I laughed, Stella turned to the girl on the couch. "Darby, are you going to buy that book ever, or just come here every day to read it?"

The woman grinned and said, "I'll take option B."

Stella laughed and shrugged, as if to say, *Fine with me.*

Best. Bookstore. Ever.

I finally found the strength to drift over to the YA section. Refreshingly, it was placed smack-dab in the middle of the store, instead of tucked into some shadowy corner in the back. I rounded the aqua bookcase, almost licking my lips in anticipation of all the pretty book jackets arrayed on the shelves like candy.

I stopped short when I saw that somebody else was in the aisle.

Not just any somebody. A boy. A boy so tall and long-limbed that his slouch against the bookshelf make him look like the letter C. A boy with fair skin, and a perfect nose and neatly shorn brown hair.

A very cute boy.

He was squinting at the cover of a paperback, but when I took a few steps down the aisle, he looked up at me. I saw a flash in his eyes. They were brown—the exact same brown of my favorite velvet chair at Granly's cottage. They had long lashes and thick brows the same wet-sand color as his buzz-cut hair.

The pretty brown eyes glanced back at his book for a moment, then quickly snapped right back to me. Now they were widened in an expression that seemed a little stunned.

This, of course, caused me to catch my breath and spin around to face the bookshelf.

That was a double take, I thought. *It was* definitely *a real-live double take! For . . . me? For me!*

A feeling of both giddiness and panic bubbled inside me. Hoping my face wasn't turning bright red, I bent toward the bookshelf and pretended to search for a particular title. Meanwhile, I could feel the boy staring at me.

My hand floated up to my ponytail, which felt like it had frizzed into a giant puffball in the heat. I twirled a lock of hair nervously around my finger.

He was still looking, I could tell.

For maybe the first time in my life, I wished I *were* a stereotypical redhead, all sassy and impulsive. I'd swing myself around and stare right back at him. My dark blue eyes would crackle impishly, and my smile would be twisty and mischievous, just like the redheads I'd read about in books but had never actually met in real life.

Of course, even those redheads might have hesitated if they'd just emerged from a three-day road trip, plus a crying jag, with barely a glance in the mirror. My sleeveless red-checked shirt, which had surely been cutely crisp and picnicky when it was first made in the 1970s, was now faded and wrinkly and had a permanent ballpoint pen stain near one of the buttons. The Revlon Red polish on my toenails was chipped, and for all I knew I had a raspberry limeade drip on my face.

I skimmed my fingertips across my chin, feeling for stickiness. Then I tapped at the corners of my mouth to make sure there were no raspberry remnants there.

Since I seemed to be drip-free, I shot the boy a sidelong glance.

He was still looking at me.

And now he was *saying* something to me.

"There's nothing on your face, you know," the boy said in a low, somewhat raspy voice.

It took a second for me to realize what he'd said and what it meant. Clearly my attempt at a subtle chin check had been anything but subtle.

"What?" I blurted.

"It looked like you were wondering if you had something on your face," he said. "Maybe mayonnaise. You know, from the coffee shop? I just thought I'd let you know, there's not."

"Oh," I said. "Um, thanks. I wasn't at the coffee shop."

"Oh, okay," he said.

We looked at each other blankly for a moment before I blurted, "Besides, I'm not so into mayo. I'm more of a mustard girl."

I cringed. *What was that? Please tell me I'm not talking to this boy about condiments!*

But the boy nodded as if this were a perfectly normal thing to say to a cute person of the opposite sex. Who knew? Maybe it was. Maybe I should ask him what kind of stuff he put on *his* ham sandwiches.

Then I imagined those words coming out of my mouth, and I clamped my lips shut to make certain that they didn't.

The boy returned to his book, which gave me the chance to stare at *him*. He looked so different from most of the boys I knew. They were always swinging their hair out of their eyes with swoops of their heads, something that I hadn't realized I found annoying until just now. This boy's hair was sleek and neat and allowed a view of his very nice forehead.

Wait a minute, I thought. *There's no such thing as a nice forehead. Foreheads aren't nice or not-nice. They're just . . . foreheads.*

What kind of weirdo admires a guy's forehead *of all things? What does* that *mean?*

But I think I already knew.

It meant that I had been struck with an instantaneous crush—a crush that was possibly mutual (there'd been that double take, after all) but just as possibly not.

I tried to think of something to say. Something breezy and bright that had nothing to do with ham sandwiches. Of course, my mind was blank—except for the part that was consumed with this boy's long fingers and his stylish Euro sneakers and (still!) his forehead.

So I just watched in silence as he turned to a wheeled cart behind him. It was stacked neatly with paperbacks. I assumed that Stella, the store owner, had left them there so she could shelve them later.

The boy took a silver pen off the cart.

It hovered over the front cover of his book.

I felt myself tense. What was he doing? Was he going to *write* something on the book cover?

Only when I heard the sound of paper tearing did I realize that he was doing something even worse. He was *slicing the cover off the book*! The pen was not a pen. It was an X-Acto knife!

Maybe Stella didn't mind if customers read her books without buying them or got vanilla wafer crumbs in the bindings. But even she wouldn't stand for this, would she?

"What are you doing!" I cried, grabbing the boy's wrist.

Now it was his turn to be shocked.

"I'm doing my job," he said. "What are *you* doing?"

I realized I was still clutching his wrist. It felt satiny smooth and warm. I dropped his arm like it had burned me.

"What kind of job involves slashing a book cover?" I demanded. "What did that book ever to do you?"

That's when something weird happened.

Weird in a wonderful way.

The boy smiled.

His teeth were very white and straight, except for one crooked eyetooth. Each of his cheeks had a dimple in it.

"It's nothing personal against the book," he said. "It's just being remaindered. These all are."

The boy gestured at the cart full of paperbacks.

"Remaindered?" I asked. "What's that?"

"They're not selling," he explained. "So we return them to the publisher. But it's too expensive to ship back the whole book, so we just send them the cover and recycle the rest of the book."

"Oh," I said, feeling stupid and sad all at once. I eyed the cart full of books.

"You're going to slice up *all* those books?" I said. "How can you stand it?"

"They're not selling," the boy repeated with a shrug. "If we don't get rid of the ones that won't sell, we won't have room for the books that will."

I plucked a tomato-red paperback off the cart.

"Waiter, There's Soup in My Fly," I read.

"Fly-fishing humor," the boy said with a sorrowful shake of his head.

"Well, I don't know why *that's* not selling," I said sarcastically. I reached for another book.

"My Life as a Cat Lady," I read with a shudder.

"I'm telling you," the boy said. With one hand he reached out to take the book from me. With the other he held up his X-Acto knife.

"No," I protested, plunking the book back onto the cart. "How can you kill off all those innocent cats?"

"Well, we *are* dog people here," the boy said, glancing toward the lounge, where E.B. was wetly gobbling another vanilla wafer. The boy rolled his eyes and shook his head.

But he also smiled, and those dimples showed up again.

My stomach fluttered. I hoped he couldn't tell. Quickly I bent down so I could peer more closely at the books on the cart—and hide my face from him.

One paperback was sunset orange. I pulled it out.

"*Coconut Dreams* by Veronica Gardner," I said. "That sounds beachy to me. I'll take it."

The boy laughed.

"You're not actually buying that," he declared.

"I'm *rescuing* it," I said, hugging the book to my chest. "This book does not deserve to die."

"Do you even know what it's about?" he said.

I glanced at the back of the book.

"It's a dollar ninety-nine on clearance," I said, eyeing the red sale sticker. "Ooh, and it's YA! That's a good start. Let's see . . ."

I began to read the description on the back cover aloud.

"'Nicole can't believe her parents have shipped her off to

camp for the summer. Even if the camp is on a tropical island—'"

I paused to snort.

"Sounds deep," the boy said, prompting me to read on.

"'Nicole is *super*-mad about it. What about hanging out at the mall with her friends? What about her job at the frozen yogurt shop? She'll miss all the parties and all the fun, which is just what Nicole's parents want! At first Camp Coconut is awful—early wake-up calls, catch-your-own-fish breakfasts, a monsoon—'"

"A monsoon!" the boy and I blurted out together.

"Okay, safe to say that's a stretch," I said with a giggle.

"'But then,'" I read on, "'everything changes. Nicole meets a local boy named Kai. Their summer love blooms like a coconut flower, but like the tide, Nicole knows it can never last.'"

This was the part where I was supposed to groan and make a joke about two bad similes in one sentence.

But instead my throat seemed to close up as I realized something—

I was reading to my new crush from a *summer romance novel.* It was about as subtle as my sticky-chin check.

Okay, I told myself. I tried to take a deep breath without *appearing* to take a deep breath. *Maybe he's not making the connection. He's a boy, and lots of boys are clueless.* *Or maybe he* isn't *clueless but he just doesn't associate* me *with a summer romance* at all.

How could I figure out which one it was? And how could I *also* find out his name, his age, and whether he'd been on Team Peeta or Team Gale? (Either one was fine, as long as he'd never been on Team Edward or Team Jacob.)

When you were in a bookstore, those were perfectly legitimate things to ask, right? So why was I still speechless?

We were just verging on an awkward silence when Stella's voice rang out from the front of the store.

"Josh, honey? You back there?"

The boy looked up at the ceiling and sighed quietly before calling out, "Yeah?"

I felt that little flutter in my stomach again.

His name is Josh.

Then the boy spoke again. "What is it, Mom?"

This time my eyebrows shot up.

His name is Josh and his parents *own the bookstore of my dreams.*

It seemed so perfect that I couldn't help but grin. My smile was unguarded, uncomplicated, and delighted. I did not have this sort of smile very often. It felt a lot like the smile that had been on Josh's face a moment ago.

Luckily, Josh was listening to his mother and not looking at me while I grinned like a big goofball. I only half-heard the question she asked him—something I didn't understand about a packing slip and a ship date.

Whatever it was, it seemed to bring Josh back to the serious worker-bee place he'd been before we'd started talking.

"It's in the office file cabinet, third drawer down in the back," Josh called. Then he added, in a mumble, "Where it was the last time you asked."

He stared at the X-Acto knife in his hand for a moment. I could tell he wasn't seeing it, though. His eyes were foggy and distant, and they were definitely not too happy.

Then he seemed to remember I was there and looked at me. He pointed at the book in my hand.

"So, are you buying that or not?" he asked gruffly. He was suddenly impatient to get rid of me so he could get back to his book destruction.

And just as suddenly my rescue of *Coconut Dreams* didn't seem cute, clever, and boy-impressing. It was silly, a waste of Josh's apparently very valuable time.

I wondered if I'd been mistaken about his double take. And maybe we *hadn't* just had an amazingly easy and fun conversation about his cart full of doomed books. Maybe I'd imagined all that, and in fact I was just another annoying customer at Josh's annoying summer job.

So now what was I supposed to do? Put the book back and skulk away? If I did, I'd have to sidle past Josh in the narrow aisle. Twice. It'd be much quicker to just make a dash for the front desk.

So I nodded at Josh.

"I'll take the book," I said quietly.

"Fine," he said, looking stony. "I'll ring it up for you."

"That's okay," I said. "Your mom can do it."

Josh shrugged—looking a little sulky—and turned back to his cart.

I headed back up the aisle toward the front desk. Just before I emerged from the stacks, I heard the awful sound—*rrriiiiip*—of another book cover getting slashed.

I couldn't meet Stella's eyes as I handed her *Coconut Dreams.*

"Well!" she said brightly. I nodded sympathetically. What else *could* you say to such a pathetic purchase? I could have told her the book was supposed to have been a joke between me and her son, but now the joke had fizzled and it was just a cheesy book on clearance that I was buying before I made a quick getaway. But that seemed like a *lot* to explain, so I just stayed silent.

Why, I asked myself mournfully for the hundredth time, *did I take my e-reader into the shower?*

"So that's a dollar ninety-nine," Stella said. I handed over two of my precious dollar bills, then dug into my pocket for the tax.

"No tax, sweetie," Stella said. "After all, that book was headed for the shredder. You rescued it!"

"That's what *I* said," I said. She grinned at me, and I half-smiled back, feeling a little less mortified.

"Okay," I sighed. "Well . . ."

I cast a glance back toward the stacks, where Josh was still hidden. Suddenly I felt a rush of tears swell behind my eyes.

How had this gone so wrong? I wanted to linger in Dog Ear. I wanted to slowly browse the stacks, then take a tall bundle of books over to the lounge. I'd flop into that cracked-leather chair, where I'd skim through six different first chapters while nibbling vanilla wafers. Then I'd buy myself a *good* book and take it straight to the beach.

But instead I'd met Josh, and somehow we'd gone from flirting to flame-out in less than five minutes. I was too mortified to stay. I had to slink out of Dog Ear, with a lame book, to boot.

It just wasn't fair.

I turned back to Stella to thank her for ringing me up, but she was peering with concern into the lounge.

"E.B.," she said with a warning tone.

The dog lifted one eyebrow at her and whimpered.

"Oh, no," Stella cried. "E.B., hold on, boy!"

She swooped down to reach for something under the counter. When she came up, she was holding a leash.

Now the dog let out a loud, rumbling groan.

"Noooo, E.B.!" Stella cried. She raced over and grabbed the dog by the collar. She clicked on the leash and hustled E.B. to the door.

"You *know* you shouldn't eat so many cookies," she scolded.

I clapped a hand over my mouth to keep from laughing out loud as Stella hustled her rotund black Lab through the door.

But a moment later I felt a presence behind me, and my urge to laugh faded.

It was him. I just *knew* it.

I paused for a moment before turning around. I inhaled sharply.

You know how some people's looks change once you get to know them? Unattractive people become better-looking when you find out how funny and smart they are. And gorgeous people can turn ugly if you find out they're evil inside.

Well, now that I'd seen Josh's surly, sullen side . . . that didn't happen at all. He was somehow cuter than ever. Which is really annoying in a boy who's made you feel like an ass (even if he did make me feel pretty amazing first).

"E.B. has a touch of irritable bowel syndrome," Josh explained.

"Am I supposed to laugh at that?" I asked.

"No," Josh said simply. "It's not a joke. It's really gross, actually."

That, of course, made me *want* to laugh. So now Josh was making me feel like an *immature* ass.

"Well, I hope he feels better. See ya," I said. Of course, I *didn't* plan to see Josh. I was already wondering how I could find out his work schedule—so I could be sure to avoid him.

"Look at this," Josh said, thrusting a book toward me. It sounded a lot like an order.

"Excuse me?" I said. I raised one eyebrow, which was a skill I'd learned recently. I'd had a lot of time to practice it during the drive from California.

It worked. Josh looked quite squirmy.

"I mean, well, I think you might like this book," he said more quietly. When I didn't take it from him, he put it on the counter next to me. I glanced at it only long enough to see that the cover was still intact. It had a photo that looked blue and watery.

"Listen, *Coconut Dreams* is not my usual kind of book," I said. "If this is *anything* like that, I think I'll pass."

"It's not, I swear," Josh said. "Look, it's not even on clearance."

I gave him a look that I hoped was deeply skeptical, and picked up the book.

I loved the look of the cover. It was an undulating underwater photo. In the turquoise water you could just make out a glimmer of fish scales, a shadowy, slender arm, and one swishy coil of red hair.

Beyond the Beneath, the book was called, and *oh*, did I want to flip through it and find out if the words were as flowy and beautiful as that cover. But I wasn't about to tell Josh that. He'd already gotten me all confused with his mixed signals and his cuteness. Plus, I only had five bucks left in my pocket, so I couldn't afford the book anyway. I was going to make my escape while I could.

"I don't think so," I said, trying to sound breezy. I tossed the book back onto the counter. "But thanks."

"Oh, okay," Josh said. He dug his hands into his pockets and looked away, the way I always did when I was disappointed.

I'm sure that's not it, I told myself. *That's probably just where he keeps his extra X-Acto knife blades.*

Josh seemed to have spotted something behind the counter. I followed his gaze to the receipt paper trailing out of the cash register. It had a bright pink stripe running along it.

"Oh, man," he muttered. "She never remembers to change the tape."

He ducked around the end of the counter and started extracting the paper roll from the register, scowling as the thing seemed to evade his grasp.

"Weird," I said.

Josh stopped fiddling with the receipt tape and looked at me. "What's weird?" he demanded.

"I think it would be a dream to work in a bookstore," I said, "and you don't seem to like it at all."

"I like it—" Josh started to say, sounding super-defensive. He stopped himself and frowned in thought. "It's not that I don't like it. It's just that, when people open a bookstore, they think it's going to be all, you know, *books.*"

"Isn't it?" I asked.

"Well, yeah," Josh said, "but it's also receipt tape. And packing slips and book orders and remembering to pay the air-conditioning bill."

"But *you* don't have to worry about that," I scoffed. "I mean, you're . . ."

"Fifteen?" Josh said. "Yeah, well, you don't have to have a

driver's license to pay the air-conditioning bill. You just have to have a tolerance for really boring chores."

At that moment he looked a lot older than a boy my age.

Even though, I couldn't help noting, he *was* a boy my age. Not college age or even my sisters' age.

I don't know why that mattered to me, though. Who cared if he was age-appropriate? Yes, he was really, really good-looking. And mature. And for about three minutes it had seemed like he thought I was pretty intriguing too.

But now I didn't know *what* to think about this boy. How could I have anything in common with someone who found a bookstore—*this* bookstore—as uninspiring as receipt tape?

And how, I wondered as I walked out the door, could I possibly feel worse leaving Dog Ear than I had before entering it?

That night my dad grilled corn and salmon, and my mom tossed an arugula salad with hazelnuts and lemon juice. Abbie and I collaborated on wildly uneven biscuits. Mine looked like shaggy little haystacks, while hers were perfectly round but as flat as pancakes. Hannah made a fruit salad, then muddled raspberries and frothed them into a pitcher of lemonade.

But instead of setting the table like usual, we piled all the food into boxes and baskets and toted them down the two blocks to the lake.

Sparrow Road was narrow and sharply curved. Though the road was paved with used-to-be-black pavement, walking it meant wending your way around various large cracks and potholes. Before you knew it, you were usually in the middle of the road. Which was fine because there were hardly ever any cars. There was no reason to drive on Sparrow unless you lived in one of the twenty-or-so houses on it.

I always loved our first shadowy walk to the lake. It was so thickly overhung with trees that by August you felt like you were in a tunnel. Of course, by August you also had to spend most of that walk slapping away mosquitoes and horseflies. But even that—after doing it my whole life—felt like a ritual.

I think we all exhaled as we rounded the last bend in the road that led to our "stop." This was a little wooden deck with a bike rack (not that anybody bothered to lock their bikes here) and a rusty spigot for hosing the sand off your feet. A little gate on the far end of the deck led to the rickety, narrow boardwalk that led to the beach.

None of us spoke as we kicked off our shoes, then walked down the boardwalk single file.

Tonight the silence seemed heavy with meaning and mourning. But actually we were always pretty quiet during our first visit to the lake. After the Pacific, so violent and crashy, the lake seemed so quiet that it always made us go quiet too. As a little kid I imagined that this water kept people's secrets. Whatever you whispered here was safe. The lake would never tell.

As we stepped—one after another—from the boardwalk onto the sand, I realized that maybe I hadn't completely outgrown that notion.

After we'd settled onto the sand (nobody had had the extra arm for a picnic blanket) my mother declared, "Dinner on the beach on our first night in Bluepointe. It's a new tradition."

Even though her voice caught on the last syllable and her eyes looked glassy in the light of the setting sun, she smiled.

I gave her my own damp-eyed smile back. It felt weird to be simultaneously so sad without Granly and so happy to be there in that moment. The smoky, charred corn was dripping with butter and the sand was still warm from the sun, which had become a painfully beautiful pink-orange. The gentle waves were making the *whooshing* sound that I loved.

When I'd finished my salmon and licked the lemony salad dressing from my fingers, I got to my feet. I scuffed through the sand, tiptoed over the strip of rocks and shells that edged the lake, and finally plunged my feet into the water. It was very, very cold.

I gasped, but forced my feet to stay submerged. The cold of the water felt important to endure for some reason. Like a cleansing of this very long day.

I glanced back at my family. Abbie was sitting with her legs splayed out while she gnawed on her cob of corn. Hannah was lying on her stomach gazing past me to the sunset. My parents were sitting side by side, both with their legs outstretched and crossed at the ankles, my mom's head resting on my dad's shoulder.

There was only one person missing.

My mind swooped to an image of Granly. If she were here right now, she'd be sitting in a folding beach chair. Maybe she'd sip a glass of wine while she searched the sky for the first stars of the night. Or she'd be efficiently packing the dishes up while she gossiped with my mom about old Chicago friends.

But then something surprising happened. Just as quickly as my mind had swooped to Granly, it swooped away again and landed on—the boy from the bookstore.

I wondered what it would be like if *he* were here on the beach with me. He didn't seem like the goofy splashing-around-in-the-water type. But I could definitely picture him taking a long, contemplative walk along the lake. Or building a sand castle with me, with all the turrets carefully lined up according to size.

I wondered if he knew the constellations and would point them out as the night sky grew darker. Or maybe he didn't like to talk much. Maybe he was more of a listener.

I tried to imagine what it might feel like to lean my head against his shoulder or snuggle into those lanky arms. And I remembered the way his face had lit up when he'd smiled at me for the first time.

But after his mom had brought him back down to earth, his face had tightened. His mouth had become a straight, serious line as he'd struggled with the receipt tape and perhaps reviewed a long to-do list of chores in his head.

It had not looked like a kissable mouth.

And those broad shoulders? It seemed there was enough leaning on them already. There was no room for my head there.

Even if there was, was Josh thinking about me in the same way?

Was he thinking about me at all? He didn't even know my name!

I couldn't stop repeating *his* name in my head. *Josh*. I loved the one-syllable simplicity of it. I loved the way it ended with a *shhhh* that you could draw out, like the soft sizzle of a Lake Michigan wave.

But I stopped myself from whispering the name out loud. If I did, I felt sure that I wouldn't be able to get it—to get *him* and my does-he-like-me? angst—out of my head.

So instead I tromped back to my family, who looked blurry and ghostly now that the sun had set.

"Isn't it time for frozen custard?" I asked.

It was funny that we had so many rituals in Bluepointe, when we had hardly any in LA.

At home we went to whatever brunch spot had the shortest line. Here we might wait for ninety minutes to get Dutch baby pancakes (and only Dutch baby pancakes) at Francie's Pancake & Waffles.

In LA my mom marked our heights on the laundry room wall whenever she remembered. Not on birthdays or New Years or anything that organized.

But in Bluepointe we always took the exact same photo on the exact same day, which was the last day of our visit. Hannah would kneel in the sand, Abbie would sit next to her, and I would lie on my stomach, my chin on my fists, at the end of the line. We even took that shot in the rain once, because there was no leaving Bluepointe without the "stack of sisters" shot.

Yet another tradition here was frozen custard on our first night in town. We always went to the Blue Moon Custard Stand.

As we drove there Hannah said, "I wonder what color it's going to be this year."

The Blue Moon got a new paint job every summer, going from bubble-gum pink to neon yellow to lime green—anything as long as it was ridiculously bright. I guess it was easy to paint, because the stand was no bigger than a backyard shed. There was barely enough room inside for two (small) people to work, and even that looked like a struggle. They always seemed to be elbowing each other away as they took orders, exchanged money, and handed cones through the stand's one tiny window.

This meant the line was always long and slow-moving, which was part of the fun of the Blue Moon.

Sure enough, when we pulled up to the stand (purple!) just outside of town, there was a crowd milling around it. But as usual nobody seemed to mind the wait. The evening air was cool and breezy, and the air was so lit up with fireflies, it made the weedy gravel lot feel like a fairy ring. Nobody was in a rush, and you didn't even have to expend mental energy mulling your custard order, because the Blue Moon had exactly two flavors: chocolate and vanilla.

We always ordered the same thing anyway. Dad and Hannah got hot fudge sundaes, hers with sprinkles, his with nuts. I got chocolate custard in a cake cone. Mom had a cup of vanilla drizzled with chopped maraschino cherries, and Abbie got a butterscotch-dipped sugar cone. We all got huge servings, even though frozen custard is about as bad for you as a bacon-topped donut, as distant from the calorie-free, pomegranate-flavored frozen yogurt of our hometown as you could get. That was exactly the point. This first-night ritual was our way of saying good-bye to California for the summer, and hello to Bluepointe, where things—until now—had always been as sweet and easy as frozen custard.

I took a giant bite of my cone as soon as the kid behind the counter handed it to me.

"Oh!" I groaned through a messy mouthful of chocolate. "Thish ish shooo good! How do I always forget the perfection that is frozen custard?"

"If you remembered," my dad said, wiping hot fudge off his chin with his napkin, "you'd never need to go back for more. And what fun would that be?"

I grinned and took another huge bite. As I swallowed, though, I felt a wave of cold surge though my head.

"Owwwwww, brain freeze!" I groaned. I turned away, squeezed my eyes shut, and slapped a hand to my forehead.

In a few seconds the yucky feeling in my frontal lobe passed, and I opened my eyes—to find myself looking right at—Josh! He was just walking away from the Blue Moon window, holding a simple vanilla cone. Behind him was his mom, digging into a sundae with about half a dozen colorful toppings on it.

Also just like me—he seemed stunned. After what felt like a *long* moment, during which we just stared at each other, he gave me a little wave.

I gave him a little smile.

And then Stella spotted me. Waving at me with her fudgy spoon, she said, "You were in Dog Ear today, weren't you, honey? How do you like that book?"

"Oh," I said, trying to sound breezy and comfortable even though I *completely* wasn't, "I haven't had a chance to start it yet."

"Well, you let me know, okay?" she said.

I nodded as, out of the corner of my eye, I saw Josh's gaze drop to the ground. He ate his frozen custard in giant, hurried bites until his mom wandered off to chat with someone else. Then he took a few steps toward me.

"You should," he said seriously.

"I should . . . what?" I asked him. I wondered how this was going to go. Was he going to be flirty Josh or surly Josh?

"You should come back to Dog Ear," he said.

I raised my eyebrows. That definitely didn't sound surly.

"I finished the remainders," Josh went on. "I promise, all the books are safe for the next few months. And . . ."

Now Josh looked a little embarrassed. "I can also promise you the staffers will be more polite."

"Oh," I said. "That sounds sort of like an apology."

"It sort of is," Josh replied.

Which might have been sweet in a different tone of voice. But Josh said it in such a somber, almost curt way, I didn't know quite *how* to take it. Was this just him doing the right thing, clearing his conscience? Or did he want me to come back to Dog Ear . . . to see him?

I didn't know what to say. What's more, my melting tower of frozen custard was beginning to tilt dangerously in my cone. And my family was not two feet behind me. I knew it wouldn't be long before they emerged from their custard hazes and noticed me talking to a boy. That would mean awkward introductions, followed by a sisterly interrogation for which I would have absolutely no answers.

What could I tell them? *This is Josh. We totally hit it off this afternoon. And then we didn't. And now I don't know* what's *going on, except that I still find him painfully cute.*

It would have made no sense to any of them. It barely made sense to me!

So I simply said to Josh, "Well, I guess I'll see you then."

As I turned back to my family, I realized I'd said pretty much the same thing when I'd left Josh at Dog Ear that afternoon. Of course, I'd been completely lying then.

Now? I hoped what I said would actually come true.

I barely tasted the rest of my frozen custard. In fact, I threw my cone away when it was only half-eaten. This was unheard of.

But, of course, everything was different this summer.

My parents hammered *that* point home as we walked back to the car, doing our best to wipe our sticky hands with flimsy paper napkins.

"Your dad and I have decided that we're going to move into Granly's room," my mom announced. "Hannah, you can have our old room so that you can have a quiet place to study. Abbie and Chelsea, we can split up the bunk beds for you if you want."

"But—" Abbie began. It was pure reflex for her to protest the injustice of Hannah getting her own room. But then it all must have sunk in, because Abbie clapped her mouth shut.

Mom and Dad were moving into Granly's room—her *empty* room.

It made sense. After all, the house was small and it was silly to leave an entire bedroom empty all summer.

But it was also incredibly depressing.

After we'd loaded ourselves soberly into the car, I pressed my knuckles to my lips.

Part of me wondered, why had we even bothered with this first-night outing? *All* our Bluepointe rituals were shattered now that the person at their center was gone.

But another (guilty) part of me was glad that we'd gone and I'd gotten another glimpse of Josh.

After we got home, I flopped into the rocker on the front porch. I didn't want to go in and watch my parents move their stuff into Granly's room. Instead I rocked slowly while the crickets sawed away outside the window screens. After a few minutes I picked up my purse from the floor where I'd tossed it and fished out my wrinkled memo pad and a pen.

What if? What if Granly was still here? What if I hadn't run to town this afternoon? What if the library had been open? That whole "butterfly causing a tsunami with one beat of its wings" thing has always made me crazy. It makes it seem like there's an either/or between everything—your grandmother living or dying. A summer spent in humongous Los Angeles or a tiny town in Michigan.

Why can't you have both sides of the either/or? If my grandma was here, maybe I wouldn't have met a cute boy today. Now I've met the cute boy, but I can't tell my grandma about him. See? Either/or. I guess that's just how life works.

I scratched out my exhausted thoughts until the pen almost fell out of my hand. Then I stumbled to my room and flopped into bed in my checkered shirt. I hadn't unpacked yet and couldn't find any of my pajamas.

In the middle of the night, I was awakened by the muffled (but still unbearable) sound of my mother crying from Granly's room on the other side of the wall.

It didn't wake Abbie up, because *nothing* ever woke Abbie up.

But just to test the theory, I grabbed the little flashlight that was always in the nightstand drawer. I flicked it on and aimed it at Abbie's face—her utterly placid, sleeping face. I wiggled the light back and forth over her eyes, but they remained stubbornly closed. Then she made a cooing noise and flipped over so she faced the wall.

It didn't seem fair that Abbie was not only sound asleep but was having a good dream.

Now in the next room I heard the low grumble of my dad's voice. He must have said the exact right thing, because my mom gave a sniffly laugh, then quieted down. Gratefully I smushed my head deeper into my pillow and resolved to laugh at my dad's next joke, no matter how corny it was.

I aimed the flashlight at the wall. It was papered instead of painted because Granly thought wallpaper was warm and cozy. The paper was barely pink and dotted with tiny impressionistic butterflies—each one just a few swipes of ink and a couple blobs of watercolor. They were the pale greens, blues, pinks, and tans of birds' eggs.

This wallpaper was in one of my earliest memories. I don't

know how old I was—young enough that I was put to bed before the sun had fully set. I was also young enough that I couldn't yet read myself to sleep. So instead I tried to follow the pattern in the wallpaper. I found the gray-blue butterfly that seemed to be dancing with the coral one, then I searched for the spot where the pair repeated. I pointed at the blue and coral butterflies over and over, working my way around the room, until my eyes became the butterfly wings and fluttered shut.

Now, at three a.m., searching out my favorite butterflies with a flashlight felt more like a hunting expedition than a relaxing way to drift off to sleep. So I groped for the nightstand and grabbed the first thing I found there.

I squinted at the book through half-closed eyes. Oh. *Coconut Dreams.*

Stella wanted to know what I thought of it. So did Josh. At least it had *seemed* that way.

So, even though I was already pretty sure what I would think of *Coconut Dreams,* I smiled as I cracked it open and started reading.

The best thing I could say about the story of Nicole's exile on the Island of Bad Similes was that it put me to sleep within three pages. The last thing I thought as my flashlight slipped out of my fingers and I fell back asleep was, *This is better than a sleeping pill. I wonder if I could stretch* Coconut Dreams *out to last two and a half months.*

With all the *what ifs* I had to think about—not to mention the *what nows*—I had a feeling I was going to need it.

Maybe it was because my dad was taking some time off work. Maybe it was because my mom was a fourth-grade teacher who thought every moment of every day should be educational.

Whatever the reason, our first weeks in Bluepointe became all about family outings.

Normally my sisters and I would have protested. Our time in Bluepointe was supposed to be lazy, so lazy that moving from the couch to the kitchen required serious consideration. So lazy that you could spend two hours in the lake, just bobbing around and counting clouds. So lazy that you'd subsist on chips and salsa for lunch *and* dinner if it would get you out of having to think about or help prepare a real meal.

But this summer, of course, was different. None of us wanted to be in the cottage much, especially me. Being home made me ache for Granly. It also gave me time to talk myself in circles about Josh. One moment, I felt certain that he liked me, and I would make *definite* (okay, definite-ish) plans to put on my cutest vintage sundress and head to Dog Ear.

The next minute, I would talk myself out of it. I wondered if I'd misread what he'd said. I pictured myself showing up at Dog Ear, clutching my long to-read list like a total dork, only to have Josh be all casual and brush-offy.

Or maybe, I thought, I'd show up and he wouldn't even be there. Then I'd have to go *back*. It might take multiple attempts to pin him down. The next thing you know, I'm a stalker.

The idea that it could all go well—that was the scenario I couldn't quite envision. I knew that kind of thing happened all the time. It had been the easiest thing in the world for Emma and Ethan. But it had never happened to me, and I just couldn't bring myself to believe that it ever would.

If I just put off going to Dog Ear, I told myself, I could delay the inevitable disappointment.

So that was how I ended up joining my family for an endless series of day trips. We went wild mushroom hunting in the Michigan woods. My parents had read about it in some foodie magazine, and they would not be deterred by the fact that choosing the *wrong* mushrooms could kill us all. (Somehow we survived. And the mushrooms actually weren't bad, if you could get past the lingering taste of dirt.)

After that we spent an afternoon churning butter at a living history museum a few towns over.

We rode inner tubes down the South Branch Galien River.

We cooked massive breakfasts and elaborate dinners, each involving new and difficult recipes that my parents had squirreled away over the course of the year.

And, oh, the antiquing. I knew we'd gone overboard with that when I found myself having a serious internal debate about which kind of quilt pattern I liked best, Double Wedding Ring or Log Cabin.

But toward the end of June it all fell apart. Abbie slipped out one morning for a "quick dunk" in the lake and never came back, so I was sent to look for her.

When I got there, she was still in the water. And even though she was just bobbing around in a bikini instead of seriously training in her Speedo, I decided I'd better not disturb her. I had no choice but to flop onto the sand and start texting with Emma. I'd just happened to stash my phone in my bag on my way out the door, along with a giant tube of sunscreen, Granly's old copy of *Sense and Sensibility*, and my bathing suit and cover-up.

You know, just in case.

One by one the rest of my family arrived. First came my dad with a soft cooler full of soft drinks. Then Hannah, who had a beach blanket and a mesh bag of clementines. And finally my mom, wearing her purse and a confused expression.

"But we're going to that artists' colony to watch them make fused glass," she complained. She was decked out in touristy clothes: capri pants, walking sandals, floppy-brimmed hat—the works.

"That sounds fascinating," Hannah said, shielding her eyes with her hand and squinting up at Mom. "But you know what would be an even *more* interesting way to spend the day?"

"What?" Mom asked.

"Lying on this beach doing absolutely nothing," Hannah said.

Without looking up from my phone—where Emma had just finished a long, dramatic story about getting caught making out with Ethan in the parking lot of the LA Ballet—I raised my fist in silent solidarity.

"There's not another glass demonstration until August," my mom protested feebly. I couldn't help but notice, though, that she kicked off her sandals as she said it.

"Maybe Hannah's right, hon," my dad said. "It's been a long few weeks. It's been a long *year*. Maybe it's time for a breather. We can go see them blow glass next time."

"*Fuse* glass . . . ," my mom said. But her teacherly voice trailed off as she gazed out at the blue-green, sun-dappled lake.

She sat down gingerly on the blanket.

"Cold Fresca?" Hannah asked, digging into the cooler for my mom's favorite drink.

Mom shrugged as she took the can and popped it open. She took a sip. It turned into a deep swig. Then she dug her toes into the sand, flopped back onto the blanket, and said to the sky, "Oh. My. Gawd."

"See?" Hannah said to her. "Nice, huh?"

I held up my hand so Hannah could high-five me, then returned to my cell phone.

That's when Abbie emerged from the lake, shaking the water out of her hair like a wet puppy.

"Uh-oh," she said, eyeing Mom. "Well, I guess it was too good to last. So what's on the agenda today? Making our own soap? Tracing Johnny Appleseed's steps through Michigan?"

"Here," Mom said as she reached into the cooler. "Have a Coke. We're not going anywhere."

"Oh. My. Gawd," Abbie said, gaping at our mother.

"She's crossed over to the dark side," Hannah said happily. Then she flopped onto her back next to my mom and closed her eyes for a nap.

At some point we got hungry. So we threw on our flip-flops and shuffled up to town.

Perhaps because it was the first café we hit on Main Street, we wandered into Dis and Dat. A little hole in the wall with mustard-yellow walls, Dis and Dat sold two things and two things only: hot dogs and french fries. Both the food and the thick-necked guys behind the counter had south-side-of-"Chicawgo" accents. They clapped their serving tongs like castanets and pointed them at you as they interrogated you about your hot dog toppings.

"You want some of dese pickles?" they'd demand. "How about some of dose peppers?"

They'd shake celery salt on your dog and announce, "A little of dis."

Then they'd squirt on some mustard and say, "And a little of dat."

I couldn't help but feel a little insider pride when Hannah marched up to the counter and barked, "Five of 'em with everything."

She knew not to say "please" and she *definitely* knew not to ask for ketchup. Chicagoans have this weird thing about ketchup on a hot dog. Ask for it, and they'll act like you said something disgusting about their mother.

"That's what I like to heah!" the guy behind the counter said to Hannah. He started tossing butterflied buns onto an orange plastic tray. Hannah couldn't have been more pleased if she'd gotten an A-plus on an exam. My dad laughed and gave her a squeeze.

"Think she'll do all right at U of C?" he asked the counterman.

"Don't you worry 'bout *her*," the counter guy said, pointing his tongs at my dad now. "A U of C girl. She's a sharpie."

"She's a genius!" my dad agreed.

"Daaaaaad," Hannah said. Her grin faded fast.

But at least the hot dogs were amazing. We sat down at one of the cramped sidewalk tables to devour them. In addition to the celery salt, peppers, pickles, and mustard, each dog was piled with chopped onions, tomatoes, and pickle relish dyed an unnatural emerald green. I sat with my back to the plate-glass window so the Dis and Dat guys wouldn't see me picking off the onions.

"Yummmm," Abbie said as she wolfed down her dog. "I'm *so* getting something from the Pop Guy for dessert."

As she peered down the street to see if the rainbow umbrella was there (it was, of course), she suddenly clutched at Hannah's arm.

"Hey," Hannah said, dropping her french fry. "That hurts."

"It's him!" Abbie hissed. She released Hannah's arm to gesture wildly at the other side of Main Street.

"Oh my God," Hannah said, covering her face with both hands. "You're such a spaz. He'll see you!"

"It's not yours," Abbie almost shouted. "It's *mine*. You know—James. Or John . . . Wait a minute—Jim? Jim! I think it's almost definitely Jim."

She crammed her last bit of hot dog into her mouth as she stood up.

"What are you doing?" Hannah asked.

"Catching up to him," Abbie declared. "Hello. We have it all planned, or did you forget?"

"Didn't the plan involve you looking hot in your swimsuit?" I said as I crammed a fry into my mouth.

"What?" Abbie said. She glanced down at the wrinkled shorts and baggy T-shirt she'd thrown over her bikini. She shrugged and whipped off her shirt, revealing her tan, muscly abs and her skimpy swimsuit top.

"No," both my parents said at the exact same time.

"You guys are so hung up," Abbie sighed as she shimmied back into her T-shirt. "It's just a body. What's the big deal?"

"Don't answer that," my mom said to my dad with a wry smile. "It's a trap."

Hannah and I rolled our eyes at each other. My parents loved it when they got to join forces and tease us. Which, if you asked me, was kind of mean. It's not like we could help being teenagers any more than they could choose not to be old and wrinkly.

Abbie knotted her T-shirt at the waist and wove her disheveled hair into two sleek braids, which rendered her instantly adorable.

The she crossed her arms over her chest and glared at me and Hannah.

"Hurry up!" she said.

"What?" I squawked. "I'm not going with you!"

I glanced over my shoulder to look at myself in the Dis and Dat window. My outfit was okay—I was wearing a gauzy vintage swim cover-up that looked better the more it wrinkled, which was a good thing, because it was *very* wrinkled. But from the neck up my look was . . . problematic. Even in the dim reflection of the window, I could see that a bunch of new freckles had popped out on my face in the morning sun. My hair was so lake-tangled that a neat braid like Abbie's was out of the question. Even my usual ponytail could barely contain it. Spiral curls sproinged out along my hairline, pointing in all different directions.

"A, yes you are going with me. Both of you," Abbie said to me and Hannah. "And B, it doesn't matter how *you* look."

Hannah looked at me and bit her lip.

"It matters a *little* bit," she said before reaching over and snatching the rubber band out of my hair. I felt my wild ringlets bounce off my shoulders.

"Hey!" I said.

"I've been wanting to do that for the past hour," my mom said with a grin. Turning in her seat next to mine, she scrunched my hair a little bit and then smiled. "I love it. It's just like Granly's."

Then her eyes went glassy.

And I really didn't want to go down that road—not after the perfect morning we'd just had. So I grabbed my beach bag and jumped up to follow Abbie, who was already halfway down the block. Hannah huffed into place behind me a moment later.

The Silver sisters began to stalk their prey.

Jim or John or James was sauntering slowly about a block ahead of us. He was totally Abbie's type. Super-tan, super-muscly, and happily aware of both. It turned out he was moving at that turtlelike pace so he could check himself out in every store window he passed. He also had to shake his long, blond-tipped bangs out of his eyes every few steps.

Hannah and I rolled our eyes at each other.

"Perfect summer fling material," she whispered to me.

"Ugh," I said. "I know where *I'd* fling him."

Abbie was so fixated on sneaking up on him, she didn't hear us. When she turned to whisper to us, her face was alight.

"I think he's heading to the Pop Guy," she whispered. "Score! I can get the boy *and* dessert!"

"If I hadn't just seen her in a bikini," I said to Hannah, "I'd swear *she* was a boy."

"'It's just a body,'" Hannah mimicked. She put her hands on her hips and swished them back and forth. "'What's the big deal?'"

I laughed so loud that Abbie turned around and glared at me. I tried, not very hard, to quiet down. Not that it mattered. Jim (or John or whoever) was completely oblivious to us.

He also didn't seem to be in the mood for a pop. Just before he reached the rainbow umbrella, he jaywalked across the street, heading for the corner.

And on the corner was—

"Oh, no," I breathed, skidding to a halt.

"What! What is it?" Abbie asked as she and Hannah hopped off the curb in pursuit.

When I didn't answer, Abbie huffed with impatience and grabbed my hand. She dragged me across the street, almost getting us hit by a pickup truck while she was at it.

Before I knew it, we were pushing through the jangly front door of Dog Ear. Immediately after feeling a rush of best-bookstore-ever happiness, I was seized with panic.

Josh couldn't see me like this! I was supposed to be wearing my favorite yellow sundress with the bell-shaped skirt. I should have on mascara and lip gloss. My nose should *not* be bright red after a morning in the sun, and my hair . . . Well, there was nothing that could be done about my hair, but a big hat would have been nice.

I froze in my tracks. Abbie, still clutching my hand, tried to get me to follow her to the lounge, where her boy was headed (probably just to snap up some free snacks without even making the pretense of reading something). But I wouldn't budge. My eyes darted around the bookstore. Behind the half-dozen stacks of books on the corner of the L-shaped counter, there was a girl with cherry-red streaks in her hair. She was sitting on a stool, reading a book and scratching her head with a neon pink pencil. A gray-haired man was unpacking a box in the kids' section, and a half-dozen people were browsing the stacks. But I didn't see Josh.

I breathed a little easier, but I wasn't in the clear yet. I decided that if he didn't surface in three minutes, he probably wasn't there and I was safe.

Until then I was staying put. I pretended to study the table full of bestsellers just inside the door.

"Oh, fine!" Abbie whispered. "I should have known I couldn't count on you in a bookstore. Come on, Hannah."

Hannah followed her to the lounge. I watched as Abbie smoothly grabbed a random book off a shelf, then flopped herself onto the couch next to her boy. She kicked off her flip-flops and plunked her feet onto the coffee table, the better for J-boy to check out her legs.

It took, oh, about thirty seconds for him to recognize Abbie and start chatting with her. Hannah perched easily on the couch arm and joined in on the banter. How did my sisters make it look so effortless?

I pulled my ragged little notepad out of my bag. I jotted down all the things that would have been going through my mind if I were Abbie:

Okay, so he remembers me, I wrote, channeling my sister, *but that doesn't mean he* likes *me. What if he doesn't?*

What if he does?

What if he does but he has a girlfriend?

What if I *become his girlfriend and then find out he kisses like a fish?*

I stopped scribbling and looked at Abbie's face. It was as open and sunny as the mason jar full of daisies on the coffee table. Clearly she was thinking *none* of these ridiculous things. I bet the only loop running through her head was: *I look awesome! This hottie is the perfect match for me. Until I dump him to head back home.*

I sighed as I flipped my notepad closed and tossed it back into my bag. When Abbie was born, she hogged all the badass genes, leaving none for me when I came along.

On the bright side, I realized, three minutes had passed and Josh hadn't emerged from a back room or from behind a bookshelf. He clearly wasn't there. Which meant I was free to dig into Dog Ear without worrying about how horrid I looked.

I glanced at Abbie and Hannah. Hannah had found a book and sunk into the leather chair to read it. Abbie was laughing with J-boy. She flicked one of her braids over her shoulder and propped her chin on her fist. She was laying it on thick! I had time.

I wondered if that book Josh had showed me, *Beyond the Beneath,* was still in stock. I started for the YA section.

But as soon as I passed the stacks of books on the corner of the counter, I realized I'd made a grave miscalculation.

The only person I'd *seen* behind the counter was the girl with the red streaks. But behind that barricade of books, there was plenty more room for another person. Especially if that person was sitting in a low chair and bent over a desk tucked below the counter.

I stifled a gasp as Josh came into my sight line. He was doing his letter C slouch again, so hunched over that you could almost see the knobby curve of his spine through the thin, white fabric of his T-shirt.

And in case you were wondering whether I thought his spine was as cute as his forehead, the answer, pathetically, is yes.

I froze in place, debating whether I should tiptoe back to the front door, where Josh couldn't see me, or dart into the stacks to hide among the books. Before I could do either, though, I got distracted by the thing on Josh's desk.

It was a huge poster. It had a blown-up image of a book cover in one corner. I couldn't read the name of the book, but I could see that it was an image of blue sky filled with perfect fluffy clouds.

Josh was inking in a sketch above the cover. It was a beautiful girl's face, gazing down at the book. She looked hazy and transparent—like she was one with the sky.

It was really, *really* good.

In another corner of the poster, Josh had made block letters in a funky, slanty font. I recognized it from the Dog Ear sign.

I glanced around at some of the other posters on the walls, each advertising an author reading or book launch party. Josh's same leaning font was on every one.

Other than that, they were all wildly different. One poster—

for a book about a London punk—featured E.B. the dog with a Mohawk, black eyeliner, and safety pins in his floppy ears. Another, for a campy zombie book, had a funny portrait of a zombie gnawing on a human arm like it was a cob of corn. Still another, for a children's picture book, had a pigeon pitching a fit from all different angles, like a police mug shot.

Clearly Josh had made all of these.

With my mouth hanging open in surprise, I glanced back at him. That's when I saw that he was staring at me!

As our eyes met I snapped my mouth shut with such force, I felt my teeth jangle a bit.

Josh did the exact same thing.

I didn't know whether to burst out laughing or to duck my disheveled head and run out of Dog Ear. Given my lack of makeup, I kind of wanted to do the latter.

But given Josh's adorable face?

I stayed.

"You finally came," he said.

He had a nervous/sweet half smile on his face. And his smooth cap of hair was kind of flattened in the one part where I guessed he'd been propping it on his hand while he drew. His shoulders were angular and adorable inside his thin T-shirt.

"Um, yeah," I said. "I've been meaning to, but things have been kind of family-intensive. I'm with my sisters right now, in fact . . ."

My voice trailed off as I gestured at them in the lounge.

What I didn't say was, "My sisters dragged me in here because I was too terrified to come by myself."

"Oh," he said. Which made me wonder what *he* wasn't saying.

"So you made all these?" I said, pointing at the framed posters lining the wall.

"Well . . ." Josh glanced at the half-finished poster on the desk, and then I *could* tell what he was thinking. He was wishing he could do a full-body dive on top of it, covering it up so I wouldn't know his secret.

"So . . . it's not all receipt tape?" I broached.

He looked squirmy again. But a sheepish smile snuck through. And even though he was trying to fight it off, it lit up his face.

"Did you ever start that book?" he said, changing the subject. "The one with the monsoon?"

"No monsoon yet," I said with a laugh. "But she did compare the rising tropical sun to a hothouse hyacinth."

"Ooh, that's bad," he said, and cringed.

"Oh, *wretched*," I said happily. "Which, you know, can sometimes be a good thing. Like Lifetime movies of the week? My sisters and I love them."

"Because you can laugh at them—"

"Not with, but at," I interjected.

"Right," Josh said. "But the point is, you do it together. Can't do that with a book."

Then his eyes lit up.

"Wait a minute," he said.

He disappeared beneath the counter. I heard a shuffling sound, and the *slap, slap, slap* of paperbacks hitting the floor. I glanced nervously at Abbie and Hannah. Hannah was completely immersed in a book that just reeked of important subject matter.

And Abbie was giving J-Boy a flirty punch in the arm. She practically batted her eyelashes at him.

Suddenly Josh reemerged. His flattened hair had popped back up. And he was holding a coverless paperback book. I pointed at it.

"Is that—"

"Coconut Dreams," Josh said. "We had two copies. This one was in the recycle box. My parents are supposed to drive the stuff over to the office supply place to get them shredded, but of course that hasn't happened yet."

This time, though, Josh seemed kind of delighted to have parents who neglected the boring bookstore chores.

"So . . . what?" I said. "You're gonna read that?"

"*We* could read it," he said. "You know, at the same time."

"Like a book club?" I said. That sounded, um, wholesome, in a middle-aged kind of way.

"Naw," Josh said. "It's like an *anti*–book club. We could both read it and make fun of it."

"So you *do* hate books," I joked.

"No, I don't!" Josh said. "There are a lot—well, some—that I think are amazing."

He dropped *Coconut Dreams* onto the desk and grabbed another book off it. It had the same cover as the book on Josh's in-progress poster. It was called *Photo Negative.*

"*This* one is amazing," Josh said, showing me the new book. "You haven't read it because it's not out yet. But when it does come out, you've got to get it."

"And the writer's coming here?" I said, nodding at his poster.

"Yeah," he said, clutching the book a little more tightly. "He is."

He looked so cutely vulnerable that I smiled. I couldn't help it. It was like I had no control over my face.

Josh smiled too—tentatively, like he'd dodged a bullet. He glanced back at his desk and seemed about to say something, when I felt Abbie *tap-tap-tap* my shoulder. I jumped.

"Hey," I said, turning to give her an irritated look. Hannah was behind her, looking amused.

Abbie whispered gleefully, "I've got good news and bad news."

She pulled me over to a display case that blocked our view of the J-boy in the lounge. It was also conveniently out of earshot of Josh.

"The bad news is," Abbie breathed, "I still don't know his name."

I looked over at Josh. His smile had faded, but it hadn't completely disappeared. He turned back to the desk.

I turned back to Abbie. She was so giddy with her impending good news that she didn't even seem to notice me making eye contact with Josh.

It probably doesn't occur to her that I could have a J-boy of my own, I thought ruefully.

"The good news is," Abbie said, "he's invited us to a party on Sunday. It's called a lantern party. I guess they do it every summer on the last day of June."

"That's weird," I said. "Why that day?"

"Oh, I don't know," Abbie said, waving her hand dismissively. "He explained it, but I didn't get the whole story. It's some small-town private joke."

"Huh," I said. I shot Hannah a dubious looks. "So he invited all of us?"

"Yeah, essentially," Hannah said. "I bet Liam will be there."

"Oh, great," I said. "So you can both go off with your boys and leave me with a bunch of strangers."

"A bunch of *potential*," Abbie declared. "We're going to be here the rest of the summer. Don't you want to make some friends? Don't tell me you want to stay home with Mom and Dad every night."

I glanced over my shoulder at Josh. He was sitting back at his desk, scribbling intensely on his poster.

I crossed my arms over my chest and faced my sisters again.

"What's a lantern party?" I asked.

"It's at the big dock at the marina," Abbie said with a shrug. "I assume they're lighting it all up with lanterns. You'll love it."

I cocked my head.

"I might like it," I said slowly.

"She's in!" Abbie blurted. She thrust her hand toward Hannah, and Hannah high-fived her. Abbie started for the door. Perfect. If she and Hannah went outside, I could finish talking to Josh.

"Oh, no!" Abbie said. She pointed at the Pop Guy's stand across the street. He was pulling down his giant umbrella, which meant he was closing up shop. "We've gotta catch him!"

She trotted to the door, then looked back and gestured wildly at us.

"Come *on*," she said. "It's so hot out, if I don't get something cold in me, I'll pass out."

"Okay, okay!" Hannah said with a laugh. She headed for the door.

"I'm going to . . . ," I began.

Hannah turned and looked at me impatiently.

"What?" she said. "Aren't you coming?"

I glanced again at Josh. His head was still down and he was frowning in concentration. Clearly he was back in work mode. I shrugged unhappily and headed for the door. Before I let it close behind me, I snuck a last peek over my shoulder—and saw *Josh* peeking around the book stacks at me! My stomach swooped. I managed a little wave before the jingly door slammed behind me.

I considered going back in to say good-bye in a less awkward way, but going back in seemed more awkward still.

And besides, he hadn't waved back.

I left so fast, he didn't have time to, I told myself as I trotted across the street after my sisters. *Right? It's not because he realized I'm a spaz with even spazzier siblings. Right? Right?*

I was lost in these neurotic thoughts as my sisters bought up the dregs of the Pop Guy's wares. As we headed down the street toward home, Hannah handed me a napkin and a creamy white frozen pop.

"What flavor is this?" I asked. I held it up. It looked like there were *raisins* in it.

"Rice pudding," Hannah said.

"Oh, yuck!" I said, curling my lip.

"Hey, at least it doesn't have tarragon or sage in it," Abbie said. "We know you hate those."

"What'd you guys get?" I said, tentatively taking a lick of

my pop. It was actually cinnamony and delicious, if I could just ignore the nubbly texture of the rice.

"Coconut jalapeño," Abbie said, hanging her tongue out. "Spicy!"

"Cherry vanilla," Hannah said. "Mmmm."

"Ooh," I said. "Let's go halvesies."

"Nope!" Hannah said. "Abbie said I could have the good one. Wingman's honor."

I grumbled as I nibbled at my pop, trying to avoid the bits of rice.

It was only when we turned off Main Street and Abbie and Hannah started debating outfits for the lantern party that my thoughts drifted back to Dog Ear. Suddenly I remembered something Josh had said.

"We could both read it."

My eyes widened. I froze mid-lick.

He asked me to form an anti–book club with him, I realized. *That's definitely more meaningful than just saying, "You should come into Dog Ear sometime," right?*

I started to get a little short of breath. I trailed behind my sisters as I debated with myself.

Okay, hold on, I told myself. *It's not like he was asking me out on a* date. *He just wants to goof on a bad book. It's not a big deal. Or is it?*

"We could both read it and make fun of it." That's what he said. So where would this fun-making take place? Over coffee? On the beach? On a picnic blanket on the beach on which he has laid out a spread of all my favorite herb-free foods?

The itchy feeling of melted ice pop dripping down my arm pulled me out of my daydream, which had been veering into the truly ridiculous anyway. As I mopped the melted milk off my wrist, I shook my head.

He just means we could have a laugh the next time I wander into Dog Ear, I admonished myself. *That's all. I bet he won't even bother to actually read it.*

But that night in bed, as I flicked on my reading light and regarded the two books on my nightstand—*Coconut Dreams* and *Sense and Sensibility*—I couldn't stop myself from grabbing the tropical romance.

As I read it, every florid paragraph seemed to have a footnote filled with the banter I could have with Josh.

And suddenly *Coconut Dreams* became a book that I really didn't want to put down.

By the day of the lantern party, we'd been in Bluepointe for almost three weeks. We'd gotten used to having nothing to do—no jobs or sports practices to rush to, no exams to study for, no friends to meet up with. Everything had slowed down. And what little we had to accomplish could be stretched out for *hours.*

Which was why, after a morning at the beach and a protracted, piecemeal lunch on the screened porch, my sisters and I spent almost the entire afternoon getting ready for our evening.

This was not our usual thing. Abbie was strictly a wash-and-wear kind of girl, and Hannah could blow-dry her hair into a perfect, sleek 'do in about three minutes. My routine mostly involved working copious amounts of product into my hair to make it go corkscrewy instead of turning into a giant poof of frizz.

But this afternoon we were a veritable movie montage of primping, perfuming, and outfit sampling.

But that was the thing about having sisters. We fought and made fun of each other and stole each other's clothes, but we also kept each other's secrets. Abbie and I, for instance, never reminded Hannah about the time she threw up in the mall food court in front of about a hundred people. And whenever Abbie lost at a swim meet, Hannah and I knew that she wanted us to be near, but silent. So we'd sit with her on the couch, turn on a dumb reality show, and hand her a big bowl of Lay's potato chips. By the time she made it to the bottom of the bowl, she was ready to talk about the meet, and we were there to listen.

So today, when all three of us turned into total girly-girls, which we definitely *weren't* in our "real" lives, we knew that nobody outside that room would ever hear about it. We could be as ridiculously giggly as we wanted.

"I can't decide!" Abbie groaned. She was looking at three outfits arranged on the big bed in Hannah's room. "I can't wear the dress, can I? That's just trying too hard."

"So you wear the white capris and the tank top," I said. I was on the floor painting my toenails a buttery yellow color. "That's more you anyway."

"Yeah, but white means I have to be careful not to get dirty," Abbie complained.

"What are you going to do?" Hannah demanded. "Roll around in the dirt with What's His Name?"

Abbie tapped a fist on her head.

"Argh," she groaned. "What *is* J-boy's name? It's too late to ask now!"

"Somebody will say it at the party," Hannah said. "You just have to keep your ears open."

"Or you could just skip right to 'honey,'" I posed. "That wouldn't freak him out at all!"

"I would *never*," Abbie gasped. "Now, 'Pooh Bear' on the other hand is completely acceptable."

"Totally," Hannah said. "You know what's even better? 'Sweet Cheeks.'"

"Love Muffin!" I yelled.

"Come here, Love Muffin," Abbie cried, grabbing a pillow and kissing it passionately.

"Ew, I sleep on that," Hannah said. She snatched the pillow away from Abbie and tossed it back onto the bed. Then she spotted my pedicure and gasped.

"Oh, *no*!" she said. She grabbed the bottle of polish remover from the dresser and plopped down in front of me. "*So* wrong."

"What?" I said. "I love this color."

"Me too," Hannah said, "but not on your feet. You're too pale. You need contrast."

She held up two bottles of polish—one shimmery hot pink, the other a bright turquoise.

"All right," I grumbled, pointing at the blue-green bottle. "But you do it. I hate painting my toes."

While Hannah polished, Abbie got busy on my hair.

"You can't keep yanking it back like you do," she said, fluffing up my hair. "You're gonna get a bald spot."

"What!" I cried, clutching at my scalp. "Is that even possible with this much hair?"

Abbie didn't answer as she rifled through her cosmetics bag. She came up with a wide elastic headband with a cute blue and green flower pattern on it. She snapped it around my head and arranged my curls behind it, with a couple tendrils popping out at the temples.

"Really?" I said skeptically. "There's just so *much* of it."

"Wear a tank top," Abbie said decisively. "Then your hair isn't competing with your sleeves."

Hannah finished my toes, and I leaned over to fan them dry with one of Hannah's *National Geographic*s.

"How come *I'm* getting all the makeover attention?" I said. "You're the ones trying to bag the love muffins."

Abbie and Hannah glanced at each other.

"What?" I demanded.

"We're just trying to help you, Chels," Hannah said.

"Why?" I demanded. "What's wrong with me?"

"Nothing, except you're a little . . . stuck," Hannah said carefully. "Uncomfortable in your skin. You need to be more confident and own who you are."

"'Own who I am'?" I said mockingly. "Who are you, Oprah?"

"Okay, smart-mouth," Abbie said. "Let's put it this way. You are standing in the way of your own hotness with this shy, bookwormy I-hate-my-hair routine. You need to lose the ponytail and stop hunching over just because you have boobs."

I could almost feel my eyebrows meet my hairline. I was literally speechless. We were always blunt with each other, but this was new terrain.

When I got over my shock, I scowled.

"I'm not shy," I said. "Just because I don't want to be the center of attention like some people I could name"—I looked pointedly at Abbie—"doesn't mean I'm an introverted freak."

"Look," Hannah said. "You're lucky. You've got two sisters who've just been through all this. We're trying to help you."

I frowned at my turquoise toenails. I hated to admit it—and I sure *wasn't* going to admit it to them—but deep down I knew Abbie and Hannah were right. Not about the hot part. Even if I did have boobs, I still couldn't fathom a version of hot that included bright red hair and freckly skin.

But it was true that I didn't exactly exude confidence. And I knew you didn't have to be gorgeous or super-popular to have it. Look at Emma. Sure, she had that graceful ballerina bod, but she also had oily skin and a hawkish nose. But it didn't matter, because Emma knew she was talented—special—and she carried herself that way. Sure enough, Ethan had fallen so hard for her that he was practically asphyxiating himself with all the kissing.

But how do you just suddenly decide you're special? Emma got on that track when she took her first baby ballet class at age four. Hannah had studied her way to brilliance, and Abbie had just been born with all that personality.

Me? I had nothin'. Reading about extraordinary people in books didn't make you extraordinary.

Of course, if I chose to believe my sisters (and that was a big *if*), I wasn't a total untouchable.

Own who you are, Hannah had said.

It would have sounded great on a greeting card, but in real life? I had no idea how to do that. I wondered if being "comfortable in my skin" was just another area in which I was doomed to fall short of my sisters.

The moment we showed up at the dock that night, just after sunset, we knew we'd wasted all that time primping.

Not that we didn't look kind of fabulous, with our fresh, color-correct mani-pedis, our summery makeup, and our bare shoulders dusted with shimmery powder. (Hannah had read about that in a magazine that was *not*, for the record, *National Geographic.*)

As Abbie had directed, I'd chosen a white sundress with skinny straps. It also had a tight bodice and a flared, knee-length skirt. The salesgirl at the vintage store where I'd bought it had told me it was made in the early 1960s.

To match my headband I'd borrowed Hannah's flat, royal blue sandals. Between those and my turquoise toes, my feet had never been so colorful. I hoped they would draw attention away from my voluminous hair.

But as it turned out, looking good at a lantern party didn't seem to be the point. At all. Most of the kids milling around the dock—which was a big square wood plank platform surrounded by anchored speedboats—looked happily disheveled in shorts and T-shirts. They had paint smears on their arms and arts-and-crafts glitter in their hair. And every one of them held an elaborate homemade lantern. Even though they weren't lit yet, presumably because there was still a bit of dusky light left, the lanterns were dazzlingly creative. There was a lantern that looked like a Japanese temple and one that looked like a fairy-tale mushroom, the kind with the white-dotted red cap. One lantern was an elaborate geometric shape that even Hannah might not have been able to identify. And there were side-by-side lanterns that looked like Fred and Wilma Flintstone.

Hannah walked over to a nearby girl who was bobbing her head to the music. Her lantern dangled from the end of a long stick. It was a cylinder made of flowery paper. Cut into the lantern was a window of waxed paper, which contained a funny silhouette of a dog.

"Love your lantern!" Hannah said as Abbie and I stood behind her. "Did you make it yourself?"

"Thanks!" the girl said, crinkling her nose happily at her lantern. "It was a hard one. It took me the whole pre-party. I guess you guys weren't there?"

"Pre-party?" Abbie said, closing in on the girl. "When was that?"

"Oh, it started around noon," the girl said. "We do it every year—get together and make our lanterns. We order in fried chicken and get all gluey. It's pretty goofy, but we've all been doing it since, like, middle school, so you know—it's a tradition now. At the end of the night there's a lantern contest."

"Wow, that sounds awesome," Abbie said flatly. If there was

anything she hated more than being left out of the loop, it was losing a contest. "Where was this pre-party?"

"It was at Jason's house," the girl said, cheerfully pointing to a far corner of the dock. There stood Abbie's J-boy, flanked by two laughing girls. He was holding up his lantern like it was a trophy. It was a very lumpy papier-mâché sculpture of Darth Vader's head. Presumably, once it was lit up, the eyes would glow.

Abbie's face darkened, but she kept her voice light as she answered, "Oh, it was at *Jason's* house. That's cool. Well, good luck in the contest."

"Thanks!" the girl chirped as Abbie drifted away.

Hannah and I gave each other a look.

"Let's see if there are any potato chips on the refreshment table," I whispered.

"She's already on her way," she said, pointing at Abbie as she made a beeline for the junk-food-laden table. Luckily, it was on the opposite side of the dock from Jason.

I arrived at Abbie's side just as she scooped a handful of chips out of a big bowl and stuffed at least four of them into her mouth.

"Well," I said brightly. I sounded just like our mom, who always got annoyingly chipper when the going got rough. "The good news is, now we know your guy's name! J-boy is Jason."

"The bad news," Abbie said grimly, "is he blew me off for someone else—*two* someone elses—before I even got here."

"Wait a minute," Hannah said as she poured soda into plastic cups for us. "You don't know that. You heard what that girl said. These people have all known each other forever. Those girls are probably just friends of his."

"Well, how do you explain the fact that he didn't invite me to the main event?" Abbie said, jabbing her thumb in the direction of a passing lantern that was about six feet tall and made to look like a tree, complete with a robin's nest and a squirrel scampering up the trunk.

"You're all confident and stuff," I said. I couldn't help but get that dig in. "Go and ask him!"

I gave her a little shove in Jason's direction. Abbie glared at me, but then she slapped her remaining chips into my palm with a crunch and headed over.

Hannah and I grinned at each other.

"Okay," she said. "One boy found. One to . . ."

Her voice trailed off as she spotted something—or rather, someone—at the other end of the refreshment table.

I followed her gaze to a boy pouring himself a big cup of sparkling water. He was dressed in khakis and a golf shirt, both of which were neat enough to give him a cute, preppy look but not so crisp as to make him look uptight.

His hair was blond and tidy. His face was sun-burnished and all-American, and he had earnest-looking blue eyes.

In other words he was *exactly* Hannah's type.

"Is that—" I started to say. "Is he—"

Hannah didn't answer me. She just pressed her cup into my hand and floated over to the boy.

"Liam?" she asked. Her tone of voice was perfect—mildly surprised and casually pleased to see him. You'd *never* guess that she'd been hoping for this moment for the past three weeks.

I tensed up as I watched the boy make eye contact with my

sister. I squinted as his face went from blank confusion to recognition to . . . delight.

Delight!

"Hannah, right?" he said. He gave her a quick hug, then stepped back to look at her admiringly. "You're back!"

Hannah shrugged. I couldn't see her face, but I didn't have to. I knew what was flashing in her eyes: triumphant relief, hopeful swooning, and just a hint of fear.

After the Elias breakup, Hannah had been single all year. She'd said it was because she was cramming for all her AP courses and applying to colleges, but Abbie and I knew that had been a convenient excuse. The truth was, she'd been truly heartbroken and afraid of being hurt again.

But now Hannah was in the lovely limbo that was Bluepointe. She'd left LA—the scene of her romance with Elias—and she hadn't yet arrived at U of C, where she'd be with the same people for the next four years.

This was her moment to have a romance that was lighthearted and fun.

I knew that if I'd come to this conclusion, Hannah would have arrived at it also. For all I knew, she'd made a whole PowerPoint presentation about it. My sister really *was* that analytical, even when it came to love. *Especially* when it came to love.

As I looked at Liam's sweet, open face, I felt hopeful for Hannah too. He looked like the perfect summer fling—cute and uncomplicated. What's more, after hugging her, Liam had let his hand linger on Hannah's arm. It looked like he was definitely interested.

I wonder what that's like? I thought a little wistfully. *To have a boy just grab you and hug you, instead of being all shy and proposing cryptic things like an anti–book club?*

I popped one of Abbie's chips into my mouth, took a swig of Hannah's drink, and turned to face the party. Nobody seemed to take much notice of me. Clearly being lanternless at a lantern party immediately consigned you to the lowest social order.

I shoved the rest of the chips into my mouth, wondering how many minutes of this party I'd have to endure before I could drag Abbie and Hannah away.

I cast a sidelong glance at Hannah and Liam. His hand was no longer on her arm, but he was standing close to her—quite close—as they chatted. He poured her some sparkling water. He let his fingers linger on hers when he handed it to her.

I grimaced and grabbed another handful of chips. It was going to be a long night.

If I was a good and loyal sister, I wouldn't have felt elated when I saw Abbie stalking toward me a few minutes later. She was so angry, you could practically see a cartoon scribble of smoke over her head.

Apparently Jason had turned out to be as jerky as he looked.

And I felt bad about that. I really did. But not as bad as I'd *been* feeling a moment earlier, when I'd been alone on the party's sidelines, glaring at all the local kids with their ridiculously clever lanterns and annoying lifelong friendships.

It was also maddening watching Hannah and Liam as they visibly swooned over each other. Hannah was doing everything right—chatting easily, laughing adorably, blushing at all the right moments. And she was clearly melting every time Liam touched her arm. Or her waist. Or her hand. (Come to think of it, Liam was a pretty handsy guy.)

It had all been very, very depressing.

So when Abbie flopped into a folding chair next to the one that I had miserably occupied for the past fifteen lonely minutes, I admit that I responded a little inappropriately.

"What happened?" I asked eagerly. "Was it really bad?"

Abbie glared at me.

"Of course it was bad!" she said. "Do I look like it was good? And why are *you* so happy?"

"I'm not," I protested. I tried—hard—to wipe the relieved grin off my face. "So what happened?"

"I don't know!" Abbie said through gritted teeth. "He seemed so interested at that bookstore. But just now he acted like he didn't even know me. It was *humiliating.*"

It was better than I'd thought! Not only was she not going to ditch me again; she was probably going to insist that we leave the party.

"Ouch," I said. "Tell me *everything.*"

"Wait," Abbie said. "Are there any chips left?"

She got up and stomped over to the refreshment table. But before she could load up on junk food and return to me, one of the local girls dragged a folding chair to the center of the dock. She stood on it and waved her lantern—a Chinese-style globe decorated with tissue paper dragonflies.

"Everybody," she screeched. "It's time to light 'em up!"

Whoops and hollers rose up from every corner of the dock. Giggling, everyone scrambled for matchbooks and lighters. I perked up too. With all my sisters' drama, I'd almost forgotten about the lanterns. I'd also failed to notice that the sky had gone black and the streetlights hanging over the dock had come on.

"Alex?" the girl shouted with one hand cupped around her mouth.

All heads swiveled toward a tall boy with an impish grin. He was fiddling with what looked like a fuse box, which was mounted on a pole at the dock entrance.

A moment later the lights went out.

"Whooo!" everyone shouted, except, of course, for me and probably Abbie. She'd disappeared in the darkness. Suddenly blind, I felt a little dizzy and gripped the seat of my chair.

"One!" the girl shouted.

There was a collective clicking noise as lighters sprang to life all over the dock. People laughed and shouted some more, waving their flames over their heads like they were at a stadium concert.

"Two!" This time the whole group chanted the number along with the leader. I gripped my chair a little harder and grinned. It was so exciting, I couldn't help but join in on the final chant, even though I had no lantern to light and nobody to enjoy this with. The other kids' fun was infectious.

"THREE!" we all shouted.

Lantern after lantern came to life!

There was a collective, quiet intake of breath as we absorbed the beauty of the lights.

The leader's buggy globe went bright orange, wobbling high

above the crowd. Fred and Wilma seemed to dance with each other. The giant tree was dazzling, emanating light from every leaf. Even Jason's stupid Darth Vader head looked amazing, with creepy yellow eyes glaring at the crowd.

At once everybody erupted into cheers.

"Whoo!" I joined in. I felt a little goofy and self-conscious jumping and clapping with everybody else, but then I brushed it off. Nobody here knew me. I was invisible to them. And for the moment, rather than being a bummer, that was a gift. I could geek out all I wanted to the perfect summery beauty of this moment without feeling embarrassed.

With my hands clasped I watched the lanterns float over my head. I gasped as I spotted the one shaped like an orange phoenix with wings outstretched, and smiled at the giant mason jar with little "fireflies" twinkling inside.

Somebody started the music back up. A ballad came on, sung by a woman with a sweet high voice, so breathy and wispy that you almost had to strain to hear her. A few couples started dancing, swaying lazily to the music. Everyone looked so pretty, almost ethereal, in the golden glow of the lanterns.

The moment was just . . . lovely. It made me swell up with happiness and feel a yearning pang all at once. It had been that way, ever since Granly had died. Every moment of joy had an ache around its edges. But when I looked at the dancing girls—this one gazing into her guy's eyes, that one whispering into her partner's ear, another laying her head on a boy's shoulder—I realized that the ache might be for something different this time.

And then my gaze shifted to the dock entrance.

I don't know what made me look, except that somehow I knew he was there.

Josh.

He was standing in the little gateway that led from the parking lot to the dock, holding on to the railing with one hand. He was wearing a short-sleeved button-down shirt in a retro checked print. His hair was glossy and neat, and his face had a recently scrubbed shine to it. In the glow of the lanterns, he looked . . . beautiful.

Or maybe he just looked that way because of the sweet, shy smile on his face. The one that seemed to be directed right at me.

I resisted the urge to turn around and make sure there wasn't some other girl behind me, one with straighter hair and a fancy lantern.

I took a halting step forward.

So did Josh.

Several steps and what felt like way too many seconds later, we faced each other.

"Hi," he said.

"Hi," I said. My voice sounded thin and fragile. I felt off balance, like the flickering of all those lantern candles was making my eyes go funny. I cleared my throat and gestured at his hands, which were empty.

"No lantern?" I asked.

"Um, no," Josh said. "It was kind of a last-minute decision. To come here, I mean."

"Oh," I said. It seemed nosy to ask why, so I just said, "They're beautiful, aren't they?"

Josh's eyes widened and he looked confused.

I gestured out to the party.

"The lanterns?" I asked. "Aren't they amazing?"

"Oh, the *lanterns*," Josh said. "Oh, yeah."

He gazed out into the party as if he were noticing the spectacle for the first time. Which was weird. They were kind of hard to miss!

He returned his gaze to me.

"Yeah," he agreed finally. "They're pretty amazing."

I smiled.

And he smiled.

And I started to wonder, even though it seemed crazy, if he had come here . . . just to see me.

A little voice in my head scoffed: *That's impossible. He couldn't have heard Abbie talking about it at Dog Ear, so he didn't know you'd be here. In fact he was probably sure you wouldn't be here, since this is just a local party.*

And yet I had this feeling that if I gave Josh a lantern pop quiz—*Are there any* Star Wars *characters in the crowd? There's one very tall lantern here. Is it a tree or a skyscraper?*—that he would fail miserably.

That's when my smile grew bigger. And, yes, more confident.

I decided I should just come out and ask him. Enough with all the mystery. I would channel Abbie and just put it out there: *You like me, don't you? And you don't know how to say it any more than I do.*

I opened my mouth.

"Josh?"

A petite, sporty-looking girl pressed out of the throng of

partiers. She had chic, close-cropped hair and white short-shorts that made her muscular, dark-skinned legs look amazing. A lantern that looked like a big, pink purse dangled from her bent arm.

"Ohmigod, the workaholic has come out of his cave," the girl squealed.

She placed the hand that wasn't holding a live flame on Josh's arm and squeezed.

"Hi, Tori," Josh said. Now he was back to looking sheepish, and I thought I saw a flush of color creep up his neck.

Wait, he's blushing? What does that *mean?*

Tori turned to me and lowered her voice, like we were besties sharing a secret.

"He's always like"—she dropped her voice an octave to imitate Josh—"'Can't make it. I have to *work*. A*gain!*' Oh, it's so boring!"

"Yeah, well." Josh shrugged lamely.

Tori shot me a sidelong look and let out another one of those conspiratorial laughs. The only thing was, I didn't know what we were conspiring about.

"So, how do you know Josh?" Tori asked bluntly.

"Dog Ear," Josh and I said at the same time, which made for more blushing.

"Oh, of course," Tori said. "Well, I'm the coxswain on his team."

"Coxswain?" I said. I was completely baffled.

"You know, his crew team?" Tori raised her eyebrows.

I nodded slowly. "Oh, right . . . crew."

"Crew is rowing," Josh explained.

"Oh!" I said with a nervous laugh. "Yeah, of course. When in lake country, right?"

Oh my God, could I be more of a dork?

"We row on the river, actually," Josh said. "The coxswain is the person who sits in the front and calls the rhythm."

"Don't forget, I steer, too!" Tori noted proudly. Then she turned to me. "I admit it. I like being able to shout orders at eight guys. They have no choice but to do my bidding."

She cackled, before adding, "The coxswain is usually a girl, because you're not supposed to weigh too much."

Then I swore she gave me one of those body-scanning looks, her eyes traveling from my neck to my ankles and back again. My curvy five feet six inches were radically different from her tiny, muscular bod. Involuntarily I crossed my arms over my chest.

The awkward silence that ensued seemed to be all Tori needed to assure herself that I was no threat to her. I could almost see the to-do list forming in her head.

1. *Wait until Josh ditches the dishrag who doesn't even know rudimentary terms like "coxswain" and "crew."*
2. *Bring Josh his favorite drink (that I just happen to know, being his coxswain and all).*
3. *Pretend to trip so he can help me to my feet and take note that I'm as light as a feather and I smell like watermelon body wash.*
4. *Let the spit-swapping ensue!*

Clearly she was confident enough about my drippiness to leave me alone with her crush.

"Ooh, I see Hazel and Callan," she said, waving wildly at two girls. When they saw Tori with Josh (and apparently overlooked me entirely), they giggled and flashed her a thumbs-up. Subtle!

"See you later, Joshie," Tori said before turning to me. "And nice to meet you . . ."

She looked at me, then back at Josh, waiting for an introduction.

Josh turned even redder. Only then did I realize he'd never asked me my name! And I'd never volunteered it.

"Chelsea," I said, unable to meet Josh's eyes. "Chelsea Silver. I'm here for the summer from LA."

"Awesome! I *love* LA," Tori said brightly. "See you around, Chelsea."

She practically skipped off to her friends, and when she reached them, they collapsed into a fit of giggles.

She couldn't have been more obvious about her intentions for Josh if she'd licked his face.

I snuck a sulky glance at him. I expected him to be gazing after Tori. How could he not? She was one of those bright-eyed, bubbly, anybody's-version-of-pretty types who *commanded* attention.

But instead Josh was looking straight at me. And there seemed to be a new light in *his* eyes.

"So . . . Chelsea Silver," he said.

"So . . . Joshie," I said. "Is that what your friends call you?"

"No!" Josh said, rolling his eyes. "And neither does Tori. I don't know *where* that came from."

Hello? I thought. *From her completely obvious crush on you.*

I wondered if mine was just as obvious.

"Oh, hey!" Josh said as if he were just remembering something. "Can you hold on a minute?"

"Uh—"

I didn't have time to respond before he darted toward the refreshments table.

Okay, I thought, insecurity washing over me. *I guess he's just really hungry. Boys are like that, right?*

That was the thing about living in a house full of women (and one not-exactly-macho accountant). Boys were a complete mystery to me. My main impression from my friends with brothers and/or boyfriends was that boys were *always* hungry. And in those rare, satiated moments when they weren't dreaming about food, they were obsessed with sex.

Which was a step up from middle-school boys, I guess. They'd seemed to devote most of their energy to coming up with new fart or burp jokes.

So when Josh dashed, I didn't know if "Hold on a minute" meant, "I'll be right back" or "Nice talking to you. Off to mingle with other cute girls now. Don't wait up!"

He was taking a long time at the refreshment table, which was pretty much a disaster by then. He poked around the wet napkins, crushed chips, half-empty soft drink bottles, and discarded paper plates.

I scanned the party for my sisters. It was hard to find anybody among the lanterns, but I finally spotted Hannah leaning back against the railing on the other side of the dock. Pressed up *really* close to her was Liam. He had one arm wrapped around her waist, and he seemed to be aiming his lips for her neck.

Hannah laughed and shoved him away—but not very far away. And she didn't seem annoyed that this guy was trying to kiss her in front of fifty strangers.

I was, though. She'd just met the guy! Okay, *re*-met him, but still. Your first kiss with someone new should be at least a *little* private, right?

Abbie clearly agreed with me, because suddenly she appeared at Hannah's side. She gave Liam a quick, insincere smile before she tugged Hannah away.

I watched them tuck their heads together for a quick conference. Surely Abbie wanted to leave.

But it looked like Hannah wanted to stay.

And me?

Well, that depended. I returned my gaze to the refreshment table and felt my heart sink.

Josh wasn't there.

I searched the rest of the party, squinting to try to find him in the sea of lights. At that moment I couldn't remember what he was wearing. All I could picture was his shy, sheepish smile.

Like he was sort of nervous/excited to see me.

Until, maybe, he realized that girls like Tori found him irresistible, and going on a "food run" had become incredibly important.

I ground my teeth in frustration and looked down at my feet. Even in the dim light I could still see my blue shoes and turquoise toenails. They were so bright, they practically glowed. And yet they'd been planted in one spot for most of the night, waiting. Waiting for my sisters, waiting for Josh.

Well, I wasn't going to wait anymore. I started to head over to Abbie and Hannah. I was going to poke my head into their little conference and announce, "That's it. We're leaving!"

And really, really hope they listened to me.

But just as I started across the dock, I heard a voice.

"Chelsea!"

I whipped around to see Josh, standing right where he'd left me. He held two red plastic cups and, in the crook of his arm, a bowl of pretzel rods.

He held one of the cups out.

"I got you something to drink," he said formally.

I smiled tentatively and walked back to him. He'd braved the gross refreshments table to get me a drink. And snacks! Nobody had ever gotten me drinks and snacks at a party before, except maybe my dad. It seemed like such a grown-up thing to do!

"It's Faygo Redpop," Josh said as I took one of the cups. "That was the only one that still had any fizz left."

Okay, *sort* of grown-up.

Josh thrust the bowl at me, and I took a pretzel rod. Not that I was even slightly interested in eating or drinking right then.

"So, I'm on page forty-two," Josh blurted. "What about you?"

"Page . . . ?" I was completely confused.

"Coconut Dreams," Josh said. "Or did you chuck it after the one-page description of Kai's smoldering brown eyes?"

I laughed out loud.

"You're not *actually* reading it," I said. "Are you?"

"Enough to get to that tragic description of the suckling pig at the luau," Josh said. "The writer laid it on a *little* thick, didn't she?"

"Oh my God, yeah," I said. "All that stuff about the singed eyelashes and little charred tail? I think she wanted us to think of the suckling pig as Wilbur and become vegan activists or something."

"Lemme tell you," Josh said, "*Charlotte's Web* is kind of a thing at Dog Ear, and Veronica Gardner is no E. B. White."

"But it's like a car wreck now," I said, and giggled. "I can't look away. Plus, the library's, like, *never* open, and I've read everything else in our cottage."

"You should get that book I showed you," Josh said. He chomped on a pretzel absently. *"Beyond the Beneath."*

"I'm pretty broke," I said. "I'm trying to save up for a new e-reader, but at this point I can barely buy myself a paperback. I guess I should look into getting some babysitting jobs, since we're here for the rest of the summer. I'm waiting until I get desperate enough."

"Oh, so you have no sympathy for suckling pigs *and* you hate children," Josh said with teasing grin.

"I like kids," I protested. "But there's only so much Candy Land and PB&J a girl can take."

"Well, how do you feel about tuna salad?" Josh asked.

"Um," I said, "I guess some kids like it, but—"

"No, I mean you," Josh said. "I happen to know that Mel and Mel's is about to put a 'Help Wanted' sign in their window."

"The coffee shop?" I asked.

The coffee shop that's right next door to the bookstore where you work every day?

"Yeah," Josh said. "Melissa's good friends with my mom. She

mentioned that they were looking for somebody new."

I pictured Mel & Mel's. It was called a coffee shop, but it wasn't the kind that had hissing espresso machines and nutmeg-dusted mochas. The coffee was pretty much regular or decaf, poured in endless refills from a potbellied glass carafe with an orange plastic handle. They sold soup and sandwiches, and for dessert they had one of those rotating pie cases. Abbie, Hannah, and I used to press our noses to that glass case when we were little, watching the towering wedges of lemon meringue and chocolate cream pies twirl slowly by. Choosing our flavors had been agonizing.

The waitresses there were old-school. They wore aprons and tucked pens behind their ears. The older ones had leathery necks and wore too much makeup. The young ones always seemed to have lots of tattoos. They called us "sweetie pie" when they plunked down our pink lemonades on the faux wood-grain table. And when they served you pie, they topped it with a big squirt of fake whipped cream, straight from the can.

"I don't know," I said, shaking my head. "Do you think they'd be looking for someone like me? I've never waited tables before."

"Do you like cats?" Josh asked.

"They're okay," I said.

"Well, *don't* say that to Melissa," Josh said. "Tell her you *love* cats, especially calicos. And before you talk to Melanie, make sure you know the score of the most recent Cubs game."

"O-kay," I said with a laugh. "Anything else I should know?"

"How are you at chopping up celery and pickles?" Josh quizzed me.

"Oh, those are my specialties," I joked.

"They'll love you," Josh said. Then suddenly he seemed to find his fizzy red drink really interesting, because he ducked his head to stare into it.

And if I could have seen better in the late-night darkness, I would have sworn he was blushing.

Shyly I looked away. That's when I saw that Abbie was motioning at me frantically from across the dock. When she saw that she'd caught my eye, she pointed dramatically at Hannah and Liam.

They were full-on making out! Yes, they were in a shadowy part of the dock with no lanterns nearby, but you could still see *everything*—Hannah's fingers in Liam's hair, his arms clasped tightly around her waist, her ankle wrapped around his.

"Oh my God!" I exclaimed.

"What?" Josh said, following my gaze.

"Never mind!" I cried. "It's nothing."

The last thing I wanted Josh to see was my *sister* macking with one of his classmates.

"It's just," I said quickly, "I came here with my sisters and I think they're ready to go."

"Oh, okay," Josh said. I was so focused on Hannah's gross PDA that I couldn't read Josh's tone. Was that disappointment I heard in his voice? Or indifference?

"But thanks for the Mel and Mel's tip," I said. "You know, I think I'm gonna go for it!"

I had only made the decision that very moment. But suddenly I desperately wanted to tie on an apron and start calling people "hon." It sounded kind of fun! More fun, anyway, than changing diapers.

Plus, I couldn't help but wonder if Josh was a regular at Mel & Mel's. It *was* just next door.

The way he smiled at me—we're talking deep dimpling—I kind of thought he might be.

"They open at seven," he said.

July

The morning after the party I left a note to my parents on the kitchen table and headed for Mel & Mel's at six forty-five.

Sparrow Road was eerily quiet, and the sunbeams filtered through the trees at a very unfamiliar angle. I was *never* up this early when I was in Bluepointe. But I told myself, maybe just a little defensively, that my job quest had nothing to do with Josh. Okay, not *much* to do with him.

I'm just being a go-getter, I thought. *Who knows how many people might be lined up for this waitress job?*

I also credited the date—the first day of July.

New month, new job—it's a fresh start. I'm already getting bored with lying around on the beach.

When I arrived at the corner of Main and Althorp, I cast a furtive glance at the not-yet-open Dog Ear, just to make sure nobody was inside. Luckily, it was dark and still, just like most of the other businesses on Main.

The brightly lit coffee shop next door looked sunny and welcoming in comparison. Just as Josh had predicted, there was a HELP WANTED sign taped to the glass door.

I peered through the door. One of the Mels, I think it was Melanie, was setting heavy china mugs out on the tables. She wore her chin-length gray hair tied back with a bandanna. Her apron—layered over jeans and a tank top—was embroidered with a calico cat.

She glanced up and saw me.

"Be right there, sweetie," she called.

"Oh, okay," I yelled back. I stepped back to the sidewalk, feeling awkward and intrusive, but Melanie (Melanie, right?) smiled sweetly as she unlocked the door.

"Well!" she said, planting her fists on her hips. "*Somebody's* really ready for chocolate chip pancakes this morning!"

"Oh, uh, no thanks," I said. "Chocolate chip pancakes really aren't my thing."

I smoothed down the marigold-colored cotton dress I'd chosen. On the plus side, it was very 1960s diner waitress. On the minus, it was horribly wrinkled. I hoped she wouldn't notice.

"Well, maybe you'd like some cinnamon streusel coffee cake?" she offered. "You would not *believe* what the secret ingredient is."

"Actually," I said, pointing back at the HELP WANTED sign, "I'm here because of the job?"

"Oh!" Mel said. She wiped her hands on her apron. "Did you just move to town?"

"Uh-huh," I said. "For the summer, anyway."

"I was kind of hoping for someone longer-term," Mel said skeptically. "What's your experience?"

"Um, I babysit for one family back in California that has four kids," I said. "Those kids can *eat*. Sometimes I feel like a short-order cook."

Melanie bit her lip. "Let me talk to my sister."

She looked over her shoulder and called, "Melanie!"

Oh! This sister wasn't Melanie; she was Melissa. That's right. It was *Melissa* who liked calico cats.

Melissa likes cats, I reminded myself. *Melanie like the Cubs. Melissa—cats. Melanie—Cubs.*

Then my stomach swooped.

I'd just remembered the other tip Josh had given me: *Make sure you know the score of the Cubs game.*

Okay, so I had no experience, I was here only for the summer, and I didn't even know who the Cubs had played last night, much less the score. I had a dim awareness that the Cubs *always* lost. I think I'd heard Granly joke about it.

So I went out on a limb as Melanie—wearing cargo shorts, a sporty-looking T-shirt, and a royal blue baseball cap with a red C on it—came out of the kitchen.

"Hi, I'm Chelsea Silver," I said, giving her a wave. "Shame about the Cubs last night, isn't it?"

"What? That they broke their losing streak?" Melanie crowed. "Three to two, baby!"

She held out her hand to Melissa for a high five. Melissa ignored the hand.

"What?" Melanie said defensively. She crossed her arms over her chest, and I noticed how tan and sinewy they looked. Melanie looked like the kind of person who spent her free time hiking up mountains or biking fifty miles or some other ridiculously outdoorsy activity. "That's a perfectly respectable score."

I laughed a little. "You remind me of me and my sisters."

"Sis*ters*?" Melanie said, shooting Melissa a teasing grin. "You have more than one? You must have a strong constitution."

"That's why you should give me a job," I blurted.

The Mels raised their eyebrows at each other. I felt a wave of nervous heat wash over my face. That probably wasn't what Abbie and Hannah had meant when they'd said I should be more confident.

"She's interested in waitressing for the summer," Melissa said to Melanie.

"Just for the summer?" Melanie said skeptically.

I glanced at the cash register at the end of the counter. It was covered with photos of calico cats, each photo sheathed in a yellowed plastic sleeve.

"Oh, are those your cats?" I said desperately. "So cute!"

Melanie ignored that and motioned Melissa over for a tête-à-tête.

I leaned against the counter in defeat. It had only taken about five minutes for me to reveal myself to be a total spaz. An *unqualified* spaz. A spaz posing as a cat-lover.

The front door opened, and a couple with two little kids walked in. Melissa waved at them.

"Just have a seat anywhere," she called with a smile. "I'll be right over."

I eyed the bin of menus mounted on the side of the counter, and shrugged. I had nothing to lose. Why not try to steal a run, as a baseball fan would (maybe?) say.

I grabbed four menus.

Then I glanced at the family as they settled into their seats, and I put two of the menus back, replacing them with kids' menus. I brought them all over to the table.

"Hi there!" I said, way too cheerily. "Can I get you something to drink?"

"I'll have coffee," the dad said. He pointed at his little girl, who looked about three. "And she'll have—Tally! Leave the salt shakers alone! Sorry. She'll have—Tally! What did I say?"

"Tally," I said, bending down to meet her pretty, round blue eyes. "Would you like some milk?"

Tally's face lit up in a shy smile.

"Juice," she said.

I glanced at her mom. She was giving her daughter one of those sappy my-baby's-growing-up smiles, which I guessed meant juice was allowed.

"Apple or orange?" I asked.

"Apple!" Tally cried, clapping her pudgy little hands together.

"Apple!" I said with a nod (and a silent prayer that the Mels had apple juice).

"Thank you!" the mom said. "And I'll have unsweetened iced tea, and, Zeke, you want OJ, right?"

As their son nodded, I said, "Okay. Coffee, iced tea, apple, and orange. Right?"

"Yup!" Zeke said.

The parents beamed some more.

"Check out the menu," I said. "You might want to try the cinnamon streusel coffee cake. You'll never guess what the secret ingredient is."

"Cake!" Tally cried.

"Thanks," the dad said to me before turning to his daughter. "Now, Tally, first eggies, *then* cake . . ."

I felt a surge of pride as I turned to walk briskly away. The surge, of course, was quickly squelched when I remembered that I had just done a bit of guerilla waitressing—and I had no idea what to do next.

The Mels were staring at me. I couldn't tell if they were mad or amused. I think it was a little of both.

"Um . . . they want a coffee, iced tea, apple juice, and OJ," I said. "Do you . . . have apple juice?"

"Lucky for you we do," Melanie said. She glanced at Melissa.

"How about we do a trial for the day," Melissa said. "And we'll see how it goes."

"Okay!" I said. "So do you want me to start now?"

"Well, you already did, didn't you?" Melanie said.

"I guess I did," I said, giving Tally a little wave. She flapped her fingers back at me.

"Melissa usually works the counter, but she can finish up with that table while I get you set up," Melanie said, hustling back toward the kitchen and beckoning me to follow her. "You do know, don't you, that taking that drink order was the easiest thing you're going to do all day?"

"Of course," I said, even though that had never crossed my mind. This was pretty much the most impulsive thing I'd ever done. I was elated and terrified all at once.

An hour later the breakfast rush started to feel more like a breakfast onslaught. And the other two waitresses—Ginny and Andrea—seemed ready to stab me with their Paper Mate pens.

That's when I started wondering which failure the Mels would reference when they told me never to come back to their coffee shop again, even to buy coffee.

Would they mention the slippery streak of ice water I trailed across the linoleum floor at least three times?

Or the moment I served four sides of bacon to the wrong table—a table that happened to be filled with vegetarians?

What about the time I jammed up the cash register, even after Ginny had taken a full five minutes (which apparently was an eternity in waitressland) to show me how to use it?

Or when I filled three pages of my waitress pad with the order of one finicky family because I didn't know any of the shorthand that the other waitresses used to communicate with Melanie in the kitchen?

If none of those gaffes sealed my doom, I was sure it was going to be the plate I dropped—the plate that had been swimming in maple syrup. It almost exploded, spraying syrup in every possible direction.

By the time the rush began to ease up, I could feel big tufts of frizz popping out of my ponytail. My armpits were so damp, I worried I might have dark circles on my dress.

The remaining customers were all in Ginny's and Andrea's sections (I'm sure that was no accident), so I slumped into one of the stools at the counter and gave Melissa a guilty look.

"Turns out," I said, "serving a restaurant full of people is more challenging than babysitting four little kids. Who knew?"

I gave a lame laugh.

Then, slowly, reluctantly, I placed my order pad on the counter and started to untie my apron. Even though the morning had been *so* hard, it had also been kind of fun. A sticky, egg-yolky, spazzy kind of fun. Plus, I'd made almost forty dollars in tips! In three and a half hours! That was way better than babysitting money.

Melissa, who had a stack of receipts piled at her elbow, glanced up from the numbers she was pounding into the cash register.

"What are you doing, sweetie pie?" she said. "Your shift isn't over for two and a half hours."

"But, but . . . I was a disaster!" I said.

"I hate to agree with her, Melissa," Andrea said as she popped a new filter full of grounds into the coffeemaker. "But she kind of was."

She sat next to me at the counter, smiling sympathetically through dark red lipstick. Andrea looked like she was in her early twenties. She had a ton of tattoos and wore Adidas sneakers with tube socks pulled up to the knee. I loved her style, and I marveled at how non-sweaty and pretty she still looked after that brutal shift.

"No offense, Chelsea," she said.

"None taken," I said sadly.

"Oh, Andie," Melissa scolded. "You on your first day, now *that* was a disaster. Remember the way you cried! 'I can't do it, Mel! I can't *do it*! Just let me wash dishes!'"

"You started me on Sunday brunch!" Andrea protested. "Talk about trial by fire! Today's only Monday! A slow Monday, at that."

"That was slow?" I squeaked.

"Moderately," Melissa admitted. Then she looked at me. "Listen, if you'd had any experience, I'd say, yes, this day was a disaster. But for someone on her first day, I'd call you, oh, a mild calamity."

"Is that good?"

Ginny breezed by on her way to a table, with a parade of oval plates stacked along the full length of her arm. She was probably in her fifties, had short salt-and-pepper ringlets, and her eyes looked tired even when she was smiling, as she was now.

"Calamity's not bad," she said encouragingly. "You'll get there. If Andie did, *anybody* can."

"Hey!" Andrea said poutily.

"So . . . do you want me to stay?" I asked Melissa cautiously.

"Well, I'll have to talk about it with Melanie," Melissa said, "but I think you might be a good fit. You are good with the little ones, and we get a lot of those in here."

"I know," I said with a grin. "I was one of those! I've been coming here for forever."

"Oh, now you're making me feel old," Melissa complained with a good-natured smile. "So, what, do your parents have a summer cottage here?"

"My grandma," I said automatically, before catching myself. "I mean, she did. I mean, the cottage is still here but my grandma . . . isn't. She passed away."

"Oh, I'm sorry to hear that," Melissa said. "What was her name?"

"Delia Roth," I said, looking down at the white Formica counter. It blurred a little bit.

"Oh, right, I did know that," Melissa said softly. "I remember Delia coming in here with all those granddaughters. That must have been you and your sisters. I should have recognized you from your—"

"Hair," I said, and sighed, smoothing back the frizzy corkscrews that had pulled out of my ponytail. "I know."

"Well, I'm sorry for your loss, sweetie pie," Melissa said.

I nodded and swallowed hard. "Thanks. It's okay."

I was glad for the distraction when Melanie called through the order window.

"All righty!" she said. "Just got my first lunch order. Turn on the specials board!"

Melissa hopped promptly off the stool behind the cash register and walked over to a glossy black screen propped on an easel next to the pie carousel. Ceremoniously she plugged it in. The specials—written in different colors of neon marker—lit up, glowing brightly.

"Wow, that's fancy!" I said.

"I know!" Melissa said, giving the light board an affectionate pat. "We just got it last season. I think it really sells the specials, don't you?"

"Melissa," said Andrea, propping her chin on her fist, "are they really specials when they're *always* the same?"

"Well," Melissa said, giving Andrea a scolding glance, "only since, you know, the *order*."

I wondered what they were talking about as I scanned the specials on the light board.

SPINACH ARTICHOKE DIP WITH TOAST POINTS . . . $4.99

EGG SALAD–CHICKEN SALAD–TUNA SALAD COMBO
ON BED OF LETTUCE . . . $8.50

PIMENTO CHEESE SANDWICH ON PUMPERNICKEL . . . $6.50

GRILLED ASPARAGUS WITH LEMON AIOLI . . . $3.99

I was starting to see a theme here. A certain ingredient that *all* the specials contained.

Then I remembered something I'd noticed that morning as I'd rushed from the dining room to the kitchen and back again. In my frantic state it had barely registered, but now that I had a moment to think, it finally clicked.

Just inside the swinging doors that led to the kitchen was a tall, chrome shelving unit. The top and bottom shelves were filled with various dinery items—spare salt and pepper shakers, red and yellow squirt bottles, a big glass jar of pickle relish, and several stacks of napkins.

But by far the predominant feature on the shelves, placed square at eye level, was the mayonnaise—jar after mammoth plastic jar of it. The industrial-size mayo containers were stacked three deep and covered two entire shelves.

Suddenly I realized why Josh had thought I had mayo-on-the-face paranoia the first day I met him.

And why he'd asked about my celery-chopping abilities.

"Melissa," I said, "what *is* the secret ingredient in the cinnamon streusel coffee cake?"

Melissa hung her head.

"Let me guess," I said. "Mayonnaise?"

Melissa nodded.

"I had a little ordering snafu," she admitted, looking a little weary. "There was . . . an extra zero."

Andrea shook her head and gave a little snort of laughter.

"The supplier wouldn't take them back," Melissa went on, "and even though the jars are sealed, there *is* an expiration date on them. So . . ."

"When life hands you mayo?" I prompted.

"Make lots and lots of tuna salad," Melissa finished. "And dips and cake and old-fashioned Jell-O molds . . . Well, it's actually kind of interesting how many uses there are for mayonnaise when pressed to the wall. It's great for moisturizing your hair. You can even use it to polish piano keys."

Melanie had wandered out to pour herself a cup of coffee during the lull.

"The only problem," she interjected, "is now we're so sick of mayonnaise, *we* can't eat it. Ugh, I *dream* about mayo. Sometimes I just want to throw it out! But little Miss Waste-Not-Want-Not over there won't let me."

Melissa glared at her sister defensively.

"It's immoral to throw away perfectly good food," she said.

"It's a *condiment*," Melanie said. "It barely counts as food."

"Hey!" I said. "What about donating it to a soup kitchen or shelter? It wouldn't go to waste there."

"Did it!" Ginny said as she swung around the counter to fill a few plastic cups with ice. "We gave 'em so much mayo, they said to please stop. They couldn't take any more."

"Wow," I said. "That's a lot of mayo."

Melanie swung her arm over Melissa's shoulders and looked mock-sorrowful.

"It is our burden to bear," she said. "And our shame."

I laughed out loud.

"Oh!" Melissa scoffed. "It could have happened to anyone."

"Sure it could, sweetie pie," Ginny said. "Don't you listen to Melanie."

Melanie scowled and gave Ginny a fake punch on the arm as Ginny strolled over to a customer sitting at a two-top near the counter.

"What can I get you, sir?" she asked the man.

"I'll have the club sandwich," he replied.

Andrea and I shrieked at the same time, "Want mayo with that?" Then we both laughed so hard that tears streamed down our faces.

The man looked very confused.

"I'm sorry, sir," Ginny said to him, giving us a glare. "I'll get right on that. And while I do, *Chelsea's* going to get you a free iced tea."

I hopped off my stool and hurried to do what Ginny ordered, a big slaphappy grin on my face.

I needed that jolt of lightness to get me through the lunch

rush, which was almost more hectic than the breakfast one. My section was full of people in work clothes, needing to eat fast and run back to their jobs.

I couldn't help but notice that Josh was not one of them. But I didn't have time to think about it. Or about Granly or about anything really, except the constant rhythm of taking orders, delivering food, checking in on customers, then checking them out. There was only, "We don't serve fries, only chips." And, "The soup of the day is spring vegetable." And "Of *course* you can have extra mayo on that."

I realized that maybe that was what I liked most about this job. It was a vacation from my vacation—the one that left me way too much time to brood about . . . everything, especially what might be going on on the other side of that wall that separated Mel & Mel's from Dog Ear.

Melissa scheduled me for the two-to-eight p.m. shift the next day, and put me down in the schedule for four afternoon shifts a week.

"We're more of a breakfast and lunch place," she told me, "so you can slow down and learn the ropes a bit."

I got to town at one fifteen the next day. But not because I wanted to get to work early.

I was going to Dog Ear.

At the corner of Main and Althorp, I paused—and hyperventilated a bit. Clutching my stomach, I ducked onto Althorp, which was really more of an alley than a street—skinny, one-way, and mostly stocked with service entrances to the stores on Main.

I smoothed down my poofy A-line skirt, adjusted the straps of my blue camisole, and tried to calm down.

What's the big deal? I asked myself. *I'm just stopping in. I'll talk to Josh, pick out some books, and be on my way.*

What's more, I'd done a mirror check right before I'd left the cottage, so I *knew* there was nothing on my face.

I gave my head a little shake, smoothed down the puff of frizz that the head shake had unleashed, and walked purposefully around the corner.

When I went into Dog Ear, Stella was behind the counter.

"Hi there!" she said, fluttering her fingers at me. "C'mon in. It's Nutter Butters today."

I grinned at her. The prospect of dribbling peanut buttery crumbs into a book that I had just *bought* made me giddy. I decided to look for a book first, and Josh second.

I was headed to the YA section when I got distracted by a chirpy voice coming out of the kids' area. I peeked over the white picket fence at a mom-ish-looking woman perched on a tiny chair. She was reading to a small crowd of toddlers who alternated between listening raptly and pointing at the pictures to shout out things like, "It's a duck!"

"Cute," I whispered to myself.

I was just heading back to the YA section, when I froze.

Between the kids' play area and the YA aisle, there was an aisle filled with picture books. Sitting on the floor of that aisle, shelving a stack of them, was Josh.

He was looking right at me.

"Hi," I stage-whispered. I didn't want to disturb the story hour.

He waved and smiled.

Which made me feel both flustered and floaty. Suddenly the thought of delaying talking to Josh in favor of shopping for books seemed really ridiculous.

After walking down the aisle, I lowered myself to the floor, trying to simultaneously be graceful and not give Josh a glimpse of my underwear. He was holding a copy of *Where the Wild Things Are* but seemed to have forgotten all about it. Instead he just stared at me.

Then we did that thing where he smiled and I smiled back and he smiled harder and so did I, and *boy* was I glad nobody else could see us right then. It comforted me to know that we were *equally* dorky.

"Listen," I said when I finally remembered that I'd actually come here to tell him something. "I was going to buy a book and then thank you. But now I'm thanking you first."

Josh smiled bigger. "You're not broke anymore?"

"No!" I said. "Look at this!"

I opened my purse and pulled out a rolled-up wad of money. It was fifty-two dollars in one-dollar bills—my final tip count from the previous day.

"That's, like, five paperbacks right there," I said.

"So, I guess you got the job?" Josh asked.

"Oh, yeah, I forgot to mention that," I said. "They started me right away. And I'm going back today for the dinner shift! So, uh, that's why I wanted to thank you—for telling me about it and giving me those pointers."

He didn't have to know how badly I'd mangled the whole calico cat/Cubs part of my interview.

"You're welcome," Josh said.

There was a moment of smiley silence, except for the voice of the reader starting a new book: "'One Sunday morning the warm sun came up and—pop!—out of the egg came a tiny and very hungry caterpillar.'"

"So," I said, because we couldn't just sit there grinning at each other for minutes on end (could we?). "I guess we'll be working next door to each other."

That's when Josh's smile faded and his face seemed to go a little pale.

And that look in his eyes—was that panic?

I felt like I'd been slapped in the face. Suddenly Josh and I were right back to the first day we'd met, when he'd started out sweet and flirty, then turned on me. Now he was doing it again. He'd *told* me about the Mel & Mel's job, and yet here he was, freaking out because I'd taken the Mel & Mel's job! Was he realizing he doesn't like me after all? Again?

"I've gotta go," I blurted.

Even though I have half an hour until my shift starts. Which I'm now going to have to kill somewhere else. What am I supposed to do, go buy fifty-two dollars' worth of fudge?

"You're leaving?" Josh said. His voice cracked a little as he said it, and he cringed.

"Yes, I'm leaving," I said frostily.

But my outfit seemed to have another idea. As I tried to get up, I realized I'd sat down on the hem of my skirt. I was pinned down!

I took a deep, long-suffering breath and started yanking my skirt out from under me. Never had my vintage habit so betrayed me! I was totally going to switch to miniskirts after this.

"'On Wednesday,'" the mom read, "'he ate through three plums, but he was still hungry.'"

"Yah!" I grunted, finally freeing myself. I smoothed the poofy skirt down, then planted my hands on the floor to push myself to my feet.

But before I got very far, Josh planted *his* hands on me! On my shoulders anyway. I fell back to the floor.

"Oof!" I grunted, giving him a *WHAT are you doing*? glare.

From the stunned look on his face, it seemed Josh was asking himself the same question.

But then his fingers tightened on my shoulders and he answered the question for both of us by leaning in—and kissing me!

It was just one kiss. By the clock it probably only lasted a few seconds. But in my head (not to mention the *rest* of me) that kiss—Josh kissing *me*—seemed to go on and on. I felt a tingly jolt in my lips. Josh's palms felt incredibly warm on my shoulders, and my arms and legs went rubbery.

No, that wasn't the right word for it. I felt *melty*.

I couldn't believe it.

Whenever I read a romantic book (and I'd read a lot of them), I'd get to the part where she "melted beneath his touch" or "melted into his arms" and roll my eyes.

That's just a goofy thing writers write, I'd told myself. *Nobody* really *melts when a boy kisses her.*

Now I knew. The melting really did happen—if you kissed the right boy. For the first time in my life, I seemed to be doing just that.

And I was doing it with a chirpy mom reading *The Very Hungry Caterpillar* literally six feet away. Not to mention all those little kids. This was . . . weird!

Also wonderful.

And very, *very* surprising.

That's surely what Josh saw in my face when we finally pulled away from each other. That and a whole lot of hot-and-bothered hair frizz.

"Um . . . ," I said.

"Um . . . ," he said.

"So I gotta . . . ," I said, pointing in the general direction of the door. Kissing Josh seemed to have rendered me half-mute.

Josh only nodded. I guess he was *fully* mute.

As I drifted to my feet, I couldn't help but wonder if that was a good or bad thing. Maybe another girl (my sister, Abbie, for instance) would have come out and *asked* him if it was a good or bad thing. But I didn't. I *couldn't.*

For one thing, there was the half-muteness.

For another, I couldn't look Josh in the eyes. Not after his lips had just been on my lips and he'd just seen my face more close-up than I'd seen it myself. It was so embarrassing!

Also amazing.

I turned and headed out of the picture book aisle, trying not to wobble as I walked. I forgot about book shopping entirely and reported to work twenty minutes early. This earned me completely unintentional brownie points, as well as the privilege of chopping up some celery for Melanie while I waited for my shift to begin.

Once it did, it took a while for my tables to fill up, which was a good thing. I was ridiculously distracted from a job I hadn't even begun to master yet.

Okay, the first question, I thought as I laid napkins and flatware on my tables, *is why! Why did Josh kiss me? Does he really like me? Or maybe kissing me was an accident, somehow. I mean, it doesn't get less sexy than* The Very Hungry Caterpillar.

And besides, I know he regretted telling me to go for the job next door. I could see it in his eyes. So why—Oop! Party of six in my section.

I hurried over to scoop up menus as three middle-aged couples settled themselves into my section's biggest table. I handed the menus out, then managed to get their drink orders correct—even if I did hand the wrong drinks to each customer, down to the very last person.

"I'm sorry!" I said as they laughed and passed their drinks around the table until each one found the person who'd ordered it. "It's only my second day."

"In that case," said one of the customers, a jolly-looking guy with thinning hair and a big grin, just the kind of guy my dad would *love* to regale with one-liners, "I'll have a chef salad with ham instead of turkey. And egg whites only, no yolks. Dressing on the side. And I'd like extra dressing."

"Okaaaay," I said, sticking my tongue in the corner of my mouth as I furiously scribbled the complicated order.

"Now the extra dressing," the man instructed, "I want on the salad. Oh, and I'd like ham instead of turkey."

"Wait a minute," I said, "didn't you just say turkey instead of ham?"

And doesn't a chef salad have both turkey and *ham?* I wondered frantically.

"Sweetie," said the woman across the table from the man, "he's messing with you! He does this every time we go to a restaurant."

Then she scowled at her husband.

"John!" she scolded. "You're scaring the girl to death."

"All right, then," the man said, grinning at me. "I'll have a burger. With everything."

I squinted at him. "Really?" I said skeptically.

"Really, sweetie," his wife said. "John! Stop!"

He chuckled and crossed his arms over his big belly as if to say, *My work here is done.*

Old people amused themselves in really weird ways.

Then again, young people could be kind of weird too. For instance, some of them planted out-of-the-blue kisses on unsuspecting girls during completely inappropriate children's story hours.

I swooped back to the kiss—to the unexpected yet wonderful kiss and the imprint of Josh's hands on my shoulders that I swore I could still feel—and completely missed the next two orders.

"I'm sorry," I said as John's wife said something about an extra plate. "Can you repeat that?"

I saw the customers exchange a look and shift in their seats.

It's going to be a long afternoon, they telegraphed to each other.

You don't know the half of it, people, I thought.

By the end of my shift, I was beyond exhausted. If Melissa thought two-to-eight was the easy shift, then she was a superhero. My feet ached and my arms were sore from lugging heavy trays. I had a greasy spot on my camisole from a salad dressing spill. I was starving, but I also had no desire to even look at food.

I was also just as bewildered by the Kiss as I'd been six hours earlier. In my few minutes of free time that afternoon, I'd sent Emma three urgent *NEED ADVICE* texts, but her phone must have been turned off. Her mean teachers at the Intensive apparently loved to snap cell phones in half if they dared to ring during class. The ballet world was so weird.

Of course, everything was seeming weird to me at that moment—customers who left tips entirely in nickels, Melanie making a gross blue and red cake in honor of the Cubs . . . Weirdest of all, of course, was Josh acting all phobic one moment, then planting the best kiss of my life on me the next.

I went to the little office off the kitchen to take off my apron and get ready to leave. I considered calling a couple other friends from back home to get their take on the Kiss, but I was too tired to explain all the backstory to them. Then I thought about talking to Hannah. With her I could speak in sisters' shorthand. Then she'd probably do that thing where she reads between the lines of what I tell her and informs me of what I'm *really* saying. Usually I find that excruciatingly annoying, but in this case I actually kind of craved it.

You've got two sisters who've just been through all this, Hannah and Abbie had told me before the lantern party.

I hated when they were right, but they were right. I decided to talk to Hannah right after I got home.

As I walked through the dining room, waving good-bye to Melissa, I pulled the rubber band out of my messy ponytail and held it between my front teeth. I pushed through the front door backward as I used both hands to smooth my hair back so I could make a new, neater pony.

But as soon as the door *swooshed* closed behind me, I heard the jingle of Dog Ear's door opening and closing as well.

I glanced up. The elastic band fell out of my mouth and my hands dropped to my sides, causing my hair to poof frizzily around my face.

Josh was standing in front of the bookstore.

He looked kind of like he wanted to dive right back inside.

For once I knew we had something in common, because I kind of wanted to do the same thing.

But I also couldn't stop staring at him. At his smooth face, his super-short hair, and his cute orange-and-green sneakers.

"Hi," I said. My voice sounded hesitant and a little raspy after talking over the clatter of dishes all day.

"Hi," Josh said, sounding just as nervous as I felt. Feeling clumsy, I grabbed my hair elastic off the sidewalk. Then Josh pointed behind him. "Are you walking this way?"

I nodded and started down Main. Josh fell into step beside me, and it felt . . . wonderful. He was so close that our arms almost touched, so close that I could feel the warmth radiating off his body.

I guess that was what made me turn off Main and head down

Althorp. Suddenly, instead of wanting to get home as soon as possible to shower, eat a mayo-free dinner, and puzzle out this Josh business with my sister, I wanted this walk—with Josh—to last as long as possible.

When we were a few feet from the end of the block, Josh stopped, turned, and looked down at me. He really was tall. His face looked sweetly sheepish and a little aggravated.

"Listen," he said. "I know you must think I'm crazy. I mean, I haven't exactly been, um, consistent. With you."

I raised my eyebrows.

"I guess it's safe to say," Josh went on, "I've been a little, how do I say this . . . taken aback."

"Taken aback?" I asked. This did *not* sound like a positive thing.

"See?" Josh said, wringing his hands. "I never say the right thing to you. It's like I don't have control over my mouth."

See? I thought. *He all but said it—he* did *kiss me by accident!*

I bit my lip, bracing myself for heartbreak.

"Chelsea," Josh said, "here's the thing. You tried to rescue those books from me. And you think *Coconut Dreams* is as fabulously horrible as I do. And you wear those vintage clothes, and you have that *hair*—"

"I hate my hair," I said, my hand instinctively springing to my head to smooth it down.

"See?" Josh repeated. "I did it again."

He looked down at the ground, suddenly even shyer.

"And then I went and . . . you know," he said. "Earlier."

"Yeah, earlier," I whispered.

"So anyway, about that," Josh said. "I'm sor—"

Josh didn't get to finish what he was saying.

Because I grabbed him by the shoulders and sprang to my tiptoes—and kissed him!

Josh stumbled backward. I started to pull away from the kiss, but he plunged his hand into my messy mane of hair and pulled me closer.

And now I wasn't kissing him and he wasn't kissing me.

We were kissing each other.

My eyes fluttered closed. I let my right hand trail down Josh's arm—which was thin but muscular and so smooth and warm—until my hand found his. Our fingers intertwined.

Josh tilted until his shoulder blades touched the brick wall behind him. I tilted along with him.

And now "melty" took on a different meaning. All the confusion and hurt I'd been feeling? All those mixed signals Josh had given me? They all melted away—canceled out by one perfect kiss after another.

My dad woke me and my sisters up early the next morning.

"I'm commandeering you for the morning," he announced. "Your mother wants some time to herself, and *I* want some time with my wayward daughters."

"Dad," I said, shoving a curl out of my eyes as I slumped out of my bed, "me having a *job* doesn't exactly make me wayward. You and Mom are the ones who make us earn all our own money."

"Well, then I guess I'm only talking about Hannah," Dad said lightly. "Anyway, be in the kitchen in five. No primping!"

I laughed as he hurried down the hall, then I whispered to Abbie, "What does he mean 'Hannah'? What's she been up to?"

"Didn't you know?" Abbie said, throwing off her covers and sitting up in bed. "She had a date with Fasthands last night. She got home after you were asleep."

"Liam?" I said.

"Yes, *Liam*," Abbie grumbled. "When she got home, she was all giggly and floaty. *Very* un-Hannah-like."

"Oh!" I said.

I hurried over to the closet and ducked inside it, ostensibly to throw on some clothes, but also because I had to hide my incredulous grin.

How had this happened? Instead of Hannah and Abbie doing all the dating, it was Hannah and *me* who'd been with boys last night.

That was very un-Chelsea-like, too.

Part of me wanted to dash to Hannah's room and ask her if she felt just like I did—all dreamy and incredulous. I kept wondering if the previous night had really happened. Then I'd touch my lips and remember what *Josh's* lips had felt like and realize, yes, it really had.

"Girls! I've got bagels toasting!"

It was my dad—giving me no time to dish with Hannah about Josh. What *was* this mystery outing? I quickly threw on some knee-length khakis and an A-line top with a swirly, psychedelic pattern on it. I grabbed some heavy-duty bobby pins off the dresser and piled my hair into a sloppy bun on top of my head.

In the kitchen my dad handed each of us a hot bagel wrapped loosely in a paper towel. He grabbed a coffee thermos and a stack of paper cups and shooed us toward the front door.

As we passed through the living room, I saw my mom standing in front of the built-in hutch. It was the centerpiece of the living room, its shelves filled with books, family photos, knickknacks, and a tiny TV. The bottom of the hutch was all cabinets. Inside of these were so many of the things that made the cottage Granly's. There were decks of mismatched playing cards and lots of battered board games. Photo albums filled an entire shelf. There was an accordion folder full of essays my mom had written in high school and college, and a dried corsage. I'd always loved Granly's sewing basket and the box of super-loud costume jewelry that she'd worn in the sixties and seventies. My sisters and I used them to play dress-up when we were little.

My mom was staring down at those cabinets. Her hands were on her hips and her eyes looked tired, even though she was usually such a morning person.

"Hi, Mom," I said quietly.

She jumped, startled. When she looked in my direction, her eyes were a little unfocused—until they crinkled into a beaming smile.

"Oh! Hi, sweetheart," she said. The perkiness in her voice was set to extra high.

Maybe I should have lingered a moment and given my mom some sympathy as she got ready to sort through Granly's cabinets.

But I just didn't want to go there. Not when a tiny remnant of last night's magic was still lingering inside me.

So I just said, "Well, have a good morning."

"You too," Mom replied. "Enjoy the fishing!"

"Fishing?" I squawked. Then I stomped outside. "Daaaad!"

He knew we hated fishing! He'd totally conned us!

Hannah and Abbie were already settled into their seats, munching their bagels. Dad had started the car. I flounced into the backseat next to Hannah and pointed an accusing finger at our father.

"Do you know where he's taking us?" I said as my dad hurriedly put the car into reverse and skidded out of the driveway. "Fishing!"

"Daaaaaad!" Abbie and Hannah complained.

"Throw me a fish bone, will you?" my dad said, with his dadly chortle. "It's the one father-son kind of thing I ever ask of you."

"Oh, poor Dad," Abbie teased. "You know you love having girls."

"I *would* love it, if you'd just put on a happy fishing face for me," Dad said, pretending to be grouchy about it.

"First of all, I don't know how Americans turned fishing into a male thing," Hannah said. "In most cultures it's the women who gather the fish."

"Second of all," I piped in, "I don't know why boys *or* girls like it. It's *boring*. Only men would define sitting and waiting for some unsuspecting fish to eat your fake bug as a sport."

"A *fashionable* sport," my dad said. He opened the car's center console and pulled out a beat-up tan hat with neon-colored lures all over it.

"Ew, it smells like fish!" Hannah said, waving her hand in front of her nose.

So much for our bagels. We put them aside in disgust, opened the windows, and teased my dad the entire drive to the South Branch Galien River.

I have to admit, it was really fun.

The river was gorgeous, all breezy and glinty in the early-morning sunshine. My sisters and I baited our hooks, plopped them into the water, and lay back on the smooth, warm, weathered wood of the dock.

But after a short while Abbie popped up.

"Daddy," she said, "since you turned us off our bagels, can't you please go get us some Casper's Donuts?"

"Abbie," Dad said, messing with a lure and his line, "I haven't even caught—"

"Toss it in," Abbie said, pointing at Dad's hook. "We'll watch if for you, I promise. Pleeease. Casper's is so close, and those donuts are *so* good."

"Pretty please," I joined in the begging.

"Pretty please with cinnamon and sugar on top?" Hannah added with a grin.

"Ooh, yeah," Abbie said. "Cinnamon sugar cake donuts. Get those!"

Dad frowned at us, then scratched his head beneath his fishy hat.

"If you promise to have a good attitude about this fishing expedition," he said, "I will get you the donuts."

"We promise," Abbie said. "Thanks, Dad."

"Oh, now I'm Dad again," my dad grumbled. "Now that you've gotten what you want."

"Bye, Daddy!" we singsonged together, laughing and waving at him.

He grinned as he drove away. The minute he pulled into the

road, Abbie planted her fists on her hips and glared at Hannah.

"You're so lucky I got rid of him before I ask you this," Abbie said to Hannah. "*What* is that?"

Abbie pointed at Hannah's neck.

Hannah gasped and pulled her loose hair tightly beneath her chin.

"Do you think Dad saw?" she asked.

"Saw what?" I sputtered. "What is it?"

"Oh, you wouldn't understand," Abbie said, brushing me off with a wave. Then she jumped at Hannah and pushed her hair back, exposing a reddish-blue mark on her neck.

"Hey!" Hannah swatted at Abbie's hand. "Stop it!"

"Ew," I said, pointing at the splotch. "What is that?"

"It's a hickey," Abbie said smugly. "Only the tackiest thing a girl could ever come home with."

Hannah looked both mortified and a little proud.

"What, you're the only one allowed to mess around with guys?" she said to Abbie. "It's no big deal."

"I bet that's what he said," Abbie scoffed. "What else does Fasthands say is no big deal?"

"I know what I'm doing," Hannah said. "I *am* older than you, you know."

"Then act like it," Abbie said.

While Hannah glared at Abbie, I jumped in.

"What did you mean, I 'wouldn't understand'?" I demanded. "I know things."

Abbie and Hannah both looked at me like I was a black fly buzzing around their heads.

"What kind of things?" Abbie said in a patronizing tone.

"I kissed a boy just last night!" I blurted.

It wasn't exactly how I'd planned to pass along this momentous information. I'd pictured a much more romantic moment—my sisters and I would be stargazing together or taking a long walk. And then I would blushingly tell them that I was deeply in like with a boy named Josh.

"What! When? Where?" Abbie and Hannah asked.

"After I got off work," I said, sticking my chin out. "On Althorp Street."

"Well, who is this boy?" Hannah said.

"He's . . ." I drifted off as I gazed out at the river. Josh's face was floating before my eyes again, with those dimples and those smiling eyes, and those *lips.*

My eyes refocused when I noticed a skimming motion on the river. I put my hand over my eyes to block the sun.

It was a long, skinny boat, sort of like a canoe, but it was as long and sharp as a needle. The person rowing the boat was bending forward and back, his long oars flashing as they skimmed over the surface. His back was to us, but I could see he was tall and skinny.

And he had very short brown hair.

He was . . .

"Josh!" I exclaimed. "That's him!"

"What?" Hannah said. "*That's* the guy you kissed. In that boat?"

"Oh my God," I whispered. "What do I do?"

Abbie cupped her hands around her mouth and hollered, "Josh!"

Josh was so startled, one of his oars missed the water and hit his canoe or whatever with a *thwack*. He peered over at us.

"Abbie!" I whisper-shrieked. "I hate you so much."

"Chelsea?" Josh called.

"Um, yeah," I yelled. "Hi."

Even when you're yelling across a body of water, it's possible to sound nervous, I noted with a cringe.

"Hi!" Josh said. He was at least fifty feet away, but I could still see his teeth because he was grinning so hard. Then he waved so energetically, he almost tipped himself off his boat.

"Hi!" I yelled back. I was up on my tiptoes, leaning against the rail, my voice catching because I felt so giddy.

"I don't have your number!" Josh yelled.

I inhaled sharply and glanced back at my sisters. They raised their eyebrows, impressed.

"I don't have yours either!" I yelled. Then Josh and I both laughed like idiots. And *then* the current took him so far past the dock that we couldn't yell to each other anymore.

I turned to my sisters, my giddiness quickly replaced by insecurity.

"I'm such a spaz," I said. "But that was good, right? I mean, him wanting my number and me wanting his? That's good?"

"That's great!" Abbie said. "Most boys are all about the arm's length. They'll do anything to *avoid* getting your number. But here yours doesn't just ask for it; he yells for it from the middle of a river!"

I grabbed Abbie and gave her a squeeze.

"Abbie! I love you so much."

Then all three of us squealed and jumped up and down.

"Chelsea has a boyfriend, Chelsea has a boyfriend," my sisters chanted while I covered my mouth with my hand and shrieked.

"Chelsea has a *boyfriend*?"

My dad's voice brought us down to earth with a thud. He was standing behind us, looking kind of disheveled and pathetic with his grease-stained brown paper bag and a quart of milk.

"Milk, Dad?" Abbie said, eyeing the carton. "What are we, ten?"

Dad got a look on his face that seemed to say, *I very much wish you were.*

A year ago I might have agreed with him. I was wearing braces then and had just gotten my first underwire bra. Every time I tried to drink coffee, it gave me the shakes and tasted awful. I was pretty much convinced that growing up meant being physically uncomfortable at all times.

But now my teeth were straight, I liked coffee (albeit with so much cream that you could barely call it beige), and I had (maybe?) a boyfriend!

I still liked milk, though, so I sidled up to my dad, gently took the carton from him, and said, "Milk is perfect for cinnamon sugar donuts. Thanks, Daddy."

He started to smile at me, but then we heard an ominous sound: *Zzzzzzzz.*

Dad glanced at his fishing rod propped against the dock railing, and shouted, "Girls!"

The pole was bending dangerously over the railing, and the

line was zipping into the river so fast, the little handle on the reel thingy was a blur.

"Oops. I guess you got a bite, Dad," Abbie said.

"You *guess*?" Dad bellowed. He thrust the food into my hands and rushed over to his rod. "You girls were supposed to keep an eye on it!"

"Chelsea had her eye on something much more interesting," Hannah explained with a glint in her eye.

"Shut up!" I said cheerfully.

"No, you shut up!" she shot back with a grin.

My dad rolled his eyes as he wrestled with his fishing rod and called out, "A little help here? I need my net and my emergency line and a donut, stat!"

Giggling, we got him everything he needed, and he eventually reeled in his fish. It was huge! Well, big enough that Dad didn't have to throw it back the way he usually did.

"I am hunter!" Dad said, beating his chest with one hand while he used the other to hold up the poor dead fish. "Hear me roar! And take my picture, somebody!"

"Ohmigod, Dad," Hannah burst out. "How reactionary can you be?"

Dad faux-scowled at her.

"You know, when we found out you were going to be a girl, everybody congratulated me," he said. "They said, 'Oh, daughters and fathers. She'll think you hung the moon.'"

"And I did think you hung the moon," Hannah shot back, "right up until you killed that fish!"

"Ha-ha!" Dad said. "You'll thank me at dinnertime."

In the car on the way home, I texted Emma:

You awake?

YEAH, YOU?

Duh, I'm texting you! And it's lunchtime out here. How's the intensive?

INTENSE! I'M DOING THE PAS DE DEUX FROM DON Q.

I have no idea what you just said. Guess what? Have news.

WHAT KIND OF NEWS!?!?!?

The boy kind.

?!?!?!?!?!?!

His name is Josh. We kissed! Last night.

DEETS!!!!!!

He works in a bookstore! He's so cute.

I stopped typing for a moment. My deets were true, but they only scratched the surface of what I liked about Josh. All the things I *really* thought of him couldn't possibly fit in a text. Which was, I thought, a very good thing. I had a big, goofy smile on my face as I typed, *How's Ethan?*

GOOD!!!! I THINK . . .

You think?

NO, NO, HE'S GOOD. HE'S JUST, WELL, IT'S NOT LIKE HE'S GOING TO JUST SIT AROUND WAITING FOR ME AFTER MY DAYS AT LAB. HE'S GOT A LIFE TOO.

Deets?

HOW'RE THINGS GOING WITH YOUR FAMILY? IS IT STILL SUPER-SAD?

I frowned at my phone. Could Emma have been more obvious

with her subject change? *Yeah, a little, but it's okay. My dad is working through it by killing small animals.*

WHAT???

We just went fishing.

OH. GROSS.

Know what's not gross anymore? Kissing! You were holding out on me.

ARE YOU KIDDING?!? I TOLD YOU EVERYTHING.

Bunhead, I was being sarcastic!

LATE FOR CLASS! LUV U.

I snapped my phone shut and frowned again. The conversation wasn't nearly as satisfying as it would have been by Emma's backyard pool with ginormous smoothies.

Then again, I reminded myself, *if I was poolside with Emma right now, I wouldn't be here in Bluepointe. With Josh.*

I smiled through the rest of the drive.

When we got home, Mom was in the vegetable garden. She was decked out in a floppy hat and gloves the color of Pepto-Bismol. She was shoveling with such force that she was out of breath, red-faced, and sweaty.

"What are you doing?" I asked. There was a big pile of dead plants and weeds next to her.

"I just couldn't stand this mess of a garden anymore," my mom said. "Something needed to be done!"

"What *are* you going to do with it?" I wondered.

"I don't know . . ." Mom trailed off, gazing at the big patch of bare earth as if she were seeing for the first time what she'd done. "I hadn't gotten that far."

She waved as Abbie and my dad carried our big cooler around the house to the back.

"How was the fishing?" Mom asked as she pulled off her gloves and tossed them to the grass.

"Check it out!" my dad said, flipping open the cooler and pulling out his big fish. It looked dull and stiff and very, very dead.

My mom clapped a hand over her mouth, and her eyes immediately welled up.

"Rachel—" my dad said in a *What did I do?* voice.

My mom shook her head and waved him off.

"I'm fine," she said. "I was just a little surprised, that's all."

"Aren't you excited to have fresh fish for dinner?" Dad asked a little wanly.

"Of course!" Mom said. Her voice was doing that perky thing, but it was choked up, too. "Listen, I'm tired after all this digging. I'm just going to take a little nap."

She almost ran to the house, and by the time we followed her in, Granly's bedroom door was closed.

My dad heaved a big sigh, then tapped on the bedroom door and went inside.

The three of us wandered into the living room. I peeked into the cabinets in the hutch. The jewelry boxes, board games, and photo albums were right where they'd always been—untouched.

Abbie gave her head a little shake and whispered to us, "Beach?"

"Let me get my stuff," Hannah whispered. "I've got some reading to do."

"I'll get some food," I said.

I went to the kitchen hoping I could find something that *wasn't* a baked good with a hole in it. As I fished some peaches out of the fruit bowl, I noticed that my mom had left her laptop open on the kitchen table.

I'd barely looked at a computer since we'd arrived. How funny that, other than texting with Emma and a couple other friends, I'd barely wondered what was going on at home. Maybe the long drive out here had made my "real" home feel far away and unreal. Or maybe it was the fact that when you're in a place like Bluepointe, it's kind of hard to believe a place like LA even exists.

Or maybe it was because I'd been preoccupied with a certain boy. . . .

It was partly guilt that made me log in to Facebook to see if I'd missed any big news. But there wasn't anything that caught my eye.

I took a big bite of peach and clicked on my messages. I scrolled quickly through them, until I got to the last e-mail. It had just arrived a few minutes earlier.

When I saw who it was from, I let out a little shriek.

It was from Josh Black, of Bluepointe, Michigan, born February fourth, the same year as me.

The message said: *Kai's long, shiny locks reminded Nicole of the black keys she'd so loathed during her years of piano lessons. But now she was just itching to touch them.*

I clapped my hand over my mouth so my family couldn't hear me laughing.

I rushed to my room and snatched my copy of *Coconut*

Dreams off my nightstand. Abbie was just snapping the strap of her swimsuit's halter top into place.

"Aren't you gonna change?" she said.

"Go on without me," I said, waving her away. "I'll meet you down there."

"O-kay," she said slowly. "Let me guess—your J-boy?"

I felt a twinge of guilt. I knew what it felt like to be the odd girl out, when everybody else seemed to be in a constant state of swooniness.

"Is that . . . is that okay?" I asked.

"Whatever," Abbie said, fishing her goggles out of her beach bag. "I'm doing my two miles, so I don't have time to hang on the beach anyway."

"Yeah, but . . ."

"Chelsea," Abbie said. She smiled at me. "It's *fine*. I mean it. He seems really sweet."

I smiled, hugged *Coconut Dreams* to my chest, and headed back to the kitchen.

I flipped through the book until I found the perfect passage.

Nicole and Kai danced on the sand, and the gossamer moonbeams danced with them, I typed. *When Nicole placed her slender fingers upon Kai's chest, she felt that his heart beat in time with her own; it beat for her.*

I bit my lip through a grin and hit send.

The chime of his reply came only a couple minutes later.

So, can I go ahead and get that number from you?

My hands shook a little as I typed my number into the reply box.

It only took a minute or two for the phone in the pocket of my khakis to start buzzing.

I felt happier than I had in a very long time. I was sure Josh would be able to tell through the phone when I answered.

But that was okay. I wanted him to.

I flipped the phone open.

"Hi," I said. "It's me."

The funny thing about dating Josh was that it took us a while to go on an actual date.

Our obvious first choice—seeing the fireworks on the Fourth of July—got squelched by a massive thunderstorm.

For days after that we were both scheduled to work. So we did a lot of flitting back and forth between Mel & Mel's and Dog Ear.

He was the first one to sit in my section, for instance, whenever I started my afternoon shift at the coffee shop.

The third time he showed up at precisely two p.m. and settled himself into my section's corner booth, I laughed and said, "Oh, you again?"

"Can I help it if I really, really like pie?" Josh asked. "I get peckish at two p.m."

"You did *not* just use the word 'peckish,'" I said.

"I read it," Josh said, holding up the book he'd brought with him. "It's no *Coconut Dreams*, but . . ."

"Oh!" I said. "Allison Katzinger? I *love* her! But . . . wait a minute! *Leaves of Trees?* I've never heard of that one, and I've read all her books. Or at least I thought I had . . ."

"This is a galley of her book that's about to come out," Josh said. "She's coming here in August and I'm doing the poster, so I thought I'd re—"

"Oh my God!" I said. I sat down across from him and grabbed the table. "Why didn't you tell me you had the new Allison Katzinger? And she's coming here? To Bluepointe?"

"Yeah," Josh said with a shrug. "My mom arranged it. *That's* her favorite part of having a bookstore."

"So, is it good?" I asked Josh. "What am I saying? Of course it's good. But is it devastatingly good? I mean, is it one of her funny ones or one of her tragic ones? I can never decide which kind I love more—"

"Listen," Josh offered, "I'll need it back, but if you want to read it, you could bor—"

Before he could finish his sentence, I'd reached across the table and snatched the book out of his hand.

"Really?" I blurted. "You know I'll read it *so* fast. I can't believe I have to wait six hours to start. I'm sooooo excited."

"I'm beginning to think you just like me for my books," Josh said.

"Just like you like me for my pie," I said. I passed the book back to him and let my fingertips touch his for a quick, thrilling moment before I stood up. "Hold that for me? I'll be right back."

When I returned, I presented him with a slice of lemon meringue.

"Is this what you normally do?" Josh said, giving me a confused smile. "Choose pie flavors for your customers?"

"I know what you were going to order," I said.

At the same time we both said, "Cherry."

"But trust me on this?" I whispered, glancing over my shoulder to make sure neither of the Mels was within earshot. "You want to go with graham cracker crust for the next couple days. Melanie's, erm, tinkering with the fruit pie crust."

"Don't tell me . . . ," Josh groaned.

"Yup," I whispered, "mayonnaise. I'm afraid to try it."

Josh grinned as he took a big bite of his lemon pie.

"Mmm, good choice," he said.

I felt a little zing. I loved that I knew Josh's favorite pie flavor, just like he knew that I took my coffee with five creamers and two sugars (even if he did make fun of me for it).

He'd told me that he loathed his dictator-like high school art teacher and had learned most of his drawing techniques on YouTube.

And I'd told him that I read *Little Women* at least once a year, but still cried every time Beth died.

Sharing things like that with Josh made kissing him even better. Knowing what was going on *inside* his head was what was really making me swoon. This was the part of having a boyfriend I'd never imagined—the best friend part. I'd dreamed about the kissing and the hand-holding. But I'd had no idea that the most mind-blowing part of dating could be the *talking*. Looking into a boy's eyes and understanding what you saw in them. And each day learning a few more of the little quirks and details that made him *him*.

It made me feel different. Changed. Sometimes when I looked in the mirror, I expected to see someone else there. Someone older, with a knowing glint in her eye (and maybe fewer freckles).

As Josh took another bite of pie, I leaned against the table and wondered, "How far do you think she can take this mayo-in-everything scheme? Can you think of anything grosser than mayo pie? I think all the egg fumes are starting to scramble her brain."

"I heard that!"

I gasped and spun around to see Melissa glaring at me with her fists on her hips. Where had she come from?

"Oh, Melissa," I gasped. "I didn't mean—"

"Listen, Melanie's *always* been that crazy," Melissa whispered. "It's not the mayo's fault. And besides, it seems like you've got mayo on the brain too!"

She tipped her head toward the specials board, where I'd scribbled a little paragraph in the empty black space beneath the list of pie flavors.

B. hoped nobody could see the shiny new horns beneath her bangs as she held out the platter. "Deviled egg?" she offered.

I shrugged and laughed.

Melissa grinned back at me.

"Do you know, since you put that up there the other day," she said, "our deviled egg order has tripled? We had to send Andrea to the market for more eggs and paprika! Where'd you get such an idea, honey?"

"Oh, I don't know," I said with a smile and a shrug. "I was just serving someone deviled eggs, and the name struck me as funny. Do you want me to erase it?"

"Are you kidding?" Melissa said. "Don't you dare. *And* stop mooning over that boy and go give menus to that four-top over there. They want two blacks, two decafs."

"You're the best, Melissa," I breathed.

When Josh left, he wrote on his check, *Your Tip* → with the arrow pointing at the Allison Katzinger book.

Of course, I *had* to stop by Dog Ear after my shift to say thank you.

And there just happened to be a wine-and-cheese happening for a local poet when I got there. Josh was working the cash register, so I stayed to chat with him during lulls. We debated Allison Katzinger's funny books versus her tragic ones. I fetched Josh a plateful of artichoke dip and little endive leaves squirted with blue cheese and olives, and we agreed that they were as delicious as they were gross-looking. We had absolutely no privacy all night except for one brief moment, when the tipsy poet knocked over a stack of books with a sweep of her bangled arm, and Josh and I crept under the table to pick them all up.

But somehow it all felt romantic. More romantic than going to a movie or eating dinner in a restaurant with candles on the tables.

I didn't know if this was because I had a warped sense of romance—or because anything I did with Josh seemed romantic, even gathering books off the floor, our fingertips touching as we reached for the same one.

But finally one afternoon a few days after the Fourth of July fireworks got rained out, Josh shook his head.

"Chelsea, look at us," he said.

"What?" I replied. We were at the Pop Guy's cart with E.B., scarfing down frozen treats during a ten-minute break. Josh was wearing shorts and one of his cute plaid shirts. He had a wad of plastic bags poking out of his pocket (kind of a must when you're taking an overweight Labrador for a walk). I was still wearing my waitress apron. My fingers had ballpoint pen and neon marker (and probably mayonnaise) on them.

"You know, people sometimes see each other for longer than ten minutes," Josh said. "Or without a cash register sitting between them. They might even get a little dressed up. It's called a date."

If only I hadn't just taken a big, cold bite of my melting pop just as he'd said that. Then I could have given him a flirty pout and said something clever like, "What took ya so long?"

The truth was, though, that despite all the hanging out we'd been doing—the quick meetings, the texts, and, of course, the kissing—the idea of going on a date had never occurred to me. It seemed so old-fashioned, so formal.

"What, are you going to come pick me up at seven and shake my dad's hand and pin a corsage on my dress?" I laughed.

"Um, that was kind of what I was thinking," Josh said, looking sheepish. "I mean, except for the corsage part. Maybe a sparkler, though? It'd be a better fit for the DFJ."

DFJ meant "Deferred Fourth of July." The rained-out fireworks had been rescheduled, and the town had posted flyers about the event all over Main Street.

"That's datey, right?" Josh said. "A picnic, fireworks, marching band music?"

"I've always found marching band music to be very romantic," I said, laughing.

"Hey, it's better than our usual sound track," Josh said. "The little bell on the cash register."

He reached out with the hand that wasn't sticky with pop drips and brushed my cheek with his fingertips. It sent a jolt through me. I imagined being alone with Josh for an entire evening. "Dreamy" didn't begin to cover it, which was why I thought there must be a catch.

"Aren't your school friends going to be having a party or something?" I said.

"Maybe," Josh said with a shrug. "I'd rather be with you."

"Oh," I whispered. Josh's habit of bluntly saying what was on his mind still made me reel. But in a good way now.

"So . . ."

"So . . . ," I said. I smiled at him, shyly at first, then with giddy excitement. "So, pick me up at seven, I guess!"

By the time I woke up the next morning, there were only a couple hours *left* in the morning. I smiled lazily and stretched.

After our first frenetic weeks in Bluepointe, with all the educational outings and sporty field trips, our family's pendulum seemed to have swung in the other direction. Life had seriously slowed down. And all that togetherness? That had tapered off too. Abbie had decided to train for a triathlon—because that was her warped idea of leisure—so her ninety-minute swim workout had expanded to include a couple hours of running and biking, too.

Each day, Hannah commandeered the swing on the screened-in porch so she could check another line off her to-read list. (I'm pretty sure she snuck in some naps on the porch swing too. It was impossible not to.)

My dad holed up for a few hours in the makeshift office he'd set up in Granly's bedroom. And I did my afternoon shift at the Mels or hung out at Dog Ear or the beach.

My mom's to-do list was to go through Granly's things—her clothes, her mementos, her artwork and wedding china and egg cups . . . the whole life she'd suddenly left behind here.

But somehow something else always seemed to come up.

There was the afternoon of antiquing she'd scheduled with an old high school friend.

"I *have* to see her. It's been years," Mom said as she put on makeup for the first time since we'd arrived in Bluepointe. Abbie and I sat on the bed watching her get ready, the way we used to do when we were little. "It's been years!"

"*Who* is she again?" Abbie said.

"ZiZi Rosbottom," my mom said. "From high school."

"Never heard of her," Abbie said. She turned to me. "You?"

"Nope." I shook my head.

"Yes, you have," my mom protested. "We edited the yearbook together. ZiZi!"

"I think we would remember a name like *ZiZi Rosbottom*," Abbie said.

"Yeah, because Abbie would have made all sorts of disgusting jokes about the fact that her name had the word 'bottom' in it," I agreed.

"Well," Mom said lightly as she breezed out of the bedroom, "maybe that's why I never mentioned her."

She made other excuses to flee the house too. She had to go to three different stores to get the right jars for making blueberry jam—even though blueberries wouldn't be in season until the end of July.

Or she passed a field full of sunflowers en route to the grocery store and had to go back and capture it with the tripod and the good camera.

This morning she was sitting on the living room floor surrounded by mounds of clothing. Most of the items looked so small, they couldn't possibly have been Granly's.

"What is that stuff, Mom?" I asked. I stood in the doorway between the living room and the hallway. I wasn't sure yet if I wanted to go in.

"Your baby clothes!" Mom said. She held up a tiny pink onesie with a duck on the front. "Well, yours and Abbie's and Hannah's. I'd forgotten they were here."

"Why *are* they here?" I asked.

"Oh, Granly and I used to say we were going to make a quilt out of them," Mom said, picking up a fuzzy little blanket and rubbing it between her fingers. "But it seemed like there was always something else to do."

"Oh," I said quietly.

Even as my hands gripped the door frame, I realized my body was tilting backward, poised for flight. I didn't want to think about yet another thing Granly wouldn't get to do. Or see.

Mom didn't seem to want to think about Granly either. She was lost in our pink, ruffly past.

"Oh!" she said, reaching for a hot-pink dress with a ribbon of orange tulle around the hem. "You and Abbie both wore this at your second birthday parties."

"Oh, yeah!" I said. "I remember the pictures."

"This would make the perfect center square for the quilt," Mom said, pawing through the tiny outfits. "And then the colors could get lighter and lighter as I move toward the edges. I can just see it!"

The thing was, I couldn't. Of course, I understood why my mom was nostalgic over baby clothes. She got all misty-eyed every time she thought about our babyhood, to the point that I sometimes felt kind of rotten about having grown up.

"You know, I should just do it," Mom announced. She began laying little dresses and sun hats and bodysuits out on the rug, organizing them in their full range of color, from powder pink to bubble gum pink to shocking pink.

"Ooh," Mom crooned. "I remember bringing you home from the hospital in this. . . ."

She was technically talking to me, but in reality I think she forgot I was even there; *she* might remember me as a baby with no teeth and chubby thighs and a little orange afro, but I didn't.

When I turned to go, she barely noticed.

I stalked through the laundry room and into the backyard. The sun was directly overhead, and the cicadas were grinding away from their invisible perches in the treetops. That sound, combined with too-long grass and the empty, dried-up garden plot, made the yard feel overheated and oppressive.

I found myself pacing back and forth along the stepping stones, my arms folded over my chest.

I should have been glad Mom had decided to do this quilt

thing. I hadn't seen her this happy and excited since we'd arrived in Bluepointe.

But . . . it just felt weird. This summer was supposed to be about Granly, not about *baby* clothes. She was walking down the wrong memory lane!

Not that I should have been complaining. I hated the thought of moving Granly's stuff. I wanted her sewing box and photo albums to stay in the hutch forever.

So I should have been happy that Mom was leaving everything untouched, right?

But I just . . . wasn't.

Because as long as we kept things just as they'd always been, we were in limbo. We were always in the process of saying goodbye to Granly . . . but never finished.

I heaved a deep sigh, then idly bent over the garden to pull a big clump of clover. My mom had done all that work turning over the soil in this garden, and then she'd abandoned that, too. Weeds were quickly creeping back in, and the dirt looked dry and cakey.

I pulled another few weeds, then cocked my head to give the garden a hard look. I went over to the shed and pulled open the squeaky screen door. I found a stiff rake, carried it back to the garden, and slammed it down into the dirt with a satisfying *whumpf.* Dragging the rake through the dirt broke it up, unearthed the baby weeds, and made a nice, straight, flat track of earth.

I could picture a row of tomatoes there.

I dropped the rake and headed back inside.

"Going to town," I called to whomever cared. I dug my phone

and a wad of tip money out of my dresser drawer, then slammed purposefully out the front door.

An hour later I returned with a rusty Radio Flyer wagon full of little plastic pots. Each held a feathery seedling. I'd gotten the plants at the fruit and vegetable stand where we always bought our corn and tomatoes. Mr. Jackson had given me a 75 percent discount because the planting season had pretty much ended.

"I don't know if they'll make it," Mr. Jackson had said to me as he'd helped arrange the seedlings neatly in the wagon. The plants looked even more spindly in his big, meaty hands. "They're pretty leggy—the ones everybody else passed over."

"And I know nothing about gardening," I'd said, biting my lip.

"Well, the good news is these are easy plants," Mr. Jackson had said. "Tomatoes, cucumbers, squash, lettuce . . . I mean, all they want to do is grow."

"Oh!" I'd said. "I forgot one more thing I wanted. Radishes. Do you have any of those?"

By dinnertime my pathetic little plants were in the ground. I'd followed exactly the instructions Mr. Jackson had written for me on a sheet torn off a yellow legal pad, spacing the tomatoes eighteen inches apart and tucking the radishes into two neat rows.

I grinned at my baby garden as I gave it a gentle spray with the hose. Then I pulled off Granly's pink gardening gloves, went inside, and opened the spice cabinet in the kitchen.

"Cayenne pepper," I whispered, finding a big bottle of the orange-red stuff near the back.

Mr. Jackson had sworn by it.

"Just sprinkle it all over the garden after you water each

morning," he'd told me. "Oh, that'll keep all the critters away."

As I dusted my garden with the red hot pepper, I pictured the beautiful basket of plum tomatoes, romaine lettuce, and crunchy pickling cucumbers I'd be pulling out of this garden in August. Not to mention the egg-shaped heirloom radishes.

I thought Granly would be proud of what I'd made of her little garden.

I couldn't help but think about what would be different by the time these little sprouts were ready to harvest (if they made it past the first week).

The summer would be almost over.

I'd be saying more good-byes—to Granly's cottage, to Bluepointe, to Josh.

But at the moment that seemed as distant and unreal as the idea that these little sprouts could grow into big, succulent vegetables.

So I just shrugged my shoulders, gave the garden one last shake of cayenne, and went inside.

I waited until the morning of the DFJ to tell my family about my date.

Mostly because it took me that long to be able to whisper the words "I have a date" without covering my mouth and giggling like an idiot.

The day of the fireworks started off feeling like any other, except for the fact that my dad was making us banana pecan pancakes instead of working.

When he plopped a trio of them onto my plate, they each had two round ears.

"Dad!" I complained. "I don't eat Mickey Mouse pancakes anymore!"

"Oh, lighten up," Hannah said. "He made them for all of us."

"Even me!" my mom said, coming to sit at the table with her own plate of Mickeys. "I don't know. Somehow they taste better with those little ears."

"Well . . . okay," I grumbled. I poured a puddle of syrup into the space between my mouse ears, and said, "So . . . what are you guys doing tonight?"

Mom and Dad glanced at each other with raised eyebrows.

"What are *we* doing tonight?" Mom said. "Um, watching the fireworks with our three daughters, of course. Why, did you have other plans?"

"Well, yes," I said. "I—I have a date."

Mom and Dad looked at each other again, and their eyebrows went even higher.

"With this boy, Josh?" my mom said.

"Of course with Josh," I said. "We've been together for, like, weeks now."

"Together when?" Dad said. His fork was poised over his own plate, but it wasn't moving.

"Well, that's the thing," I said. "We've only seen each other before and after work. And during, sometimes. So he asked me out for the DFJ. You know, fireworks, picnic, marching band music?"

"Marching band music?" Abbie snorted.

"It's a figure of speech," I growled. I sliced an ear off one of my Mickey Mouse pancakes and shoved it into my mouth.

"How old is Josh?" Dad asked. "If he's your boyfriend now, we need to meet him."

"That's the whole plan!" I said. "He's fifteen, and he's picking me up at seven. You can meet him then."

"Honey," Mom said gently, "we were really looking forward to spending the evening with you girls. I mean, you've been working so much, and Hannah—well, who knows if she'll be with us on the Fourth next year. Right after breakfast your dad and I are going shopping for a really nice dinner on the beach."

"It's not even the real Fourth of July," I complained. "It's just the *Deferred* Fourth of July. Anyway, when did this holiday—whatever it is—suddenly become as important as Thanksgiving? I don't remember you ever caring that much about us being together for it before."

"Well, that was before," Mom said. Her lips went thin, and she dropped her fork to her plate with a clatter. "I'm not going to *order* you to have dinner with us. I'm going to ask you to do the right thing. You could always ask your friend to join us for dessert and the fireworks."

"How about I have dinner with you, and then Josh can come meet you when we're done?" I negotiated. "And then he and I can watch the fireworks by ourselves?"

Once again I watched my parents' eyeballs do their silent summit.

"All right," my mom said after a long moment. "Home by ten thirty."

"You let me stay out until midnight when I go out with Hannah and Abbie," I complained.

"*Because* you are with Hannah and Abbie," my dad said pleasantly. "Don't push it, Chels."

I brooded through the rest of my pancakes, wondering how I was going to tell Josh that my parents were being ridiculously clingy.

I was just putting my syrupy plate in the sink when my phone rang.

"Hi!" I said to Josh, rushing out onto the screened porch and shutting the front door behind me.

"Hi," he said. "Listen, I have something really awkward to tell you."

"O-kay," I said, feeling nervous heat prickle along my hairline.

"My parents have somehow decided that the DFJ might as well be Christmas," Josh said. "And you know, my dad's been in Chicago a lot for work, teaching that seminar at Loyola, but he has four days off in Bluepointe—"

"And they're not letting you ditch dinner?" I interjected gleefully.

Josh cleared his throat.

"Okay, that's not the reaction I was expecting," he said.

"No, it's just that mine got all weird about the DFJ too," I said. "We're in the same boat. I'm free for fireworks, though."

"Fireworks," Josh said. "I'll make it happen."

"Oh, but first you have to meet my parents," I said. "I can text you to let you know where to find us on the beach."

"Okay," Josh said, sounding less assured this time. "I can make that happen too."

"Don't worry," I said. "They're not too scary. And remember I have two older sisters. By the time they get around to doing all the parental requirements on me—you know, making me eat my broccoli, scheduling extra teacher conferences, meeting boyfriends—they've kind of lost their steam."

"Ha," Josh said. "Wonder what my parents' excuse is, then."

I bit my lip.

Josh and I hadn't talked much about his parents. All I knew was that his dad was a philosophy professor, which pretty much meant he thought of life as a series of hypotheticals.

"It's when it gets real," Josh had told me one day during a slow walk home after we'd both gotten off work, "as in a clogged toilet or remembering to go to the Bluepointe Business Association meetings, that he kind of loses interest. I don't think any of his ancient philosophers ever had do stuff like stock bookshelves and break down the boxes."

"Well, what about your mom?" I'd asked him. "I mean, Dog Ear is more her thing, right?"

"Yeah, but you know my mom," Josh said. "She thinks if she makes things charming enough, people will forgive anything, even lack of electricity."

"Maybe she's right," I said. "Dog Ear is the most amazing bookstore I've ever been in. You should feel good that you're helping her make it happen."

"You're right, I should," Josh said. "I wish I were superpassionate about Dog Ear. But like you said, it's my mom's thing.

It's not mine, really. Except now it has to be because it's the family business."

"And you *are* really good at doing all that organizing," I told him.

Josh rolled his eyes.

"Glad I could impress you with my file labels," he said. "I know they're really sexy."

I laughed before I pressed on.

"What about your posters?" I asked. "Josh, they're *really* good. I can't wait to see what you do with the Allison Katzinger."

Josh had smiled in thanks but changed the subject.

Now he did it again.

"So, should I wear a tie or something to meet your folks tonight?" he asked.

"Oh, definitely," I joked. "Bow tie, shined shoes, the works. And bring my mother flowers. Her favorite is the hothouse hyacinth."

"Oh, Nicole," Josh said, the way he always did when we quoted *Coconut Dreams.*

"Oh, Kai." I gave him my standard reply with a giggle in my voice. "See you tonight."

Instead of going to our usual beach that night, we went to the public stretch closest to town, where they'd be setting off the fireworks. My mom insisted we go early so we could stake out enough space for this elaborate picnic she and my dad had planned.

"Can't I meet you there?" I said. "If we go early, it'll still be all hot and muggy out. I don't want to get all sweaty and gross for . . . for later."

Which was kind of ridiculous. Most of the time Josh saw me, I was coming off six hours of hustling around Mel & Mel's. Even though I took time to wash my face, redo my hair, and put on lip gloss before I saw him, I knew it could only help so much. I probably smelled like a combination of dishwasher steam and deviled eggs.

But on a date (okay, half a date) you were supposed to look different. You opened your door, and your guy did a double take because you'd done something different to your hair and put on jewelry. Your heels made you two inches taller. You were supposed to smell like shampoo and perfume, not like the fishy end-of-day wind that comes off Lake Michigan in the heat of the summer.

"Chelsea," Mom said, putting her hands on her hips. I noticed a couple of Band-Aids on her fingers—she kept stabbing herself with pins as she pieced together the baby clothes quilt. "I'm asking for one thing—that we be together for the Deferred Fourth of July. Please? For me?"

"All right," I grumbled.

It wasn't until we set out for the beach late that afternoon that I realized why Mom wanted this family moment so badly. It wasn't because of the (non) holiday.

It was because she'd decided that this would be Gatsby night.

Granly had always insisted that we do Gatsby night at least once every time we visited her. That was just her name for a fancy picnic where the adults drank champagne and the kids had sparkling grape juice in bowl-shaped goblets.

The food was always very fussy: crustless cucumber sandwiches, slivered carrots and celery with spinach dip, tiny pickles and expensive olives, hearts of palm salad, and baked oysters. It was something we'd always done—like the stack-of-sisters photo on the beach—that I hadn't thought about too much. I'd assumed my mom had kind of taken it for granted too.

But obviously I'd been wrong.

As we all headed toward town that afternoon with a heavy picnic basket, blankets, and another basket full of clinking dishes and champagne glasses, I whispered to Hannah, "Why didn't she just say it was Gatsby night?"

Hannah shrugged.

"It was always kind of spontaneous when Granly did it," she whispered back. "Y'know, like one morning she'd just snap her fingers and announce it, and we'd all spend the day pitting olives and peeling shrimp. Remember?"

I did. I remembered my sisters and me getting giggly and excited about Gatsby nights. We'd put on satiny "dress-up" clothes and steal Granly's pink lipstick and say things like "Ooh la *la*!"

My mom was really different from Granly. Granly had always had a bright manicure, and she wore big rings with chunks of turquoise or lapis lazuli in them. When she talked with her hands, they made a *clickety-clack* sound.

My mother's nails were always short and unpainted. The only ring she ever wore was her narrow platinum wedding bad. Her wavy, chin-length hair was as different from Granly's wild red curls as hair could be.

When Granly threw a Gatsby picnic, it was fun, a little dramatic, and most of all effortless.

My mom's Gatsby night came less naturally to her. It took more work.

So when we made it to the beach and laid out our fancy spread—with the votive candles and the tiny silver forks and everything—I think I appreciated it more than I ever had when Granly was alive.

"Now, Chelsea," my mom said, arranging food on my plate while I texted Josh with our location, "I know you usually don't like goat cheese, but just try a little with this pepper jelly. I bet you'll love it."

"Looks yummy," I said.

My mom looked up in surprise.

"Really?" she said, giving me a skeptical smile. "Well, how about some smoked oysters?"

"Eh, let's not push it," I said with a laugh.

I didn't really like the goat cheese either, but I didn't tell my mom that. It didn't matter anyway. I loved the olive tapenade and the artichoke torte and lots of the other fancy stuff she and my dad had made.

And Abbie cracked us up with a story about Estelle, the crazy art gallery owner, who'd had another one of her famous tantrums recently.

People we knew from town started claiming spots around us and saying sweet, funny things about our hoity-toity picnic.

Dad passed around a small bowl of the first blueberries of the season. They were tiny and on the sour side, just the way we all liked them. We nibbled them as we watched the sun go down. It was so fun and the sunset was so mesmerizing that I almost forgot to be nervous about my date.

So of course that was just when Josh showed up.

I didn't realize he was there until I saw him standing at the edge of the picnic blanket, holding a cute little bouquet of daisies and gaping at our fancy china and champagne goblets and candlelight.

"Josh!" I said, quickly swallowing the blueberry in my mouth and hoping desperately that I didn't have any food in my teeth. "You're here!"

I jumped to my feet, smoothing down my yellow halter dress with one hand and tucking the frizz away from my hairline with the other.

As I gave him an awkward we're-in-front-of-my-family hug hello, he whispered, "I didn't think you meant it about the bow tie!"

"I didn't!" I said with a laugh.

He was wearing a white T-shirt with a cool, faded American flag on it, rolled up khakis, and had bare feet. He gave our fancy dishes and silverware a glance, then looked back at me with raised eyebrows.

"Oh, this is just something we do," I scoffed, waving my hand at the Gatsby picnic. "For a laugh. We're not *really* fancy."

"Speak for yourself," Abbie said. She was leaning on one elbow, popping blueberries into her mouth.

"That's my sister Abbie," I told Josh. "And this is Hannah, and, um, my parents."

"I'm Adam," my dad said, standing up to say hello.

"And I'm Rachel," my mother said as she pulled some dessert plates out of our picnic hamper. "We were just about to have dessert if you want to join us."

"Oh, that's okay," Josh said. Then he seemed to remember his daisies and thrust them toward my mom.

"For you," he said bluntly.

My mom and I raised our eyebrows at each other as Josh whispered to me, "I didn't know what the heck a hyacinth was."

"Those are perfect," I said.

Which was true. They were simple and sweet. They were just the kind of not-fancy flowers my mom loved. She smiled as she gave the little bouquet a sniff, then plunked it into her water glass.

It made for an easy, guilt-free exit.

"I'll be home by ten thirty, I promise," I told her, crouching down to say good-bye. "Thanks for the Gatsby night. It was . . ."

I couldn't say it was perfect. Because perfect would have included Granly.

"Well, I really loved it," I said.

And that was the truth.

I guess since I'd forgotten to feel nervous before Josh arrived, all my nerves hit during our walk down the beach. I couldn't think of anything to say as we picked our way around shrieking packs of little kids and college students laughing as they popped the caps off bottles.

I wanted to hold Josh's hand, but the wind was picking up and I needed my hands to hold my skirt down.

Josh was quiet too. He asked a couple polite questions about my parents and my sisters.

Then I asked him how dinner had been with his parents.

"Oh, fine," he said. "Some of those poets who like to come into Dog Ear set up right next to us, and they started improvising."

"Ooh," I groaned. "Improv poetry? That sounds painful."

"Oh, my dad ate it up," Josh said. "He likes that kind of thing. He went to Woodstock, but don't ask him about it unless you want to listen to him go on about it for three hours."

"Woodstock!" I said. "But how— How old—"

"Sixty-six," Josh said, answering the question I couldn't quite bring myself to ask. "He was fifty-one when I was born, and my mom was forty."

"Wow," I said. "I mean, I knew they were, you know, on the older side . . ."

"Yeah." Josh shrugged. "That's why they only had me. But I think that's what they wanted anyway. I mean, my parents have never been the romp-around-with-a-bunch-of-little-kids types."

"Oh," I said.

I hadn't really thought before about how different our lives really were. I'd grown up in a suburban house where there had always been us three kids (and usually a few of our friends) hanging out in our TV room, raiding the fridge, or playing in the backyard.

Meanwhile, Josh had never even *had* a backyard. Before moving to Bluepointe he and his parents had lived in an apartment in

Chicago, and Josh had taken the subway everywhere he needed to go. Now they lived in one of the lofts that overlooked Main Street, just a few steps away from Dog Ear.

It seemed very sophisticated and grown-up.

Maybe that was why Josh had proposed a "real" date, when I'd just been content to hang out wherever we landed. *And* why he felt the kind of responsibility for Dog Ear that never would have occurred to me.

We arrived at a spot where the picnic blankets were sparser and there was an empty patch of sand in front of the dune grass.

"This looks like a good place to see the fireworks," Josh said.

We sat and stared at the darkening sky for a few long moments. For some reason I was at a loss for words again.

"I wonder when they're going to start," was what I finally came up with.

Then I started to feel miserable. Why was I suddenly making small talk? This was *Josh*, with whom everything had been so easy and fun and *right* ever since our first kiss.

Josh reached over and took my hand, but just like my small talk, it felt forced. Like what you're *supposed* to do on a date, instead of what he wanted to do.

"Well . . . ," Josh said, staring out at the horizon just as I was, "this is weird."

"I know!" I said, exhaling with relief and turning to look at him. "Did my family freak you out?"

"No!" Josh said. "I liked them. I mean, from the three minutes or so I spent with them. Your mom seems like such a normal mom."

"What, like June Cleaver?" I said with a laugh.

"No, she just seems, I don't know, comfortable in that mom role," he said. "She seems kind of sad, too."

"Yeah," I said, hanging my head. "My grandma."

"I know," Josh said. His hand tightened around mine. "Listen, do you want to go back? We could watch the fireworks with them, if you want. Or . . . you could be alone with them."

I looked up at Josh's face, searching for what he *really* meant. I wanted to know what he was thinking just from gazing into the depths of his eyes. I wanted to be back on that road that we'd started on, the one where we just *got* each other and being together felt completely natural.

But now Josh felt opaque. I couldn't figure out what he meant by his offer. Was he being selfless? Or was he pushing me away?

"I don't want to go back there," I said.

"Okay," Josh said with a nod.

"No," I said urgently. "I mean back to how things were when we first met, and I liked you and you liked me, but both of us were too scared to say anything about it. And you sent me all those mixed signals . . ."

Josh frowned.

"What mixed signals?"

"You know!" I said. "When we first met. You were all hot and cold. You were sweet, then you were surly. You told me about the job at Mel and Mel's, but then when I got it, I swear your face went *white*."

"And then I kissed you," Josh said quietly. He looked like he wanted to kiss me right then, but I wasn't having it.

"Yeah!" I said. "You can see how I was a little confused. But then, well . . ."

I grabbed Josh's hand, loving how familiar his long, slim fingers felt and how neatly and automatically they crisscrossed with mine.

"But then I thought we were all figured out. I mean, it's been amazing. Until tonight."

Josh cocked his head and said, "Chelsea, you of all people should know nobody gets 'figured out.' You *never* figure it all out—but you keep trying."

Now I cocked my head at him.

"That's a funny thing for *you* to say," I said.

"Why?"

"Well, I hope this doesn't sound bad," I said, "but I think you've got some issues with, you know, control."

Josh smiled a tiny bit, then took his hand back and leaned into the sand, propping himself up on his elbows. He gave me an *I'm listening* look.

"Well, there's the way you have a folder or drawer or cubby for every little thing at Dog Ear," I said.

"That's true." Josh nodded.

"And you do this sport that's all about precision and timing," I said. "And what about your friends? You skipped that whole lantern-making extravaganza even though I can think of one person—one *girl*—who would have really liked to see you there."

Josh snorted.

"And then there's your hair," I said.

"My *hair*?" Josh said, slapping his hand on top of his head.

"No, no, I love your hair!" I said, getting up on my knees so I could reach over and stroke his sleek, spiky hair. His eyes fluttered closed for a moment. "It's just that it's so different from a lot of boys' hair. It's so close-cropped, it never gets messy, never gets in your eyes. It's very . . . practical."

Josh shook his head slowly as he gazed at me. And in the almost darkness I couldn't quite tell what was going on in his face. Was he mad?

"But attractive," I said with an earnest nod. "Did I mention th—"

I didn't get to finish what I was saying, because Josh was on his knees too, wrapping his arms around me and kissing me hard. He came at me with such force—or maybe just because it was too dark for him to have good depth perception—that we toppled over into the sand. We landed, our arms still tangled up together, on our sides.

This made us burst out laughing. But then, quickly, we were kissing again, our hands buried in each other's hair and our bodies pressed together. When we finally broke apart, we were breathing hard. We lay on our backs for a moment, staring up into the black sky.

Then Josh rolled over so that he was facing me, and I rolled toward him. He put his hand on my cheek.

"I think you *do* have me pegged," he said.

"Oh, I don't know," I said with a coy smile. "I think I've got to do some more investigating."

Josh moved his hand up to my temple. He pulled free a curl

that had poofed out of my ponytail and spiraled it around his finger. Automatically I reached up to tuck it back behind my ear, but he stopped me.

"You like *your* hair under control too," he said. "But I loved it that day you came into Dog Ear with your sisters. It was all loose and wild."

"And *red*," I said with a long-suffering sigh.

"And red," Josh said, but from the way he said it, I could tell he thought it was a good thing.

Also because he started kissing me again.

But then abruptly he stopped and pulled back far enough to look me in the eyes. I wished I could see the pretty, velvety brown of his eyes, but it was too dark to see colors. We'd become black and white, like an old movie.

"You make me want to, I don't know," Josh said with a little self-conscious laugh, "not *lose* control so much as release it."

"That's the nicest thing-that-I-don't-completely-understand that anybody's ever said to me," I teased.

Josh shrugged happily.

"Like I said, that's the whole point," he said. "Not-figuring each other out."

I touched his hair again.

"I'm enjoying not-figuring you out," I said.

"I'm enjoying not-figuring you out too," Josh said. Then he squelched my laugh with another kiss—a kiss so long and deep that it made me feel dizzy, especially in the pitch-dark of our little nest near the dune. I sank into the kissing so deeply that I forgot where we were.

Which is why I was startled when we were interrupted by a huge *Pow!*

Only when I saw bright red sparks tendrilling down through the sky over the lake did I remember.

"The fireworks!" I said.

Josh's hand was on his chest.

"I forgot too!" he said breathlessly.

Pow!

The next one was gold and shimmery. It made a sizzling noise after it exploded.

I sighed and leaned against Josh. He swung his arm around my shoulders, and I snuggled in even closer.

Usually, watching fireworks made me feel tiny, almost consumed by the huge starbursts looming above me. But in Josh's arms I felt different. Safe and not quite as small as before. But way more exhilarated.

"I've changed my mind," I said to Josh during one of those breathless pauses between explosions. "I think I like dates after all."

"Me too," Josh said. "I think we should go on another one"—he paused for another big *Pow*—"as soon as possible."

And that's why Josh showed up at my house on my very next day off—carrying two giant paddles.

"This one's yours," he said, thrusting one of them at me with a big grin.

"You've got to be kidding," I said, stepping off the front steps into the gravel with my arms crossed. I was wearing my favorite bathing suit, the high-waisted black halter with the white polka dots. It wasn't vintage but looked it. Over that I wore my gauzy, flowy cover-up. "I thought we were going to the lake!"

"We are," Josh said. "Just not Lake Michigan. We're going to Wex Pond. Well, to be specific, we're getting into a boat on Wex Pond. My parents' landlord has a little rowboat there, and he said we can use it whenever we want."

Wex Pond is what Bluepointers called the Albert R. Wechsler Reservoir, because that was a pretty fancy name for what was really just a big bowl of water surrounded by farmland, some crooked trees, and a few docks.

I propped the oar on its end next to me and looked at it dubiously.

"I think you've got the advantage here," I said dryly. "Is this thing gonna give me blisters?"

"How about we just try it," Josh proposed. "I packed us a mayo-free lunch and everything. If you don't like it, we can go back to the beach. I promise."

I couldn't help but smile and nod my consent. It was so easy to be adventurous with Josh. I think I would have even agreed to go fishing with him, even though that would have driven my dad crazy.

"Let me just water the plants," I said, laying the oars down in the gravel and leading him to the backyard.

"Oh, yeah. How's the garden?" Josh asked. He walked over to check it out while I unwound the hose from its reel on the back of the house.

"Wow!" he said.

"I know!" I said, proudly pulling a couple weeds from around the lettuce plants. "I mean, about half of the radishes croaked, and one of my cucumber vines is looking pretty puny, but everything else is getting *huge*."

It was a little embarrassing how proud I was of my garden. The tomato plants got visibly bigger and fluffier every day. The pale-green romaine leaves were looking less delicate and translucent. They stood straight up. And most of the other plants had started sprouting trumpet-shaped yellow flowers.

"Hey, look!" Josh said, bending over to peer closely at the biggest tomato plant.

I crouched next to him to squint at the fuzzy branch. Then I gasped.

One cluster of little yellow blossoms had been replaced by tiny tomatoes! They were as green as Granny Smith apples and just as hard, but they were unmistakably tomatoes. Each had a little cap of pointy leaves that made it look like a gift-wrapped present.

"That was so fast!" I exclaimed. I did a quick inspection of the other plants and shrieked again when I found a collection of little cucumbers, curled under the big, flat leaves like shy caterpillars.

I jumped up and down with my garden hose, accidentally spraying Josh a little bit.

"Sorry!" I said. "I just can't believe I actually grew something. I mean, all I did was stick them in the ground and water them, but still! Pretty cool, huh?"

"Pretty cool," Josh said with a crooked smile and a hint of a tease in his voice.

"Okay, I know it's dorky," I said. "But I don't care. I'm super-proud of my little vegetables, and I will not be inviting you over for salad when they're ready."

"No!" Josh said, rushing over to put his arms around me. "Salad vegetables are the only ones I like. Please?"

"I'll consider it," I said. I finished spraying the soil. The July heat was getting so bad that the dirt caked right back up by late afternoon. I put the hose back and grabbed my jar of cayenne pepper from the windowsill. After giving the plants a quick sprinkle, I led Josh inside.

My mom was at the kitchen table, pinning pink and pinker squares together in a complicated pattern.

"Hi, Josh," she said warmly. Even though I still thought her baby clothes quilt was a little weird, I was happy to hear a normal warmth in her voice again, instead of that forced perkiness that had been there when we'd first arrived in June.

"I'm just going to get my bag from the bedroom," I told Josh, slipping into the hall.

When I got there, Abbie was sitting on the floor with her legs stretched out to the sides. On the rug between them were various piles of papers. They were in all different sizes, colors, and states of wrinkliness, but they all looked old.

"What're those?" I asked lightly as I headed for the closet.

"Granly's letters," Abbie said. "Most of them to and from Grandpa."

I froze at the closet door and turned to stare at my sister.

"Wh-what?" I stammered. "Why are you looking at them?"

"Listen," Abbie said brusquely as she slapped one of the letters into a pile, then scooped up another from a box sitting at her hip. "Mom has abdicated. We both know this quilt project of hers is not about getting all nostalgic about us as babies. It's about *avoiding* thinking about Granly!"

"Well," I murmured, "I think it's a little of both. . . ."

"Whatever," Abbie said. "You have a date with Josh, Hannah is off getting hickeys or whatever with Fasthands. And *I'm* here. So I might as well go through Granly's things myself. I mean, isn't that the point of us being here all summer?"

I felt terrible.

"Listen," I said, sinking to the floor just outside her circle of paper piles. "You shouldn't have to do that by yourself. Do you want me to say something to Mom? Or I could—"

Abbie held up her hand to stop me.

"You know what?" she said. Her face and voice softened. "I actually kind of like it."

She picked up the letter that she'd just slapped down, and smoothed it out on her leg, as if apologizing to it for the rough treatment. Then she read from it. With her head bowed and her hair spilling forward, I couldn't see her face, but her voice sounded a little different—slower and more lilting. Less like Abbie and more like Granly.

"'Dear Artie,'" Abbie read. That's what everyone had called Grandpa, though his real name had been Arthur. "'It feels funny to be so looking forward to the summer when *last* summer was so beastly. But my New Year's resolution was to look forward, not back, and I have been better at keeping at that than I have been at studying for my statistics exam. I really don't believe stats have anything to do with library science, and no (boring) thing you can say will convince me otherwise. By the way, you did catch what I said about last summer, didn't you, Artie? Now what, or whom, do you think is the reason for *that*?'"

As Abbie read, I put my hand over my mouth without realizing it. I could just *hear* my grandmother saying those words, even if they were in my sister's voice.

But then again I couldn't. Because that had been a Granly I never knew, the Granly who was young, writing a love letter to her boyfriend when she was supposed to be studying. And that "beastly" summer. What was *that* about?

"You know what I think she's talking about? That summer?" Abbie said as if she'd seen the question in my eyes. "I think they broke up."

"But we never heard about that!" I whispered, glancing at the door.

"Well, obviously it all worked out in the end," Abbie said with a laugh. "It's funny, isn't it, how someone's story can change? Maybe when Granly wrote that letter, *that* was their story, that they had come close to saying good-bye to each other forever."

"Which would have meant no Mom," I whispered, shaking my head in wonder. "No us."

"Yeah, and once they were married, who knows if they ever thought about it again. Maybe when your big picture is in place, all those bumps in the road along the way get sort of smoothed over."

I thought about that.

"Do you ever feel like," I asked, "right now, it's nothing but bumps?"

"Oh, yeah," Abbie said, nodding in recognition. "Why do you think I love to swim so much? There're no bumps in water."

Abbie replaced Granly's letter in its pile and smoothed it out carefully.

"Anyway, I think you should read these letters . . . sometime. Mom, too. When you're ready."

I picked another letter up, holding the dry, crackly-feeling paper between my thumb and forefinger.

"I . . . I might be ready."

Abbie shook her head.

"I know you're not," she said. "But that's okay. I am. I don't know why I am, but I am. So I'm going to get them all *organized* for you in little folders, which I know Hannah will approve of, and we can take them home with us. And when you're ready—they will be too."

I teetered over the piles of paper to give Abbie a thank-you hug.

"Aren't *we* huggy," Abbie said, pushing me away with a grin. "You're clearly getting some action."

"Shut up!" I whispered, glancing again at the bedroom door as I got to my feet. "You're so gross."

"Maybe," she said. "But I also know what I'm talking about."

I laughed as I checked myself in the mirror. I'd worn my hair half-down as a concession to Josh, with only the front sections pulled back into a big tortoiseshell clip. But there was nothing I could do about my freckles, other than smear them with tons of sunscreen and hope no more popped out after my day in the sun. I grabbed my bag, blew my sister a kiss, and met Josh out front.

By the time we arrived at Wex Pond, which was about a two-mile walk from Sparrow Road, we were both hot and sweaty.

Josh led me to the end of one of the rickety, rocking docks. There, bouncing against the timbers, was a shabby once-white rowboat that looked barely big enough for the two of us. The interior of the boat was blackened with dirt and a little puddle of water. There was one seat in the center that hardly looked big enough for two backsides.

"Isn't it great?" Josh said, jumping easily into the boat and holding out his hands so I could hand him the oars and our bags.

"Um, do you want an honest answer?" I said as I shuffled my feet out of their flip-flops.

"Of course not," Josh said with a smile. He got a sly look in his eyes as he pulled a nylon picnic blanket out of his bag. He spread it out on the bottom of the boat. Then he produced a little pillow and tucked it into the back of the boat (or maybe it was the front, I couldn't quite tell).

"I was lying about you having to row," Josh said. "You get to sit there while I row you around. You can pretend you're Daisy Buchanan."

My mouth dropped open. "Seriously?"

"Well, you like playing Gatsby, don't you?" Josh held out a hand to help me climb into the boat. "And, conveniently, my English class read that book this year. If I get tired of rowing, I'll peel you a grape."

I burst out laughing.

"I'm not *that* much of a princess, you know," I said. "I'm a waitress! And I'm pretty good with a garden rake."

"All the more reason you deserve to relax," Josh said. "If you want something to do, think of another installment for *Diablo and the Mels.* The same bit's been on the specials board for the past three days."

"No pressure or anything," I said as I sank into the little waterproof nest he'd made me. "Besides, it's a good bit, right? 'B. smites that low tipper.' I should leave it up longer as a cautionary tale."

Josh laughed, which made me smile—it always did. And he was right. Even though I could feel the cold of the puddle beneath the blanket, and it smelled kind of moldy down there, lounging while he rowed me around the pond *did* make me feel kind of like a princess.

My perch also gave me a great view of Josh's arms flexing as he leaned forward and back, pulling at the oars.

"Do you need me to be your coxswain," I said. I imitated Tori's cute, squeaky voice and pointed. "A little to the right, *Joshie*."

"Har-har," Josh said, a little out of breath with the rowing. "By the way, you don't say 'right'; you say 'starboard.'"

"Oh," I said. I watched him take a few more pulls on the oars. "What do you like about rowing?" I asked.

Josh cocked his head to think for a moment.

"I like the efficiency of it," he said. "One stroke can take you a whole boat-length down the river. And I like how a whole row of guys can all be communicating with each other, matching each other's rhythm, putting extra muscle into it, sprinting for the win, all without saying a word."

I nodded slowly, imagining the steady, strong back-and-forth motion of a queue of boys, all with shaggy hair fluttering in the breeze, save one.

That communication without words but through breath and rhythm and some sort of telepathy . . . it fascinated me.

Sometimes I felt that Josh and I had that kind of silent way of speaking to each other, with our eyes and our gestures.

And of course with kissing.

Everything seemed to make me think about kissing lately. But I didn't want *Josh* to know that (even though I had a feeling that he felt much the same way). So I grabbed my bag and rooted around in it until I found *Someone New*, an Allison Katzinger novel that I was rereading after finding my own left-behind copy on Granly's bookshelf.

"You brought a book?" Josh squawked.

"Of course," I said, blinking at him. "What, you don't have one?"

"Do you just bring a book with you everywhere you go?" Josh said. He looked like he was trying to decide if this was maddening or cute.

"Um, pretty much, yeah," I said. "I mean, if I still had my e-reader, I might not have brought it onto a *boat*. Then again, I probably would have. That's kind of why I don't have an e-reader anymore."

I sighed, remembering my little electronic tablet fondly.

"Anyway, I thought you wanted me to relax," I said, giving his leg a nudge with bare toes.

"That *is* what I said, isn't it?" Josh said. He angled the oars so they backchurned the water, slowing the boat down. He kept on working the oars until we'd pretty much stopped.

Then he grinned at me.

"Wouldn't want you to get seasick."

"Oh, really?" I said. "Well, fine!"

I tossed my book back into my bag, pulled myself up, and plopped down on the seat next to him. Grabbing the oar out of his right hand, I said, "Teach me to row."

"Yeah?" Josh said, squinting at me.

"Yeah! You make it sound so magical. I want to try it."

"Okay," Josh instructed, "flatten your oar while you're pulling back, then turn it just as you hit the water, like you're scooping ice cream. I'll count, and you go with that rhythm, okay?"

I nodded.

But every time Josh brought his paddle forward, mine seemed to go backward. And vice versa.

And then somehow I was paddling twice as fast as he was, but when he sped up, I slowed down.

The upshot was that our rowboat was spinning around in circles, and I was laughing so hard, I couldn't row anymore.

"I hate to say this," Josh gasped between laughs, "but I think you have no future as a coxswain."

"*Now* do I get to read my book?" I joked. I stood up to turn around so I could settle back into my nice waterproof nest.

But the boat was still twirling a bit. So Josh, trying to be helpful, dug an oar into the water to stop it.

Which tossed me off balance, and well, you can guess what happened next.

Splash!

It took Josh about two seconds to jump in after me.

"Are you okay?" he cried.

My feet found the bottom of the pond, and I stood up. The water only reached my shoulders.

"I think I'll make it!" I replied, laughing as I wiped water off my face. "I'm not even ruining any clothes."

I reached down and peeled my soaked cover-up over my head and tossed it into the boat.

"But thanks for coming to my rescue," I said, giving Josh a light kiss on the lips.

"Anytime," Josh said, giving me a bigger kiss in return.

I turned to float on my back. My fingertips grazed his torso as I fluttered my hand to keep myself balanced.

"It's so peaceful in here," I said. "So different from the big lake. I could stay out here forever."

Josh said something, but with my ears underwater, it was garbled. I splashed myself back to a standing position.

"What was that?" I asked.

Josh looked down at the water for a moment, pensive, "I said 'I wish you would.'"

My easy smirk faded.

"When do you leave again?" Josh asked.

Automatically I waved my hand—a *Not for forever* gesture. Because that's how this summer had seemed for so long—like an endless stretch of days, each longer and hotter and lazier than the last. The ending felt so distant, I'd stopped believing it would ever arrive.

But now that Josh had asked me to think in terms of the calendar, my eyes widened.

"We leave the third week of August," I said. "We've got to give Hannah time to get home and pack and fly back out for school in September."

Josh looked down at the water. Our hands flittered back and forth beneath the surface, keeping us upright.

"That's about a month away," he said.

"A month," I said. My voice sounded craggy suddenly.

"Well, that's better than weeks," Josh said, and I could tell he was adding brightness to his words, the way my mom perked up faded fabric in her quilt by edging it with sunshine-yellow thread.

"*Much* better than days," I added.

It didn't feel quite real that these rowboat, beach, and blueberry days . . . were going to end. That my life was going to go back to slamming locker doors, and spiral-bound notebooks, and babysitting, instead of slinging mayonnaise and reading nothing but novels. And being with Josh.

It didn't seem real, and yet, when Josh pulled me to him, there was a new urgency in the way we kissed.

I let my hands linger on his bare shoulders, trying to memorize all his curves and angles.

He lifted a hand to smooth back my hair and sent water trickling down my face. It felt like tears.

I let my feet leave the soft, loamy mud at the bottom of the pond so that I was afloat, held in place only by Josh's arm around my waist.

And we kissed as if we had all day. If we pretended the day was endless, then a month was nothing to fear.

Suddenly signs of summer ending were everywhere. The days were getting hotter, but they were also getting shorter.

My dad started working less as his clients got ready to make the "great migration" to their August vacations. And Hannah started taking long afternoon naps, as if she wanted to cram in as much sleep as she could before she started pulling all-nighters at U of C.

Finally, on a day when she knew I wasn't working at the Mels, my mom pulled the stack of tin buckets out of the hall closet.

The buckets meant blueberry picking. And blueberry picking meant—inescapably—that it was the last week in July.

This was the week we always went picking when we were in Bluepointe, because it fell right before the berry season peaked and the orchards got crowded. Late July was also when the berries were still small and tart. None of us could stand a super-ripe, sweet, squishy blueberry. It must have been genetic.

"Mom," I said as she clanked the stack of buckets onto the kitchen table. "Is it okay if I invite Josh to go picking with us? I'm working the next few days, and I'd really like to hang out with him."

My mom frowned and glanced at the other end of the table, which had pretty much been permanently overtaken by her baby quilt.

"I don't know, honey," she said. "We've always gone with just us."

I followed her gaze to the quilt top. It was really starting to take shape, with cone-shaped swatches of fabric making a shell-like spiral in the center, framed by small squares. It was amazing, but I knew I didn't see in it what my mother saw. She looked at it and was carried back to the powdery smell of our baby heads, and the satin feeling of our baby skin, our fuzzy never-cut hair, and our mouths that looked like little rosebuds.

I just saw a bunch of cute old onesies.

"Listen," I said, "if you want, I won't invite him. But . . . everything's different this summer anyway."

Mom's eyes got glassy for the first time in a while—at least that I'd seen. I felt guilty.

But I also wanted her to say yes.

She nodded slowly and said, "See if he wants to come. Tell Hannah she can ask Liam, too, if she wants."

Abbie had just walked into the kitchen to pull a snack out of the fridge when Mom made that proposal. She snorted.

"I can guarantee Fast—I mean Liam—doesn't want to go on a family berry-picking outing with us," Abbie said. "He prefers to see Hannah alone. At night. Where nobody can see anybody's *necks*."

"Abbie!" I growled, looking shiftily at Mom.

My mom rolled her eyes.

"Do you think I didn't see that hickey on Hannah's neck?" she asked us. "And did you think I didn't already have a discussion with her about it? Please. Always remember"—she looked straight at me then, and her eyes did *not* look glassy anymore. Instead they were her steely *Don't mess with me, I'm a teacher* eyes—"there's not much about you girls that I don't know."

I think she did know how I felt about Josh—which was why she'd said he could come blueberry picking with us. I flashed a grateful smile and trotted toward my room to start getting ready while I called him.

Before I could finish dialing, though, my phone rang! I didn't even check to see if it was Josh.

"Hiiiii," I crooned into the phone.

"Chelsea? You sound weird."

"Emma!" I blurted with a laugh. "Um, I thought you were—"

"Josh?" Emma said. "Wow. So things are good, huh?"

I could tell by the flat tone of her voice that she had not called me—at six a.m. California time!—to dish about my boyfriend.

"What's wrong?" I asked, flicking on my closet light and stepping inside. I pulled out a dress I'd been thinking would be perfect for blueberry picking—very 1940s housedress, but in a cute way—and tossed it onto my bed.

"Nothing!" Emma replied quickly. "Tell me about Josh."

"Well—"

"It's just that— Oh, Chelsea! I'm totally wrecking things!"

"With Ethan?" I said. I pulled out a pair of red-and-white pedal pushers and tossed those onto the bed too. "What are you talking about?"

"I don't know!" she said. "I just love him so much. And I don't have a lot of time, what with the intensive and rehearsals for *Don* Q on top of that."

"So, you're dying because you don't have time to see him?" I said.

"When I have the time, he doesn't," Emma said. "And when I don't have the time, he does! Supposedly. I'm starting to think he's just making that up. I think I'm getting on his nerves. But I can't help it. I think about him all the time. I can't sleep! I almost want to quit the Intensive so I can have time for him. Maybe that would help?"

"Emma, no!" I gasped, dropping the tank top I was holding. "What are you talking about? That's crazy!"

"I know, but love makes you do crazy things," Emma said. "*You* know."

"I guess?" I said, even though I wasn't sure I *did* know what she was talking about.

"Okay, like, how do you handle it when you want to call Josh for the third time that day?" Emma asked.

"Um, I don't think that's happened," I said. I sat on the edge of the bed and frowned in thought. "But I guess I would just . . . call him?"

"And what would he do?"

"Well, if he was working, he'd probably let it go and call me back later?" I said. I wasn't really sure what she was driving at.

"See?" Emma said. "Ethan, too! Doesn't that make you crazy?"

"No," I said. I was starting to feel weird. Was it *supposed* to make me crazy? "Listen, Josh and I talk every night before we go to bed. So, I know I'll talk to him then."

"You dooooo?" Emma said yearningly. "That's soooo romantic."

And she was right. It was. But it was also what Josh and I had done since the day after our first kiss. We'd just fallen into that sweet pattern, and I'd already gotten used to it. I hadn't known it was so revolutionary. To me—to us, I was pretty sure—it was just the natural thing to do.

I wondered if I was truly crazy about Josh if I wasn't feeling *crazy* about Josh. Being with him made me feel kind of floaty and giddy. And I had noticed that everything seemed a little more intense since I'd started dating him. Like my dad's bad jokes started to seem funny, and kittens or cute commercials on TV made me go all crumple-faced and sappy. And food tasted really delicious.

But did I feel crazy or desperate the way Emma did? I didn't think so.

I guess it helped that when I called Josh after hanging up with Emma, he sounded so happy to hear my voice. And when I invited him to go berry picking, he dropped what he was doing to say yes. (He literally did! I heard a big stack of books hit the counter with a thud!)

I couldn't stop smiling as I hung up the phone and plucked the 1940s frock off the pile on the bed.

If Emma had it right, being with Josh was supposed to make me act either cagey or crazy. And falling for Josh was supposed to make me feel lost.

But instead I felt found. And if that meant I was doing this relationship thing wrong, I decided not to care.

Not surprisingly, my family always went to the same blueberry farm: Chloe and Ken's U-Pick Farm and Art Gallery.

"Oh, yeah," Josh said when we told him where we were

going. "I know them. Did you know they're selling free-range eggs now?"

My dad clapped his hands and laughed.

"Of course they are!" he said. "And I bet they're miserable about it."

"Totally miserable!" Josh said with a grin.

Ken and Chloe desperately wanted to be brilliant starving artists who made a meager living with their blueberry farm. Instead they were wildly successful blueberry farmers who made really bad art. Chloe worked with clay—wobbly vases that looked like she'd caught them in midair just as they'd careened off her potter's wheel, or little animals with drunken, hooded eyes and buck teeth. Ken was always carving up wood. He made sculptures and woodcuts, all of them splintery and angry.

It seemed like the more frustrated Chloe and Ken got as artists, the more their farm thrived, just to spite them.

Sure enough, when we pulled off the flat, dusty dirt highway, their rows of bushes were fluffy and heavy with berries. Cute little white hens clucked and pecked around the bushes. Up on a hill just behind the rows of blueberry bushes, several rows of boxy hives were swarming with so many honeybees, you could see the clouds of them from the driveway.

When we got out of the car, we were met by Ken, looking long-faced in paint-smeared overalls.

"The place looks good, Ken," my dad said. "Won't you *please* take my card. You need an accountant to manage all this money you're making!"

Ken winced. My dad had said that as if it were a *good* thing.

"We started raising these chickens," he said morosely. "People *really* like the eggs. And, well, the chickens fertilize the berries, so *they're* doing really well. And the bees are making so much honey, we had to add fifteen more hives."

Ken hung his head and sighed.

"Oh!" Mom said. She had her perky voice on, and she was pointing at a tall, crooked log planted vertically in the ground. "Ken, I see you're doing something new. Um, is that a totem pole?"

"Chainsaw carving!" Ken said, perking up. "Let me tell you about it. . . ."

My sisters and I looked at each other in alarm.

Run away! Abbie mouthed.

I grabbed Josh by one hand and a stack of buckets in another, and the four of us dashed into the nearest thicket of bushes, all of us snorting with laughter.

"Quick," I whispered, "before we get sucked into the vortex of bad art."

We headed for the back of the orchard, twice almost tripping over lazy chickens.

"I think we're safe," Hannah said with a laugh. She plucked a few berries from a bush and dropped them into her pail.

"Kerplink, kerplank, kerplunk," she said.

"Ah, *Blueberries for Sal*!" Josh said. "That's a big favorite at the kids' story hours at Dog Ear."

Of course, thinking about the children's story hour at Dog Ear made me remember our weird, wonderful first kiss. And *that* made me want to kiss him right then.

I gave Josh a shy glance and caught him giving *me* a shy glance. His Adam's apple was bobbing up and down, and I could tell he was thinking the same thing.

"You know," I said to my sisters, "these berries look too big and squishy. I think Josh and I are going to try a couple rows over."

"Oh, yeah," Abbie said, nodding vigorously. "The kissing will be much better over there."

"Abbie!" I squawked.

"Oh, did I say 'kissing'?" she said with a mock gasp. "I meant '*berries*.' The *berries* will be much better over there."

"You're awful," I told her before ducking through a couple of bushes with Josh to get to the next row. We kept pushing through until we couldn't hear Abbie giggling anymore.

Josh grinned at me when we emerged from the last row of bushes.

"She's awful," I repeated.

"Oh, yeah, awful," Josh said, smiling as he bent over to kiss me.

And kiss me and kiss me until—*clang*—I dropped my bucket into the dirt and we broke apart, laughing.

"Your sister's right, though," Josh said. "The kissing *is* much better over here."

"I hate it when she's right," I said with a grin.

I scooped up my bucket and added, "Come on. We have to pick a *lot* or they'll know what we were up to."

"They know anyway," Josh said. He snaked his arm around my waist and kissed the top of my head, which for some reason made me feel just as melty as when he kissed me on the lips.

"Kerplink, kerplank, kerplunk," I reminded him, twisting away so I could start picking berries.

"All right, all right," he murmured.

But he still stood so close to me that every time he reached for a branch, his arm brushed mine.

Or he would bend for some low-hanging berries, and his fingertips would graze my leg.

Or he would find my version of the perfect blueberry—just tender enough that it wasn't lip-puckeringly sour, but nowhere near as ripe as many people like them—and pop it into my mouth.

It took a while for our berries to stop *kerplink*ing against the bottoms of our buckets. And when we'd finally filled them and headed back to the car, my family had been waiting so long that they'd actually gotten roped into buying some of Chloe's bad pottery.

"Look, Chelsea," Mom said, her voice so perky that it had gone up a whole octave. Chloe was there too, wearing overalls that exactly matched Ken's. Chloe was beaming proudly. "Aren't they, uh, cute?" Mom said.

She was holding two little ceramic chickens, made of rough-looking red clay with plenty of visible fingerprints. They had bulgy eyes with big, bluish lids half-closed over them. Their beaks looked sort of smushed-in. One was a rooster, the other a hen.

"We're calling them Josh and Chelsea," Hannah said with a glare.

I turned to Josh.

"You know we're totally getting sterilizing duty for this."

Sterilizing the jars is the worst part of making jam. You have to hand wash every jar in steaming hot water, then submerge them in boiling water for at least twenty minutes. We always used Granly's roasting pan, balanced over the stove's two back burners, to boil the jars, while two pots of sugared blueberries frothed away on the front two. You had to plunge your arm through the sticky blueberry steam to fish out the clean jars with a pair of wobbly metal tongs, timing it so they were still freshly scalded when the blueberries reached the right temperature and you could pour them into the jars—bubbling and spitting and flecking your clothes with tiny purple dots.

Sure enough, when we got home with our buckets of berries, my mom pointed Josh and me to the sink, where two dozen Ball mason jars were waiting to be scrubbed.

"Here," Hannah said, placing Chloe's clay chickens on the windowsill above the sink. "They can keep you company."

She placed them beak to beak so it looked like they were kissing.

"Now *you're* awful," I said, rolling my eyes at her. I gave Josh a sheepish glance. His face was definitely a little pink, but maybe that was just from the sun and the steam, because he refused to inch away from his spot right next to me at the double sink. He stood so close that my hip nestled comfortably against his leg, and every time he handed me a soapy jar to rinse, our forearms brushed against each other. I noticed the downy hair on his arm had gone blond, and his skin was a bit more golden than it had been when we'd first met. That was back when he'd spent most of his time at Dog Ear, back before he'd had a reason to escape to berry patches and Wex Pond.

Just when the kitchen started to feel oppressive, with the windows steamed up and the air smelling syrupy, my mom put one of Granly's Beatles CDs into the little countertop stereo. Abbie and Hannah started dancing each other around the kitchen, dripping blueberry syrup onto the floor and laughing hysterically. Josh and I bumped hips (or my hip and his leg) and clinked jars together like they were cymbals.

I thought of those stacks of paper that Abbie had made on our bedroom floor, and I knew—this was one of those days that I needed to write down. Maybe on a scrap of paper that nobody ever saw. Maybe in a letter to Josh. It didn't matter. All that mattered was that my pen on paper preserve this moment, so I could know it had really happened when I was back in LA.

That it hadn't been a dream.

The dreamy feeling didn't go away after Josh headed home for dinner—a jar of still-warm blueberry preserves in each hand. Hannah and I crawled around the kitchen with hot soapy rags, scrubbing at the worst of the jam drips, while my mom got ready to go over the whole floor with Granly's old string mop.

Meanwhile Abbie scrubbed pots in the sink. She kept making new sticky splashes on the floor, and we laughed and screeched at her.

Finally cleanup was done, and the only sounds we heard were the jars of jam settling on the kitchen table. The cooling, and some law of physics that Hannah could probably teach us, sucked the mason jar caps downward. Eventually they would all have slight scoops to them, which meant they were safely sealed. As this happened, the jar tops made little *pings* and *pops* and *squeaks.* It gave the strangely cozy illusion that the jam jars were alive. Which I guess was why I winced a little bit when my dad arrived home from a long walk and excitedly popped open one of the jars so he could spread some of the new jam on toast.

While my dad munched and he and my mom chatted, the rest of us drifted away from the kitchen. I went to get my book off my nightstand, and Hannah headed out to the screened porch, dialing her phone. Abbie flopped onto the living room couch and clicked on the TV.

That's when we were all summoned to the living room by a loud whoop.

"What is it?" I yelled, dashing in, my book still open in my hand.

"Look!" Abbie said, grinning and pointing at the TV screen. "Next up: *Till Death Do Us Part?*"

"No. Way!" I screamed.

"What happened?" Hannah said, her hand pressed to her phone to block out our noise.

"Lifetime movie!" Abbie and I shouted at her.

"It's one we've never seen, and it's just starting," I said, flopping down onto the couch with Abbie. I crossed my fingers, closed my eyes, and chanted, "Please let it star Jennifer Love Hewitt!"

"Either her or Valerie Bertinelli," my mom chimed in, flopping down next to me.

Hannah murmured into her phone, "I'll have to call you back, okay? It's kind of important." Then she sank onto the floor in front of the couch and said, "I want Meredith Baxter. She does crazy really well. I think her eyes are a little off their track."

We watched hungrily as the movie started, with melodramatic swells of violins. As the opening credits flashed past in a blocky font that screamed "low-budget" we realized there were no famous B-list actors in the cast. Or even C- or D-list actors. They were total unknowns.

Or maybe Canadians.

That meant the production values were going to be wretched, the acting awful, and the screenplay riddled with melodrama and awkward catchphrases.

"Ooh, it's going to be *so* bad!" I squealed, clapping my hands.

"Honey," my mom called to the kitchen. "Could you make us some popcorn? And is there any wine left from last night?"

"And *please* tell me we have marshmallows," Abbie called.

The marshmallows weren't for eating, of course. They were for tossing at the TV screen during bad lines.

It turned out *Till Death Do Us Part?* was about bigamy, true love, murder, and reconstructive surgery, not necessarily in that order. I knew we had a winner when wife number one raged at her husband, "John, I supported you through law school so you could study jurisprudence, not mess around with some woman named Prudence!"

When wife number two started lacing John's scrambled eggs with arsenic, Hannah and I screamed, "*Flowers in the Attic*!" at the exact same time. We high-fived each other before throwing our last marshmallows at the screen.

We lost Mom when wife number one got killed off. She left

with Dad to pick up a pizza for dinner. But my sisters and I stayed until the bitter end, when—*duh duh DUH*—there was a shocking appearance from wife number THREE.

We turned down the volume during the final credits but couldn't bear to turn it off.

"Best bad movie *ever*," I said, collapsing into the couch cushions and hugging myself. "When are they gonna be back with that pizza? I'm starving! I hope Dad got extra mushrooms."

Abbie and Hannah glanced at each other over my head and exchanged some secret signals.

"What?" I said. "What have you guys been saying about me *now*?"

"She's showing all the signs," Hannah said to Abbie.

"Of what?" I said, alarmed.

"'Of a force stronger than the law, and more brutal than the laws of *nature*,'" Abbie cried, quoting the movie while shaking her fists at the heavens.

I laughed—until I realized what she meant. Then I swallowed my laughter with a quick gulp.

Hannah gave me a smile that was a little wistful as she said, "Does all food taste incredibly delicious? And does all music seem like it's really about you?"

"Do you suddenly think Josh is a completely unique name," Abbie asked, "even though it's really just another one of those blend-together J-boy names?"

"No it's not!" I said automatically. "It's *so* much better than John or Jim or Jason."

"See!" Abbie said, pointing at me.

I sank back into the couch, feeling floaty and on the verge of elated. Were my sisters right? Was I in love with Josh? How could I know for sure? It wasn't like there was some lever inside you that switched from *like* to *love* one day with an audible click.

It made me feel a little feverish to think about it, so of course I lobbed the issue back to Hannah.

"Well, what about you?" I said. "What's going on with Liam?"

"Liam?" Hannah said, blinking rapidly as if she didn't know who I was talking about.

"Yes, Liam, the boy who likes to give you hickeys?" I demanded.

"Oh my God," Hannah groaned. "It was *one* hickey, you guys! Grow up!"

"We will if you will," Abbie said with a little glower.

"What do you mean by that?" Hannah said.

"I mean, are you really finding it *fun* to hang out with some-one who's so . . . blond?"

"Whoa," I said, swinging around to look at Abbie. I was always sensitive to hair-color pigeonholing. "Stereotype much?"

"It's a figure of speech," Abbie said, jutting out her chin. "I just mean Hannah deserves someone less generic. More like . . ."

Just before I could say *Josh*, Hannah whispered, "Elias."

I bit my lip and shot Abbie a look. Looking regretful, she put a hand on Hannah's shoulder.

"I didn't mean to—"

"Listen, Eliases don't come along every day," Hannah said. "But in the absence of one, I think I'm allowed to have some fun."

She pointed accusingly at Abbie.

"You do it all the time!" she said. "You date like it's a sport, just like swimming, but with more contact."

"Yeah," Abbie agreed. "But you're not me."

That, of course, was an understatement. Sometimes I didn't understand how the three of us could be so very different—yet understand each other so well.

Hannah shrugged, grabbed the empty popcorn bowl off the coffee table, and headed for the kitchen, stomping on a couple marshmallows as she went. Which was another way of admitting that Abbie was right. Not that Abbie seemed to enjoy it. She flounced off the couch and headed to our room, stepping on more marshmallows.

I could just picture what Granly would say if she saw us smushing marshmallows into her Persian rug. I slid to the floor (which was easy enough because I was feeling a little weak and rubbery) and crawled around, picking up the flattened marshmallows. I scooped them into the skirt of my cute sepia-colored blueberry-picking dress.

Then I just sat still for a moment and tried to gather my thoughts. I heard a tinny *ping* come from the kitchen as another jar of jam sealed itself closed. That was followed by the soft *thwack* of one of Hannah's textbooks hitting the kitchen table, then flipping open.

I found that the only thoughts I had to gather were ones of Josh, of the way his fingertips felt grazing my cheek, of the dimples that seemed to always go deeper whenever I was around. I pictured the black ink smudge he always had on his middle finger after he'd been working on his Allison Katzinger book launch poster. I could almost smell him, a smell that was warm and clean with a hint of vanilla (maybe from all the cookies floating around Dog Ear).

And then my phone rang, and I knew it was him, and I also knew—with a sudden, breathtaking certainty—that I *was* in love.

I loved Josh's too-long arms and the little cowlick in his left eyebrow. I loved the way he slouched over his coffee cup, and I loved his cherry pie rut. I even loved the way he read books so differently from the way I read them—all businesslike and analytical, always thinking about whether they would sell or sit on the shelf.

But my feelings for Josh went deeper than the details. I just loved . . . him. The him beneath the surface, the him that maybe only I really knew.

I dashed to find my phone, which was on its way to vibrating off the kitchen counter. It felt a little sticky when I scooped it up. I fumbled as I snapped it open, and grinned when I saw Josh's number on the screen and knew that I'd been right.

"Hi," I said, not able to catch my breath somehow. I headed back toward the living room and waited for him to ask what had made me so out of breath.

Would I tell him? *How* do you tell someone something like that?

So, guess what? I just realized that I love you.

I shuddered and shook my head. Then I shrugged and smiled to myself.

The one thing I did know about being with Josh was that there *would* be a time and a way to tell him how I felt, and when it arrived, it would feel natural and sweet and right.

"So, was your mom excited about the jam?" I asked Josh. "Tell her not to put it out in Dog Ear. It'll get gobbled up in a few hours. We worked too hard for that, right? Kerplink, kerplunk . . ."

My voice trailed off. The silence on Josh's end of the line was . . . too silent.

Something was wrong.

"Josh?"

When Josh finally spoke, it came in a rush.

"While I was gone," he said, "my parents were looking at the book delivery schedule. They found my order for the Allison Katzinger books . . . which I never sent out."

"Oh, um, is that bad?" I asked haltingly. "Her reading is in less than two weeks, right?"

"Yes, it's bad," Josh said quickly. "We were supposed to have a hundred of her books here for her signing, and now we probably won't be able to get any, not in time anyway. And it was my fault. I messed up."

"Josh," I began, "you shouldn't have to—"

"But I do, Chelsea." I didn't like the way he cut me off, or the way my name sounded when he said it. "I do have to do these things. My dad's always in Chicago, and my mom—well, she's not handling it, is she? She just doesn't get it. So it's up to me or the store goes under and everything changes and it's all because of *me*."

"Okay, okay," I said, trying to make my voice soothing. "I think—"

Josh cut me off again.

"Listen, I know you want to make me feel better," he said. "But me feeling better isn't going to solve this problem. You know what will? Me doing my job. I need to focus—to *re*focus on what matters. Dog Ear."

"But . . . ," I whispered, "don't I matter too? To you? Because you—"

"You . . . you know you do. But I need to focus."

"You already said that," I said, hating that my voice sounded tear-choked. "So what are you saying? You want to see each other less?"

There was an awful silence on the other end of the phone.

"Oh," I whispered. "We won't see each other . . . at all."

Josh sighed deeply.

"I can't think of another way," he said.

I tried to make my voice go as cold as his.

"Or you won't think of another way," I said.

"Chelsea—"

"No, I get it," I said. "I'll let you go."

"Chelsea, this . . . isn't what I want," Josh protested. "It's what I have to do."

"Sure, Josh," I snapped. "You do what you have to do."

Then I clapped my phone closed. I looked around. I didn't remember coming back into the living room, but there I was. I stared at my reflection in the mirror hanging above the mantel. My hair was a frizzy, tangled mess, but that wasn't unusual. It was my face that I didn't recognize.

Well, actually, I did.

I remembered looking into the bathroom mirror in LA right

after my dad told me about Granly's stroke, and seeing that same version of me in the mirror—pale, confused, blindsided, and very, very upset.

I'd known I would have to say good-bye to Josh. But it wasn't supposed to be like this! What had just happened?

The front door swung open, and I jumped.

"Hi, sweetie!" my mom said, her face lighting up at the sight of me. My dad was behind her, holding two large pizza boxes. "We got your favorite—extra mushrooms!"

I don't know why *that* was what finally made me crumple to the floor and start crying.

"I want to go home," I sobbed as my mom knelt down next to me, wrapping her arms around my shoulders.

"I don't understand," she said, her voice immediately thick with empathetic tears.

I shook my head slowly, closing my eyes and feeling a fresh river of tears roll down my cheeks.

"Neither do I."

August

It's strange what will drag you out of bed the morning after your heart's been broken.

Food won't do it, even if your dad is making bacon and blueberry pancakes. Even if he has deferred to the fact that his daughter's soul is crushed and he has promised to skip the mouse ears.

Needing something to read won't do it. I couldn't read through the tears in my eyes anyway. The words blurred, or worse—were replaced by images of Josh's face. Either way the pages got wet and splotchy, and I ended up reading the same sentence about six hundred times.

Having to pee? Okay, that made me get up, but it doesn't count if you make it quick and jump directly back into bed.

Being scheduled to work also wouldn't rouse me. If I called in sick that afternoon, I decided, it wouldn't even be a lie. I *was* sick. Heartsick, headsick, and actually a little queasy and headachy, although maybe that was due to lack of food.

So what *did* make me crawl out of bed at around eleven in the morning?

My garden.

My first impression of this first day of August, other than the fact that it was a dismal, awful, oh-the-humanity kind of day (for me anyway) was that it was hot. Not cheery, sunshiny, let's-go-to-the-beach hot. No, this was a ruthless white heat, a wilting, joy-sapping, punishing heat. A garden-destroying heat.

My plants needed me.

Ever since mid-July the garden had required daily watering. If I skipped even one morning, I noticed the plants began to wilt. The stems sagged and the leaves curled inward as if to protect themselves from the sun's glare. The half-red tomatoes would wrinkle, and the cucumbers would take on a dusty cast.

When that happened, I'd feel as guilty as if I'd neglected a pet.

What's more, the garden was on the verge of being edible. The tomatoes were looking plumper and redder each day. The cucumbers had outgrown their gherkin infancy and had grown into stout little pre-pickles. And my squash were getting so pot-bellied, my dad promised to use them the next time he made shish kebabs on the grill.

How lame would it be to let the garden shrivel up now, just because my heart was a raisin?

Maybe it was Granly's ghost who made me roll out of bed and slump to the backyard to unreel the hose. Maybe it was just stubbornness or force of habit. Either way, I did it. I didn't bother to change out of my nightshirt or put on flip-flops before I plodded outside.

I felt like I was watching myself from a distance as I uncoiled the hose and started spraying my plants. I got no satisfaction from watching the dry, dusty dirt become wet, squishy, and nourishing. Nor from the spiky yellow-green scent that sprang off the tomatoes when I watered them. I didn't even feel happy when my spray uncovered a whole new trove of baby cukes, some of them still wearing their shriveled yellow blossoms.

I cared enough to keep the garden alive, but the daily joy it had given me all month? That was gone.

I was numb.

I finished watering and turned off the spigot. Then I leaned against the house and tried to think of something, anything, I wanted to do for the rest of the day.

Beaching it with my sisters would be awful. They'd be all careful and sweet around me, and it would break my heart further.

If I spent time with either one of my parents, I knew I would just curl up into a ball and cry.

Then I thought about Mel & Mel's, and the clatter of dishes *whooshing* out of the Hobart, of filter baskets being slammed into the geriatric coffeemaker, and the constant scrape of chairs on the floor and fork tines on china. I realized that *that* was where I wanted to go. It was the only even remotely tolerable place I could imagine spending this awful day.

But what about Josh on the other side of the brick wall?

I was *almost* certain he wouldn't come into Mel & Mel's. Even if he'd become a cold workaholic robot, he wouldn't be *that* cruel, would he?

Or maybe he'd stay away simply for the time it would save. After all, girlfriend drama or, say, eating would cut into his busy schedule.

Now, I knew, Josh would do *anything* to avoid that.

By the time I left for work, I *thought* I'd pulled myself together. I'd put on makeup. (Well, except for mascara. The last thing I needed was telltale black streaks trailing down my cheeks.)

I'd pulled my hair into its usual ponytail but refrained from twisting it into an angsty bun.

I even decided against my first impulse outfit—a dour black T-shirt and dull, army green cargo shorts—and forced myself to wear a butter-yellow tank top and some stretchy denim shorts.

I looked almost presentable. Certainly not like someone who'd realized she was giddy-in-love just minutes before being brutally dumped.

I even felt a little hopeful as I walked my roundabout Dog Ear–avoiding route to Mel & Mel's. Nobody there had to know what had happened. I could immerse myself in the rhythm of greeting/serving/clearing. The white noise of the coffee shop clatter would cancel out the turmoil in my head. My body would propel itself through what had become routine motions, and the exhaustion I felt at the end of the day would be welcome.

Maybe I'd leave work somehow feeling a little better.

Maybe I would even sleep that night.

But I only had to step through Mel & Mel's door for my whole suffer-in-silence plan to crash down around me.

"Oh, Chelsea!" Andrea cried when she saw me. She'd been en route to the kitchen with a tray full of dishes, but she immediately put it down on a table and rushed over. "What happened?"

"What?" I said, my voice squeaky. "What are you talking about?"

"Well, clearly something's really wrong," Andrea said. "It's all over your face."

"But I put on makeup!" I protested while Andrea guided me to a stool at the counter. Melissa popped up from behind it like a gopher sniffing for trouble.

"Let me get you a drink, hon," she said. She made me my favorite—iced tea and lemonade. "Now spill."

"It's nothing," I said, shaking my head and pushing away the icy drink. It was already beading up with condensation in the steamy heat.

"Drink up," Melissa said in a harsh Big Mama voice. It was so different from the firm sweetness of my own mother's voice, but somehow it was just as effective.

"Okay," I said. I took a huge, delicious swallow. It was so cold and sweet, it made my teeth hurt, but it was also delicious. I could have put a straw into a pitcher of it and drunk the whole thing right there. It was the first thing I'd tasted that day that hadn't made me want to gag.

Finally I plunked my glass back onto the counter, wiped my mouth with the back of my hand, and announced, "Josh broke up with me. He said he needs to focus on the store."

"What?" Andrea cried, putting both hands to her face in shock.

"Well!" Melissa said. "I can't believe it! I mean, I can because he's a *boy* and *they* do crazy things all the time, but . . . *Josh*? That boy is in love with you. We could all see it. Am I right, Al?"

Al Thayer had just walked in and was heading to his usual

table in my section, but when Melissa spoke to him, he wheeled right around and came to join us at the counter. He hopped onto the stool next to mine, which was pretty impressive, considering that Mr. Thayer was pushing eighty. He was also my favorite regular, so it gave me a tiny lift to see him.

"How's my favorite little waitress?" he said, tweaking my ponytail.

"A, that's kind of sexist, Mr. Thayer," Andrea said, crossing her arms over her chest. "And B, I thought *I* was your favorite little waitress."

"Did I ever say, Andie," Mr. Thayer said, his white eyebrows crunching into a bushy line over his big nose, "that you weren't *also* my favorite? You can have more than one, you know."

"No you can't," Andrea and I said at the same time, which made her laugh and made me *almost* smile.

"Well, *I* can," Mr. Thayer said. "Besides, did *you* ever write me into a serial, Andrea?"

He glanced at the specials board, where the latest installment of *Diablo and the Mels* was still glowing beneath the list of pie flavors.

B. didn't like Thayer. She of all people (or whatever) didn't trust a man who ate his eggs with hot sauce. That was her *thing.*

"I expect B. and me to have a grand battle, my dear," Mr. Thayer said. "Make it happen."

I tried to laugh, but all that came out was a pathetic little honk.

"So, what's the problem?" Mr. Thayer asked.

"Josh," Melissa, Andrea, and I said at once.

"I thought as much," Mr. Thayer said. "What happened?"

"He's choosing career over love," Andrea said dramatically. "Men!"

"I don't think you can call Dog Ear Josh's career," I said wanly. "I mean, he hasn't even graduated from high school!"

"He's a good boy," Mr. Thayer said. I felt my eyes well up. My tongue went so thick in my mouth that I couldn't talk, but I nodded. Because I couldn't help agreeing with Mr. Thayer. Even though I was hating Josh for choosing his parents over me, I also loved him for it. He *was* a good boy.

"But," Mr. Thayer went on, "being good doesn't mean you're always right. And being a boy, a young man—well, that's a trial-by-error time if there ever was one."

"So you think he made a mistake?" I choked out. I didn't know why this filled me with such hope. I guessed it was because Mr. Thayer was old. And a man. So he knew more about this honor and manhood thing than I did.

"If he did," Mr. Thayer said, "I don't think Josh will be too proud to admit it. He's a good boy. And I am thirsty. Can I have one of those Arnold Palmers, young lady?"

He pointed at my almost-empty glass. I hopped off my stool, nodding hard and flicking the moisture from beneath my eyes at the same time.

Soon after, a summer swim team came in, celebrating a win and wanting massive amounts of food. After that there was the dinner rush. So, just as I'd hoped, I didn't have time to think.

Which wasn't to say I forgot about Josh. He was always there in the back of my mind.

The fact was, he'd been in that spot, hovering in my consciousness, ever since I'd met him. First he lodged in my head as a curiosity, then as a delight. Now he was a wound, a fresh paper cut that wouldn't stop stinging.

When my shift was almost over, and my section was down to one table—a couple nursing cold drinks—I slumped against the counter and breathed a long, tired sigh.

But I followed it up with a little smile. I'd been right to come in today. I put my elbows on the counter and propped my chin on my fists.

"Do you know what, Melissa?" I said to Mel as she did her nightly receipt tally. "I've made a decision. When I go back to LA, I'm not taking any more babysitting jobs. I'm going to wait tables."

"Put me down as a reference, sweetie," Melissa muttered without looking up from her receipts. But a moment later she stopped herself and looked at me.

"You know, I almost forgot you were from LA!" she said. "You seem so . . . Bluepointe. And you never talk about your life back home."

I bit my lip and glanced at the Dog Ear wall. I hadn't been thinking about my life back home either. I glanced at the little calico cat calendar that Melissa kept tacked up next to the cash register. I quickly added up the days we had left in Bluepointe.

Twenty-one.

Twenty-one days that Josh and I could have been spending together. It wasn't much. On the other hand, you could cram a whole lot of fun—and a whole lot of love—into twenty-one days if you wanted to.

"Too bad he doesn't want to," I muttered to myself, shaking my head.

But then I frowned and replayed (for, oh, about the fortieth time) the things that Josh had said to me the previous night.

"This isn't what I want; it's what I have to do."

I bowed my head, scrunching my fingers into my hair. *How* could Josh think that this was right? He meant well, but if his mom *knew* what he'd done—

I lifted my head abruptly.

Of *course*, Stella didn't know. That was the whole point. Josh's mom was sweet, but kind of clueless. I would have bet she had no idea how much Josh was doing—and sacrificing—for Dog Ear.

I hopped off the stool and untied my apron at the same time. As I hurried toward the kitchen to hang up my stuff, I called to Andrea.

"Can you do me a favor and check out my last table? Please?"

Andrea looked at me in confusion.

"There's something I've gotta do," I said. "Now. Before I lose my nerve."

Andrea glanced over her shoulder at the Dog Ear wall, then looked back at me and nodded excitedly.

"Only if you promise to come back after and tell me everything that happened," she said.

"I hope there's something to tell," I said with a nervous grin. "Thanks, Andie."

I darted into the bathroom and dabbed at my shiny face with a damp paper towel. I rubbed at the circles under my eyes, until

I remembered that I wasn't wearing mascara and those circles weren't going anywhere. I took out my hair elastic and cringed as my curls—which looked even brighter after two months in the sun—sprang out in a Medusa-like puff. I pulled the front bits back and let the rest of my hair coil around my shoulders.

Then I gave myself a last, hard look in the mirror, stalked out of Mel & Mel's, and went next door.

Every other time that I'd walked into Dog Ear, I'd felt elation swell up inside me. It wasn't just about Josh, either, though that had been the biggest part of it. I just loved the place, with its pretty yellow walls and goofy rainbow review cards, the picket fence and Josh's broody posters. I loved that there was always some kid running around with a book in one hand and a yo-yo in the other, and of course I loved the couch and the snacks.

Maybe that's why my eyes teared up the moment I walked in. Because I was afraid of losing Dog Ear in addition to Josh.

As the door jingled closed behind me, E.B. ambled over. He pushed his big, blocky head beneath my hand for an ear scratch. I whispered hello to him and nervously scanned the store for Josh.

I didn't see him, but I was sure he was there. Somehow I could feel him there, the same way I knew it was him whenever he called me.

Isobel was at the cash register. I gave her a little wave and walked toward the stacks. E.B. shuffled along behind me until he realized that I wasn't heading toward the lounge—where there was a basket of Triscuits and a can of spray cheese on the coffee table. He gave a little snort and trotted away.

I couldn't quite believe where I finally found Josh. He was sitting on the floor in the children's aisle, the exact same spot where we'd had our first kiss.

For some reason this gave me hope. Maybe we could somehow go back in time, to the improbable perfection of that kiss and . . .

I stopped there, because even if time travel were possible, I wasn't sure how it would fix things.

Josh looked up at me, his eyes wide and startled. They weren't nearly as cold as his voice had been on the phone the night before. They also had gray shadows that exactly matched the ones under my eyes.

But once Josh got over the shock of seeing me, he clenched his jaw and frowned.

"Chelsea, I—"

I shook my head and gave him a stern *Let me talk* look. Then I knelt before him, glad that I was wearing pants today instead of one of the poofy skirts that could make a quick exit difficult.

"Have you ever told them?" I asked Josh. He went a little pale and cringed. Once upon a time I might have been offended. But now that I knew Josh, I knew what that expression meant. He didn't want to get rid of me. He wanted me to stay—and keep talking.

"What do you mean?" Josh asked me.

"Your parents," I said impatiently. "Do they even know how you feel? Do they know that you grind your teeth every time you have to change the receipt tape or update the store's website?

That *they're* living this owning-a-bookstore dream because *you're* the one with your feet on the ground?"

"Of course they know," Josh said. Now he sounded impatient with me. "How could they not?"

"You're a good son," I said with a shrug. "Maybe they just assume this is your dream too."

"That's the thing," Josh said. He grabbed a book off the shelf and held it up. "This isn't a dream. This is a store. A business. It's like this . . . *beast* that needs to be fed. And if we don't keep up with the feedings, the store goes under, my parents lose piles of money, and where does that leave them?"

"And you?" I added. "You know, you're allowed to put yourself into that equation too."

I pulled the picture book gently from Josh's hands and laid it on the floor. I knew not to shelve it out of order and create more work for him.

"I think if your mom is anything like mine," I said, "she would prefer that you did think of yourself, at least a little bit."

"What do you mean?" Josh said.

"I mean, you should talk to your parents," I said, getting to my feet. "Tell them what's been going on with you, Josh. Tell them—"

I looked down sharply, trying to contain the tears that had suddenly welled up in my eyes.

"Tell them everything," I said. "And tell them what *you* want, for once. I think they might surprise you."

Then I turned to leave. I wanted to take a last, lingering look at Josh's face, but I knew if I did, I would burst into tears. I didn't want that, and not just because it would have been mortifying. I also didn't want to manipulate Josh into coming back to me. I wanted him to do it because being with me made him happy. I wanted it for him as much as for myself.

I guess if I wanted a confirmation that I really did love Josh, then that was it—even if it was too late.

I went straight to bed after I got home. Despite my head's best efforts to keep me awake with a looping tally of anxieties, my exhausted body dragged me into sleep.

And when I woke up, it wasn't quite as hard to get myself out of bed. There was a tiny kernel of hope that maybe I'd gotten through to Josh. And maybe I'd hear from him.

Even if I didn't, at least I'd tried. I'd done *something*. I'd gotten my say. It wasn't exactly cheering, but it made me feel a little better about this whole breakup thing.

I had to water again. The sun was as searing as ever, even at nine thirty in the morning. I had breakfast with my sisters first. They were quietly watchful but didn't crowd me with a *How're you doing?* inquisition. I showered and threw on a blue sundress. It was the one dress I had that happened to have pockets, which meant I could keep my phone on me at all times. You know, just in case. Then I headed into the backyard.

As soon as I stepped off the laundry room steps, I knew something was wrong.

My mom was standing in front of the garden with one hand covering her mouth. She saw me and took a halting step toward me.

"I just got back from a walk," she said. "I thought I'd check to see if there were any tomatoes ripe enough for lunch, and . . . Oh, honey, I'm sorry."

I shook my head in confusion as I walked toward her, but as soon as I got a look at the garden, I knew what she was talking about.

It had been decimated.

The ground beneath the tomato plant was littered with half-gnawed fruit, including lots of green tomatoes. The lettuce leaves were riddled with rodenty bite marks, and two of the cucumber vines had been torn out of the ground altogether. As for the radishes, it was like they'd never even been there.

I slapped both hands on top of my head.

"Yesterday," I croaked, "when I watered, I forgot the cayenne pepper!"

I couldn't believe how quickly my garden had been destroyed. It was like the animals were getting back at me for my spicy repellant.

"I'm sure it was deer," my mom said. "They can tear a garden to pieces just like that."

I thought of Granly, sitting at the kitchen table, watching beautiful forest animals sample her veggies, loving how delicately the deer tiptoed through the plants.

I dropped to my knees at the edge of the garden, not caring if I got dirt on my pale blue dress. I began yanking the stringy remains of my lettuce plants out of the earth. I tossed them into a messy pile at my side.

And it was only when my mom crouched down to put her arms around me that I realized I was sobbing.

"I wanted it to be different!" I said through angry tears.

"Different? What do you mean?" Mom asked.

"From Granly's garden," I cried. "Hers got all eaten up, but mine was supposed to be different. It was almost there!"

"Wait, look!" my mom pointed at the one cucumber plant that was left intact. Then she stepped into the garden and said, "And there's a lot of squash still here, and I found three lettuce plants that they missed."

"Okay," I said quietly, wondering why I wasn't comforted at all.

Mom picked her way back through the messy thatch of plants. She handed me a big, unscathed squash, its yellow skin waxy and perfect.

"Thanks," I muttered, swiping away my tears. Only when she sat next to me did I realize she was crying too.

"I'm sorry, Chelsea," she sighed. "About . . . everything."

I nodded sadly. Then we sat there in silence but for the occasional sniffle and, of course, the hot-day hum of the cicadas.

"Why do you think it was so important to you," Mom wondered, "that your garden turn out differently from Granly's?"

I shrugged.

"I guess," I said, feeling guilt wash over me, "I kind of wanted to . . . move on? To not always be stuck in this place where it feels like we have to do all these things that she did, but without her. I guess I just want to get to that place where she's not here but life goes on and . . . and it's bearable."

It felt kind of terrible to utter all these things out loud, especially to my mom. But it also felt kind of wonderful to say them, like something that had been clamped down on me had suddenly released its grip.

Mom sighed.

"It *has* become more bearable, hasn't it?" she said. "I think being here has made it so."

I blinked. It was true. Living in the cottage with Granly's furniture and her photo albums, and even her egg cups, had gotten a little easier.

"But not to the point where you can go through Granly's stuff," I pointed out.

"It's funny. I was just pondering that on my walk," Mom said. "I was thinking that maybe I *am* ready, and I think it's because I'm getting to the end of my quilt."

"It's going to be really pretty," I said. "The quilt."

Mom nodded absentmindedly.

"You know," she said, "I was doing some pattern research online, and I found this article about mourning quilts."

"Morning quilts?" I said. "Like for cold mornings?"

"No, the other kind of mourning," my mom said. "An Appalachian woman, when she suffered a loss, would make a quilt. All that piecing and batting and hand-stitching—it's so absorbing. It doesn't make your pain go away, but it gets you through it. Making the quilt both distracts you and makes you focus on the person you lost. The work carries you through the days. It is true, you know, that cliché about time. It does heal all wounds.

"The funny thing about the mourning quilt is, once it was finished, it was just another quilt to throw on the bed," Mom went on. "It wasn't made into a shrine to hang on the wall or put in a chest. They didn't have that luxury. And besides, the mourning quilt was about the process, not the product."

"Has it been that way for you?" I asked.

"I think so," Mom said, nodding thoughtfully. "I think I've been mourning more than just Granly. I've been sewing up these baby clothes, and sometimes I just can't *believe* you ever wore them. You're all so grown-up. And Hannah's leaving—"

Mom's voice caught, and she shook her head apologetically while I wrapped my arms around her and squeezed.

"I'm not graduating for ages," I reminded her. "I can't even drive yet! You've got me trapped."

Mom laughed and squeezed me back.

"You know that's not what I want," she said

I nodded. I *did* know. And if it was hard to feel exactly lucky right then, what with my phone still silent in my pocket, I did feel grateful.

"Mom?"

My mom and I turned to see Abbie hesitating at the back door. She was holding a big storage bin—the plastic kind with the locking lid. And she had a funny look on her face.

"I found this in the back of Granly's closet," she said as Mom and I stood up and walked over to her. "I thought it was gonna be clothes, but look . . ."

Mom and I peered into the bin. Inside there was a neat stack of cardboard boxes. They were closed loosely, without tape, and on each one Granly had written a name.

Our names.

My mom inhaled sharply, then shook her head.

"She told me about those boxes," she whispered. "Such a long time ago. I'd forgotten."

"What are they?" I asked as my mom took the bin from Abbie and carried it to the kitchen table.

"Adam?" my mom called down the hall. "Hannah? Can you come in here?"

Then she turned to me to answer my question.

"These are the things Granly wanted each of us to have after she died," Mom said bluntly. "During one of our visits here, just before she was taking that trip to Scandinavia, she sat me down and told me where the key to her safe deposit box was and where all her passwords were and things like that. And she told me about this box of things she'd set aside for us. I didn't pay much attention because she was so young. I told her she'd be around for forever."

Mom's voice wobbled but she pressed on.

"When she died," Mom said, "I did remember about the bank vault and the passwords, but somehow I forgot about this."

My dad came into the kitchen, with Hannah right behind him.

"What are those?" Hannah asked, peeking into the bin.

My mom pulled out the box with Hannah's name on it.

"Presents!" Mom said. Tears were streaming down her cheeks, but she was smiling through them.

Granly hadn't written my name on my box in careful calligraphy or anything precious like that. It was just a quick scrawl with a Sharpie. But it still brought me to tears to see her handwriting.

As each of my family members opened their boxes and silently read the notes Granly had written to them, the whole kitchen filled with sniffles. Even my dad's eyes brimmed as he held up a men's watch with a satiny ivory face and gold Roman numerals.

"It's Grandpa's watch," he said, immediately buckling the worn leather band onto his wrist.

Abbie pulled two framed works of art out of her box. They were two of the red Conté nudes that Granly had loved to collect. Both female figures were in motion—their muscular bodies leaping through the air, their hair flying out behind them.

"I remember these!" Abbie said, wiping at her cheek with the back of her hand. "I always loved them."

"She gave me Grandpa's passport holder," Hannah cried, holding up a brown leather wallet embossed with Grandpa's name in gold.

Mom was the only one who wasn't surprised by her gift.

"I always told her I wanted this," she said, lifting a string of pearls out of her box. The clasp looked like a blossom—a cluster of gold petals. "She used to wear these pearls every Saturday night when she'd go on dates with Grandpa."

I was the last one to open my box. Inside I found a thin stack of familiar leather-bound notebooks. Granly's journals. Flipping one open, I saw more of Granly's handwriting—some of it in ink, some of it in smudgy pencil—pages and pages of it.

Two more of the journals were filled up, but the fourth was blank.

I opened the card that Granly had written to me.

For my Chelsea, who's a writer (too). Enough with those scraps of paper! With all my love, Granly.

I opened my mouth to speak, then closed it again. I was speechless.

Chelsea, who's a writer?

Where had Granly gotten that idea? I was a *reader*. And yeah, I wrote stuff down on those scraps of paper. But that didn't count.

Did it?

Timidly I opened the first of Granly's notebooks again.

Daddy and Mother want to go to the South Shore for all of June, and I think I'll just die if I have to go with.

My eyebrows shot upward. That was a pretty good beginning. And a familiar one.

I couldn't wait to read more.

For the rest of the morning our cottage was very quiet. We all drifted apart, each of us deep in thought, each of us saying our own thank-yous to Granly's ghost.

But eventually I stopped reading Granly's journals—which were part diary, part very funny short-story collection. I didn't want to tear through them. I wanted to make them last.

Besides, I was starving.

When I wandered into the kitchen, I found Abbie peering into the fridge.

"I think I'm officially sick of blueberries," she said, closing the door with a curled lip.

"Better not be," I said. "The blueberry festival's next week, you know."

"Oh, yeah," Abbie said. "I almost forgot about that crazy festival."

"You wouldn't have if you worked on Main Street," I said. "Every electrical pole is plastered with flyers. Mel's got three different kinds of blueberry pie on the menu. And at Dog Ear—"

I'd been about to tell Abbie about the cute blueberry-themed window display Stella had made for the bookshop. But I decided to just let that one go.

"Were you and Josh going to go together," Abbie asked quietly. "To the festival?"

I shrugged.

"We hadn't talked about it yet," I said.

But I was sure we would have gone to the festival together. Ever since the DFJ, Josh and I had just known—without having to say it—that we'd share all the summer's big events. All its little ones too.

Before I could explain that to Abbie, I heard a knock at the front door. A loud, urgent knock.

"Who is that?" I said in alarm.

Abbie and I jumped up and headed to the door. Nobody ever knocked on Granly's door. Sparrow Road was too remote for salesmen, and anybody who knew us would have just opened the unlocked door and called, "Anybody home?"

Abbie opened the door a crack and peeked outside. Then she turned toward me, flashed me a huge grin, and opened the door wide.

Standing on the screened porch, looking red-cheeked, breathless, and pretty terrified (but also really, really cute) was Josh.

His bike lay on its side in the drive behind him, its front wheel still spinning. I watched that wheel twirl around and around and wondered if my eyes were doing the exact same thing.

"Chelsea," Josh huffed, "can I talk to you?"

I couldn't quite form words, so I just nodded and stepped outside. The moment Abbie closed the door, Josh spoke in a rush.

"I did it," he announced. He flopped triumphantly onto the smushy couch. I sat—way more tentatively—next to him.

"You did . . . what?"

"I did what you told me to do," Josh said, breaking into an elated smile. "I talked to my parents. Both of 'em."

"Well, what did you say?"

"I asked them to step it up at the bookstore," he said. "Because it was their choice to buy Dog Ear, not mine. That I was doing all this stuff to keep the store afloat for *them*, but that it wasn't making *me* very happy. In fact, I told them, I've given up a lot for Dog Ear. And I was pretty okay with that until . . . well, until I lost you."

Josh looked so earnest and serious, I *had* to touch him, just to make sure this was really happening. I reached over and rested my fingertips lightly on the back of his hand.

Josh heaved a shuddering sigh and closed his eyes.

"What did they say?" I asked him.

Josh gave a little laugh.

"You were right," he said, looking at me shyly. "They had no idea. And they were pretty mad at me for keeping it a secret all this time. Then my mom promised to do more practical stuff, though she might need a little training."

My smile felt tremulous.

"Does this training," I broached, "have to happen within, say, the next twenty days?"

Josh leaned in, his face so close to mine that it made me feel dizzy in the best way.

"Not a chance," he breathed.

I closed my eyes and felt his arms wrap around me, so tightly that I gasped. And then he was kissing me. It was the perfect kiss—full of apology and relief and passion.

In an instant I felt like I'd rewound the past two days and landed right back in that moment when my cell phone had rung and I'd just *known* how I felt about Josh. I was feeling it all again.

It turned out I wasn't the only one.

"Chelsea," Josh murmured when the kiss finally ended. "Can you forgive me for being an idiot?"

"Well, you were being an honorable idiot," I whispered with a little laugh.

"Is that a yes?" Josh asked, twining a lock of my hair around his finger.

I grinned and leaned in until my forehead was touching his. I rested my hands on the back of his neck and whispered, "Yes."

"Good, because you know what?" Josh said.

"What?"

"I'm in love with you, Chelsea. I think I have been since the first time I ever saw you, when you tried to rescue that book from my X-Acto knife."

Tears sprang to my eyes, but they couldn't have felt more different from the ones I'd been crying for the past two days.

"What a coincidence," I said. "That's when I fell in love with you, too."

Josh covered my mouth with his. We didn't say anything else—nothing else needed to be said—for a long, long time.

When you see the boy you love through a crowd, he can look completely familiar and be a complete surprise, all at once.

I thought I knew everything there was to know about Josh's face. I knew that his left eye got a little more squinty than the right one when he smiled. And that his chin was square, rather than pointed, if you really looked at it. I'd watched the sun turn his hair the color of milky caramel over the course of the summer. It had also gotten long enough to actually look tousled. I knew that the back of Josh's neck flushed when he got overheated after rowing or, say, rushing over to my house a week earlier to tell me that he loved me.

But when I spotted him in the middle of a throng of people at the Blueberry Dreams Festival, I didn't recognize him for an instant. Was that him? Was that boy, so tan and tall and *gorgeous*, Josh? *My* Josh?

Suddenly he saw me, and I could swear I saw him blink too—before he smiled an incredulous, giddy smile.

We wove our way through the people crowding the Bluepointe town square. Every adult seemed to be sipping a tall, purple cocktail, and every little kid was sweating inside a puffy blueberry costume. Everybody in between, like me, wore face paint, their cheeks dotted with berries. Or they had on funny blueberry beanies, with tufts of green leaves on the crowns instead of propellers.

Josh and I had just seen each other that morning at the beach, but we hugged as if it had been days.

"You look really pretty," Josh said, putting a hand on my still-damp-from-the-shower hair.

"So do you," I said. I laughed before kissing him lightly on the lips. "Should we do a walk around?"

The square was lined with tents in which people were hawking blueberry honey, blueberry syrup, blueberry baked goods, and of course, a whole lot of blueberry art.

We ambled along lazily, our hands clasped, checking out the ceramic blueberry bowls and purple paintings. Only when we got to Chloe and Ken's tent did we *have* to stop.

They were both sitting in the back of their tent looking miserable. Their space was fronted by two folding tables. One was *full* of ceramic animals, wobbly bowls, and rough-hewn wood sculptures. The other table was almost empty. That's where Chloe and Ken had set out their blueberries, eggs, and honey. They had all clearly been snapped up by shoppers.

Josh met my eyes. He cringed, feeling Chloe and Ken's pain.

Then he pulled out his wallet and reached for something in the center of the table.

It was a small chunk of wood that Ken had carved into a little rowboat. It looked craggy and splintery, but it was also the exact same shape as the shabby little boat that Josh and I had floated into Wex Pond.

"Would you take ten dollars for this, Ken?" Josh asked. "It's really awesome."

I've never seen a man's face go from dour to lit-up that fast.

"Absolutely," Ken said, jumping up to take Josh's money. "Would you like some blueberry jam to go with that? Gratis!"

"Oh, no," I said. "We're good, really. We're *awash* in blueberry jam."

Ken shrugged and turned to give his wife a happy kiss on the cheek. As Josh and I walked away, he handed the little rowboat to me.

"You could put the kissing chickens in it," he said, "and put them in the bathtub."

I laughed.

"It's the most romantic present I ever got," I said, kissing *him* on the cheek. "Also the ugliest, but that's okay!"

"You just don't appreciate good art," he said.

"Oh, I think I do," I said with confidence.

I thought about the poster Josh had shown me the day before, the one he'd finally finished for Allison Katzinger's book party. It was dreamy and shadowy and layered with one beautiful image after another. It was perfect. And luckily, it wouldn't be wasted. After Josh's big talk with his parents, Stella had spent an entire afternoon making calls. She'd managed to round up more than a hundred copies of *Leaves of Trees* for the party.

Josh and I approached the Dog Ear tent, where lots of books and big piles of blue Dog Ear T-shirts and baseball caps had been transplanted for the day. E.B. was stationed out front, panting smilingly at the passersby.

I put a hand on Josh's arm.

"Maybe we should go the other way," I suggested. "You know

if you go in there, you're gonna start working. You won't be able to help yourself."

Josh didn't answer. He just quietly watched what was happening in the tent.

His dad was stationed at the front table, working the cash box. His gray hair was hidden under a Dog Ear baseball cap and he was chatting amiably with one customer after another. He didn't look like he was talking about philosophy or academia or anything very serious. He also looked like he was having a ball.

Meanwhile, Stella was hand-selling in the back of the tent, chatting up various books. She pointed one teenage girl to Josh's Allison Katzinger poster. Clearly she was urging her to come to the book party.

"They're kicking butt in there!" I said.

"I know!" Josh replied, staring in awe. "But how . . ."

"I told you they'd surprise you," I said. "Parents sometimes do."

I craned my neck to see if my parents were still where I'd left them a few minutes earlier, talking to some of their friends. They were. In fact, my dad had just told one of his awful jokes. I could tell by the way my mom was rolling her eyes and the way the other couple were shaking their heads as they laughed.

"Aaaand," I added, "sometimes they don't."

"Josh?"

At the sound of a girl's surprised voice, Josh and I turned. A sweet-faced girl with a blueberry beanie was trotting toward us.

"Hi!" she gushed, giving Josh a quick hug. "How's your summer been?"

Josh smiled and slipped his arm around my waist.

"Really good," he said. "Chelsea, this is Aubrey. We go to the same school."

"Oh my God, you guys are *cute* together," Aubrey said.

"Um, thanks," I said with a shy smile. "Hey, didn't I see you at the lantern party? You had that pretty lantern with the dog."

"Yeah!" Aubrey said. "That was me. And *this* guy has been AWOL ever since!"

She gave Josh a poke in the ribs.

"I guess we have you to blame for that, Chelsea?" she said.

"Well, I—"

"Actually," Josh said, looking down at me with an easy smile, "I just got an e-mail about a post-festival party at the dock. I was gonna ask you if you wanted to go."

"Really?" Aubrey and I said at the same time.

Josh held up his hands defensively.

"Hey, I'm not *that* antisocial," he said.

Aubrey and I looked at each other with matching one-eyebrow-lifted looks of skepticism, which made us both dissolve into laughter.

"Well, maybe I'm feeling a little *more* social these days," Josh said, giving my hair a quick stroke. "For some reason."

"We'll be there," I told Aubrey quietly. Then I shot a quick look at Josh. He seemed a little different, suddenly. More confident, more comfortable in his skin.

Was it all because of . . . me?

"Awesome," Aubrey said, breaking into my thoughts with her bubbly response. Then she cocked her head like a dog listening for a distant whistle. "Music's starting. Let's go!"

She pushed through the crowd toward the gazebo, where a band was indeed setting up. It was a quartet of hipster dudes with lots of facial hair and old-timey instruments—an accordion, banjo, and fiddle.

"Ooh," I said, fluffing up my purple poodle skirt. "My kind of band!"

A crowd gathered before the gazebo steps. Josh and I made our way toward its center. As soon as the band started up with a twangy rockabilly tune, everyone around us started dancing.

Josh looked at me with a touch of panic in his eyes.

"I'm a terrible dancer," he admitted.

"Me too," I said.

Then I started wiggling my hips around and pumping my hands in the air. Josh threw his head back and laughed, then shrugged and joined me.

Did we find each other's rhythm and start twirling around as a beautiful unit, our love making us effortlessly graceful, perfectly synchronized?

Not even close. We were even more awkward dancing together than we were on our own. We were the absolute antithesis of Emma and Ethan.

And I was beyond fine with that.

At the end of the song, we fell into each other's arms laughing. We pushed our way out of the crowd, and Josh said, "Let's find the Pop Guy. I'm dying of thirst."

We were headed to his rainbow umbrella when we were intercepted by Abbie and . . . Hannah! Hannah's eyes were red-rimmed, and one of the spaghetti straps on her tank top was ripped. She was using her hand to hold her top up.

"What's going on?" I said. "I thought you were with Liam."

"She was," Abbie said fiercely, "but she's not anymore!"

It didn't take me long to figure out who was behind Hannah's torn strap.

"Hannah?" I said, my voice thin and scared. "Are you okay?"

Hannah nodded quickly.

"I am, I promise," she said. "But I won't be seeing Liam anymore."

Abbie whispered into my ear so Josh wouldn't hear, "He might not be walking for the rest of the day either. He got the big ol' knee from Hannah!"

My mouth dropped open.

"You didn't," I gasped.

"I did," Hannah said, glancing down at her broken strap. "He deserved it."

I turned to Josh regretfully.

"I think I need a little sister time," I said.

Josh nodded quickly.

"No problem," he said, giving me a quick, sweet kiss. "I'll see you."

Hannah seemed a little shaky, so we went to sit on a bench that was hidden behind a cluster of tents.

"I'm getting you some blueberry lemonade," Abbie declared. "Back in a minute."

Hannah pulled her knees up to her chin and wrapped her free arm around her shins.

"I'm such an idiot," she said, shaking her head.

I hated to agree, but . . .

"Why *were* you hanging out with that guy?" I said.

"I don't know. It felt nice to get all that attention," she said. "It's been kind of a lonely year, you know."

"But why did you want *Liam's* attention," I asked. "I mean, he's cute and preppy and all, but he's not exactly a brilliant conversationalist."

"Yeah." Hannah shrugged. "He's just, you know, kind of normal. Average."

"Hannah," I said, "you've never made a C in your life. You need above-average."

Hannah leaned her head back and groaned.

"So I've been told for forever," she said. "I'm kind of over it! Or let's just say I felt like taking a little break from my pigeonhole. Studious, serious, smart Hannah, you know?

The thing was, I *didn't* know.

"I always thought it would be cool to have a *place*," I said. "Like, an identity. Abbie's an athlete, and you're this pre-premed whiz. You know, you're *defined*."

"But if you're not, you can do anything!" Hannah pointed out. "You've got freedom!"

As she said this, Abbie returned and handed Hannah a plastic cup of purple-tinted lemonade. She sat down on the bench so that Hannah was sandwiched between us.

"Is that what you want?" she asked Hannah. "Freedom? Do

you regret choosing such an intense school? Because you could always transfer to UCLA."

She rested her head on Hannah's shoulder.

"Please?" she added.

Hannah tipped her head to rest on Abbie's.

"I'm going to miss you, too," she said. "But no, U of C *is* what I want. Liam proved that to me. I mean, besides being *way* too handsy, the guy was a *bore*. Have you ever met somebody who's never heard of the Human Genome Project? I didn't think that was even *possible*."

Abbie and I rolled our eyes at each other.

"Yeah, she's ready for U of C," I said.

Hannah shook her head in disbelief.

"It is coming up really soon, though," she said. "I'm kind of terrified."

I was too. Unlike Hannah, I'd never known a world without my two sisters in it every day.

So many endings were looming. This summer in Bluepointe. Hannah.

Josh.

But then my eye wandered across the square to the Dog Ear tent. It was still spilling over with people, many of them immobilized because they were so absorbed in their books. I thought about the blank journal Granly had left me.

I'd already filled a few pages. And it had started me thinking—maybe this summer wasn't just about endings and goodbyes. Maybe it was a beginning as well.

Choosing my outfit for the Allison Katzinger party required major strategy. I knew that she was super-stylish from the pictures she sometimes posted on her blog. She always wore big colorful jewelry and cute little dresses. She had a huge collection of funky glasses, not to mention rotating choices of hair colors.

I didn't want to just look pretty when I met one of my favorite authors. I wanted to look memorable.

(Well, to say I'd be *meeting* Allison Katzinger was a stretch. What I'd really be doing was waiting in line for half an hour before I got to stand in front of her for ten seconds. She'd read my name off a sticky note and inscribe my book before giving me a quick smile. Then Isobel or Stella would usher me away so the next person in line could have his or her ten seconds. But still, even ten seconds with Allison Katzinger called for a killer outfit.)

The other problem was that for six hours before Allison's party, I'd be at Mel & Mel's, slinging supper. So my outfit also needed to be mayonnaise-proof.

That was why I might have gone a little overboard with the patterns. Nothing would show up on a tropically flowered skirt with gray, yellow, and purple in it, right? To tone the skirt down, I went with a simple gray tank top, but then *that* needed jazzing up, so I threw on one of Granly's chunky costume necklaces and stuck some glinty chopsticks into my bun.

And *then* I felt so overdone that I wanted to change completely, but it was too late.

Luckily, I didn't have time to be nervous/excited about the party, because we were slammed at Mel & Mel's. I hustled for two hours straight, serving a group of office workers who'd come in after playing in some goofy kickball tournament.

I was just rushing a giant order of artichoke dip to the kick-ballers when Ginny swept over and lifted my tray out of my hands.

"I'll take that, hon!" she said. "You're on break."

"Break?" I squawked. "What are you talking about?"

Melissa scooched up next to me, untied my apron, and looped it around her own waist.

"We're covering for you, Chels," she said. "No arguments. Josh has it all arranged."

She nodded at the coffee shop door. I spun around and saw Josh peeking through the glass. As always, I felt my face light up at the sight of him.

"Josh!" I said as he opened the door. "What's going on? I'm going to see you in just a few hours at the par—"

I choked on my next word. Because walking in behind Josh was Allison Katzinger!

She looked much smaller than I'd imagined. She was wearing a fabulous silky wrap dress and a chunky necklace just like mine. Her hair was a warm blond, and her glasses frames were red.

As soon as she walked into the coffee shop, with these long, purposeful strides and a big wide-mouthed grin, I realized she was bigger than she seemed in her pictures too. Personality just radiated off her.

She hustled right up to me and gave me a hug.

Allison Katzinger. Hugged. Me!

"Hi!" I blurted. "Um, hi! Wow, it's really nice to meet you."

I gave Josh a hurried *What the heck is going on?* look, so he explained, "Allison is here for a late lunch."

"Oh, sure," I said, nodding quickly. "Okay. Let me get you a menu."

"No," Josh said. "A late lunch . . . with you. *And* me. And my mom's going to join us soon. She's just finishing up some work at the store."

I gaped at him.

"There are so many awesome things in that sentence, I don't even know which to respond to first," I breathed.

"Well, let's choose lunch, shall we?" Allison said. She rubbed her hands together hungrily. "I hear you've got a lot of mayonnaise here. I'm Southern, so I speak mayo fluently. Lay it on me."

I laughed loudly—because Allison was funny, but also because I was crazy nervous. I smoothed back my hair and adjusted my skirt as Melissa led us ceremoniously to the best four-top in the house.

"You look fabulous," Josh whispered into my ear as I sat down.

I shot him a grateful look.

Then I stared across the table at Allison Katzinger and wondered what I could possibly think of to say to her.

Luckily, she had that covered.

"So," she said, after ordering a pimento cheese sandwich and a sweet iced tea from Melissa, "Josh tells me you're a writer."

"I am not!" I gasped. "I mean, I jot stuff down here and there."

"What else is writing but a lot of jotting?" Allison said. "With a narrative arc and subplots and lots of dialogue and drama and . . . I'm exhausted just thinking about it. Why do I do this again?"

"Because of people like me?" I suggested. "Who love to read your books?"

Allison grinned and nodded.

"That's definitely the happy by-product, yes," she said. "But believe it or not, I don't think about you readers when I'm writing. I write because, well, I have no choice. The stories are in me, and I *have* to get them down. Just like I have to read myself to sleep every night."

"I do too!" I said. "I'm always falling asleep with the reading light on."

"I hear ya!" Allison said in her twangy Southern accent. "LED bulbs. That's the solution."

Then she asked, "What are you reading now?"

"Well . . ." I was little embarrassed because it seemed so fawning. "You! I'm rereading *Apples and Oranges.* I love it."

"Oh, so you like the star-crossed lovers thing?" Allison said. "Is that you two?"

She looked at Josh, then me.

"You definitely seem to have everyone's stamp of approval," Allison observed. She nodded at Melissa, who was grinning at us like a doting aunt.

"Yeah, there's no feud or anything," I said. "It's just, well, I live in California, and Josh is here. I head home in less than a week."

"Ah." Allison nodded. "Well, that's where writing really comes in handy. And an imagination. And an open mind."

Josh and I looked at each other. I didn't know *exactly* what

Allison was talking about, but I had a feeling I should file it away. For later.

Allison adjusted her (vintage!) cat-eye glasses as she peered at the specials board.

"Do you want a piece of pie?" I said, twisting in my seat to see what flavors were left on the board.

"No, I'm looking at that paragraph there at the bottom," Allison said. She read it out loud, which made it sound kind of . . . cool!

"'B. wondered if this was the moment of her destruction. Thayer had discovered the one chink in her armor. Since she was technically an arachnid, that was no mean feat. But he didn't have to be so smug about it! What Thayer didn't know was that B. had almost a dozen lives to spare, and she was tiring of this one anyway.'"

"It's a serial," I said with a shrug. "If you haven't read the rest of it . . ."

"It's your basic hellhound arrives in a small town, gets a job as a waitress, wreaks havoc, and smites the regulars sort of story," Josh provided for her.

Allison looked impressed.

"You've got a voice," she told me. "You've definitely got a voice. Let me ask you this. If you could never write another word . . ."

She paused, waiting for me to fill in the blank.

"Um, I'm having trouble picturing that scenario," I said. "I really don't know what I'd do!"

"Yup." Allison nodded at Josh and picked up her pimento

cheese sandwich. "She's a writer. Oh, she's got it bad."

I felt both proud and terrified as Allison pronounced this about me, like it was a diagnosis. Was it even possible that *I* could someday be like *her*?

I twisted in my seat and took another look at the little passage I'd written about B., the hellhound in an apron.

It was just a paragraph.

But maybe it really was, as Allison said, more than that. It was my voice and no one else's. It was my imagination.

It was, perhaps, the start of something I'd never dared to dream about.

But first there had to be an ending.

I tried not to dwell on the days ticking away. If anything, the fact that I was leaving very, *very* soon made every minute I had with Josh that much better. I forced myself to enjoy every kiss, every call, every lazy morning lolling together in a boat or on the beach with a cooler full of sodas and a book.

Had it been my fourteenth summer, I'm not sure I would have been able to keep smiling and savoring like that. But this summer I knew not to waste the time we had. I knew to celebrate but not cling. I think that knowledge was another gift I got from Granly, one that hadn't come in a box.

And besides, saying good-bye to Josh might not be good-bye forever. My parents, after shipping home several boxes of letters, photos, and other Granly relics, had decided to keep the cottage.

"At least while Hannah's in school in Chicago," Dad told us, giving Hannah a squeeze. "It'll give us an excuse to come visit her more often!"

"Oh, great," Hannah mock-moaned.

I didn't ask if we would come back to Bluepointe next summer. I didn't want to plan for that or think that far ahead. Because if it didn't happen . . .

Whatever happened with Josh, I realized, wouldn't change the singular miracle that was this summer—the summer I fell in love for the first time. The summer I learned to live without Granly. And the summer when (maybe, just maybe) I first looked in the mirror and saw a writer looking back.

It was even the summer that I started to feel a glimmer of affection for my red curls. After all, I found out on my last night with Josh, it was the hair that had first hooked him.

We'd decided to make our last date a non-date, since that's what we did best. We packed a picnic and took an endless walk on the beach, holding hands and talking—talking fast, as if we could fit it all in. Of course that was impossible. I couldn't imagine an end to the things Josh and I wanted to talk about.

We kept sneaking looks at each other's faces—memorizing.

And of course we kissed. We lay in the sand between tufts of dune grass, the sun pulling away inch by inch, as if drawing a blanket of shadows over us.

It was here that Josh wrapped a handful of my hair around his fingers and groaned.

"I remember the first time I saw this hair of yours," he said.

"It's one of the reasons I acted so freaked out. I'd never seen anything so beautiful."

I started to reach for my automatic I-hate-my-hair response, but then I stopped myself. Because I didn't. Not anymore. How could I hate Granly's legacy? How could I hate something that Josh adored?

"That's why I wanted you to buy this book," Josh said. He reached into the bag that contained our romantic picnic dinner, which we hadn't had the appetite to eat yet. The book he pulled out was wrapped in classic Dog Ear style—plain brown paper with a whimsical tuft of bright ribbons and a stamped image of E.B. with his tongue lolling out.

I opened the wrapper to find *Beyond the Beneath*, the book with the mysterious red-headed mermaid on the cover.

"Oh, I *wanted* this," I breathed, thanking him with a long kiss.

"The whole time we were talking that first day, all I could think about was this book," Josh said. "And that you *had* to read it."

"And then I rejected it," I said with a horrified laugh.

"You were so stubborn," Josh said.

"I was also broke!" I reminded him, kissing the corner of his mouth. "Now, thanks to you, I'm less so."

"Broke or stubborn?" Josh asked.

"Both," I said. I ran my fingers through his hair, loving how every-which-way it was now that it had grown out some.

"You know, I've saved up enough tip money to get myself a new e-reader," I said.

"Are you going to?" Josh asked. He ran a fingertip over my collarbone, making me shiver.

I shook my head.

"I don't think so," I said. "You know, I really like bookstores. Well, one in particular."

Josh smiled—a little wanly.

"It's not going to be the same without you, Chelsea," he said.

"That's a good thing, isn't it?" I asked.

He nodded as he leaned in to kiss me again. And again and again. I only pulled away when I just had to get one more word in. Two tears spilled down my cheeks, but I smiled through them.

"I won't ever be the same either," I told Josh.

It was true. Josh was my first love. Even if I never saw him again, that—he—would always be a part of me.

ACKNOWLEDGMENTS

Many thanks . . .

To Jennifer Klonsky for another whirlwind summer.

To all the friends who shared the south shore of Lake Michigan with me, particularly the Berkelhamer family and "the BC."

To Little Shop of Stories in Decatur, Georgia—the bookstore that inspired Dog Ear.

To my parents, for all the child care and cheerleading.

To my sweet daughters, for understanding when mom is fiction-addled.

And most of all to Paul. Thank you for being there with me every step of the way and for clearing the way for me to write.

Sixteenth Summer

With special thanks to Elizabeth Lenhard

For Paul, for six summers and counting . . .

The first time you lay eyes on someone who is going to become *someone* to you—*your* someone—you're supposed to feel the earth shift beneath your feet, right? Sparks will course through your fingertips and there'll definitely be fireworks. There are *always* fireworks.

But it doesn't really happen that way. It's messier than that—and much better.

Trust me, I know. I know how it feels to have a *someone.*

To be in love.

But the day after my sophomore year ended, I didn't know *anything.* At least, that's the way it feels now.

Let me clarify that. It's not like I was a complete numbskull. I'd just gotten a report card full of A's. And one B-minus. (What can I say. Geometry is my sworn enemy.)

And I knew just about everything there was to know about Dune Island. That's the little sliver of sand, sea oats, and sno-cones off the coast of Georgia where I've lived for my entire sixteen-year existence.

I knew, for instance, where to get the spiciest low-country boil (The Swamp) and the sweetest oysters (Fiddlehead). Finding the most life-changing ice cream cone was an easy one. You went to The Scoop, which just happened to be owned by my parents.

While the "shoobees" who invaded the island every summer tiptoed around our famously delicate dunes (in their spotless, still-sporting-the-price-tag rubber shoes), I knew how to pick my way through the long, fuzzy grass without crushing a single blade.

And I definitely knew every boy in my high school. Most of us had known one another since we were all at the Little Sea Turtle Play School on the north end of the island. Which is to say, I'd seen most of them cry, throw up blue modeling clay, or stick Cheetos up their noses.

It's hard to fall for a guy once you've seen him with a nostril full of snack food, even if he was only three at the time.

And here's one other thing I knew as I pedaled my bike to the beach on that first night of my sixteenth summer. Or at least, I *thought* I knew. I knew exactly what to expect of the season. It was going to be just like the summer before it, and the summer before that.

I'd spend my mornings on the North Peninsula, where tourists rarely venture. Probably because the sole retail establishment there is Angelo's BeachMart. Angelo's looks so salt-torn and shacky, you'd never know they make these incredible gourmet po' boys at a counter in the back. It's also about the only place on Dune Island where you *can't* find any fudge or commemorative T-shirts.

Then I'd ride my bike south to the boardwalk and spend my afternoon coning up ice cream and shaving ice for sno-cones at The Scoop.

Every night after dinner, Sam, Caroline, and I would call

around to find out where everyone was hanging that night. We'd all land at the beach, the deck behind The Swamp, Angelo's parking lot, or one of the other hideouts we'd claimed over the years.

Home by eleven.

Rinse salt water out of hair.

Repeat.

This was why I was trying hard not to yawn as I pedaled down Highway 80. I was headed for the bonfire on the South Shore.

That's right, the *annual* bonfire that kicked off the Dune Island summer, year after year after year.

One thing that kept me alert was the caravan of summer people driving their groaning vans and SUVs just a little too weavily down the highway. I don't know if it was the blazing, so-gorgeous-it-hurt sunset that was distracting them or my gold beach cruiser with the giant bundle of sticks bungeed to the basket. Either way, I was relieved when I swooped off the road and onto the boardwalk.

I tapped my kickstand down and had just started to unhook my pack of firewood when I heard Caroline's throaty voice coming at me from down the boardwalk. I turned with a smile.

But when I saw that Caroline was with Sam—and they were holding hands—I couldn't help but feel shocked for a moment.

In the next instant, of course, I remembered—this was our new normal. Sam and Caroline were no longer just my best friends. They were each other's soul mate.

As of two Saturdays earlier, that was.

I don't know why I was still weirded out by the fact that Sam and Caroline had gotten together that night. Or why I cringed whenever they gazed into each other's eyes or held hands. (Thankfully, I hadn't seen them kissing. Yet.)

Because the Sam-and-Caroline thing? It was really no surprise at all. There'd always been this *thing* between them ever since Sam moved to the island at age eight and settled into my and Caroline's friendship as easily as a scoop of ice cream nests in a cone.

We even joked about it. When Sam made fun of Caroline's raspy voice and she teased him about his gangly height; when she goosed him in the ribs and he pulled her long, white-blond ponytail, I'd roll my eyes and say, "Guys! Get a room."

Both of them would recoil in horror.

"Oh gross, Anna!" Caroline would say, sputtering and laughing all at once.

Inevitably, Sam would respond with another ponytail tug, Caroline would retaliate with a tickle, and the whole song and dance of denial would start all over again.

But now it had actually happened. Sam and Caroline had become a Couple. And I was realizing that I'd kind of *liked* the denial.

Now I felt like I was hovering outside a magical bubble—a shiny, blissed-out world that I just didn't get. Sam and Caroline were inside the bubble. Together.

Soon after they'd first kissed, both of them had assured me that nothing would change in our friendship, which, of course, had changed everything.

Still, Sam and Caroline were sweetly worried about my third-wheel self. And they were clearly giddy over their fresh-hatched love. So I was trying to be supportive. Which meant quickly hoisting my smile back up at the sight of them looking all cute and coupley on the boardwalk.

I eyed their empty hands (the ones that weren't clasped tightly together, that was) and raised one eyebrow.

"Don't tell me you didn't bring firewood," I complained. "I hate being the only one who did her homework."

"Naw," Sam said in his slow surfer-boy drawl. "We already piled it on the beach. The fire's going to be huge this year!"

"We were collecting wood all afternoon," Caroline said sunnily.

I couldn't help it, my smile faded a bit.

I guess this is how it's going to be, I thought. Sam and Caroline collecting firewood is now Sam and Caroline On a Date—third wheel not invited.

Caroline caught my disappointment. Of course she did. Ever since The Kiss, she'd been giving me lots of long, searching looks to make sure I was okay with everything. I was starting to feel like a fish in a bowl.

"We would have called you," she stammered, "but didn't you have sib duty today?"

She was right. I did have to go to my little sister's end-of-the-year ballet recital.

So why did I feel this little twinge of hurt? I'd had countless sleepovers with Caroline that didn't, obviously, include Sam. And Sam and I had a regular ritual of going to The Swamp for giant buckets of crawfish that were strictly boycotted by Caroline. The girl pretty much lived on fruit, nuts and seeds, and supersweet iced tea.

But ever since Sam and Caroline had gotten together, a kernel of insecurity had been burrowing into the back of my head. All I wanted to do was shake it off. But like an especially stubborn sandbur, it wasn't budging.

This is stupid, I scolded myself. *All that matters is that Sam and Caroline still love me and I love them.*

Just not, the whiny voice in my head couldn't help adding, *the mysterious way they love each other.*

I sighed the tiniest of sighs. But then my friends released each other's hands and Sam plucked the firewood bundle out of my arms. He hopped lightly from the boardwalk onto the sand and headed south. Caroline hooked her arm through mine and we followed him. I ordered myself to stop obsessing and just be normal; just be with my friends.

"Cyrus is already *so* drunk," Caroline said with a hearty laugh and an eye roll. "We have a pool going on how early he's going to pass out in the dune grass."

I pulled back in alarm.

"There's beer here?" I asked. "That's, um, not good."

The bonfire was not more than a quarter mile down the beach from The Scoop, where my mom was working the post-dinner rush. And when you make the most to-die-for ice cream on a small island, everybody's your best friend. Which meant, if there was a keg at this party, it would take approximately seventeen seconds for the information to get to my mom.

Luckily, Caroline shook her head.

"No, the party's dry," she assured me. "Cyrus raided his dad's beer cooler before he got here. What an idiot."

Down the beach, just about everybody from our tiny high school was tossing sticks and bits of driftwood onto a steadily growing pyramid. By now, the sun had been swallowed up by the horizon, leaving an indigo sky with brushstrokes of fire around its edges. Against the deep blue glow, my friends looked like Chinese shadow puppets. All I could see were the shapes of skinny, shirtless boys loping about and girls with long hair fanning out as they spun to music that played, distant and tinny, from a small speaker.

But even in silhouette I could recognize many of the people. I spotted Eve Sachman's sproingy halo of curls and Jackson Tate's hammy football player's arms. It was easy to spot impossibly tall Sam. He tossed my firewood on top of the pyre, then waved off the laughter that erupted when most of the sticks tumbled right back down into the sand.

I laughed too, and expected the same from Caroline. She was one of those girls who laughed—no, *guffawed*—constantly.

But now she was silent. So silent, I could swear she was holding her breath. And even in the dusky light, I could see that her heart-shaped face was lit up. Her eyes literally danced and her lips seemed to be wavering between a pucker and a secret smile.

I looked away quickly and gazed at the waves. The moon was getting brighter now, its reflection shimmering in each wave as it curled and crashed. I zoned out for a moment on the sizzle of the surf and the ocean's calming inhale and exhale.

But before I could get really zen, I felt an *umph* in my middle, and then I was airborne.

Landon Smith had thrown his arms around my waist, scooped me up, and was now running toward the waves.

If I hadn't been so busy kicking and screaming, I would have shaken my head and sighed.

This is what happens when you're five feet one inch with, as my grandma puts it, "the bones of a sparrow." People are always patting you on the head, marveling at your size 5 feet, and hoisting you up in the air. My mom, who is all of five feet two and a half, says I might grow a little more, but I'm not betting on it.

Landon stopped short of tossing me full-on into the surf. He just plunked me knee-deep into the waves. Since I was wearing short denim cutoffs and (of course) no shoes, this was a bit of an anticlimax. I looked around awkwardly. Was I supposed to shriek and slap at Landon in that cute, flirty way that so many girls do? I hoped not, because that wasn't going to happen. After a lifetime of tininess, I was allergic to being cute.

I'm not saying I cut my hair with a bowl or anything. I'd actually taken a little extra care with my look for the bonfire. Over my favorite dark cutoffs, I was wearing a white camisole with a spray of fluttery gauze flowers at the neckline. I'd blown out my long, blond-streaked brown hair instead of letting it go wavy and wild the way I usually did. I'd put dark brown mascara on my sun-bleached lashes. And instead of my plain old gold hoop earrings, I was wearing delicate aqua glass dangles that brightened up my slate-blue eyes. (Or so my sister Sophie had told me. She's fourteen and reads fashion sites like some people read the Bible, searching for the answers to all of life's problems.)

While Landon laughed and galloped doggily back onto the dry sand, I said, "Har, har."

But instead of sounding light and breezy, as I'd intended, it came out hard and humorless. Maybe because I was just realizing that Landon's shoulder had gouged me beneath the ribs, leaving a throbbing, bruised feeling. And because everyone was staring at me, their smiles fading just a bit.

I felt heat rush to my face. I wanted to turn back toward the ocean, to breathe in the cloudy, dark blue scent of it and let salt mist my cheeks.

But that would only make everyone think I was *really* annoyed, or worse, fighting back tears.

Which I *wasn't.*

What I was feeling was tired. Not literally. That afternoon I'd downed half a pint of my latest invention, dark chocolate ice cream with espresso beans and creamless Oreo cookies. (I *might* have eaten the cream from the cookies as well.) My brain was buzzing with caffeine and sugar.

But my soul? It was sighing at the prospect of another familiar bonfire. Another same old summer. A whole new round of nothing new.

Except for this restlessness, I thought with a frown.

That *was* new. I was almost sure I hadn't felt this way the previous summer. I remembered being giddy about getting my learner's permit. I dreamed up my very first ice cream flavors, and some of them were even pretty tasty. I graduated from an A cup to a B cup. (I'm pretty sure all growth in that area has halted as well.) And I was thrilled to have three months to bum around with Sam and Caroline. The things we'd always done—hunting for ghost crabs and digging up clams with our toes, eating shaved ice until our lips turned blue, seeing how many people could nap in one hammock at once—had still felt fresh.

But this summer already felt like day-old bread.

I shook my head again and remembered one of those first ice cream flavors: Rummy Bread Pudding.

If I'd turned stale bread into magic once, I could do it again, right?

It was this bit of inner chipperness that finally made me laugh out loud.

Because me channeling Mary Poppins was about as realistic as Caroline singing opera. And life was not ice cream.

Who was I kidding? Nothing was going to change. Not for the next three months, anyway. On Dune Island, summer was the only season that mattered, and this summer, just like all the others, I wasn't going anywhere.

After the bonfire was lit, I rallied, of course. It's hard to be too moody when people are skewering anything from turkey legs to Twinkies and roasting them on a fire the size of a truck.

I'd already toasted up a large handful of marshmallows and was contemplating the wisdom of a fire-roasted Snickers bar when Caroline trotted up to me. Sam was right behind her, of course. Since Caroline didn't like anything that tasted of smoke, she was just drinking this year's Official Bonfire Cocktail: a blueberry-pomegranate slushie garnished with burgundy cherries.

"This was a terrible idea," Caroline said, taking a giant sip of her drink. "Everybody's teeth are turning purple. But *mmmm*, it's so yummy, I can't stop."

She slurped noisily on her straw.

"Real attractive, Caroline," Sam joked. But from the uncharacteristic lilt in his monotone, I could tell he wasn't joking. He really *was* swooning.

Caroline responded by taking another slurp of her slushie, this one so loud it almost drowned out the crackling of the fire.

I threw back my head and laughed.

And then—because what did I care if I had purple teeth in this crowd?—I reached for her plastic cup to steal a sip of the slushie.

"Get your own, Anna!" Caroline teased. Holding her cup above her head, she shuffled backward in the sand, then turned and darted into the surf.

Laughing again, I ran after her, kicking a spray of water at her back. Caroline scurried back up to Sam, still cackling. She threw her free arm around Sam's waist and nestled against him. He slung a long arm around her shoulders. It was such a smooth, natural motion, you'd think they'd been snuggling like that all their lives.

I didn't want them to know that their PDA was making me regret all those marshmallows, so I grinned, waved—and turned my gaze away.

And that's when I saw him.

Will.

Of course, I didn't know his name yet.

At that moment, actually, I didn't know much of anything. I suddenly forgot about SamAndCaroline. And the too-sweet marshmallow taste in my mouth. And the fact that you don't—you just don't—openly stare at a boy only fifteen yards away, letting long seconds, maybe even minutes, pass while you feast your eyes upon him.

But I couldn't help it. It was like I forgot I had a body. There was no swiping away the long strands of hair that had blown into my face. I didn't worry about what to do with my hands. I didn't cock my hip, scuff my feet in the sand, or make any of my other standard nervous motions.

There were just my eyes and this boy.

His hands were stuffed deep into the pockets of well-worn khakis, which were carelessly rolled up to expose his nicely muscled calves.

His hair—I'm pretty sure it was a chocolaty brown, though it was hard to tell in the shadowy night light—had perfect waves that fluttered in the breeze.

His skin looked a bit pale; hungry for sun. Obviously, he was a summer guy, though (thank God) he wasn't wearing shoes on the beach. And he didn't have that "isn't this all so quaint?" vibe that some vacationers exuded.

Instead, he simply looked comfortable in his skin, washed-out though it might have been. He shot a casual glance at the party milling around the bonfire, then looked down at his feet.

He did that thing you do when you're a summer person getting your first delicious taste of the beach. He dug his toes into the sand, kicked a bit at the surf, then crouched down and let the water fizz through his fingers.

He stared at his glistening hand for a moment, as if he was thinking hard about something. Then he looked up—and straight at me.

I wish I could say that I smiled at him. Or gave him a look that struck the perfect balance between curious and cool.

But since I was still floating somewhere outside my body, it's entirely possible that my mouth dropped open and I just kept on *staring* at him.

It's not that he had the face of a god or anything. At first glance, I didn't even think of him as beautiful.

But the squinty softness of his big, dark eyes, the strong angle of his jaw, a nose that stopped just short of being too thin, that swoop of tousled hair, and the bit of melancholy around his mouth—it all made me feel something like déjà vu.

It was like his was the face I'd always been looking for. It was foreign *and* familiar, both in the best way.

Looking at this boy's face made me feel, not that famous jolt of electricity, but something more like an expansion. Like this oh-so-finite Dune Island beach, which I knew so well, had suddenly turned huge. Endless. Full of possibility.

"Who's the shoobee?"

Caroline's voice brought me back with a thud. I must have been holding my breath, because it whooshed out of me.

I closed my eyes, then turned around. When I opened them,

I was looking at my friend. But I wasn't really seeing her. I was feeling the boy's gaze. It was still on me, I was sure of it.

"He's . . . he's not wearing shoes," I pointed out to Caroline. "Which means he's not a shoobee. Not technically."

Caroline shrugged and peered over my shoulder at him. I was dying—*dying*—to turn around and look too, but I bit my lip and made myself stay put.

"He's kind of hot, for a short guy," Caroline said idly.

"He's not short," I huffed.

"Hmm, maybe five nine," Caroline allowed. "Of course, compared to you, *everybody's* tall."

"And compared to Sam," I reminded her, "everybody's short."

"Maybe that's it," Caroline said with a giggle.

I gaped. Caroline did *not* giggle. She cackled. She brayed. Was *this* what love did to a girl?

Caroline's eyes widened slowly. Was she wondering the same thing?

If so, she didn't let on. Instead, her focus returned to the mysterious boy down the beach.

"You should go talk to him," she said.

"No!" That's when my heart actually did leap into my throat. But it wasn't a love-at-first-sight thing. It was abject terror.

Which Caroline didn't notice at all.

"Look, this is totally low-risk," she said. "I saw him checking you out, so he's probably interested. And if he isn't, or if you screw it up, well, he leaves at the end of the week and you can forget all about him."

"Thanks for the vote of confidence," I said dryly. "But have you considered the other possibility? That he doesn't leave until the end of the *summer*? And I run into him everywhere I go, my humiliation festering like an infected wound?"

"There is that," Caroline agreed with a laugh. I was happy to hear that she'd gone back to the bray. "Or . . . it could go really well."

Could it? As Caroline danced back to the fire, I glanced the boy's way again. He was sitting on the ground now. Clearly, he didn't care at all if he got those nicely threadbare khakis wet or gritty. His bare heels were dug into the sand. His forearms rested on his bent knees. They looked strong and a little ropey and were completely mesmerizing. To me, at least.

The boy was gazing out at the ocean. I didn't get the sense that he was itching to join the bonfire. Or, for that matter, that he was burning to talk to me.

At least, that's what I thought until I saw him sneak another glance in my direction.

Before I could look away, he caught my gaze. And then *neither* of us could look away.

Instantly, I felt like I *had* to know what color his eyes were.

I wanted to hear what his voice sounded like.

I needed to know his name.

Caroline was right. I really had no choice.

I was going to talk to him.

Unless I had a heart attack as I walked across the sand, I was going to talk to him.

One of my feet inched forward as if it were testing to make sure the sand hadn't magically turned quick, ready to suck me under.

I took another, slightly bigger, step.

The boy got to his feet.

The sadness that had been dragging at the corners of his mouth and eyes was gone. He was starting to smi—

"Will!"

The boy turned away. He squinted beyond the fire at a woman on the deck of one of the beach's smaller cottages. Even from this distance, I could see the weary sag in her shoulders.

"Will," she called again, "can you come back in? We've got three big suitcases left to unpack and I just can't face them."

The boy—Will—paused for a moment.

And then, without another glance at me, he began to tromp across the beach to the house. His mom had gone back inside to what sure sounded like a whole summer's worth of unpacking.

I stood there watching him go. Now I felt like a speck on this newly big beach, as invisible as one of the ghost crabs that darted around the sand waving their ineffectual little claws.

But then everything changed again.

When Will had almost reached the rickety little bridge that connected the beach to his cottage's deck, I got the second of the summer's many surprises.

He turned around and looked right back at me. He shrugged and smiled, a rueful, crooked *what're you gonna do?* smile.

Then he lifted his arm in a loose half wave. His smile widened before he turned and jumped gracefully onto the bridge. He crossed it with long, almost-bouncing strides.

Maybe that was just the way he always walked, I thought as I watched him bound away.

Or maybe, just maybe, *I* was the spring in his step. Maybe he'd seen something in *my* face that was foreignly familiar too.

In the coming days, I'd kick myself for just *standing* there as Will waved at me, too dumbstruck to wave back or even smile.

I'd play out different running-into-Will scenes in my head. It would happen back on the beach or in the nickel-candy aisle at Angelo's or under the North Shore pier.

I'd think of his name, Will, and wonder if it was going to move to the tip of my tongue.

So what if it wasn't fireworks the first time I saw Will? Fireworks are all pow and wow and then—nothing. Nothing except black ash dusting the waves.

But me and Will? I thought we could be something. If I was lucky. If he'd seen the same spark in my eyes that I'd seen in his. If, somehow, this summer was going to be different from all the others.

The possibility of that was much better than fireworks.

"Has *any*one seen my wrap?" I'd just stalked into the screened porch that covers the entire front of our house. My parents and sisters, Sophie and Kat, were at the long, beat-up dining table, munching buttered Belgian waffles (leftovers from The Scoop). My five-year-old brother, Benjie, was sitting on the floor feeding his breakfast to his pet tortoise.

Not one of them even glanced at me.

Sophie ignored me completely. My mom didn't seem to hear

me. Kat shrugged her shoulders. And my dad's eyes never left his smart phone as he said, "Nope!"

"Thanks for the help," I muttered.

It was Wednesday, four days after the bonfire (not that I'd been counting or anything), and I was *trying* to get ready to go to the beach. And yet I didn't seem to be getting any closer to the front door.

First, I hadn't been able to find my swimsuit top. I should have known to look for it in Kat's room. Lately, Kat, who was seven, had been obsessed with breasts. She kept stealing bras and swimsuit tops from the laundry room and trying them on.

Sure enough, I found my blue-flowered bandeau crumpled on Kat's bedroom floor. Only then did I realize that I didn't have my wrap!

And girls on Dune Island never went to the beach without their wraps. Unless they were shoobees, that was.

The summer people lugged all sorts of unwieldy stuff to the beach: folding chairs, umbrellas, voluminous beach towels, all piled on top of giant, snack-stuffed coolers on wheels.

Local girls took three things and three things only—big sports bottles of something cold and caffeinated, reading material, and our wraps.

Wraps were homemade and usually hemless, so their edges were always fraying. They were made of a light, crumply fabric that could stretch to the size of a small tarp or be wadded into your back pocket. We used them for everything. Your wrap was both beach blanket and towel. It was a sarong, a tube top, or even a long-tailed bandanna. When the noon sun got too sizzly, you could drench your wrap in water and tent it over yourself.

Every April, which was when the sun on Dune Island started to graduate from merely sultry to scorching, we all made new wraps. We wore them until they were shredded, which conveniently happened right around Labor Day.

I loved the wrap I'd made this spring. It was pumpkin orange with a white tie-dye design in the middle in the shape of a giant eye. I'd been going for a crescent moon, but when I'd gotten an eye, I'd shrugged and kept it. Sophie always dyes and re-dyes her wraps, going for perfect, but that's just too girlie-girl for me.

Sophie had *always* desired the feminine stuff I couldn't fathom—popularity, a fabulous wardrobe, boys raising their eyebrows when she walked by.

But me? I didn't know exactly *what* I wanted. Sometimes I wanted to dance and laugh with my friends until midnight, and sometimes I wanted to screen all calls and hide away with a tragic novel and a bag of candy. Sometimes I spent an hour trying to pretty myself up, and sometimes I could barely be bothered to comb the knots out of my hair before I left the house.

Sometimes I wanted to know what it felt like to tell a boy all my secrets. Other times, that seemed as impossible as waking up one morning to find myself fluent in a foreign language.

Sometimes I felt better alone than I did with people. And sometimes that just felt lonely.

It didn't seem normal to be so wishy-washy. That was a term my mom used a lot, and it always made me think of gray laundry water, swishing around and around in circles before it drained away. And as anyone can tell you, gray is the most invisible color there is.

Orange is better.

Orange is a color people notice, people like . . . Will.

And there I was, thinking about this stranger named Will *again*. I was picturing that smile, that half wave, and the way he'd looked in his khakis. It made me want get out of the house faster than ever.

It was irrational—actually, it bordered on crazy—but here's what I was thinking as I frantically searched my cluttered house for the wrap: *I'm late for The Moment.*

That's right. I was certain that somehow Will and I were supposed to meet—*really* meet—right then.

At that very instant, I was *supposed* to be on my way to the beach and Will was *supposed* to be somewhere along that way, and I was *supposed* to bump into him.

Then I'd actually, *finally*, get to talk to him and . . .

Well, I had no idea what would happen after that. Destiny? Bitter dejection? Or some vague place in between the two? *That* seemed like the worst fate of all. But at this point, I would've welcomed even a lame Will interface—say, in front of my parents or something equally mortifying—if it would just *happen* already.

But it wasn't going to happen, my newly superstitious mind was telling me now. Because while I was searching for my wrap, the magic window of time—in which a boy bumps into a girl at that perfect moment when her teeth are freshly brushed, she's wearing her favorite bikini, and she has the whole morning to herself—was closing.

I was late. I was going to miss him.

Just like I'd probably missed him the night before when I'd somehow gotten a big gob of sunscreen in my hair and had to quickly shampoo it before going out with Sam and Caroline. And the day before *that* when I'd completely forgotten about a fishing party at the southern pier and had instead spent the afternoon at home doing ice cream experiments.

Those ice creams, by the way, had all tasted wretched. Probably because the spot in my brain where deliciousness usually dwelled was filled instead with all these made-up missed connections with Will.

All this was why I was pretty darn grouchy when I began searching our cluttered screened porch for my wrap. I barely looked at the plate of fluffy waffles or the sweaty pitcher of minty iced tea on the table. I made eye contact with no one and sighed loudly as I pulled cushions off the couch and rockers, peered behind the porch swing, and even rifled through the magazine rack next to the hammock.

I could *not* find my wrap anywhere.

I almost considered leaving for the beach without it. But the thing was, when you'd low-maintenanced yourself down to a single item, you *really* needed that item.

I sighed louder. And finally my mother looked up from the Scoop accounting books. She'd been poring over them with a pained squint. (Not because business was hurting. Numbers just made my mother's head hurt. It was one of the things, besides shortness, we had in common.)

"What're you looking for, honey?" she asked, her eyes a little bleary.

"My wrap?" I said, trying to keep my voice from sounding shrill. "The wrap I asked you about fifteen minutes ago?"

Glancing up from her magazine, Sophie snorted.

"Okay, five," I allowed.

"Mmm." Mom cocked her head, thought for about half a second and said, "Pantry. Next to the bread."

Now Sophie laughed, and I heaved one more sigh, this one equal parts irritation and gratitude.

I had no doubt that the wrap would be exactly where my mother said it was. My mom is famous for random brilliance like that. Which is kind of a surprise because both my parents are—how to put this delicately?—a bit scattered. Their very existence on this island was sort of an accident. They came here from Fond du Lac, Wisconsin when my mom was pregnant with me. And then they just . . . never left.

They'd stumbled into the ice cream biz too, when a kitchen fiasco led my mom to invent The Scoop's most famous best-seller, Maple Bacon Crunch. (Trust me, it's much better than it sounds.)

My parents had added onto our house as they'd added more kids to the family, and now it kind of reminded me of Sam—a kid who'd grown too tall, too fast. With all the new nooks and crannies, our place was pretty much chaos. But it was a chaos that my mom had a mysterious mastery over.

She'd decorated with mismatched vintage wallpaper, funky estate-sale furniture, and painted floors. She'd added a fancy marble pastry counter to the kitchen, but kept the creaky, pink sixty-year-old oven. She stored everything from safety pins to sugar in old mason jars, then stashed them on random window-sills or bookshelves.

And this morning she could remember exactly where she'd spotted my wrap—but it had never occurred to her to move it to a place where I might *ever* have considered looking for it.

Like Maple Bacon Crunch ice cream, my mother's world should have been a mess, but instead it was sort of sublime. You can only imagine how annoying *that* was.

I gritted my teeth while I thanked my mother. Then I knotted my wrap around my waist and flew out the door.

But I'd been right about missing that Magic Moment.

Even though I took the most roundabout route possible to the North Peninsula, I didn't see Will anywhere.

So then I sped through the end of my novel, requiring a trip to the library for reinforcements. But Will wasn't there, either.

Finally I committed an act of desperation. I convinced Sam and Caroline to go to the touristy end of the boardwalk for lunch.

"Ah, Crabby's Crab Shack," Sam said sarcastically as we walked into the café. The screened-in dining room was artfully distressed, with deliberately peeling turquoise paint, paper towel rolls on every table, and a big fish tank so crowded with pirate, mermaid, and fisherman figurines, I wondered how there was any room for the fish.

"My grandparents love this place," Sam continued. "So 'authentic.'"

"Oh, shut up," I said, looking around with shifty eyes. The tables looked way too shiny and the floorboards had been oddly swept clean of sand. "You know you love their curly fries."

"The cheesiest food *ever,*" Caroline said.

She snorted so loud that all the sunburned shoobees twisted to stare at her before returning to their fried shrimp baskets. Not one of those flushed faces was Will's, I noted with a quick but thorough scan of the joint. I was both crestfallen and relieved.

If Will *was* at Crabby's Crab Shack, I wanted it to be ironically. Or because he'd been dragged there by a clueless parent. Or because he was laughing at, not with, the curly fries.

But I knew it was too much to hope that Will would understand all these requirements just a few days into his summer here. From my experience of shoobees, there was a *lot* they didn't understand about us, and vice versa.

Dune Islanders live inland in candy-colored cottages. Our houses hide like turtles' nests on twisty cul-de-sacs and overgrown dead ends off Highway 80.

The shoobees' vacation rentals on the South Shore stand on stilts above prime real estate. The houses stand shoulder to shoulder like a barricade. They face the waves, casting long shadows behind them.

When inlanders cross the highway to go to work in bike rental shops, boardwalk bars, beachmarts, and sno-cone stands, we don't see the ocean. Our view is of the summer people's trash cans.

Okay, that sounds a little dramatic. It's not like shoobees and inlanders are Sharks and Jets, staging rumbles on the beach. It's just that we live in separate worlds. They're on one side of the cash register, and we're on the other.

"If you're so desperate for Crabby's," Sam said after we'd settled into a table that smelled of cleaning solution and fish, "does that mean you're paying, Anna?"

"I'm not *desperate*," I said, glancing through the screen at the boardwalk. "I just need a change. I've eaten at Angelo's for the past four days."

"Yeah," Sam said with a grin. "The same fried shrimp you can get on the other side of the island, but for five bucks more? That *is* a refreshing change."

I would have responded with a crack of my own, but I was distracted by the faces passing by outside the screen. *Not Will, not Will, definitely not Will, two more not-Wills* . . .

"Hey, who are you looking for?" Sam blurted, jolting me back to our table. "Is it Landon Smith?"

"Landon Smith?" I said. My voice was as flat as an algae-covered pond.

"Landon Smith!" Sam said. "Hello?"

"Sam thinks he likes you," Caroline said. She glanced at Sam. He glanced back. His eyes crinkled into a secret smile, and her lips pursed into a gossipy grin. Clearly they'd already discussed the possibility of a romance between me and—

"Landon Smith?" I said with a little laugh. "I don't *think* so."

"The guy made a clear gesture at the bonfire," Sam insisted.

I laughed again.

"Oh, would that have been this gesture?" I asked, swinging

my arms around like an ape. "I guess I didn't realize that was a declaration of like."

"Duh," Sam said.

"Maybe he should have made himself more clear," Caroline suggested, grinning at me. "He could have dumped a smoothie over your head."

"Or *broken* some of my ribs," I suggested with my own grin, "instead of just bruising them. Swoon!"

I clasped my hands under my chin and fluttered my eyelashes.

"I'm just saying," Sam said, "you should think about Landon. The guy digs you. I can tell."

But the preposterous idea of me-and-Landon evaporated from my mind almost immediately. As Sam and Caroline started chatting about something else, my gaze drifted back to the boardwalk and its seeming flood of not-Wills.

I'd been so sure that he'd "dug" me that night at the bonfire. But now, after days of not running into him on this very small island, I was starting to think that perhaps I just wasn't meant to see him again. Maybe Will's sweet smile and cute shrug had meant nothing, and the spark I'd seen in his eyes had just been a reflection of the dancing fire. Maybe the beach was the same size as always.

I decided right then that it was time to give up on this boy named Will. We didn't have a destiny together. We didn't have some Magic Moment.

Coming to this decision in Crabby's Crab Shack, across the table from my mad-in-love best friends, was so depressing that I ended up ordering an extra-large curly fries from the waitress in the pirate hat. *And* a fried shrimp basket with cocktail sauce. So when I stumbled into work at The Scoop after lunch, I had greasy skin and clothes that smelled like fried fish, not to mention a stomachache. After two hours of ice cream scooping, I was also sticky and sweaty, with my hair pulled back in a sloppy bun and an apron smeared with hot fudge.

So of course *that* was the moment—during the lull between the afternoon-snack crowd and the ice-cream-for-dinner crowd—that Will walked through the door.

Will was with another boy, who was the same height as him but with lighter hair, broader shoulders, and lots of freckles. Still, he was clearly Will's brother. They had the exact same pointy chin and the same squinty eyes. But Will, it had to be said, was much cuter.

I'd been right about Will's eyes. They were brown, but a much darker, richer, prettier brown than I could ever have imagined.

Will's brother didn't even notice me. Like most customers, he went straight for the glass cases, peering down at the tubs of Mexican Chocolate, Grapefruit Mint sorbet, and Buttertoe (a Butterfinger bar smashed into vanilla ice cream with some toasted coconut thrown in). I think he might have asked me if I preferred the Salted Caramel to the Pecan Praline. And I might have mumbled a reply.

But I'm pretty sure I just stared at Will and thought two things: (1) *It's him!* And (2) *Oh, crap!*

Will had clearly spent the day on the beach. He was wearing faded red swim trunks and a worn-to-almost-transparent gray T-shirt. I wanted to reach over the ice cream case and touch it. Luckily, that would have involved some not-terribly-subtle climbing up on the counter, so it wasn't too hard to restrain myself.

There was also the fact that as good as Will looked, that's how gross I felt.

Maybe, I thought with a mixture of hope and dread, *he won't even recognize me, with my hair up and ice cream toppings all over my apron. For all I know, I've got Marshmallow Fluff on my face.*

A quick swipe at my sweaty forehead came away Fluff free, but it was small comfort.

I glanced at my dad, who was sitting on a tall stool behind the cash register, his nose buried in a copy of *Time* magazine. I could only hope he'd stay this oblivious until Will left.

I managed to eke out a panicked smile at Will, then quickly spun around and pretended to attend to the chrome hot-fudge warmer. In actuality, I was peering at my distorted reflection in the silver cube. My face was supershiny. I grabbed a paper towel, blotted surreptitiously, then tucked a few errant strands of hair behind my ears. I would have loved to pull my hair out of its rubber band and whisk off my chocolaty apron, too. But that would have been ridiculously obvious, so I just took a breath and tried to recapture the feeling I'd had after my lunch with Sam and Caroline, when I'd written Will off and resigned myself to a summer without him.

A summer alone.

And yes, what I'd felt was sort of empty. Maybe even a little tragic.

But I hadn't curled up and died or anything. I'd survived.

So what did it matter that Will was here, and that he was likely to take one look at me and try to forget he'd ever smiled at me? (That was, if he even recognized me.) Since I'd already lost him, the stakes couldn't have been lower, right?

Then why was my face feeling hot (and probably getting even pinker and shinier)? And why was I having trouble getting enough oxygen into my lungs to make my brain work correctly?

Luckily, I could scoop ice cream in my sleep, so when Will's brother finally decided on a sugar cone full of Sticky Toffee Pudding Pop, I was able to dish it up without any disasters.

But then I had to look at Will.

I mean, he was the next customer in line. I had no choice.

Unlike his brother, Will wasn't studying ice cream flavors. Or searching for an open booth or admiring the hundred vintage ice cream scoops that dangled from the ceiling.

He was looking *right at me*.

His eyes were a little wide. And his hands were suddenly digging deep into his pockets, sending his shoulders up to his ears.

Oh yeah, he remembered me all right.

But I had no idea if this was a good or a bad thing.

"Um . . . ," I croaked out. "Ice cream?"

I gestured with my scoop at the bank of ice cream cases. You know, just in case he hadn't noticed the two tons of electronic equipment that stood between us, humming loudly.

"I . . ." Will's voice was on the froggy side, too.

Wait a minute. Was Will as tongue-tied as I was?

"I'm not really into sweets," Will said. "He is."

He glanced over at his brother with a shrug. The broader, blonder version of Will, meanwhile, was kind of moaning his way through his ice cream. Clearly, he was the sugar fiend in the family.

"I can't believe you don't want some of this," he said to Will with his mouth full. "It's the best stuff."

"Yeah, it is! My daughter invented that flavor!"

I froze. Was that actually my *dad* inserting himself into the most awful, yet potentially fabulous, moment of my life?

"Um . . . ?" I squeaked.

Dad had shoved his reading glasses up so they rested on top of his endless forehead. He was pointing his rolled-up *Time* at Will's brother's ice cream cone.

"Sticky Toffee Pudding Pop, right?" Dad said. "That's Anna's!"

Now he was pointing the magazine at me—at a shocked and mortified me.

"My daughter," Dad went on, getting off his stool, "is an ice cream genius."

He grabbed a tiny sample spoon, scooped up a little chunk of Pineapple Ginger Ale gelato, and thrust it over the counter at Will.

"Try it," he ordered Will.

"Dad, he just said he doesn't like sweets," I said. My voice sounded reedy, as if my throat had completely closed up. Because it had.

But Will gave a little smile as he took the spoon from my dad and popped the ice cream sample into his mouth.

I cringed. I assumed my dad had chosen Pineapple Ginger Ale because it was *his* favorite. I had to admit, it was one of my favorites too. When I'd come up with it a few months earlier, it had emerged from the churn both spicy and subtle, bubbly and sophisticated. It had been the first time that I'd felt like an alchemist in the kitchen, instead of just someone who messed around with cream and sugar, hoping for a happy accident.

Still, Pineapple Ginger Ale definitely wasn't for everyone. I wished my dad had picked something easier to love, like Peanut Butter Crisp or Mud Pie.

I watched Will's face as the ice cream melted in his mouth. His dark eyebrows shot upward. The corners of his mouth slowly lifted into a surprised, and very satisfied, smile.

He looked at me and said, "I'll have a double."

I bit my lip and looked down at my feet, trying to keep a dorky grin from erupting on my face. I failed completely, of course. But hopefully Will didn't see me beaming as I ducked into the ice cream case and dished up his two scoops. I hovered in the case for a moment, my eyes closed, feeling a cloud of sugar-scented coldness billow over my hot cheeks. It felt wonderful.

But it couldn't compare to the knowledge that Will loved my ice cream.

Or, I realized, he *didn't*, but had ordered it to be polite. Which you would do only if you really cared what the creator of that ice cream thought of you!

Either scenario seemed shockingly promising.

I carefully stacked Will's scoops into a deep brown waffle cone.

"It's a gingerbread cone," I explained as I handed it to him. "It really brings out the zing in the ice cream."

Will smiled at me for two beats too long, as if he didn't know what to say but wanted to say *something.*

I wanted to say something too. I felt my head buzz as I searched for the perfect witticism.

"I just don't understand people who don't like sugar," I blurted. "I'm obsessed with it."

Um, *what* was that?

I so badly wanted to bite my words back, I think I might have clacked my teeth together.

Of course, I couldn't take the words back. So for the next minute or so, I squirmed because I'd basically just called Will a sugar-hating freak. And Will took galumphing bites of his ice cream, probably thinking that the sooner he finished the stuff, the sooner he could get out of The Scoop and never come back.

We were saved from all this awkwardness by Will's brother, who spoke up once again as he paid my dad for the two cones. I liked that guy already.

"I know, right?" he said to me. "*How* does anyone not like sweets? Of course, you've never seen anyone more obsessed with salt than Will. He used to buy those giant soft pretzels on the street and cover them with mustard. Then he'd lick the mustard off, along with all the rock salt, and throw the pretzel part away.

It was like nails on a chalkboard listening to him crunch that salt between his teeth."

This made Will stop eating. His mouth dropped open and he gave his brother one of those *how am I related to you?* looks. I knew that look well.

I glanced at my dad, who was now cleaning out the milk-shake machine, his *Time* open on the counter next to the sink so he could read and (messily) work at the same time.

Well, Will and I already have something in common, I thought, feeling shaky and exhilarated at the same time. *Familial humiliation.*

Will returned his gaze to me.

"We're from New York," he explained. "There's a lot of street food there."

"I know," I said quickly. "I love New York."

Which was true. I *had* absolutely loved New York during the three days my family had vacationed there when I was twelve. I'd loved it so much that my daydreams about my future self were almost all set there. I always pictured myself—taller and with shorter hair—striding down those impossibly busy streets. I carried a cute little short-handled purse under my arm and often ducked into one of those subway stairwells with the wrought-iron railings and the globes that glowed green or red.

What this future self was doing in New York, and how she would get there, was a mystery. More than that, really. It seemed just as fantastical as, say, becoming magic. People in movies and books did it *all* the time, but in real life? It just didn't happen. Likewise, it didn't seem possible that a girl who'd lived her entire life on a nine-mile-long island could end up in New York City.

"I never had a pretzel when I was in New York," I told Will. "But I remember having a knish from a street cart. It was delicious."

Suddenly, Will's mouth started twitching. He looked like his was trying mightily to suppress a laugh.

His brother didn't even try, though. He guffawed.

"It's *kuh-nish*," he said, correcting me. "Not *nish*."

"Oh . . . ," I choked out.

Will gave his head a little shake, then took a few more enormous bites of ice cream. The silence between us grew awkward. And *more* awkward, until . . .

"Did you know," Will blurted, making me jump, "that if you leave your beach towel on the sand at seven p.m., it'll pretty much be sucked out to sea the minute you turn your back?"

I shrugged and said, "Well, yeah. This time of year, that's right before high tide."

"High tide," Will said with a shy smile. "I always thought that was just a saying."

I was floored. Not only was Will (probably) choking his way through my ice cream just to be nice, but he'd admitted to flubbing something as basic as the tide.

Or, I supposed, as basic as the pronunciation of "knish."

And even though it's much cooler to be a big-city guy who's ignorant about Dune Island than a backwater babe for whom Manhattan is practically Mars, I decided that we were even.

So now I didn't even try to hide my smile from Will. I just laid one on him. A big, toothy smile.

Will returned the smile, and instantly, I was back at one end of that wire-thin connection I'd sensed between us. I was feeling the glow of the bonfire all over again.

And I wasn't just *wishing* I could hear Will's voice or see his eyes up close. I was listening and seeing—and feeling so floaty, I was a little embarrassed.

Until Will's brother broke the spell by grabbing Will's waffle cone.

"You're dripping," he said, helping Will out by taking several large bites around the base of the scoop.

"Gross, Owen," Will said, snatching the cone back.

Will's brother looked bewildered for a moment, then glanced at me. His eyebrows shot up and he murmured, "Ohhhhh."

Then he leaned over and whispered—good and loud—in Will's ear, "So *that's* the girl from the bonfire. I think the dad said her name is Anna."

"Shut *up*," Will hissed.

Owen just gave a little laugh, then strolled over to the bulletin board by the front door and peered at the rental flyers, lost cat photos, and join-my-band pleas.

Will avoided my eyes until his ice cream started dripping again and he had to scramble for a napkin from the box on top of the freezer case. I tried to make myself busy until he spoke again.

"That bonfire the other night," he said, "was it fun?"

"Oh, yeah." I shrugged. "I guess."

"So those people were . . ."

". . . pretty much everyone in my school," I said. "It was an end-of-the-year thing."

"Yeah . . . " Will said, trailing off. "And then where does everybody go? For the summer?"

I opened my arms and gestured to my right and left. Since The Scoop was smack-dab in the center of the boardwalk, there were cafés and candy shops, surf shops and beachmarts on either side of us. I probably knew a kid who worked in every one of the boardwalk's stores.

"Oh, yeah, I should have known that," Will said. "We usually stay home for the summer too. Other people go to the Hamptons or the Catskills or places like that, but we just stay in the city and sizzle. It's actually kind of fun. New York just empties out every August."

I didn't tell Will that *I* had been in New York in August—and thought I'd never seen so many people smashed into one place.

"So . . . ," Will said after popping the soggy end of his cone into his mouth. "I guess you're going to the thing tonight?"

"The . . . thing?" I was confused. Sam had said something about folks going to The Swamp to watch a Braves game later. But how did Will know about . . .

"The Movie on the Beach?" Will asked. "I think it's *Raiders of the Lost Ark*."

"Oh, *that*," I said. "That's a shoob—"

I caught myself, then said diplomatically, "That's the first movie of the summer. They happen every other week."

"Pretty cool," Will said, ignoring my squirming. "Where do they put the screen?"

"It's kind of funny," I said, leaning against the ice cream case.

"The guy who does it is a movie nut. He's the dad of someone I go to school with. And every year he tries a different screen placement. Once he put it on the pier, but the sound of the waves on the wood drowned out the movie. Then he put the screen on these poles literally in the water. But the wind kept blowing it down, you know, like a sail? So he had to cut these little semicircles all over the screen to let the air through. Ever since, the people in the movies looked like they had terrible skin or black things hanging out of their noses, or . . ."

I stopped myself. Once again I was putting my foot in my mouth, making fun of something that Will obviously thought was cool. He had no idea that my friends and I only went to Movies on the Beach when there was *absolutely* nothing better to do.

And when we went, we laughed at the holey screen, or drifted into loud, jokey conversation halfway through the movie, ignoring the glares and shushes of the summer people who found the whole scene so enchanting.

I could tell Will could see the lame alert on my face.

"So I guess you have something else going on tonight, then?" he broached.

I caught my breath. Had he just been about to ask me to the movie? And had I just completely blown it by being snarky?

Once again I became painfully aware of my father, who'd finished cleaning the milk-shake blender. Now he was loading a fresh tub of Jittery Joe into the ice cream case just to the left of me. He was so close I could feel a gust of cold air from the freezer. The blond down on my arm popped up in instant goose bumps, which only added to the shivery way I was feeling as I talked to Will.

"Um, well, my friends are kind of having a thing . . . ," I said weakly.

"Yeah, that's cool . . . ," Will said, stuffing his hands back in his pockets. "I heard about a party going on tonight, too, actually. It'd be funny if it was the same one."

I was incredulous. And hopeful.

"At The Swamp?" I asked—at the exact moment that Will said, "At the Beach Club pool."

"Oh," I said, deflating a bit.

Of *course*, Will hadn't heard of The Swamp. The dark little bar and grill, surrounded by an alligator moat, was hidden in a mosquitoey thicket off Highway 80. It had no sign, just a break in the kudzu and a gravel driveway. The only shoobees who ever found it were Lonely Planet types who tromped in with giant backpacks and paid for their boiled peanuts and hush puppies with fistfuls of crumpled dollar bills.

And the only locals who went to the Beach Club were the retirees who lived on the South Shore year-round. Mostly the Beach Club was filled with summer people from Atlanta who wanted to hang out with their country club friends—in a different country club.

Suddenly, it became clear that almost everything about The Moment was going *badly*. I was a muscle twitch away from just hustling Will out the door with a chipper, *Have fun tonight. Maybe I'll see you the next time you want some Pineapple Ginger Ale. Unless, of course, you hated it* and *you think I'm drippier than your ice cream cone! Ta!*

But before I had a chance, Will stepped closer to the ice

cream case. He rested a hand on top of it in a way that was probably supposed to look casual. The only problem with that was Will's hand was knotted into a white-knuckled fist.

I felt a prickly wave of heat wash over my face. He was about to say something. Something that mattered. I would have sworn on it.

"Why don't you come with me to the party?" Will blurted.

"Or to the movie, if you want," he added quickly. "But at a movie, you can't really talk. And it'd be kind of . . . nice. To talk. I mean, if you want to . . . and you don't mind ditching the, um, swamp?"

Then *I* was hanging onto the ice cream case for dear life, too. I felt another head-rushy wave, but it didn't feel at all bad.

Even so, I wasn't sure at first what I should say. As cheesy went, Movie on the Beach was a stack of American slices—so bad it was kind of good. But a party at the Beach Club pool was more like stinky French cheese—you could swallow it, but only if you held your nose. I definitely would have preferred pockmarked Harrison Ford to the fusty air-conditioning, horrid wallpaper, and uniformed "staff" of the Beach Club.

But Will wanted to *talk*.

Fuzzy though my mind was at that moment, my gut told me this was a good thing.

It was such a good thing that I sort of wanted to start the conversation right there. That very minute. But one sideways glance reminded me that my dad was still there, fumbling around the cash register and *so* obviously eavesdropping on me as a boy asked me out for the very first time.

And then there was Will's brother, Owen. He was still

stationed at the bulletin board but had his head cocked in such a way that it was *just* as obvious that he was listening in too.

And *then,* the wind chime on the screen door tinkled as a quartet of locals—most of whom I knew of course—came in for their sugar fix.

I had to make a decision and I had to make it immediately.

So I said yes to the Beach Club pool party. To a night of eating bad hors d'ouevres among an army of shoobees . . . and to a date with Will.

"Meet you there at eight?" I proposed.

Will grinned and nodded. Then grinned some more and nodded again until finally Owen came over and grabbed his arm, muttering, "I'm gonna save you from yourself, here, mm-kay? Let's go."

They left so fast, I barely had time to squeak out a "See you later." I was too floored to form complete sentences anyway.

After that, I nodded my way through four ice cream orders before I realized I hadn't heard a word the customers had said. After I asked them to repeat themselves, I got half the orders wrong anyway. But I didn't really care. How could I when all my hopes and dreams (at least, all my hopes and dreams of the past four days) had come true?

Will and I had had our Moment. Our weird, awkward, yet somehow amazing, Moment. It hadn't been destiny, but it *had* made me excited about going to the Beach Club of all places. So maybe it actually *had* been magic.

Time, I thought, looking anxiously at the clock over the screen door, would tell.

I had an hour and a half left in my shift. If I'd been keeping a log, here's how it would have read:

5:05: Went to the walk-in cooler and called Caroline to tell her I had a date. But hung up when I got her voice mail. Leaving this information on a message seemed jinxy somehow. A recorded declaration of swooning would only come back to bite me later, right?

5:07: Began a catalog (on a paper napkin) of all the date-worthy outfits I owned.

5:08: Despaired at lack of date-worthy outfits in closet. Began a catalog (on several paper napkins) of Sophie's date-worthy outfits.

5:14: Plotted sister bribery for that pale blue halter dress.

5:16: Decided the blue halter dress was trying too hard and I should just wear jeans.

5:18: Called Caroline to confirm. Hung up on voice mail again.

5:19: Okay, I would compromise with a skirt and top.

5:20: Realized I'd been in the cooler for fifteen minutes and was freezing. Returned to work. Dad was scooping away and messing up all the orders. I took over and Dad reminded me that *he* preferred to be the backstage operator at The Scoop, before slinking into the kitchen to make a batch of Strawberry Rhubarb.

5:44: Scooped for a group of shoobees who looked less like individuals than just a tangle of sunburned limbs and expensive sunglasses. Occurred to me that Will might not have been asking me out for a *date* per se. Maybe he'd just meant for it to be a group thing. A join-the-crowd kind of thing. That's what a party really *was*, wasn't it?

5:53: Called Caroline to confirm suspicion. Voice mail *again*. She was probably too busy making out with Sam (ew) to answer. Hung up. Again.

6:03: Certain now that I was delusional. Of course Will wasn't asking me out! It was just a "Maybe I'll see you at the Beach Club party" invitation. Right? What *were* his exact words? Obviously, goose bumps had impaired my hearing.

6:06: Considered asking my dad for his impression. Questioned own sanity. Ate extra-large scoop of Maple Bacon Crunch to calm nerves.

6:10: Worried about having bacon breath at party.

6:11: He was definitely not asking me out on a date. Wondered if I should even go.

6:15: Okay, I would go, but I wasn't dressing up.

6:17: Wait a minute, Dune Island was *my* turf. Decided I should just call Will and tell him I was going to The Swamp. "And maybe I'll see *you* there."

6:18: Realized I didn't have Will's number. Despaired.

6:19: Went back into the cooler. Breathed in stale fridge smell and tried to get zen. But goose bumps on arms reminded me of conversation with Will, so went back to work.

6:23: Epiphany! Called Caroline. Actually left a message.

6:29: Shift (almost) over! Tore my dad away from his backstage maneuvering and hightailed it out of there.

* * *

Just as I was getting home, my phone rang.

"Is this The Scoop?" Caroline rasped in my ear. "I'd like one Nutty Buddy, please. Oh, wait, I've already got one."

"Oh my God," I said. "We don't have time for your corny jokes. I've got an emergency."

"So I heard after about eighteen hang-ups," Caroline said. "It was the other part of your message that must have gotten mangled in my voice mail. You didn't *actually* say you want me and Sam to come to a party at the Beach Club pool, did you?"

"*He* invited me," I whispered as ran up the stairs and into the screened porch. Kat was on the porch swing eating a bowl of bright orange macaroni and cheese.

"Ugh!" I said, looking away. I was already queasy, and watching Kat eat fake food as she swung in long, lazy swoops gave *me* motion sickness.

Kat pointed a bright orange fork at me and said, "That was rude!"

I gave her an apologetic shrug, then headed up the stairs. Hoping not to run into (and possibly offend) any other family members, I darted down the wide second-floor hallway, then ducked into the steep, narrow staircase that led to my room.

Meanwhile, Caroline was chattering in my ear.

"What 'he'?" she said. "*That* he? The he from the bonfire?"

"Yes!" I said as I flopped into my unmade bed. I stared through my skylight at a wispy, strung-out cloud. My parents had finished the attic for me and Sophie three years ago. Well, it was *their* version of finished, which meant floorboards painted with pink and orange polka dots to hide their unevenness, curtains made out of vintage bedsheets, and in the bathroom, a claw-foot bathtub that my parents had gotten cheap because someone had painted the entire thing lime green.

Sophie and I had been granted one wish each for our room. She'd wished for a walk-in closet, of course. I'd asked for a skylight over my double bed, so I could watch the stars blink at me as I fell asleep. I'd somehow forgotten about the flip side of stargazing—blinding laser beams of light waking me up every morning. But it was worth it. I loved looking through the glass dome just over my pillow. It made me feel like I was outside, even when I was in; like I could just float away, weightless and free, at any moment.

As I pulled the rubber band out of my hair, letting it fan over the cool pillowcase, the view of the sky calmed me. For a brief moment I forgot about my armoire full of non-datey clothes and about the fusty Beach Club.

I only thought about him.

"The he from the bonfire is named Will," I told Caroline. It came out as a sigh—the kind of simpering, love-struck sigh I usually mocked on TV.

But hearing the sigh in my own voice felt, strangely, kind of good.

It also brought all my nervousness rushing back.

"He asked you to the *Beach Club pool party*?" Caroline said. I knew she was curling her thin upper lip.

"Yeah, but I don't think he knows what it's like there," I said defensively. "I bet he just heard about the party from people on the beach."

"From the other shoobees he's been hanging around with," Caroline insisted. "Is that who *you* want to be with tonight?"

I thought about all the summer people who'd ever called me a "townie." Most of them didn't even know there was anything obnoxious about that word. They weren't malicious so much as clueless, which was somehow even harder to swallow.

If this date (or whatever it was) with Will was a bust, the presence of all those shoobees would only make me feel worse. That was why I needed backup.

"Look," I pleaded with Caroline. "I've basically been your third wheel ever since you and Sam got together. Now it's your turn. You guys *have* to go with me tonight. Just in case."

"In case of what?" Caroline said.

In case my heart gets broken, I thought.

Then I shook my head in disbelief. A broken heart? I'd never used that phrase in my life. I didn't believe in broken hearts. Or guardian angels, destined soul mates, or any of the other things that my sister and her friends giggled about when they rented romantic comedies.

I knew that the tide wasn't mystical; it was just the rotation of the Earth relative to the positions of the sun and moon. I knew that ice cream wasn't magic; it was an emulsion of fat, milk solids, and sugar. And I knew that girls like me became chic New Yorkers only in the movies.

I also knew another thing from Sophie's favorite flicks. The "townie" who got swept off her feet by a big-city boy usually found out she'd been played.

That was why I needed Sam and Caroline to come with me. Because if I'd misunderstood Will and this *was* a group thing, *they* were my group.

And if my heart did get shattered, they'd be my shoulders to cry on.

I pictured myself standing on the sand in front of the Beach Club with my head literally on Caroline's shoulder (because Sam's shoulder is impossible for me to reach).

The image made me smile through my nervousness.

But then I imagined Sam in this scenario. He'd be standing on Caroline's other side, holding her hand.

And that made me sigh wearily.

I slithered off my rumpled bed and went over to my dresser. The first thing I saw in the top drawer was the slightly crumpled camisole I'd worn to the bonfire.

The top was silky with thin, delicate straps. When I'd tried it on while I was getting ready, it had looked soft and romantic, like something a ballerina would wear with a long tulle skirt. It had made me feel pretty, almost *too* pretty for the Dune Island High bonfire. But if I'd stashed the camisole away for a special occasion, I might have found myself waiting forever to wear it. So I'd gone ahead and kept it on.

Little had I known, I'd been going somewhere special after all.

And maybe tonight I'd be surprised again.

"Can you meet me at the club at eight?" I asked Caroline.

Maybe she heard a change in my voice. I was no longer the girl who'd shrugged Will off over a plate of curly fries that afternoon.

Now I actually had something to lose.

And though it filled me with a sort of hopeful dread, I had to see this night through; see who this boy was who'd (most likely) lied about liking my ice cream and who'd asked me out in front of my dad.

He wasn't afraid to look foolish. So the least I could do was show up.

Even if it ended up breaking my heart.

I hadn't been to the Beach Club since The Scoop catered an ice cream social there two years earlier. As I walked in that night with Sam and Caroline, the entry hall smelled exactly as I remembered it—of slightly fishy ice and Sterno.

I knew the odor emanated from the ice sculptures and chafing dishes in the large main room. But I always imagined the smell came from the club's hideous wallpaper. The pattern, a burgundy and gold paisley with forest green borders, made me imagine horrible things usually seen only under microscopes. Just looking at it made my queasiness return. Or maybe I was just nauseous over the prospect of this nebulous perhaps-date with Will.

Sam wasn't exactly making me feel better.

"Anna, if you tell anybody I ditched the Braves versus the Padres to go to *this*," he threatened, "I'll seriously have to kill you."

"I'm sure there are plenty of guys out there who can tell you the score," I said, pointing at the wall of windows and French doors on the other side of the ballroom. Through them we could see the pool deck, packed with men in wheat-colored blazers and women in pastel shifts; boys in long shorts and golf shirts, and girls in tube tops and A-line skirts. It was like they'd all gotten an e-mail instructing them to wear a uniform. They skimmed back and forth on the other side of the glass like a bunch of extremely white fish in an aquarium.

"Yeah, right, I'll ask *them* the score," Sam muttered. He looked even more gangly than usual in the low-ceilinged foyer.

"You are going to keep it together, right?" Caroline asked Sam. "*Please* don't get in another fight."

"What are you talking about?" Sam said. "Fight?"

"You know what I'm talking about!" Caroline said. She'd been jokey at first, but now her voice had a bit of an edge to it.

"Anderson Lowell's party," Caroline and I said together.

"Last August?" Sam squawked. "Well, that was totally provoked!"

"What, a shoobee simply *showing up* at one of our parties forced you to punch him in the head?" Caroline said.

"What *was* that, anyway?" I asked, with one eye on the French doors. I still didn't see Will. "I always meant to ask you. I thought you Neanderthal boys always went for the nose or the chin. But you hit him on the *head*."

"I didn't mean to," Sam said, a semiproud smile tugging up one corner of his mouth. "The guy was so short, I couldn't reach his face."

"Oh my God," Caroline said, rolling her eyes. "I can't believe I allow myself to be seen with you in public."

She was joking, of course. But I could hear a thin shard of impatience in her voice.

And in Sam's there was a touch of wheedling as he said, "You know that's not me, Caroline. The guy was a complete jerkwad, throwing his weight around. It was just . . . a bad moment, I guess."

"Well, remind *me* never to make you have a bad moment," Caroline said.

"You could never . . . ," Sam began, but Caroline had already waved him off. She was peering out at partygoers.

"Looks like skirts were indeed the way to go, Anna," she said.

She and I were both wearing skirts, if not the A-line uniform of the shoobee girls. Caroline's was short and sporty. Mine was more flowy, tickling my ankles when the hem fluttered.

Even though we'd ditched our cutoffs for the evening, I knew Caroline and I didn't look like those girls. And it wasn't just because they had bleached teeth and manicures and we didn't. There was a shininess to the shoobees. And a chilly breeziness. In my mind, these qualities created a sort of force field around them that deflected funky odors and ugliness. Not to mention insecurities about vague date requests from strange boys.

I was the one who lived here year-round, yet in this "club," it felt like they owned the whole island.

"Oh!" Caroline rasped. She grabbed my arm and pointed through the windows to the left side of the pool deck. Thinking she'd spotted Will, I felt my stomach swoop.

"Daiquiris!" Caroline exclaimed. She was pointing, it turned out, at a bar where people were ordering frozen fruity drinks in voluptuous glasses. "I forgot this place serves the best virgin daiquiris."

"Caroline," Sam said. "There's nothing less cool than a virgin daiquiri."

"Of course there is," Caroline said, motioning to the entire pool deck.

Sam and Caroline both dissolved into snorts of laughter.

I wanted to swat them on the backs of their heads Three Stooges–style, but then I thought of the alternative: Caroline curling her lip at the shoobee girls, Sam swaggering by the shoobee guys, then everyone jumping down to the beach for a good old-fashioned fistfight.

A little derisive laughter, I decided, was definitely preferable.

"Listen, can you get me a drink too?" I asked Caroline. At that moment I had as little interest in a virgin daiquiri as I did in geometry. But I was pulling out the trick my mom always used on Kat and Benjie when they were acting insufferable—she distracted them with a task.

"I'll see you out there, okay?" I said, pointing vaguely toward the right side of the pool deck.

Then I headed across the ballroom to the French doors. Just before I reached them, I had an impulse to run to the ladies room, where I could check my teeth for food particles, blot my shiny face, and fruitlessly attempt to pee.

But at that point I was annoying *myself* with all the nervousness, so I just gritted my teeth and plunged through the double doors. They automatically swung shut behind me, actually making a little squelching sound as they closed. They reminded me of spaceship movies where people get sucked out of the airlock.

What am I doing *here?* flashed across my mind.

Then I was scanning the crowd dizzily. The people really did all look alike to me. But none of them looked like—

Will.

There he was, leaning against the pool deck railing. He wore a pumpkin-colored T-shirt and faded jeans. With the sand and darkening ocean behind him, he almost seemed to glow. In just four days on the island, he had gotten very tan. Somehow I hadn't noticed in the fluorescent lighting of The Scoop.

His brown hair had also gotten cutely frazzled by all the salty breezes.

But did Will have one of those shiny force fields around him?

That I couldn't tell yet.

When he saw me, though, he lurched off the railing so hard that an ice cube flew out of the Coke he was holding.

I couldn't help but laugh.

He laughed too as he hurried around the pool to come meet me. I relaxed a little as I wondered if he was as scared, and exhilarated, by this moment as I was.

If he *was* really different from the other shoobees.

And if this was going to be a night that I'd always remember.

* * *

"Hi," Will said as he sort of skidded to a stop in front of me.

"Hi," I said.

Then we both tried, and failed, to stop grinning unrelentingly.

Will smoothed down his flyaway hair with his palm and straightened his slightly wrinkled T-shirt. I marveled at how pleasurable it was just to look at him.

Then we started talking—and things spiraled downward from there.

"So," Will said as we found a couple of deck chairs to perch on, "it's pretty cool that this isn't a members-only club. Anybody can go, right? It's so different in New York. You can't even get into most apartment buildings without a birth certificate."

"Yeah . . . ," I said. I glanced at the Beach Clubbers as my voice trailed off. My smile went plastic. How could I tell Will—without sounding like I had a big, fat attitude—that the Beach Club *felt* like the most exclusive place in town? It was about the only place on the island where I didn't feel absolutely comfortable.

"So . . . how'd you find out about this party?" I asked. It was a lame conversation starter, but it appeared to be all I had.

"Oh, my brother, Owen," Will said with a laugh. "He found out about it from someone he met on the beach. Of course. The guy can't ride the subway without becoming best friends with everybody within five feet of him."

"Oh," I said. "That's not normal?"

In Georgia, when you pass someone on the street, you not only say hello, you ask after her mama and find something—*anything*—about her outfit to compliment.

"No way," Will said with a laugh that made me feel like a yokel. "You don't talk to anybody on the subway. Unless you're Owen."

Or, I thought, *me*.

"So . . . Owen's here with you?" I asked.

Yes, my wit was positively sparkling.

"Well, he wanted to come," Will said. "But I kind of didn't want him to."

He gave me a shy smile and I . . . had no idea how to respond. What did he mean? Had Will ditched his brother because he'd wanted to be alone with me? Or was it just because he and Owen didn't get along? Was Will trying to tell me that he sometimes felt overshadowed by Owen the Extrovert? I could totally bond with him about that! But how to broach this subject without potentially dissing his brother? What if they were actually *really* close and I offended him and . . .

Yes, as you've guessed, the silence that ensued while I pondered all these scenarios was long. And awkward.

Will swirled his ice cubes around in his glass—*clink, clink, clink*—until finally he broke the silence with some more (nervous, I think) chatter.

"Anyway," he said, "my mom roped him into going to this place for dinner. I think it's called Caleb's?"

"Oh yeah," I said. "Out on Highway 80. It's, um, nice."

Once again I was censoring myself. Caleb's, a restaurant in a semicrumbling, Civil War–era mansion, was more than nice. The food was so decadently Southern, it drawled. But I loved Caleb's because whenever my family went there for dinner, Sophie and I made up stories about all the ghosts that haunted the old house. As Kat and Benjie gripped their deep-fried drumsticks harder and harder, our stories got more and more grisly. Then one of the kids either cried or freaked out and we had to get our dessert to go.

It was tradition. Even my parents kind of liked it, despite the nightmares the kids usually had afterward.

But telling Will about these goofy family dinners would make me feel about twelve years old. It was out of the question.

"Well, all I know is my mom used to go there when she was a kid," Will said. "It's the only place from that time that's still around, so she decided she *had* to go. And Owen never, *ever* turns down a free meal."

I grinned, and Will pressed on.

"That's why we're here," he said. "My mom's on a nostalgia trip. She spent summers here when she was a teenager. We're even staying in the same cottage her parents rented every year. Of course, the place has been totally redecorated. Mom's kind of heartbroken that the owners got rid of the orange shag carpeting."

"My parents always go on about shag carpeting too!" I said, grateful that I finally had something to say, even if it did invoke my parents. I took comfort in the fact that Will had done it first.

"Oh, my mom's got it bad," Will said. "She gets all misty-eyed over everything from the good old boardwalk to the smell of the seaweed that washes up on the beach every morning."

"I ate seaweed once," I volunteered with a shudder. "In a sushi restaurant in Savannah. It tasted exactly like that stuff on the beach smells."

The moment the words left my mouth, I regretted them. First of all, gross. Second, could I sound like any more of a hick? New Yorkers probably ate sushi for their after-school snacks.

A waiter walked by with a tray of goat cheese mushroom puffs or some other fussy party food. I glanced at him and realized that the server in the red polyester jacket and too-short black pants was Jeremy Davison, a boy I knew from school.

Being spotted by Jeremy just as I'd revealed my sushiphobia made me feel doubly dumb.

At that point I pretty much clammed up—until Will gave a little jump, sending another ice cube flying.

"Oh my God, I just realized," he said, "you don't have anything to drink." He made it sound like this was a *really serious problem*.

"It's okay," I assured him. "I'm not thirsty."

Because you can't drink anything when your throat has closed up.

"But I invited you here," Will said, jumping to his feet. "I should have gotten you a Coke. Do you want a Coke?"

"It's okay," I said, getting up too. "I don't like . . . I mean, I don't *need* anything to drink."

"Here's your daiquiri!"

I closed my eyes for an agonized moment. Of course. That was Caroline, bouncing over—with the drink I'd requested.

The slushie she thrust into my hand was the color of a sunset.

"It's peach-raspberry," Caroline said. "*So* good. I got strawberry-lime. Want a taste?"

"No, thanks," I muttered.

"Um, hi?" Will said. He was clearly confused. He looked from Caroline to me. Then Sam strolled up, swigging a Coke from the bottle.

"This is Sam and Caroline," I offered lamely. "This is Will."

"Hey," Sam said, giving Will a floppy wave.

"Hi, Will," Caroline said. "How do you like Dune Island?"

"I love it," Will said, nodding for too long. He gestured politely toward the clubhouse. "This place is great."

All four of us froze.

Out of the corner of my eye, I saw Caroline squeeze Sam's forearm, warning him with a dig of her nails not to make One. Obnoxious. Comment.

I felt, bizarrely, like I might burst into tears.

And Will looked even more confused.

Then Sam shook off Caroline's claws and blurted, "Dude, *seriously*?"

"What?" Will said. His eyes went wide.

"You *like* the Beach Club?" Sam said. "*Nobody* likes the Beach Club."

"Sam . . . ," I said.

Will gaped at Sam. Then he glanced to the right as another waiter walked by with a tray of smoky-smelling Scotch glasses. To our left, a woman wearing a *lot* of jangly jewelry came through the French doors, bringing a gust of stale-smelling air-conditioning with her.

"So you guys don't hang out here," Will said. It wasn't a question.

As Will processed this information, I literally saw a crease between his eyebrows melt away.

"You know," Will said after yet another awkward beat, "a month ago I wiped out playing basketball on an asphalt court. I had this big scrape all down the left side of my calf. And when it scabbed over . . . it looked *just* like that wallpaper in there."

I blinked. Had Will just done what I thought he'd done?

When Caroline started laughing, I knew that he had.

From the moment this awkward date had begun, I'd felt like there was a barrier between me and Will—that invisible wall between the ice cream scooper and the guy paying for the cone.

But with one little joke, Will had batted that barrier away as easily as if he were slapping a mosquito. I laughed, as much from relief as from Will's quip.

Sam gave Will a friendly wallop on the back.

"So do you want to get out of here?" he proposed. "You heard of The Swamp?"

"I have, actually," Will said, looking at me. A smile played around the corners of his mouth, but it was only a small one. The rest of his face was not very smiley at all.

Will's eyes shifted quickly to Sam and Caroline, then back to me. Then they dropped to his glass of ice cubes. *Clink, clink, clink.*

With a sinking sensation, I realized I'd blown it.

This hadn't been a group thing.

It *had* been a date.

And I'd invited not one, but *two* friends to come along. All because I was worried that a date at the Beach Club had meant a date with a Beach Clubber.

I mean, would that even have been so bad? I thought. Now that I knew Will wasn't one of *them,* I was feeling magnanimous about the people at the party. I took a quick survey. A boy with eyelash-skimming bangs pulled a flask out of his pocket and dumped some clear liquid into his Coke. The girl who was flirting with him *flip, flip, flipped* her long, blond hair. An older couple laughed as they woozed their way toward the bar.

Um, yes, it would have been very *bad,* I told myself with an inward and, okay, smug giggle.

When I returned my gaze to Will, though, all self-congratulation ceased. I would have bet that Will wasn't sizing me up nearly this exactingly. He hadn't even smirked at my sushi gaffe. All he'd wanted to do when he'd asked me out was *talk,* but I'd been too freaked-out to be even remotely charming—or charmed.

Until now. Was it too late?

I wanted to find out. And I didn't want to do it with my friends at The Swamp. Pulling Will into my world felt like cheating somehow. No, I wanted to get to know him there, at the Beach Club.

Or *maybe,* I brainstormed, breaking out my first confident grin of the evening, *not* quite *at the Beach Club.*

"You know what, guys?" I said. I was talking to Sam and

Caroline but I was looking at Will. "You go on to The Swamp. I think we're going to do our own thing."

That "we" felt strange and wonderful to say. Maybe Will caught it too. His thick eyebrows shot up.

I didn't have to ask Sam and Caroline twice. Caroline gave Will a little wave as she slurped up the dregs of her daiquiri. Sam gave him a fist-bump. But Will seemed to be looking at *me* during the entire exchange.

Ever-watchful Caroline noticed and flashed me a quick grin.

It was official. My friends liked Will. It seemed like something I should be glad about. Everyone knew that was a classic sign of boyfriend worthiness.

But at that moment, I didn't feel in a position to be testing Will. Quite the opposite. I had some making up to do.

As Caroline and Sam drifted away, I tried to smile lightly at Will. I pointed to the railing at the edge of the pool deck, the one that overlooked the beach.

"Can you go wait for me over there?" I asked. "I'll be just a minute."

I was being cryptic, I knew. Will looked skeptical and I couldn't blame him. He probably thought I was sending him into another ambush—my parents, say, ready to hop out and interview him about his credentials and intentions.

But to Will's credit, he just shrugged and also tried to smile. Then he headed over to the rail.

I ducked into the crowd of partiers.

My plan took longer than I'd thought. By the time I headed back toward Will, a good ten minutes had gone by and I could see he was getting annoyed. He tipped his plastic cup to his lips, clearly forgetting that his ice cubes had melted long ago. Then he carefully knelt to put the empty cup on the edge of the pool deck, stretching his orange T-shirt tightly across his shoulder blades. He hadn't seen me yet, which was a good thing, because looking at his back made me stop and take a deep, wide-eyed, admiring breath.

Looking at Will was so *different* from looking at other boys. When you live on an island, you don't even think about seeing boys' bodies. They're just always . . . there. I barely noticed when Sam whipped off one of his holey T-shirts to go galloping into the surf. My friends' tan skin, broad shoulders, and angular shoulder blades all sort of looked alike.

But here was Will, so fully clothed even his *ankles* were covered, and I was practically hyperventilating.

Which was not good, given all the plates, glasses, and foodstuffs I was balancing in my arms.

When Will straightened up and glimpsed me, I could swear he gave his own little gasp. His smile was instant, and natural this time, lighting up his entire face from his crinkling eyes to his slightly scruffy chin.

He simply looked happy to see me, which, given all the confusion of the past half hour, seemed like a feat.

Suddenly I felt like the old independent me—the one who thinks nothing of cutting her friends free and committing acts of petty larceny all over the Dune Island Beach Club.

I found myself beaming right back at Will.

"Come on," I said, transferring a few of my more awkward items into Will's hands. I sat on the floor, swung my legs out, and inched beneath the railing's lowest bar until I'd landed in the sand below. I kicked off my flip-flops, then started collecting my loot from the edge of the pool deck.

"Am I supposed to come down there too?" Will said, glancing furtively over his shoulder.

"Yeah," I said. "Make a break for it before they notice all the stuff I took."

Will grunted as he squished himself through the railing. His T-shirt scrunched up to his rib cage and I tried not to stare. Instead I bent over and sidled under the deck, which was about four feet off the ground. The sand felt cool and slithery under my bare feet. I smoothed a patch of it into a makeshift table, then arranged on it all the dishes and napkin-wrapped bundles I'd collected.

"Has anybody ever told you," Will said, grunting again as he crab-walked under the deck to join me, "that you're really small?"

"Watch it, bub," I muttered with a laugh.

As Will settled in on the other side of my little sand table, I arranged votive candles in a circle around us. We were quiet as I lit them. The party chatter over our heads was muffled by the stone deck, but the crash/sizzle of the waves seemed to echo all around us. The candlelight danced on the blond fuzz on Will's arms and made my own hands look almost graceful as I pulled a burgundy cloth napkin off a dinner plate. It was piled with hors d'oeuvres.

"What's this?" Will asked, taking in the crab puffs, hot artichoke dip and crackers, spinach pies, and bacon-wrapped dates.

"A picnic," I said, using a toothpick to pluck up a crispy date for him. "A tremendously old-school picnic. I don't think the Beach Club has updated their menu since before we were born."

"When *were* you born?" Will asked with a curious smile.

That's when I realized—we didn't know anything about each other. I didn't know Will's age. I didn't even know his last name!

I looked down so he wouldn't see the momentary panic flutter across my face. I busied myself with cracking open a bottle of lemony sparkling water and pouring it into two champagne flutes. I felt a little sheepish about the flutes. When I'd filched them from the bar, I thought they were sophisticated and romantic. Now they seemed way too heart-shaped-hot-tub for comfort.

"I'm sixteen," I told Will.

"Seventeen," Will said, tapping his chest with his fingertips. Then he reached for the flute of fizzing water and said, "What's with these skinny glasses, anyway? I mean, where do you put your nose?"

Confirmed. The glasses had been a cheesy choice. I pointed at the pool deck above us. "So much of *that* just baffles me," I said. "I mean, a bathroom attendant to hand you your paper towel? *Really*?"

"You're right," Will said, popping the date into his mouth. "That's just dumb."

I skewered my own date and twirled the toothpick between my thumb and forefinger.

"Is that what it's like in New York?" I asked. "Poshness everywhere?"

Will shrugged.

"Eh, there's a lot of posh, I guess," he said. "Just not necessarily in *my* house. Especially lately . . ."

His voice trailed off and he took a quick sip of sparkling water.

"Um, what . . . ," I stammered. "Why. . ."

I didn't want to pry. But on the other hand, I *seriously* wanted to pry.

"It's nothing," Will said, still looking down at his crossed legs. "Just—my parents split up in February."

"Oh, I'm sorry," I said.

"It's okay," he said. "I mean, it wasn't a scandal or anything. My dad didn't slink out in the dead of night or leave my mom for a younger woman. He just moved into a studio a few blocks away."

"Did they fight a lot?" I asked. Which seemed *very* prying, but I couldn't stop myself.

"Naw," Will said. "That was one of the things that was weird about it. One of many, many things. They just—I think they stopped seeing each other, you know? Stopped talking. I had a feeling that when Owen and I weren't around, our apartment was just . . . silent. I could almost feel it when I got back home—this heaviness."

I thought about my own house, where the front door was always open, letting in the breezes from the screened porch. Where the floors were often crunchy with sand and dried dune grass and waffle crumbs. There was always chatter in my house, and cooking smells, clashing cell phone rings, and somebody calling up or down the stairs. Heavy, it definitely wasn't.

I braced myself, wondering if a barrier would rise up between us again. A wall with Dune Island on one side, New York on the other; big, happy family on one side, fractured home life on the other; inscrutable boy on one side, confused girl on the other.

And maybe that *would* have happened if I hadn't been so focused on what Will was saying. If my interest in *him* hadn't drowned out my own self-consciousness.

"After the divorce," Will went on, "my mom and Owen and I had to move, too. We rented a two-bedroom, which meant I had to share a room with my brother for the first time since we were little kids."

"I share a room with my sister too," I said. "It definitely can suck sometimes."

"Yeah . . ." Will picked up one of the triangular spinach pies. He peeled off the top layer of crispy phyllo. But instead of popping it into his mouth, he crumbled it between his fingers. I had a feeling he didn't even realize he was doing it.

"The truth is, and this is going to sound really dorky," Will said, "but it was actually kind of nice to share a room with my brother. He just graduated and he's moving out to go to NYU in the fall. So it was the last time we'd ever be living under the same roof in New York.

"Plus"—Will crushed up another layer of the phyllo before tossing the spinach pie back on the plate—"Owen's the only one who can understand what it's like to be in my family. To go out for sad Chinese food with my dad on Sundays or pretend not to hear my mom crying some nights."

I felt a little choky just imagining such a bleak scene.

Then I knew why I sometimes saw that melancholy dragging down on the corners of Will's mouth.

Of course, I hadn't seen it since we'd ducked under the pool deck, which made me feel a little thrill as Will kept on talking.

"My dad left right before Valentine's Day," he said. I had a feeling he hadn't talked about this very much and was sort of unleashing. I leaned forward a little, not nodding or going, "Hmm." Just listening.

"It was Owen's idea to take my mom out for an anti-Valentine's Day," Will said. "I never would have thought of it. We went over to the Bowery to watch the garbage barges. For dinner we had street meat, these disgusting gyros you buy from carts on the street. With extra onions, of course. Then we went to a horror movie."

"That's brilliant," I said with a laugh. "I hate Valentine's Day in general. But that one must have really been awful."

"Why do you hate Valentine's Day?" Will asked. He was looking at me seriously, almost sadly.

"Oh, well . . ."

Suddenly I felt stammery. How did I tell Will that I hated Valentine's Day because nobody had ever wanted me to be his valentine? Every year on February 14, my school was overrun by cheesy red and white carnations—the bigger your bouquet, the greater your social status. I'd gotten plenty of flowers, but they'd always been white, signifying friendship. Not love.

"Valentine's Day is so . . . schmaltzy, don't you think?" I said.

"And you don't like schmaltz?" Will asked. He lifted his

champagne flute of bubbly water and took a giant gulp. "Could have fooled me."

I felt myself turn bright red.

But then I looked at Will's eyes, which were all sparkly in the candlelight. They were also filled with warm humor, and not a speck of judgment.

So I decided to get over myself and just enjoy this okay-I'm-just-going-to-call-it-an-official-date.

Because I *was* enjoying it. Against all odds, I really, really was.

Will and I talked until the votive candles sputtered out. We emerged from our little cave under the pool deck and Will snuck back under the railing to return our plates and glasses.

I waited in the sand, feeling pleasantly overwhelmed by the big, black sky after the intense coziness of our picnic.

Or maybe I was whooshy-headed because I'd been chatting with a boy for over an hour and it had felt like five minutes. It had been as fun and easy as coasting my bike down an endless, gently sloping hill.

Will came back to the railing. This time, instead of sliding under it, he vaulted over it. He sailed over the rail so easily that he almost looked buoyant, as if he were in the water rather than the air. He landed in the sand, stumbled, then righted himself with a self-mocking grin.

Okay, there's the catch, I thought, trying not to laugh out loud. *He can fly. He's a superhero, like one of Benjie's action figures.*

Then I did end up snorting as I imagined Caroline shaking me by the shoulders and saying, "Get a grip, Anna. Just because you finally decide to like a boy doesn't mean he's Superman!"

The Caroline in my head was right. I was being an incredible dork.

"What are you laughing about?" Will asked as he kicked off his shoes. "Or should I say, what are you laughing *at*? Did I just look incredibly klutzy jumping down here?"

In quick succession, I thought:

1. No, he hadn't looked klutzy *at all*.

2. I loved that he'd even asked. And . . .

3. The fantasy Caroline in my head had been right. I liked Will. I really liked him.

And *that* made me feel so overwhelmed that I had to catch my breath.

Except that I couldn't. I continued to feel hopelessly breathless and giddy. So I ran. I ran down to the frothy edge of the surf, which was already cooling down for the night. Plunging my feet into the churning water calmed me, as it always does.

Will jogged up and joined me. We didn't make eye contact. Instead we both gazed out at the violet-black horizon. One point of light was twinkling brightly and I wondered if it was a star or a satellite. I decided it was a star.

I extricated a bit of hair that had flown into my mouth and smoothed it behind my ear. I scratched an itch on my neck. They were the completely mundane fidgets I did all the time and never noticed. But now, they felt *weird* because I was doing them next to this boy. Will was standing so close to me,

I could almost feel warmth radiating off his arm. It felt pretty amazing.

I wondered what Will had noticed about me. The fact that I walk just a tiny bit pigeon-toed? That my nose was peeling because I'd forgotten my sunscreen a week earlier? That I was having a pretty good hair day? I hoped he'd noticed that this silence between us wasn't awkward in the least. It was lovely, in fact.

"I love this feeling," Will said, looking down at his feet, which were planted ankle-deep in water that was rushing back out to sea. "The sand sort of sweeps out from under your feet and you feel weightless for a second, you know?"

"Yeah, I do," I said, looking down at my own legs, submerged to the ankle. They looked so twiggy next to Will's muscley calves. "I love it, too, now that I think about it."

"Do you know, when you walk on the sand," Will said, "you don't even stumble? It's like you're walking across a perfectly flat floor or something. How do you *do* that? I feel like I'm picking my way through wet cement out there."

He jabbed over his shoulder with his thumb, pointing at the part of the beach that was feather-soft, drifty, and seriously uneven.

So, I guess *that's* what Will had noticed about me. I smiled, feeling proud. So what if he was basically complimenting me on my ability to *walk*, which was a fairly basic skill.

"I think I took my first steps on sand," I said to Will with a shrug. "And pretty much took it from there. It's a local thing, I guess. But don't worry, you've got a whole summer to get the hang of it."

"Or you could just cast a voodoo spell to help me skip the pesky learning curve," Will suggested.

"What?!" I blurted with a laugh.

"Oh, come on," Will said, grinning. "You must have some spells going on at The Scoop, for instance, to lure in unsuspecting tourists. There's no way normal ice cream can taste that good."

"Oh yeah, that's it," I said with a sly smile. "Next time you come to The Scoop, just ignore that pentagram smeared on the door with chicken blood."

Okay, what was *that*?

That was me trying to be clever and quippy. That was my sushi comment all over again, but even more disgusting.

The only thing different was that it was two hours later. And I wasn't mortified by the dorky thing I'd said. I just laughed my way through it, the way I would with anyone I knew.

Sure enough, Will didn't recoil in horror. He just laughed and said, "Gross, Anna."

"You're the one who brought up the voodoo." I giggled.

I cocked my head and gave Will a quizzical look.

"Can I ask you something?" I said. "Are you glad to be here? I mean, you seem pretty *urban*. And it's for the whole summer."

"This place is a loooong way from New York," Will admitted. He glanced over at me. "I was a little anti at first. But I gotta say, Dune Island's growing on me."

I was glad it was so dark out. My blushing, I could tell from the heat on my face, was intense.

"Besides, I wasn't going to take this summer away from my mom," Will said, turning away from me and gazing out at the sea. "First my dad left, next Owen's leaving. She's kind of a basket case right now.

"So—the find-yourself mission," I said with a nod.

"Pretty much," Will replied. "The get-back-to-your-roots, find-yourself, and forget-your-ex-husband mission."

"My parents have basically been finding themselves my whole life," I commiserated.

"Oh, they're not from around here?"

"No way," I said. "They're refugees from Wisconsin. Every Christmas, they tell these epic tales of the awful Midwestern winters. You know, snowdrifts up to the roof, digging out the driveway, clunking radiators, the whole bit. And then they go on and on about the paradise that is Dune Island."

"Oh my God, that's *so* my mom," Will exclaimed. "If I have to hear once more how much better all the food tastes here in the fresh sea air, I'm going on a hunger strike."

"Besides which," I said, "there's no way we have better food than you do in New York."

"Well, they don't have Pineapple Ginger Ale ice cream in New York," Will said.

"Pineapple Ginger Ale," I said with a sly smile. "What kind of twisted mind came up with that?"

"That's what I intend to find out," Will said with a sly smile of his own.

I looked down and nudged the sand with my bare toes so he couldn't see how hard I was grinning.

"So I have a question for you," Will said, "now that we're on a last-name basis, Anna Patrick."

Last names had been one of the things we'd covered under the pool deck.

"What's that, Will Cooper?" I asked.

"Can I have your phone number?"

I laughed. Because his asking for my number *after* this amazing date seemed so backward.

And because I was overjoyed that Will wanted it.

And finally because I couldn't wait to see Will again. Yes, the night wasn't over yet and I could still enjoy the sight of Will's hair blowing into his eyes, the way his back muscles rippled under his shirt when he threw a clod of sand into the water, and the way the scruff on his chin glinted in the moonlight.

But I was already looking forward to more.

I wish I could say I dreamed about Will that night. But that would have made the date a little too perfect. Untoppably perfect. When you think about it, you really don't want that on the first date.

So I suppose I should have been grateful that when I got home a squeak after curfew, I stubbed my toe on the front steps because the porch lights were off.

Then I realized I was famished because I'd forgotten to eat more than a couple of dates during my picnic with Will. And when I went to the kitchen to grab a snack, I accidentally tipped over a glass of tea that someone had left on the counter.

After mopping up the spill, I grabbed a few crackers and tried not to crunch as I tiptoed up to my room. I didn't want to wake anybody and have to talk about my date. It would have broken the night's spell.

Or worse, someone (probably Sophie) might have pointed out that there had been no spell; that it had just been an ordinary night, complete with soggy spinach pies and more than a few verbal gaffes on my part. That I really had no reason to be so gaga.

Luckily, I made it to my room without waking anybody. When I slunk through the bedroom door, Sophie was breathing evenly, deep in her own dreams. I went straight to the bathroom, closed the door, then sank onto the round stool at the vanity. Sophie and I both loved our antique wooden vanity, which was ornate and curvy and had a slightly pink cast to it. It had lots of tiny drawers, niches, and cabinets where we used to stash things like Barbie shoes, gumball-machine jewelry, and illegal candy.

Now most of the nooks were taken up with Sophie's makeup and perfumes, but I'd staked out one drawer all for myself. In it I put keepsakes that only I could decipher.

I'd saved a piece of sea glass, for instance, that I'd picked up during my last beach walk with my grandfather before he died.

I had my childhood hair comb, the one with the mermaid on the handle, which I'd never been able to pass on to Kat.

There were pebbles, shells, and notes passed in class that I could sift through when I wanted to recall certain perfect afternoons, moments of hilarity, or even waves of sadness.

Now I pulled from my skirt pocket a green plastic toothpick.

It was shaped like a pirate's sword, with a D-shaped handle and a flattened, pointed blade. It was ridiculously cheesy and pure Dune Island Beach Club. I stashed it in my little drawer, tucking it under the torn-off bits of paper and the smooth, flat sea glass.

Then I reached across to the sink, soaked a soft washcloth, and dabbed it on my face. I felt too luxuriously dreamy to stand in front of the sink and be all efficient with my washing up. I stretched out my legs, gazed out the window, and enjoyed the feel of the cool, damp terrycloth on my hot forehead and cheeks.

As I swabbed off my neck, I glanced at myself in the vanity's cloudy round mirror. My skin was both summer gold and flushed from my bike ride. My hair was wind tousled. There was a speck of pale green artichoke dip on the scoop neck of my T-shirt.

I didn't look exactly ravishing but I *felt* sort of extraordinary. Not polished like one of the shoobee girls from the club or effortlessly buoyant like my sister or casually confident like Caroline. I suppose I felt like myself, only slightly shinier. Lighter. Happier.

And that was the girl who fell into a blissfully zonked, dreamless sleep that night. I didn't completely understand why Will and I had clicked so well. In truth, I couldn't fathom what exactly he saw in me.

But I was confident I would find out the very next day—as soon as Will called.

There was one problem with that little scenario.

Will *didn't* call the next day.

Which was perfectly fine at first. Good, even. That way I

could spend the morning floating around inside my own fuzzy head, replaying the entire date like it was my favorite movie. I could pause on Will's face when I handed him that silly champagne flute. I could fast-forward through the early, awkward bits. And I could scene-scan my way through all our conversations.

I also imagined what our phone call would be like.

In detail.

It went something like this . . .

Will: Nobody ever made me a picnic before.

Me: Oh, it's no big deal.

Will: True, the food *was* pretty bad . . .

Me: Hey, *I'm* not the one who chose the Beach Club and their antique artichoke dip.

Will: Well, at least I chose the right girl. You gotta give me credit for that, right?

Me: Oh . . .

Will: Anna? You didn't really think I cared about the food, did you?

Me: Oh . . .

Will: Tell me you'll have dinner with me again. A *real* dinner this time. Tonight.

I'd go on with my fantasy banter, but you're probably throwing up a little in your mouth right now.

Believe me, I was just as mocking of myself. I just *wasn't* a romantic. One time I found a yellowed bodice ripper in my parents' bookshelf and reading it had made me feel like I was eating corn syrup. Yet here I was spinning so much schmaltz you'd think my brain had been replaced by a cotton candy machine.

It wasn't that I wanted Will to be Prince Charming. I didn't, believe me. I guess this crazy dialogue was just my brain adjusting to life on the other side. On the other side of a fabulous first date.

On the other side of falling in like for the first time.

On the other side of Will.

Meanwhile, on the other side of Dune Island? Will continued to Not Call.

He didn't call while I was at the beach dishing with Caroline. He didn't call during my shift at The Scoop. He didn't call while I was in the shower or during *any* of the inconvenient moments when, Murphy's Law, he was *supposed* to call.

By that evening I resolved to call *him*. He'd given me his number, too, after all.

But first I needed sustenance.

Since my parents were both at The Scoop with Kat and Benjie, it was a fend-for-yourself night dinner-wise. I shuffled down to the kitchen and tried to decide if I wanted sweet (ice cream of course) or savory.

I decided spicy was better for my pre-call state of mind. It would wake me up, whereas ice cream always lulled me into a happy stupor.

As I was sizzling up some bacon for a sandwich, Sophie strutted in from the porch. She had her hot-pink wrap knotted around her waist and her sparkly pink cell phone clamped to her ear.

"Okay, so you're signing us up?" she was asking.

I heard a high-pitched voice on the other end of the phone. It reminded me of a mosquito's whine.

"I thought we decided the team name," Sophie said. "Summer Lovin', right? I know—love it! Okay, buh-bye, babe."

Strangely enough, I could completely translate that cryptic conversation.

"So that's the name of your team?" I said. "For the sand castle competition?"

The Dune Island tourist bureau staged the competition every August, just when things started to get impossibly sleepy around here. My sister and a gaggle of her friends entered every summer. Castle building was one of Sophie's random obsessions, along with gymnastics and a crocheted bracelet business she'd started with yet more of her friends. Sophie pretty much had people buzzing around her at all times. It made me claustrophobic just thinking about it, but she was one of those people who hated being alone.

I suppose that's why she hung around in the kitchen while I poked at the bacon strips on the griddle.

"Yeah, we're calling the team Summer Lovin'," Sophie said. "It's that song from *Grease*. Sung by *Sandy*? Get it?"

"Got it," I said dryly. "It's definitely better than Days of our Lives, from last year. Though I still think you're flirting with copyright infringement there."

"Um, *what*?" Sophie said, slouching into a chair at the kitchen table.

"Nothing," I said, shaking my head. "Do you want a sandwich? PBJ?"

"What am I, eight?" Sophie balked.

"Not *that* PBJ," I retorted. "It's peanut butter, bacon, and jalapeño. Very gourmet!"

"Ugh!" Sophie said. She flounced off her chair and headed to the walk-in pantry to forage for something else to eat. "Your diet is so weird. I don't know why you don't weigh a hundred and fifty pounds."

"The one perk of our genes, I guess," I said. Like me, Sophie was short and bird boned. Unlike me, she preferred her food bland, predictable, and in tiny portions.

"Come on, try my sandwich," I cajoled her. "It's like Mom's bacon ice cream. You think it's going to be awful, but it ends up being awesome. And don't worry, the jalapeños are pickled. They barely even burn."

"Guh-ross!" Sophie squealed.

I smeared some peanut butter on a butter knife, topped it with a crispy crumb of bacon, and thrust it toward her.

"So-phiiiiieee," I singsonged like a ghost out of one of our Caleb's stories. "Eeeeat me! Eeeeat meeee, So-phiiiiieee."

"Oh my God," Sophie said, dodging my sticky butter knife. "Why are you always trying to be so weird?"

I laughed, shrugged, and turned back to the counter. After I'd assembled my sandwich, I sat at the table with Sophie, who'd decided on a (boring) bowl of granola.

"You know, I don't *try* to be weird," I said after I'd taken my first (delicious, I might add) bite of my dinner. "Everyone *is* weird. *You're* the one who's trying to hide."

"Hide what?" Sophie demanded.

"You're trying to hide your inherent weirdness," I said. "It's futile, you know. Nobody's *really* normal."

"See?!" Sophie screeched, slapping her cereal with her spoon and sloshing milk on the table. "That's such an abnormal thing to say! That's what makes you weird!"

"Fine, Soph." I sighed. "Whatever you think."

I glanced at my cell phone, which was perched not inconspicuously on the corner of the kitchen table. If Sophie hadn't been there, I would have checked it to make sure the ringer was set on loud. But she was, and besides, I'd already checked the ringtone status. Twice.

"Are you waiting for him to call?" Sophie blurted. "That guy you went out with last night?"

Clearly, I hadn't been surreptitious enough for my sister.

"No," I said. "I mean, I'm not *not* wanting him to call. I'm just . . . well, I'll probably just call him. Just to say hey. No big deal, right?"

"Yes big deal!" Sophie cried. Suddenly, she sat up straight in her chair. "You can't call him."

"Um, yes, I can, Sophie," I said. "This isn't the movies and it's not 1950. You can call a boy after you've had a great time together."

"So it was good, then!" Sophie said. She raised her eyebrows.

"*Yes,* it was good," I said defensively. "Don't be so surprised."

Sophie waved off my bruised ego. She was too intent on issuing orders.

"First of all, you *think* the date went well," she said. "But you can never be sure. He could have a different story altogether. That's why you have to wait for him to call. If he does, you *know*. But if you call *him*, you never will. Plus you'll look desperate."

"Why doesn't it make him look desperate if *he* calls?" I sputtered.

That one stopped Sophie. She frowned, looked confused for a moment, and then got irritated (because she clearly didn't have an answer).

"This is just the way it is!" she declared. "I can't believe you don't know that."

Part of me was *glad* I didn't know that. I'd always zoned out a little when Sophie or Caroline dissected the latest social dramas at our school. I knew just enough of the "rules" to get through school without humiliating myself, but not enough to play all the little games. Because I'd always hated games. I read my way through whatever school sporting events Caroline and Sam dragged me to. And I could never get through more than a few minutes of Monopoly with my family.

Sophie, of course, adored Monopoly—and she always won. Which was why it was hard for me to completely ignore what she'd just said.

So I didn't call Will.

I didn't sleep much that night either.

And when I left for the beach the next morning, my wrap pulled around my shoulders like a dowdy shawl, I was officially depressed.

By the time I got to the North Peninsula, though, I was officially *mad*. I mean, *what* kind of boy asks for your number, then doesn't call? A boy who wants to mess with your head, that's who!

That must have been why *my* head felt hot and buzzy and the hair sticking to my temples was as maddening as a swarm of mosquitoes.

I tossed my wrap onto the sand, then ran into the surf. I dove head-first into a seething whitecap, then swam a few frantic laps back and forth along the shoreline. The hissing and churning of the water felt like a perfect match for what was going on inside me.

Only when I could dive beneath the surface and actually feel a hint of the peace I usually got in the water did I allow myself to stop swimming and just drift.

I dove down and skimmed my hands across the sand. My fingers felt floaty. The wet sand sifted through them, weightless and velvety. As I often did while swimming, I gave in to the illusion that I was part of the island, as elemental as the sea oats or the sandbars that emerged every day at low tide.

Still sifting, I uncovered a sand dollar. I zinged it from one hand to the other before flipping it back to the ocean floor. Then I swam by pressing my legs together and undulating them like a tail. My sister and I had taught ourselves to do that when we were little, imagining that we could go faster if we swam like mermaids. I'm not sure if it worked, but the habit had stuck with me.

Swimming like that now made me remember when mastering a mermaid kick (or a cartwheel or double Dutch) had seemed to matter so much and had been so *hard*.

They seemed easy now compared with all the mental gymnastics it took to just sit on my butt and wait for one boy to call me.

The thought of my silent cell phone got me simmering again,

and I pushed out of the water with a big splash and gasp. After blinking the ocean out of my eyes, I spotted Caroline on the beach, waving her pale blue wrap at me.

I trudged up to join her.

"Where's Sam?" I asked her as I collapsed onto the sand. I didn't even bother to spread my wrap out beneath me, but just let my soaked arms and legs get breaded like a fish fillet.

"Where's Will?" Caroline retorted.

The fish fillet gave Caroline the fish eye.

"He hasn't called?" Caroline asked with a little gulp that she quickly tried to cover up with a cough.

"So that's bad, right?" I said. I flipped out the straw on my sports bottle and took a big gulp of sugary, minty iced tea.

Caroline started to stay something, then reconsidered and clamped her mouth shut. Then she inhaled again, but cocked her head and clammed up a second time.

"What?!" I sputtered, breaking into the debate Caroline was having with herself. "Just say it! Will is blowing me off, isn't he?"

"That's the thing," she said with a helpless shrug. "I don't know *what* to say. I don't know if Will not calling is tragic or totally fine. I might have a boyfriend, but I haven't figured any of this stuff out yet. I mean, Sam and I didn't go through the mating dance when we got together because we already knew each other so well."

"Yeah, I guess it's different," I said. I'd been propped up on my elbows but now I flopped flat on my back, not even caring that I'd have to scrub sand out of my hair later. "Why couldn't I have given my number to someone *I've* known forever?"

"Because that's the whole point," Caroline said. She was sitting cross-legged on her wrap, picking at one of its many loose threads. "You don't know Will at all and *that's* the appeal. He's a mystery. He's nothing but possibility."

"Or *im*possibility." I sighed. "That's what's killing me. If this were Sam, I would *know* what was going on at his end. I'd know that he was working a double shift at the bike shop or having an emergency band practice for a gig. Or I'd know that the more caffeine he drinks at night, the later he sleeps the next day."

"Yeah, well, you never know *everything* about a boy," Caroline said before lying down herself.

I lifted my head and squinted over at her.

"Wait a minute," I said. "Is everything okay with Sam? Where *is* he, anyway?"

"What? Sam? Oh, everything's fine," Caroline said with a brusque wave of her hand. "He's just where you said. Double shift at the bike shop."

I plopped my head back down, then laid a hand on my stomach, which was feeling a little queasy.

"Uch," I said. "I think I sucked in too much salt water. Let's go to Angelo's for some sour candy."

"I'm way ahead of you," Caroline said. She pulled out a white paper sack filled with unnatural colors and flavors.

Angelo's was the closest beachmart to both Dune Island schools, so naturally, it was the island's best candy source. In fact, its bulk candy bins were legendary. During the school year, Angelo's was like a stock market floor every afternoon, complete with jostling, negotiating, and trading.

But in the summertime Angelo's was sleepier, so he was lazier with his stock. You might end up with nothing in your candy bag but popcorn-flavored jelly beans or Bit-O-Honeys.

"The pickings weren't that bad today," Caroline said. "I got a ton of sour straws. All the apple, cherry, and watermelons were gone, though. We have to make do with blue raspberry."

"Too bad Benjie's not here, he'd love that," I joked, fishing a long, cobalt-blue gummy straw out of the bag. The sour sugar made my mouth smart for a moment before the man-made deliciousness of the gummy took over. I took another bite before musing, "Remember when all it took to make us happy was mermaid kicking and some blue candy?"

"Um, no!" Caroline said. She stared at me and gave her head a frustrated little shake. "Anna, that stuff has *never* made you happy. You've always been waiting for something better to come along."

"I have?" I said. Now I sat up, feeling little rivulets of sand slide off my limbs. "What do you mean?"

"I don't know," Caroline said. "I mean, it's not extreme. You don't do that whole 'I hate my small-town life so I'm going to dye my hair matte black and start piercing myself' thing."

"So cliché," we said at the exact same time.

After we stopped laughing, Caroline got serious again.

"Sometimes it just feels like you're not completely here," she tried to explain. She pointed at the water. "When you swim laps out there, like you were just doing, sometimes I wonder if you want to just keep going. Like you wish you could swim all the way across the ocean or something. I mean, Anna . . . did you *really* think Dune Islanders were going to go for Cardamom Hibiscus ice cream?"

I laughed again.

"Holy non sequitur," I said. But Caroline only half smiled.

Of course, she was right about the ice cream. That lurid orange stuff had sat almost untouched in the ice cream case for two weeks before my dad had hauled the poor freezer-burned tub out and tossed it.

But just because I made some exotic ice cream didn't mean I wanted to run away to India tomorrow.

Right?

"Maybe that's why none of the Dune Island boys are good enough for you," Caroline went on. She looked down in her lap and fiddled with her gummy straw. "And why you were so instantly into this guy from New York."

"*Good* enough for me?" I said. "That's *so* not it. Especially since Will isn't even like that. He's way more like us than a shoobee. I *told* you what we talked about the other night."

"I'm just saying," Caroline said, looking away from my confused face and gazing out at the water, "it *is* possible to go out with someone you know. Someone who *would* call the next day."

My mouth dropped open. I had a million retorts to this, but also—none.

I'd never really thought about why the Landon Smiths of my world held no interest for me.

It also hadn't occurred to me that I might like Will simply because he was different; because he was from someplace else.

Especially since right then he couldn't have felt *farther* away and I definitely *didn't* like that. Already our date was starting to feel hazy to me and I wondered if I hadn't invented some of its swooniest parts. Maybe I'd been the only one who'd felt like the night had flown by in about five minutes—and left me wanting more.

I didn't know which was a more depressing thought. That I liked Will only because I was a pathetic small towner and he was a glamorous city boy.

Or that this boy I liked so much seemed to have forgotten about *me* entirely.

I crammed the last of my gummy straw into my mouth, then said, "It's hot. You want to swim?"

Caroline peered at me, one eye squinted shut against the sun.

"I promise not to make a break for England," I said with a forced laugh.

"Your lips are bright blue," Caroline said as we got to our feet.

I laughed, feeling a little bit better.

I mean, other than the black hole of rejection that was eating up my insides.

Perhaps to fill that hole, I reached into the candy bag for one more mouthful of sugar therapy before we headed into the water. Since the gummy straws were all gone, I popped three sticky Swedish fish into my mouth.

When I straightened up, I almost choked on them. Because walking toward me, with a bright red rental bike kickstanded in the parking lot way behind him, was Will. He was still far away, waving as if we were in a crowd on Fifth Avenue and not all by ourselves on this empty stretch of sand.

I grabbed Caroline's arm with one hand and waved weakly at

Will with the other. Then I began chewing like my life depended on it. It pretty much did. If Will walked over to find me—encrusted with sand, red-eyed from my salty swim—*and* with a mouth glued together with candy, I might have literally died.

Luckily, Caroline was my lifeguard. As Will approached, *she* spoke in my place.

"Well, hello, Will!" she called with a little too much joviality.

Then she crossed her arms over her chest, and my sigh of relief got caught in my throat. Because Caroline's stance was the same one she takes before a varsity volleyball game or a debate over fossil fuels with her dad—or before putting annoying shoobees in their place.

The annoying shoobee of the moment was clearly Will.

I started chewing much faster, hoping I didn't look like a rabbit.

"Hey!" Will said. He was trying to be polite and look at Caroline, but he kept peeking at me. I tried to chew between glances, promising myself that if I was *ever* able to swallow these ridiculous gummy fish, I'd never eat candy again.

Well . . . not in front of boys at least.

"That bike looks familiar," Caroline said, pointing at Will's shiny red beach cruiser. She wasn't smiling.

"Yeah!" Will said. It looked like the blue laser beams Caroline was shooting him with her eyes were making him a little sweaty. "I went to rent it and there was Sam!"

"And he told you where we hung out," Caroline provided for him.

"Uh-huh," Will said. He turned to check out our almost-empty beach (while I *finally* swallowed). There was nothing there but Angelo's and its cracked parking lot, a spindly looking fishing pier, and a big, sloping dune that hid all of it from Highway 80. "This is amazing. So this is why I don't ever see you at the south beach."

Caroline shrugged.

"Sam and I sometimes hang down there," she said, "but Anna's a loner."

"No, I'm not!" I protested. "I'm a . . . reader."

I pointed wanly at my novel, which was tossed into the sand next to my wrap.

"*Beloved*?" Will said. "Kind of heavy for the beginning of the summer, isn't it?"

"Have you read it?" I asked. "I love it. When it's not, you know, tearing out my soul and stomping on it."

"I had to read it for school," Will said. "I go to this kind of intense private school because my mom teaches there. They're always making us read books that feel like they're in a foreign language, even though they're in English. But *Beloved* was one of the ones I actually really dug by the time I finished it. Writing a term paper on it? Not so much."

I felt a pang. So Will dug impossible books like *Beloved*? Even if he'd read it reluctantly, that was definitely another checkmark on his growing list of pros.

Caroline rolled her eyes at my lit-geekery and stepped in again.

"I'm just curious," she said to Will, "what brought you to the bike shop?"

Will shrugged.

"Just wanted to do some exploring, I guess," Will said. "I still have a lot of the island to see. I didn't even *know* about this peninsula. It's awesome."

"I know somebody who could have given you a tour," Caroline said. Her folded arms tightened. She was practically a pretzel. "But you'd have to have, you know, *called* her."

"Caroline," I whisper-shrieked.

"Oh yeah?" Will said. "Dune Island does seem to have a lot of, like, *really* passionate volunteer types. Especially those people who camp out to protect the sea turtle nests? I met one the other night. She was a little scary, I've got to admit . . ."

"Not as scary as *some* people I could name," I said, glaring at Caroline.

"You know what's scary?" Caroline said, glaring back at me, then shifting her laser beams to Will. "Being caught in a new place without a *phone*. I mean, you're practically paralyzed if you lose your cell phone. That ever happen to you, Will?"

"Um, no . . ." Will was looking at Caroline in confusion. Then suddenly his eyes went wide. He'd realized what she was *really* talking about.

He looked at me in alarm.

"Wait a minute," he blurted. "My brother told me not to call you for thirty-six hours."

"Thirty-six hours?" I said. Now I was confused. "Is that like not swimming for a half hour after you eat? Because you know that's a myth, right?"

My voice was as flat as my feelings. I wondered if Will's

thirty-six-hour spiel was going to be more or less lame than a couldn't-find-your-number one.

"It just seemed like . . . what you're supposed to do," Will said.

"Why?" I blurted. Just as I had with Sophie.

"Because . . ." Will shook his head as if he had a sudden case of fuzzbrain. "You know, it seemed like a good idea at the time. But now . . ."

Will looked at me. And his expression was something I'd never quite seen before. Call it a meeting of delight and nausea.

Which was pretty much exactly how I'd been feeling ever since our date.

Could that be what smitten looked like?

I glanced at Caroline. Her blue laser beams had softened and her mouth was slowly widening into a big grin of recognition.

The next thing I knew, she was scooping up her wrap. She whipped it around her waist so fast that she covered both me and Will with a spray of sand.

"I just remembered," she said, "I told Sam I'd meet him for coffee on his break."

Sam didn't drink coffee. I was about to point this out when I stopped myself—and smiled slyly.

Caroline, of course, *knew* that Sam didn't drink coffee. She was speaking in code, which seemed almost as silly as Owen's thirty-six-hour rule. It also felt, somehow, very sophisticated. If the language of love was French, the language of dating seemed to be some sort of spy code. Like being in the CIA, boy-girl relations were all about intrigue and subterfuge and wearing cute outfits.

"Well, tell Sam thanks," Will said as Caroline began to walk away. "I never would have found this beach if he hadn't pointed me in the right direction."

"You should really call that tour guide," Caroline said, grinning at Will. She gave the knotted waist of her wrap one more tug, then strode over to her bike, which was propped next to mine in front of Angelo's.

After Caroline left, Will and I stood in uncomfortable silence for a moment. And suddenly I became painfully aware of what I was wearing.

A bathing suit.

A bikini, to be specific. And nothing else, unless you counted a whole lot of sand. When Will had arrived, I'd been so focused on my mouthful of candy that I hadn't even thought to consider the rest of my body and every curve, freckle, and scar on it—all just laid out there for Will to size up.

Now it was my turn to whip my wrap off the ground. I quickly sausaged myself within it while simultaneously dusting sand off my arms and legs.

"My brother . . . ," Will began.

"Oh, say no more," I said, holding up my hand.

Which was sort of a mistake, because he *did* say no more. At least for a minute.

But when Will finally found his voice again, what he said made my jaw drop.

"Nobody's ever made me a picnic before," he said.

He paused to look even more queasy/delighted—and I gaped at him. He hadn't *really* just said that, had he?

It sounded much less cheesy than it had in my daydream. It was just straightforward and sweet. I was starting to think that Will would make a terrible spy.

I pointed at his bike.

"So are you renting that by the hour?"

"Sam actually gave me a deal on it for the summer," Will said. "Even if I knew how to drive, we don't have a car here, so . . ."

"You don't know how to drive?" I said.

"I know, it's embarrassing," Will said. "But, listen, it's impressive that I can even ride a bike! A lot of people I grew up with can't even do that because their parents never lugged them over to Central Park to teach them."

"I can't even remember not being able to ride a bike," I said. "I don't know what I'd do without Allison."

I pointed over in the direction of Angelo's.

"Oh, is that who taught you to ride?" Will asked, following my gaze.

"Um, no, that's my bike, Allison Porchnik," I stammered, suddenly realizing how dumb that sounded. "You know, from *Annie Hall*, the Woody Allen movie?"

I'd always named my bikes, from my first trike (Lulu) to my old green Schwinn (Kermit) to my current gold cruiser with the white seat and the super-wide handlebars. The bike was so seventies fabulous that I'd *had* to give her a name from that era. After watching every movie in my parents' Woody Allen collection one rainy weekend, I'd come up with a perfect one: Allison Porchnik, one of Woody's dry-witted, golden-haired ex-wives.

Will was giving me a funny look.

And suddenly I realized something else.

"Oh my God," I said, covering my mouth with my hand. "My mouth is bright blue, isn't it? Caroline got us these horrible gummy straws and—"

"No, no." Will waved me off. "It's just . . . Woody Allen. The guy from New York?"

"Um, he's kind of more than 'the guy from New York'!" I said. "He's like the best filmmaker ever. Or he was, anyway . . ."

"Yeah, decades ago." Will shrugged.

"Yeah, that's when he was at his best!" I insisted. "You know, 'especially the early, funny ones'?"

Will looked at me blankly, and I smiled and rolled my eyes. So much for us having an instant private joke.

"That was a line from *Stardust Memories*," I told Will. "You *have* to rent it sometime."

"Well, if I *have* to," Will said, teasing me. Then he glanced over his shoulder at his bike.

"So," he added casually, "do you and Allison Porchnik want to go for a ride?"

I looked down at my toes so he wouldn't see how hard I was beaming. Who cared about private jokes? I was about to go on my second date with Will Cooper.

It had been a long time since I'd ridden the entire nine miles of Highway 80. I usually was too busy getting from point A to point B to just tool around for the pleasure of it.

But it was fun listening to Will's amazed exclamations as we skimmed down the endless stretch of asphalt. On our right was a prairie of swamp grass, emerald green and practically vibrating with cicadas, frogs, and dragonflies. On our left was the ocean, shooting flashes of gold at us every time the sun hit a wave.

With Will beside me, I slowed down, and not just because his red bike was a heavy clunker. The traffic was sleepy and we rode side by side, with me playing tour guide.

"We could go to the lighthouse at the south end of the island," I said. "That's what the chamber of commerce would have us do."

"Ah yes, the lighthouse from all the T-shirts and mugs and mouse pads?" Will said. "I've been there already with my mom and her *Let's Go* book."

"Dune Island's got a travel book?" I gasped.

"Um, no," Will said with a laugh. "It's more like three pages *in* a travel book. But they're a really packed three pages!"

I laughed.

"Well, does the travel book mention our water tower on the west side?" I asked. "Because I think it's a much better view than the lighthouse. If you ask me, the swamp is a little more interesting from that high up. Every time you go up there, the tidal pools are in different places. They make a picture."

"Of what?" Will asked, lazily looping his bike back and forth across the highway.

"I usually see Van Gogh," I said. "You know, all those swirls and swoops like in *Starry Night*? Most people just see Jesus."

"Seriously? Like the people who see him in cinnamon buns and water stains on the wall?"

"Will," I said gently, "Remember, you're in the South now. There's a *lot* of Jesus down here."

"Believe me," Will said. "I can tell just by talking to you."

"What?!" I sputtered. "I don't have a Southern accent. My family is from up North."

"Um, I hate to break it you . . ."

Will lifted one hand off his handlebars to give me a helpless shrug.

"Okay!" I admitted. "So I say 'y'all.' I suppose that sounds pretty Southern. But come on. 'You guys'?! That just sounds so . . . wrong."

"Yeah," Will agreed, "if you have a Southern accent."

I coasted for a moment, staring at the glinty ocean.

"Well, that's kind of a big bummer." I sighed.

"Why?" Will asked.

"Because everyone thinks that people with Southern accents are dumb," I complained. "Even *presidents* are totally mocked for their Southern accents."

"Well, you're not dumb," Will said. "Anybody who talked to you for more than two minutes would know that."

It took my breath away, it really did. Will said these things to me so matter-of-factly, as if he wasn't giving me the most lovely compliment but simply stating the obvious that anybody could see.

He didn't know that, up until then, nobody else had.

"And besides," Will added, "I like your accent."

See what I mean?

"My second favorite view," I said, pedaling harder so I could get a bit of breeze on my now flaming face, "is from the biggest dune on the island. It's way south, past the boardwalk. But you can't go there at this time of year. The panic grass is just sprouting, so it's too delicate to even *look* at."

"Maybe *I'm* dumb because I didn't understand a word you just said," Will said. "You call that dune grass 'panic grass'? Why?"

"That's just what it's called," I said. "I don't even know why, actually. All I know is, as soon as you learn to walk on this island, all you hear from your parents is, 'Watch out for the sea oats! Mind the panic grass!' Maybe that's why. They sound so *panicky* about it. I mean, if you thought the turtle nest sitters were scary, wait until you meet a dune grass guard. They're very, very passionate about erosion."

"Well, after Toni Morrison books, erosion is my favorite subject," Will cracked, with that half smile that was already starting to feel sweetly familiar. "I mean, I could go on and on and on."

I threw back my head and laughed.

And then we did talk on and on and on. Not about erosion, of course. Mostly Will asked me questions about Dune Island. Like why the gas station at the south end of the island is called Psycho Sisters. (It's a long story involving the Robinson twins, a sweet sixteen party, and a way-too-red red velvet cake.)

"Okay, and why, when I went to the library," Will asked, "was there an entire shelf with nothing but copies of *Love Story* on it? There were fifteen! I had to count them. I mean, that many *Love Story*s in a one-room library is pretty weird."

"Oh, yeah, the *Love Storys*." I sighed. "There's an island-wide book club, and someone had the fabulous idea of having *that* be the selection a couple of summers ago. Everywhere you went, women were reading this cheesy book and just *crying*."

Will had started laughing halfway through my explanation and I had to laugh too. It was kind of fun recounting these random little Dune Island details that I'd always just known and never thought twice about.

Before I knew it, we were at the southern tip of the island, which was as different from the North Peninsula as could be. The north juts out into the Atlantic with absolutely nothing to shelter it. It's craggy and lunar and feels as deserted as, well, a desert if you turn your back to the beachmart and the pier.

But the southern end of the island hugs the coast of Georgia like a baby curling against its mother. There's a sandy path there that leads into a giant tangle that my friends and I have always called the jungle. It's lush with out-of-control ivy, dinosaur-size shrubs, and big, gnarled magnolias, palms, and live oaks. The sun shoots through breaks in the greenery like spotlights, and the sounds of bugs and frogs and lizards spin a constant drone. In the middle of the jungle is a clearing, and in the middle of that are some half-decayed tree trunks arranged into a sort of lounge.

Without even discussing it, Will and I got off our bikes and walked down the path toward it.

For the first time in a while, Will didn't ask me any questions. I was quiet too. This cranny of the island suddenly felt special. Not just someplace to go with my friends to break the monotony of our beach/Swamp/Angelo's loop, but like something out of a fairy tale—my very own Secret Garden.

I hadn't done anything to make all this teeming life happen, of course. Still, showing the jungle to Will, like the rest of the island, made it somehow feel like mine. So instead of rustling quickly over the path, just trying to jet to the clearing, I found myself lingering over things. I stroked feathery ferns with my finger, enjoyed the dry, green scent of an elephant ear plant brushing my cheek, and pulled a dangling swatch of palm bark free from the trunk that was still clinging to it.

It was all very romantic, until Will started cursing under his breath and slapping at his calves.

"Oh, the mosquitoes," I said. "I can help with that. Come on."

We hiked back to the head of the path, and because we were hurrying against the drone of the bugs, we got there in only a few minutes. I pulled a little plastic box out from beneath my bike seat. In it I had an emergency stash of sunscreen, bug spray, and sno-cone money.

I held out the spray bottle, but instead of taking it, Will cocked his leg in my direction.

I hesitated for a moment, then dropped to one knee to spritz the fumy stuff on Will's ankles and calves. I tried not to fixate on Will's muscles, the hair on his legs that was somewhere between light brown and sun-bleached gold, or the way his frayed khaki cutoffs grazed the top of my hand when I stood up to mist his arms.

I guess I held the bottle a little too close when I sprayed the back of Will's neck, because the repellant pooled up in a little froth just below his hairline.

"Man, that's cold!" Will said.

"Sorry!" I giggled, then used my fingertips to rub the stuff in.

Touching Will's neck seemed shockingly intimate. Part of me wanted to jerk my hand away. Another wanted to put my other hand on his neck too, and maybe give him a little massage.

But instead I just swiped the bug spray away quickly and said, "You know, my shift at The Scoop starts kind of soon. I should probably . . ."

Will nodded, smiled, and walked toward his bike.

I had no idea if he'd thought of that moment as A Moment—or if he'd just been grateful for the bug repellant.

Either way, I felt calmer as we walked our bikes back to the highway and headed to town.

Because whatever that moment had been, I now felt pretty certain that it wouldn't be our last.

Over the next couple of weeks, Will and I fell into such a comfortable groove, it was almost hard to remember that day and a half of *will he call or won't he?* Because Will did call, whenever he felt like it.

Or I called *him*.

One morning he wandered over to the North Peninsula with a beach towel, a paperback book, and a giant iced coffee, just because he knew I'd be there.

And one evening I stashed some ice cream in a cooler and

drifted over to the crooked little boardwalk that connected his rental cottage to the beach, because he'd told me that he liked to sit there at night, dangling his legs over the tall grass and listening to music.

We covered every corner of Dune Island, me on Allison Porchnik and Will on Zelig. That's the name, from another Woody Allen movie, I'd come up with for his chunky red bike.

But with each day that went by, I realized we hadn't given our bikes the right names at all.

Unlike Zelig, the character who traveled the world pretending to be all sorts of people he wasn't, Will was incredibly honest—but sweet about it. (For instance, he eventually told me that he *had* noticed my blue lips that morning on the beach. But he also told me he'd thought they were cute.)

And after Will chucked Owen's thirty-six-hour rule, I never felt like jilted Allison Porchnik again.

It was thrillingly comfortable being with Will.

But also uncomfortably thrilling.

Every time I saw him, I felt like my eyes opened a little wider and my breath got just little quicker. I felt *intense*, like I was getting more oxygen than usual. And even though this was preferable to the way I'd felt when I'd first met Will—and couldn't get enough air *in*—it still made me a little self-conscious.

I worried that I looked like a chipmunk in a Disney cartoon, all fluttery lashes and big, goofy smiles—basically, the worst incarnation of cute.

But I couldn't stop the swooning. Every day I discovered

another little bit of Will. One afternoon he told me he'd been the resident haunter in his old apartment building. Every year on Halloween, he'd dressed up in a different creepy costume to scare the sour candy out of the kids trick-or-treating in the hallways.

Another time he reminisced about spotting his dad one day eating alone at a diner. He said he'd almost burst into tears, right there at 66th and Lex.

All these layers made me like Will more and more.

But was I *falling* for him?

That was the big question—that I had no idea how to answer.

"How did you know?" I asked Caroline one day. It was the third week in June and the heat had gotten to that point where you could see it waving at you as it shimmied off the hot asphalt. We were sitting on a shaded bench at the far end of the boardwalk, eating coconut sno-cones. We shoveled the crushed ice into our mouths, trying to eat it before it melted into syrupy puddles.

"How did I know what?" Caroline slurred. Her tongue was ice-paralyzed.

"That Sam was *it*," I said.

Caroline looked down into her Styrofoam cup, then smiled a private smile, remembering.

"You're gonna think it's dumb," she said.

"Caroline," I said urgently. "This is research. I'm totally objective."

She gave me a funny, searching look, but then went dreamy again as she thought about Sam. About their Moment.

"It was almost nothing," Caroline said. "We were out at the Crash Pad."

The Crash Pad was Caroline's dad's bizarro version of a play set. He had this ancient Airstream trailer that the family used to take out for long camping trips. But when Caroline was eight, her mom had put her foot down and said she'd rather live in a yurt made from recently slaughtered yak skin than spend one more night in that camper.

So Caroline's dad had moved the Airstream into the backyard. Then he'd put an old trampoline next to the camper and connected the two with a slide.

And *that* was what we'd grown up playing on. Now the camper was completely taken over by kudzu and the slide was no longer slippery, but the huge trampoline still had some bounce. We'd named it the Crash Pad, the perfect place to look at the stars through a halo of crape myrtle branches or to just goof around, jumping between snacks and snacking between jumps.

"We were just sprawled on the trampoline, talking about some school drama," Caroline reminisced. "I don't even remember what it was. But then a wind came and blew all these pink crape myrtle blossoms all over us. A bunch of them stuck in my hair and Sam started pulling them out. He was so gentle, so careful not to pull even one strand. And when they were all out, he made this tiny bouquet out of them and handed them to me."

I wanted to laugh, because this was just the sort of goofy thing that Sam did all the time.

But obviously, this time it had been different. It hadn't been a joke. And somehow they'd both known it.

"For me," Caroline said, "it was kind of like when my dad got new glasses. He wandered around for two days just so happy because everything suddenly looked more clear and crisp and colorful. Well, suddenly *Sam* looked, not *different*. Just more vivid, I guess. More interesting. More *Sam*."

My own eyes went wide. That sounded a *lot* like what I was feeling for Will.

"I just *knew*," Caroline said with a happy shrug. "And somehow he *knew* that I knew and he told me that he'd loved me for more than a year!"

"Really?" I gasped. "He kept it a secret all that time?"

"Well, what if I hadn't felt the same way?" Caroline posed. "Can you imagine how crushing that would be?

Yes, *that* I could imagine.

Like Sam, I didn't know how Will felt about me. Of course, I knew that he liked me. But did he like me like *that*?

Had he gone shivery all over when I'd touched his neck, or had he forgotten it before his mosquito bites had even healed?

And how much of all this time together was happening because there was nobody *else* here for him hang with except his brother and his mom?

The only time I asked myself these questions, though, was when Will wasn't around. When we were together, I was having too much fun to think about the nuances of his feelings. We could be bobbing in the waves, talking, and suddenly two hours had gone by and I was a total prune, late for my shift at work.

We'd get lunch and I'd be too busy talking to eat it.

Strolling down the boardwalk, he'd make me laugh so hard I'd forget that I hated attracting the attention of nosy islanders.

Will didn't mind people looking at him. He seemed to actually like the fact that we couldn't go anywhere without people saying, "Hey, Anna! What's the flavor du jour?" Or, "Anna, tell your mom Kat left her goggles at our house." Or especially, "Anna, who's your friend?"

"At home," Will told me as he was walking me to work one afternoon, "you're always walking through this sea of strangers. Here it's like everyone's family."

"Yeah," I said. "And what does family do? Nose into your business, remind you of embarrassing things you did when you were four, and never fail to let you know when you need a haircut. You don't know how good you have it."

"Yeah, well . . ." Will drifted off as we arrived at The Scoop. He looked through the window and as I followed his gaze, I cringed.

My entire family was inside.

Sophie was behind the ice cream case with a friend, sneaking samples. My dad was settling Kat and Benjie at one of the kiddie tables with some sorbet, and my mom was scooping for a small crowd of customers.

They looked like, well, my family. Chaotic and dreamy and . . . happy.

And *together.*

They were everything Will's family wasn't. And I'd just stuck my big, sandy foot in my mouth.

While I was wondering if I should apologize or if that would just make things worse, Will opened The Scoop's warped screen door and went inside.

I froze.

This was new. Will had walked me to work once before, but I'd said a quick good-bye before we'd arrived. I hadn't wanted to subject him to my dad's clueless questions, my mom's big, over-eager smiles, or God forbid, Sophie scanning him from head to toe for fashion appropriateness.

Plus, bringing Will home to meet my family (because The Scoop was home just as much as our house was) seemed so old-fashioned. So girlfriendy. And we weren't there.

Yet.

Yet?

I watched Will pause inside the door and glance back at me with a look that said, *Aren't you coming in?*

There were a million ways I could have analyzed Will walking into The Scoop. But I tried (really hard) not to.

Whatever was happening between me and Will—whether it was a "relationship" or just a friendship—would make itself clear soon.

It has to, right? I asked myself. *How many dates can you have without any handholding, kissing, or sappy declarations of like before you realize that they're* non-*dates? They're just two friends (one of whom has an unrequited and possibly tragic crush) hanging out.*

Something would happen, I told myself, or *not* happen, soon.

And I just had to keep myself together until then.

With that I gulped and went with Will as he met my entire family.

* * *

My peace-love-and-gelato parents are not exactly the types to give boys bone-crunching handshakes or a threatening mention of my eleven o' clock curfew. When I introduced them to Will, they only wanted to foist heaps of ice cream on him.

"Will, I want you to taste this," my mom said from behind the counter. Her voice sounded a little shrill and overenthusiastic. I was both touched and mortified that she was trying to make a good impression on Will. My parents hadn't asked me much about this boy I'd been spending so much time with, but clearly they'd been curious. As my mom mixed up something at the marble slab, she kept shooting Will quick, probing glances. She must have been wondering if this introduction to Will Meant Something.

Of course, I was wondering the same thing.

Mom plopped a huge, shaggy scoop of ice cream into a bowl and placed it on the counter.

"This," she told Will, "is a mix-in I've been playing around with."

"Mom," I interjected, "I don't think—"

"Looks good, Mrs. Patrick," Will interrupted, giving me a nervous glance. "I'll give it a try."

I didn't know whether to laugh at all this posturing or leap in to save Will. My mother was an ice cream genius, but somehow her mix-in ideas were almost always awful.

Will took a very large first bite. He started chewing. And chewing. His eyes practically watered from the effort.

"Mom?" I quavered. "What's in there?"

"Maple Bacon Crunch ice cream with mandarin oranges and sliced almonds," my mom announced proudly. "It's my play on duck a l'orange."

"But," I sputtered, "bacon is *not* duck. And anyway, *duck ice cream?*"

I think it took Will a full minute to choke his mouthful down.

"You don't have to eat any more," I assured him. "My mom won't care, right, Mom?"

"Well, I guess not, sweetie," Mom said. "But, Will, maybe you should tell us what *you* think."

She looked at him eagerly.

I watched Will's jaw tense. Either he was trying to figure out what to say, or he was working the horrible taste out of his mouth.

"Well . . . ," he said carefully, "it's very, um, textured. Yeah. A *lot* of textures going on in there."

"Do you want a palate cleanser?" my dad offered. He jumped off his stool behind the register. "Some sorbet?"

"No!" Will burst out. Then he reddened. "I mean, no thanks . . . sir."

At this Sophie and her friend dissolved into giggles. I had to stifle a laugh too as I grabbed Will by the elbow and pulled him into the kids area.

"*Sir?*" I said.

"Well, like you've said," Will said defensively, "it's the South. I figured where there's a lot of Jesus, there are probably plenty of ma'ams and sirs, too."

"That's true," I admitted, "but believe me, not with my *dad*."

"Oh," Will said. He shook his head wearily. And then . . . he shrugged it off. He pointed at the doodles Kat and Benjie were making on their chalkboard table.

"Hey, what's that you're drawing?" he asked. "Is it an Ewok?"

An instant later Will was sitting with my brother and sister, doing a Darth Vader voice. He seemed completely recovered from the duck a l'orange, not to mention meeting my parents.

So what does that mean? I started to ask myself. But before I could even begin to ponder that question, I gave my head a little shake.

Don't analyze, don't analyze, don't analyze, I ordered myself. *Just because he isn't traumatized after kind of bombing with Mom and Dad doesn't necessarily mean he's not interested in me.*

After another few minutes of amusing my brother and sister, Will stood up to leave.

"So my brother wants us to try ghost-crabbing tonight," he told me.

"Ah, yes," I teased. "For those who don't like cow-tipping, there's always ghost crabbing."

"You know I have to do it," Will said. "It's so Dune Island."

"Yeah, you kind of have to," I agreed with a grin. "Well, you and Owen have fun."

"Um, Anna," Will said, clearing his throat. "That was sort of me asking you if you wanted to come."

"Oh!" I said, rolling my eyes and grinning. I hesitated before answering, though. A date with a boy and his brother was definitely a non-date, wasn't it?

Just like this powwow with my family seemed to be too.

It was all just so *friendly*.

My heart sank a little bit. But then Will grinned at me, and he shrugged his bony, broad shoulders and I noticed a small hole in the neck of his faded navy T-shirt. It all made me feel that familiar Will-induced intensity once more.

So what could I do? I said yes. But in the back of my mind, I was also steeling myself.

Crabbing with Will's brother isn't exactly a setup for a first kiss. I might as well face it—it's not going to happen tonight.

I didn't want to think about the bigger picture, though, which was this: If we didn't kiss soon, there was clearly not going to be any romance between me and Will Cooper.

"Wow," I said to Owen and Will that night on the beach. "It's a good thing I'm here. You guys *really* don't know anything about crabs."

Both of them were crouching next to a little hole in the sand, shining their flashlights down it. They looked at me, bewildered.

"Yeah, where *are* they?" Owen said. "It's eight thirty and finally cooling off. I heard this was prime ghost crab time."

I laughed, walked over to the brothers, and turned their flashlights off.

"Give your eyes a minute to adjust," I said. "Then listen . . ."

The three of us stood very still.

Except I didn't feel still.

Ever since I'd made that secret pact with myself at The Scoop, I'd felt buzzy. Like a quivering pitch fork. Like a ticking timer.

All I wanted was for Will to put his hand on my arm or shoulder, to quiet all that nervous vibration.

But he didn't—because Owen was there, cracking jokes.

Or maybe Owen was there so that Will would have the perfect excuse to keep his distance.

Maybe this was his signal.

Maybe this was how it was going to be. Me and Will—and Owen. And Caroline and Sam and my parents and siblings . . .

Maybe we would just be friends.

I was trying to be fine with this. I mean, this evening had been fun so far. Until I'd turned off their flashlights, Will and Owen had been splashing water on each other and romping on the beach. Like all boys, they reminded me of dogs. (In a good way.)

Also, Owen—who would apparently do *anything* for a laugh—had actually checked out one of those *Love Story*s from the library. He kept tossing the book's cheesiest lines out at the most perfect moments, cracking us all up.

And I'd forgotten how ridiculously fun ghost-crabbing could be.

That was, if I could get the crabs to actually recover from Will's and Owen's flashlights.

I told Owen to stop talking.

"Just listen," I whispered.

Then I heard that familiar crunchy skittering and my

instincts took over. I snatched Owen's flashlight out of his hand and clicked it on, illuminating four tiny crabs zipping sideways over the wet sand.

If not for their darting, spidery movements, we never would have seen them. Ghost crabs were often smaller than your palm and a mottled beige, the exact color of the beach. They camouflaged themselves so perfectly, they were always a surprise, even to ghost crab lifers like me.

"There!" I shrieked.

"Aaah!" Owen and Will yelled together as the crabs scattered. Will grabbed the tin bucket they'd brought with them, pounced at one of the crabs, and scooped.

Which left him with a bucket of sand, water, and probably some crab poop.

"Oh my God," Owen huffed, bending at the waist and putting his hands on his shins. "Those things are *scary*. And so fast! I mean, they're worse than roaches."

"Naw, they're cute!" I said. "Let's try again. This time let me do it."

While Will laughed at Owen, we turned off our flashlights. Soon the creepy crawling sound returned and I leaped into the fray. Cornering one crab, I hopped around it, blocking its escape with my ankles. Then I scooped it up. You had to hold ghost crabs carefully on the sides of their bodies. Their front claws were little, but they could still pinch you until you cried. I thrust my little crab toward Owen and Will and it wiggled its many limbs in annoyance.

"That was simultaneously the most ridiculous and cool thing

I've ever seen," Will said, cracking up as the crab writhed in my hand. I put it down and it darted into the water.

"I'm so freaked out right now," Owen said, glancing at the sand nervously. "Keep your lights on so they don't come back!"

"You should see him when there's a spider," Will said. "He screams like a little girl."

"I do not," Owen started to say, when his phone buzzed.

"Oh my God, Mir," he said as he answered. "You would not believe what we're doing right now . . ."

Owen wandered down the beach as he talked.

"So much for Owen," Will said. "That's Miriam, his girlfriend. They'll be talking for the next hour at least."

I cocked my head. Will didn't sound disappointed.

"Clearly, he can't handle the crabs, anyway," Will said. He grinned and I could see his teeth shining in the moonlight.

"So you're the bug killer in the family," I said. "So am I. Well, except for spiders, because we need all of those we can get to eat the mosquitoes. And crickets, of course. They're good luck. And bees and butterflies—"

"Pollinators," Will filled in. "What about ghost crabs? Do you ever, you know, *cook* them?"

"Uch." I laughed. "Believe me, those things aren't for eating."

Will started to laugh with me, but before he could, he whooped and jumped to the side, kicking his right leg around frantically.

"I think one just crawled over my foot!" he yelled.

I burst out laughing.

"Who can't handle the crabs now?" I asked.

"Oooh," Will said, shuddering. "You win. I was trying to be all macho, but those things are skeeving me out!"

"I've got to go ghost-crabbing, Anna," I said in a deep voice. "It's *so* Dune Island."

This was me embracing the just-friends thing. Because you don't mock boys that you're angling to kiss, right?

Will uttered a faux growl and turned his flashlight on himself, making a gruesome face in the shadows.

I just laughed again, then pointed at his feet.

"There goes another one," I announced.

"Where, where?" Will yelled, running with pumping knees into the water.

"Oh, it must have just been your toes, wiggling around," I said.

"Oh, really," Will said.

"Yes, really," I replied, trying not to giggle. "It was an honest mistake."

"Like this?"

And suddenly Will jumped back onto the sand, grabbed me around the waist, and plunked me into the water.

I was just wearing cutoffs and a striped tank top, so I didn't care about getting wet.

I also couldn't remember *what* I'd always found so unlikable about boys scooping me up and dunking me into the ocean. Will's arms around me had felt as different from Landon Smith's as a hammock feels from a desk chair.

Will stepped back and pointed at my splashed clothes.

"Oh, it was an honest mistake!" he teased. "I'm sorry."

Then he splashed me some more.

I started to laugh, but it got caught in my throat when I looked at Will's smile in the moonlight. I still felt wonderful, but no longer in a giggly way. I wanted Will's arms around me again. I wanted to know what his lips felt like. I just plain wanted. Him.

Will's smile, too, faded and in midsplash he retreated, dropping his hand by his side.

Then, with a couple of quick strides, Will closed the open space between us and he *was* holding me. He pulled me tightly to him. I looked up into his eyes, feeling both surprised and . . . *finally.*

I didn't know how I could have doubted it. *This* was the place we'd been moving toward on all those walks and bike rides. Toward Will's warm, firm arms around my shoulders. Toward my hand on Will's back, feeling his muscles shifting under his clean-smelling T-shirt.

Toward this kiss.

This soft, sweet, so-worth-the-wait kiss.

July

First off, the kissing.

Kissing Will felt like so many things. Like the time I swan dived off the lighthouse catwalk and felt, for just an instant, like I might swoop into the sky instead of plunging into the water.

It felt like a sun-warmed beach towel snuggled around you after the first chilly swim in April.

It felt both zingy and cozy; breathless and . . . like breathing. Like I could do it all day.

As June gave way to July and the days *stretched* out, kissing Will seemed like the only thing worth doing.

Of course, I couldn't tell Will that; tell him that the day after our first kiss, I'd woken up thinking about his perfect jawline and imperfectly beautiful nose.

That after I'd gotten out of bed, I'd zoned out in front of the bathroom mirror for a good ten minutes, my fingertips resting on my lips. I'd stood in a trance, remembering how we'd kissed while the ocean bubbled around our knees and indignant ghost crabs skirted our ankles.

That while I made a batch of Raspberry Bellini sorbet that morning, the peaches had reminded me of his breath.

Yes, I was so smitten, I was thinking swoony thoughts about Will's *breath*.

When he'd called that afternoon during my shift at The Scoop, it had felt strange to hear his voice but not be able to touch his smooth, callused fingertips, or put my cheek against his shoulder.

I still wanted to talk to him, though. I headed back to the cooler, flashing my dad a *be back in five* signal and trying not to grin like a complete fool.

"So I realized something," Will said as the cooler door *whoosh*ed shut behind me, "about last night."

"Um, what's that?"

His serious tone made me nervous suddenly. After all this—was something wrong?

Nervousness was the one emotion I'd forgotten to feel in the blissed-out hours since our kiss. Now it caught me by such surprise that I stubbed my toe on a milk crate and had to sit down on the floor. I felt myself bracing for whatever Will had to say, but couldn't imagine what it would be.

"I never did," Will said, "catch a ghost crab."

Now I heard the laugh in his voice—and something more. A sweetness. An *I really like you, Anna Patrick* lilt.

"Yeah, you really fell down on the job, didn't you?" I flirted.

"Well, something got in the way," Will flirted back.

"Some*thing*?" I said.

"Some*one*," Will corrected. "A terrible distraction, really."

"Oh, yes," I said, trying *hard* not to giggle. "Terrible."

The throbbing in my toe had stopped completely. All the

blood had clearly rushed from my foot to my flaming, grinning face. The blood certainly *wasn't* flowing to my brain. This conversation was vapidly cute, the kind of banter that always made me roll my eyes when I saw *other* people engaging in it.

Well, how could I have known that flirting could be so *fun*?

I decided that I should read a really dark and existential book to counteract the cuteness suddenly flooding my soul. It'd be penance for my hypocrisy. I vowed to go to the library the next morning—and plunged right back into the flirtfest.

"So what are we going to do about this ghost crab problem?" I said. "Try, try again?"

I imagined us going back to the beach that night after sunset, and once again my mind flashed on me and Will tangled up together in the surf. A strand of my hair had blown against his cheek as we'd kissed, and he'd smoothed it back, gently looping it behind my ear. Then he'd let his fingers flutter down my neck before resting on my shoulder.

I shivered as I remembered it, and not from the chill in the cooler.

"How about we try again," Will posed, "*minus* the ghost crabs?"

"Don't worry," I said through my smile. "There are plenty of other things you can do to bulk up your Dune Island cred."

"Well, that's what I was thinking," Will said. "There's another Movie on the Beach tonight. I know it's dorky. But come on. They're showing *E.T.* How can you not like that little alien? He's all big-eyed and . . . lumpy."

"Lumpy." I laughed. "How can I resist?"

I was *so* grateful to be locked in the dark, damp cooler right then. Nobody could see me *glowing* at the thought of snuggling up with Will on a blanket. We'd lean back on our elbows as we ate candy, whispered jokes to each other about the movie, then tried to suppress our laughter as adults shushed us. Sitting nearby might be some girl of thirteen who had no idea (yet) what it meant to like a boy this much. She would roll her eyes because we were so disgustingly smitten.

"Anna?" Will said. "Are you there? Is the idea of going to a Movie on the Beach *that* bad?"

"No, no, it's not that," I said. "I was just wondering if they have any books by Sartre or Camus at the Dune Island library."

"Oh-kay," Will said, clearly confused.

"So, Will?" I said. I cradled the phone between my head and shoulder and ran my fingernail across the side of an ice cream tub, scraping a wavy trail through the frost. "What do you like at the movies—popcorn or Twizzlers?"

When I returned to the front, my arms covered with goose bumps, my mom was just walking in with Kat and Benjie for the evening shift. The kids immediately ran to the chalkboard tables and began scribbling. The Scoop was sleepy at the moment. No gaggles of summer people in sight.

I saw my mom's eyes flicker to my phone, and thus, mine did as well. Only then did I notice that I was clutching it like it was a staff of life. I stuffed it into the pocket of my cutoffs like it was something private and personal instead of just . . . a phone.

"Getting ready to go?" my mom said. She walked behind the counter, gave my dad a quick kiss on the cheek, then started neatening the stacks of cups and bowls.

"I think I'm gonna head to the Movie on the Beach," I said, trying not to cringe as I admitted it out loud.

"Oh," Mom said with forced casualness. "Are you going with Will?"

"Yeah," I said with just as much false breeziness.

My mom knew *just* what my friends and I thought of the cheesefest that was a Movie on the Beach. I was as much as coming out and telling her that I was going on a Date with a capital D.

"Well, I thought he was very sweet, when he was in here yesterday," Mom said. "Didn't you, honey?"

She looked pointedly at my dad.

"Oh, sure," my dad said jovially. "A very nice boy."

Oh my God. That made Will sound about as sexy as a puppy. A neutered one.

"You know, he kind of reminds me of your dad when we first met," my mom said, her smile going all dreamy.

Wow, she'd actually come up with an image that was even less sexy than a neutered puppy.

"You know, back when your dad had more of it," Mom went on, "his hair was kind of shaggy like Will's."

"Okay, no offense to Dad?" I said. "But I've seen old pictures of him. There is *no* resemblance between him and Will. Mom, he had a mustache."

"Eh, I was going through a phase," Dad said, waving his hand.

"Well, everyone thought *you* were a phase I was going through, remember?" Mom teased him. "There I was, all set to go to *law school* . . ."

When my mom talked about her near miss with the legal profession, she always made it sound like she'd caught the last lifeboat off the *Titanic*.

". . . and instead I find myself on Dune Island, Georgia, with this guy!"

"Yeah, yeah, just some guy," my dad scoffed. "That's all I was to you."

"Well, they all are," my mom said. She glanced in my direction. "Until one is more than just some guy."

"Yeah!" Kat piped up. She'd just meandered over from the kids area and was studying the day's ice cream flavors. "And that's the boy you *kiss*. Right, Anna?"

"No!" I sputtered. I felt myself turn bright red.

When I looked at my parents, standing side by side behind the ice cream case, they looked a little green. My mom quickly went back to fussing with all the ice cream paraphernalia, but I could tell when she accidentally plunked the sticky hot-fudge ladle into the ice cream scoop bin that the kissing comment had flummoxed her a bit.

"Well, anyway," she said brightly, "it just shows that you have to keep an open mind in life, right? I chucked the world of suits for a life on a crazy island. And you, Anna—"

She looked up from the counter to smile at me with the same happy/sad/freaked-out expression she always had when I did something for the first time, whether it was riding a bike or muddling through my first batch of ice cream.

"—you gave a 'shoobee' a chance," she said.

I shrugged and tried not to grin swoonily.

"You know, Mom, they're not all shoobees," I said.

"I know that," Mom said. "Like I said, he's a very nice boy. I'm glad we got to meet him, sweetie."

The whole exchange, so different from our usual recaps of Dune Island gossip or check-ins about school, made me feel sort of floaty as I went to the bathroom to freshen up for my date. I couldn't help feeling happy about their thumbs-up for Will.

And not just because it validated my sense that he was special and different. My parents were raising four sandy-footed, Southern-speaking (allegedly) Dune Islanders. But if they could see me with Will, perhaps they also had an inkling of the future Anna that I envisioned. The one who rode subways, had been on plenty of dates, and had a card to a library twenty times the size of Dune Island's.

Somehow that made getting ready for *this* date that much more exciting.

Will and I sat a bit apart from all the other moviegoers, in a pocket of sand surrounded by a narrow horseshoe of panic grass.

Since I'd come to the movie straight from The Scoop, I'd had nothing to bring but some Italian sodas and a bag of broken waffle cones, still warm.

Will provided the picnic blanket, a classic red-and-black plaid one. As we stretched it out between us, our eyes met, and Will smiled. His grin started out quiet and shy, then grew.

I wondered if he was feeling the same way I was. My emotions were so up and down, I felt like my head was on a seesaw.

First I thought, *I almost can't believe it happened. We actually kissed, after all that* yearning. *And then we went right back to being normal and hanging out. Which makes it kind of hard to imagine doing the kissing again.*

This quickly led to:

If I don't kiss Will again, and soon, my head might explode.

Followed by:

How do you go about kissing a second *time? The first time was this grand fit of passion. But after that it's sort of premeditated, isn't it? Which sounds awkward. And probably not as exciting, right?*

Then I was back to:

No, seriously, my head will *explode.*

I felt self-conscious crawling onto the blanket with Will. The sun had already set, leaving blue-gray dusk, a light in which everything looked a bit fuzzy and everyone seemed to be at loose ends, just waiting for something to begin.

For most of the folks here, that something was the movie.

For me, of course, it was that inevitable liplock. I wondered when the kissing would happen. Would Will sneak one in during the movie?

Or maybe he'd see me home and kiss me good night at the door, the way they always did on TV shows.

Whenever it was going to happen, I couldn't stop thinking

about the fact that it *would* happen. It was just *out* there, this destination, this sure thing. I didn't know whether to be excited or terrified.

The one thing I *did* know—I hoped Will would take the lead. Despite the perfection of the previous night's kissing, I was now feeling a little shy.

I arranged my snacks on the blanket and said, "Sorry, it's not much. I figured ice cream would get too melty."

"It's awesome," Will said. "I love waffle cones. I brought snacks too."

He reached into the backpack he'd brought with him and pulled out a familiar-looking white paper sack.

"Is that . . . ?"

"It's candy from Angelo's," Will said with a grin. "Didn't you say that was your favorite beachmart on the island?"

I was stunned. I peeked into the bag and saw a garish rainbow of gummies, a packet of Sugar Babies, and some Good & Plenty.

"I didn't know your favorites," Will said with a shrug, "so I got a range."

Clutching the bag in my lap, I gaped at Will.

I wanted to tell him that he'd somehow picked *all* my favorites. That he'd paid attention to me, and to the little things that delighted me, in a way that few people had ever done. That he'd looked into my soul—and seen high-fructose corn syrup.

But I couldn't seem to form any words that would express all that.

So I did the only thing that *could* demonstrate how I was feeling right then.

I threw my arms around Will's neck and I kissed him.

A big part of me didn't want to have another date like the one at the Movie on the Beach.

Don't get me wrong. The snuggling on the picnic blanket was great. The candy and kissing? Even better.

I even loved the movie, despite the fact that the holey screen made little Drew Barrymore look like she had chicken pox. Watching such a kiddie flick with Will made me feel somehow grown-up. I listened to the kids around us squealing when E.T. got left behind by his spaceship, and I could remember so vividly when that was me. Mermaid-kicking, cartwheeling, boys-are-gross me.

But those days also felt very far away. In the course of just a few weeks, I felt like I'd crossed a divide from childhood into . . . I didn't quite know what. A place that wasn't quite adulthood but was way more complicated than being a kid.

All of it made me feel 80 percent thrilled, 10 percent baffled, and 10 percent freaked-out, the way I'd feel if I woke up one morning to find myself several inches taller. (Not that *that* was ever going to happen. I was more sure of that with every day in my puny body.)

I even got into the goofy date-nightness of the Movie on the Beach. I looked at the couples around us—the other young people lounging on blankets with their ankles lazily intertwined; the parental types in fancy folding chairs, pouring each other plastic cups of wine. For the first time in my life, I felt like I had something in common with them. Like we shared a secret.

It was just . . . lovely, it really was.

But, after years of mocking the Movie on the Beachers, it also made me *cringe.*

I just wanted to be a tourist in the land of cheesy dates. I didn't want to move in.

So when we talked on the phone the next morning, I told Will, "I have to admit, I liked our little Movie on the Beach. . . "

"Wait a minute," Will squawked. "'*Little* Movie on the Beach'? *E.T.* terrified you!"

"No it didn't!" I sputtered.

"You're telling me you *didn't* grab me and spill all the Good & Plenty when the government agents swooped in to grab E.T.?"

"Well," I muttered, "guys in hazmat suits are always scary."

I shuddered at the memory of the cute little alien trapped in an isolation tank. Then I pressed on.

"Will, that doesn't make the whole Movie on the Beach scenario less corny."

"So what are you saying?" Will asked, a laugh in his throat.

I chose to ignore it as I declared, "No more dates out of a romantic comedy. No tandem bicycle rides, no milk shake with two straws, no mini-golf. I *refuse.*"

"Mini-golf?!" Will exclaimed.

I couldn't see his face, but I could tell it was lighting up like the Statue of Liberty's torch.

And *that* was how I ended up at Putt Putt Dune Island! (exclamation point not mine), strolling the Astroturf with Will, clunking my neon pink ball into holes, and—despite my best efforts—loving every minute.

What made this even more implausible was that I was possibly the worst mini-golfer in the history of mini-golf. That's probably a pretty short history, but still . . .

"How is it," I asked Will when I failed for the third time to clear the puddle (excuse me, *water trap*) on the seventh green, "that you're so much better at this than I am? You've never played mini-golf in your life. I *lived* here when I was a little kid."

"Maybe it's an attitude thing," Will teased me. "Or maybe it's your stance. You keep ducking your head, afraid that someone will see you."

"No worries," I said with a laugh in my voice. "My crowd doesn't come here anymore. Not since *every* single kid in the third grade had his or her birthday party here. After that, putt putt was *so* over."

Will got that look on his face again. The one that was a cross between *who* is *this girl?* and *I* like *this girl*.

Before I knew it, he'd crossed our little putting green and wrapped me in a hug that took my breath away.

"So if we're basically all alone here," he said, burying his face in the crook of my neck, "I guess you won't mind a little PDA?"

Will smelled wonderful, like clean ocean water and a little bit of coconut. I found myself wondering if he was different here on Dune Island than he was back home. Surely he couldn't smell like this during a New York winter, could he? And would he have been this *demonstrative* if we were on a busy Manhattan street?

I contemplated asking Will this. But when he planted a soft, smiley kiss on my lips, all contemplating ceased. All that mattered was Will in this very instant. And in this instant, he was pretty—

"Amazing."

I startled. "Amazing" was exactly the word I'd been thinking, but the voice wasn't mine. It was sarcastic and exasperated and *loud,* coming from behind the windmill at the next hole.

And if I didn't know better, I'd have been sure that voice belonged to . . .

I pulled away from Will and said, "It can't be."

I stalked over to the windmill, peeked around it, and saw—Caroline! Her fists were planted on her hips and she was staring, no, *glaring,* at Sam.

"Um, hi?" I blurted.

Caroline saw me and Will and threw up her hands.

"Oh, that's just *great,*" she sputtered. She scooped her neon yellow golf ball off the green and tossed it over her shoulder.

Sam spun around.

"What are you doing here?" he demanded.

"What are *you* doing here?" I retorted.

Caroline pointed at Sam—just as I pointed at Will.

I coughed, trying not to laugh.

Will covered his mouth with his fist, clearly working hard to keep a straight face.

And this was the part where all four of us were supposed to

crack up, right? We'd been caught in the act of the goofiest dating ritual of all time.

But the tension between Caroline and Sam quashed it.

"Okay, okay," I said. "What happened, y'all? Did Sam start doing the Caroline voice again?"

I rasped my way through a bad imitation of *Sam's* bad imitation of Caroline's voice.

At which point Will really *did* crack up.

But Caroline just looked down at the Astroturf and bit her lip.

I stopped my little comedy routine with a lurchy feeling in my stomach. Something really *was* wrong.

"Caroline?" I said, reaching out for her arm.

She sidestepped me.

"Whatever," she said. She acted as if she was shrugging it off—whatever *it* was. But I could tell she was upset. She had those two pink spots that always flame up on the apples of her cheeks when she's trying to keep her emotions in check.

Then she waved one hand back and forth in front of her face, the same irritated flutter she'd use to shoo a horsefly.

"I'm just . . ." she said. She took a deep breath and started over. "I used to be the putt putt champ!"

"I know, right?" I said with a little laugh. "Is it that we're too tall now for these little clubs?"

"Anna," Sam said, the defeated S-shape of his torso straightening a bit. "I don't think you're too tall for much of anything."

"Yeah, yeah," I said with a grin. "Heard it all before, Jolly Green."

Sam always laughed smugly when I called him a giant, but this time he just gave me a weak smile. Caroline wandered away, idly swinging her putter around her ankles. The leaf-green tape on its handle was frayed and faded after years of being clutched by sweaty kid hands.

"This was supposed to be . . ." Sam trailed off. "I don't know what. But whatever I thought, it's not happening. We should just go to The Swamp or something."

I didn't know if he was talking to Caroline alone or if he wanted me and Will to join them. I glanced at Will, who gave me a little smile and a shrug.

"I think it's kind of fun," Will said apologetically.

"Well, we set the bar pretty low," I allowed. "Seeing as you dragged me here kicking and screaming."

"You know you love it like you love curly fries," Will said.

"See?" I said indignantly. "I tell you my dirty secrets and you just throw them back in my face."

As Will laughed, I realized I'd turned toward him—and away from Sam and Caroline. For a moment I'd even forgotten they were there. Feeling strangely guilty, I spun around to discuss plan B with them.

But they'd already headed for the cinder-block building—painted the same swimming pool blue as Will's golf ball—to turn in their clubs.

"Do you want to go with them?" Will asked. "Seems like there's something going on there. Maybe . . ."

I bit my lip as I regarded the foot or so of space between my friends as they walked through the course. Sam refrained from leapfrogging the giant red mushroom at the eleventh green or jumping the stepping-stones that crossed the "rushing river" at the eighteenth hole. This was definitely out of character for him. Then again, Sam was a boyfriend now. Maybe maturity, even while playing mini-golf, came with the territory?

I didn't know, probably because the ways of boyfriends and girlfriends were as mysterious to me as math. It wasn't as if I'd learned much yet from being with Will. And besides, he wasn't my boyfriend. At least, I didn't think he was.

Wait a minute, *was* he?

Bubbles of happiness at the idea began to fizz up in my brain, but I tried to shake them away and focus on what was going on with Sam and Caroline. I couldn't imagine their issue was anything that couldn't be solved by a little loud music and chili-laced grub at The Swamp.

So I said to Will, "Oh, they're fine. Sam and Caroline bicker. They always have. I think they had a little hiatus when they first started going out and now . . ."

"The honeymoon's over?" Will said. "Well, we won't let that happen to us, will we?"

He said it casually, before dropping his golf ball on the faux grass and nudging it toward the tee with his putter. I was glad he wasn't looking at me, because I was suddenly feeling almost dizzy.

I couldn't imagine anything more boyfriendy than what Will had just said.

I also truly believed it. Will and I were our own little island,

and nobody else's rules applied to us, not even Sam and Caroline's.

I suppose this was just another version of me being a loner, like Caroline always said.

The only difference was, this time I wasn't *alone* alone. I was with Will, who seemed to fit me like my favorite T-shirt but also felt more like a wonderful surprise with each day that I knew him.

Every year my parents throw a big Fourth of July barbecue. I mean *big*. Every bar, restaurant, and sno-cone stand on Dune Island is run by skeleton crews that night because everybody *else* is in my backyard.

The day starts at sunrise, when a bunch of other dads show up in their grubbiest clothes and help my dad dig a pit somewhere between the vegetable garden and Benjie's sandbox. They fill it with smoldering hickory wood and—a pig. Snout and all. Twelve hours later, he or she is the main course. (I try to avoid learning whether the pig *is* a he or she, and my siblings and I definitely don't name the pig, ever since our great Wilbur boycott of a few years ago.)

Also on the menu are bourbon-boiled peanuts, ambrosia salad, cheese straws, dog head biscuits, boiled shrimp, pickled okra, and basically every other super-Southern morsel that my Midwestern parents find fascinating. If you could put grits on a stick, they'd serve that, too.

The one thing they don't serve is ice cream. Oh, it's there of course. We roll an entire eight-tub freezer out of The Scoop and transplant it onto the screened porch. My mom always makes up a special one-day-only flavor for the party. But it's a rule that nobody in our family is allowed to scoop. It's our holiday. The guests make a big deal of putting on aprons and paper soda-jerk hats. Then they take turns dipping gargantuan scoops and making lopsided cones and sundaes that shed gobs of marshmallow and fudge across the grass.

When everybody's good and full and sticky, we all head to the field out back. It's a big, shaggy mess of wildflowers and scratchy grass that's separated from our (slightly) more groomed yard by a thicket of blueberry bushes. The field is tree free, which makes it the perfect viewing spot for the Beach Club fireworks, about half a mile due east.

Inevitably, when the fireworks finish, someone starts singing patriotic songs and somebody *else* tells them to shut up. Then the parents make more spiked Arnold Palmers, the kids twirl with sparklers and gobble fizzy candy, and everybody stays up way past midnight.

I hadn't thought twice about inviting Will to the barbecue. I'd even told him to bring his mom and Owen. (I mean, our *mailman* comes to the Fourth of July barbecue.)

It was only after the three of them arrived that night at seven o'clock—and stopped cold in our red dirt driveway to gape at Figgy Pudding—that I saw the party from an outsider's eyes.

Oh yeah, I realized, *this must look kind of weird.*

My family (and the rest of Dune Island, for that matter) are so used to our Fourth of July tree, otherwise known as Figgy

Pudding, that even Sophie isn't embarrassed by it. It's just part of our summer landscape, along with sea turtle nests, sunburned tourists, and the constant *slap-slap-slap* of flip-flops.

Figgy Pudding became Dune Island's tackiest icon when I was still a baby. One of my parents decided that since the Fourth of July in a beach town is like Christmas everywhere else, it required a tree. But not some tasteful fir swagged with garlands and earnest ornaments. They chose the sprawling fig in the center of our front yard.

From then on, instead of bringing covered dishes to the barbecue, guests have brought strange things to drape on Figgy's branches. The ornaments are different every year, but platform shoes and feather boas are always popular, as are stuffed animals and Slinkys. People make scary fairies out of twigs and feathers. They also hang kooky cooking utensils and, of course, ice cream scoops.

After everyone has looped their decorations around the tree's branches—plucking handfuls of sticky, purple figs while they're at it—the poor tree looks like a huge, bedraggled drag queen on the morning after Mardi Gras. Enterprising tourists have even been known to come out and snap pictures of it.

We keep Figgy in her finery until the first rain turns everything to muck. Then Sophie and I climb the branches and throw down the decapitated fairies, sogged-up feather boas, and musty shoes, returning the tree to her natural state.

Benjie always cries about the dismantling of poor Figgy Pudding, but I've never thought much about it. I've always known she'd be back the following year.

And now Will and his family were meeting Figgy for the first time. Even though she was only halfway to her full gaudy glory when they arrived, she was still kind of a shock to the system.

As usual the decorations were pink, white, and blue (but heavy on the pink). Figgy was bedecked with lawn flamingos, pinwheels, and even a pink bicycle, its wheels straddling the point where the trunk split into two thick branches. There were many shoes and feather boas, of course, somebody's collection of troll dolls, and a shocking pink stuffed boa constrictor twining around the trunk. The Garden of Eden gone wild—that was my front yard.

Once they got past Figgy Pudding, I realized, Will and his family were going to see the pig, the tipsy adults making *jokes* about the pig, the not-completely-ironic pastel mini-marshmallows in the ambrosia salad, and half a dozen other possibly mortifying things.

For a moment I considered saving face by shrugging off the party as an obligation I didn't really like; a parental eccentricity.

But then I looked at Will—who was grinning like mad at the tree, while his mom shook her head in amazement—and reconsidered.

Will liked my (allegedly) Southern accent. He fed my gummy habit without judgment. He didn't think it was weird that sometimes I'd rather spend my time alone with an ice cream churn than with my friends on the South Shore.

And unless I'd been very misguided, he'd like our wacky barbecue, too.

Even though I'd never really stopped to think about it, *I*

loved our Fourth of July party. It was one of my favorite nights of the year. On the Fourth of July, I felt like we were one big, crazy, happy family—me and the Dune Islanders.

And I wanted Will to be a part of it too.

So I swallowed my self-consciousness and smiled at Will's mom. She was pretty in a mom-ish kind of way—thin, with an upturned nose and freckles. She wore her hair in a slightly frizzy blond bob, and she had the same pointy chin as Will and Owen.

"Ms. Dempsey?" I asked. (Will had told me she'd gone back to her maiden name after the divorce.) "Can I get you an Arnold Palmer?"

Will didn't like the party.

He loved it.

He loved the fact that Ellie Dunlap, Dune Island's mayor, was singing old standards with a karaoke machine on the back porch.

He loved that there were kids (and grown-ups, too) swooping on our swing, which hangs from a high branch in an ancient water oak.

He was nuts about the food, especially, as a matter of fact, the boiled peanuts.

He loved it all so much that I worried (just a little bit) that *I* was being overshadowed. I mean, how could I—even in the cute navy-and-white-striped halter dress I'd fished out of Sophie's closet—compete with the *feeling* of this party? With food that made your mouth sing, in a yard strung with so many white lights that the stars were superfluous, while on the porch a town leader in white braids and overalls sang, *"If you don't like them peaches, don't shake my tree . . ."*

But then Mayor Dunlap started a new tune. The song was clearly very old. It made me think of women wearing silk stockings with seams up the backs. Mayor Dunlap's clear, pretty soprano was both lilting and melancholy, making the couples dancing on the patio sink into one another and sway more slowly. As for me, I recognized the sweet yearning—and reward—in the lyrics.

"I wished on the moon, for something I never knew," Mayor Dunlap sang.

And Will asked me to dance.

"Seriously?" I asked. I was sprawled on the porch steps, one arm propped on the banister, the other dunked into a bowl of butter mints. I did *not* look, I was sure, like the kind of girl you asked for a waltz.

"Anna," Will said, standing over me with one hand extended. "Don't make me lose my nerve."

I laughed with a whoosh of relief.

"Okay, so this *isn't* something you routinely do in New York?" I said.

"Trust me," Will said, looking at the other dancing couples. Most of them were senior citizens. "I *never* do this."

"So it's okay if I step on your toes?"

"Considering you're barefoot?" Will said with a grin. "Not a problem. In fact . . ."

Will kicked off his own flip-flops, stashing them next to the stairs.

"Now we're even," he said.

"I *do* wear shoes, you know . . . ," I said as I took his hand and got up.

"Oh, I saw them," Will said with a nod and a sly smile. "You had 'em on for about five minutes before you ditched them."

He was right. As we walked to the patio, I tried to remember where those cream-colored espadrilles even *were*. But then Will put his arms around my waist and began to sway me in a gentle circle to the music. And suddenly I could barely remember my middle name.

My hands were on Will's shoulders. And I wasn't stepping on his feet, because he was leading me, with a soft, gentle pressure, in a loop around the patio.

I felt like I should say something. Something that poked fun at the two of us; that made this dance a lark instead of a love song.

But swaying in Will's arms didn't feel jokey. It felt serious in the most wonderful way. Will pulled back a little bit and looked down at me. Our eyes met for a long moment, much longer than would have been comfortable with anyone else.

I knew he wanted to kiss me as much as I wanted to kiss him. That if we weren't out here in front of our parents, the mayor, and the mailman, we'd be kissing.

Instead, I lightly laid my cheek against Will's shoulder. His arms tightened around me, and I closed my eyes as we danced on.

The lyrics in Mayor Dunlap's antique song might have been corny, but suddenly they made perfect sense to me.

"I looked for every loveliness. It all came true. I wished on the moon . . . for you."

Mayor Dunlap's pretty voice trailed off. The crowd clapped and cheered while she pulled at the seams of her overall legs and did a mock curtsy.

I didn't really want to let go of Will, but I had to, especially when the mayor announced, "That's it for me, folks. I've got to get over to the pit before that pig is completely gone. But stick around for a couple minutes and we'll have something *completely* different for y'all."

During the lull between acts, Will and I wandered over to the drinks table. The lingering swooniness of our dance made me want something special, so I made a spritzer of limeade, sparkling water, and a handful of raspberries. Will was reaching for the iced tea pitcher when his mother walked over arm in arm with our neighbor Mrs. Sumner. Mr. Sumner trailed behind them, looking bemused.

"Will!" Ms. Dempsey gushed. "I want you to meet Marlene Tifton and Bobby Sumner! Well, she's Marlene Sumner now. I knew the two of them when I was fourteen years old, if you can believe it."

"Well, *I* can't believe Sissy's back for the summer!" Mrs. Sumner gushed, giving Ms. Dempsey a squeeze.

"*Sissy?*" Will said to his mother.

"Oh, you know your uncle Roy was always the star when we were down here," she explained. "So for a while I was just known as his little sister."

"Sissy means sister," I said, translating Southernese for Will.

"Good thing she wasn't a little brother. Then she would have been Bubba."

"Bubba means *brother*?" Will gaped.

"What else would it mean, son?" Mr. Sumner said in his loud, booming voice.

"I think this is why I teach so much Faulkner in my lit classes," Ms. Dempsey said with a laugh.

"Oh, I know I sound like a redneck," Mrs. Sumner said with a shrug. "But, Sissy, I just can't call you by your real name. *Lizzy.* It sounds so *formal.*"

The three of them guffawed like teenagers, then drifted toward the barbecue pit.

"Your mom seems happy," I said to Will with a grin.

"Yeah," he agreed, gazing after her with raised eyebrows. "Huh!"

Before he could say anything else, a twangy crash rang out from the back porch. I grinned. I'd almost forgotten about the next act. They were shuffling onto the porch, lugging their instruments and equipment with them. I led Will back to the patio.

"I think you'll like this band," I told him. "They're called Undertoad."

"Cool name," Will said.

As Undertoad's four guys set up their stuff, every Dune Island High kid at the barbecue (especially Sophie and her posse of girlfriends) crowded around the steps and cheered. I saw Owen in the crowd too, slurping lemonade and chatting with some kids as if they'd known one another forever.

I nudged Will and pointed at the lead singer.

"See anyone you know?" I asked.

His eyes went wide.

"You didn't tell me Sam was in a band," Will said.

"Don't worry," I said with an elbow in his ribs. "You don't have to pretend to like them. They're actually good."

"How did you know what I was thinking?" Will said, shaking his head at me.

I shrugged and laughed. The fact that I'd successfully read Will's mind exhilarated me like a shot of espresso.

Apparently, the feeling was mutual. Will and I grinned at each other so hard you could probably see little cartoon birdies tweeting around our heads. Our own personal Disney movie was mercifully interrupted when Sam cleared his throat into the mic.

"Uh, hi, y'all," he said. "We'll be right with you. Just give us a chance to plug in."

As the guys started messing around with their equipment, Caroline came up, sipping peach cider from a mason jar.

"The pig's so cute this year," she said with a shudder. "I can't stand it."

"Cute . . . and tasty!" Will said, his grin turning devilish.

"So you're a carnivore just like Sam, huh?" Caroline asked.

"I think it kind of comes with the gender," I said sympathetically.

"Then what's your excuse?" Caroline said to me. "Didn't I see you gnawing on a big, juicy rib earlier?"

"I was *not* gnawing," I protested, giving Will a shifty glance. "I was . . . nibbling."

"Oh yeah," she replied. "You always drip barbecue sauce down your chin when you 'nibble.'"

I gasped in horror until Caroline leaned across me and said to Will, "I'm kidding, of course. Our Anna is the picture of manners and decorum."

"Well, let's not go too far," I said while Will cracked up.

But before the quipping could continue, Sam hunched over his battered black guitar and started tuning it.

Twang, twang, twaaaaang.

The endless string-plucking, combined with a squeal of feedback from the bass player's mic, made for some awkward squirming in the audience.

Some of the guys started hooting, "Sam-MEH!" Sam waved them off.

I laughed, but Caroline just huffed and shifted from foot to foot, taking agitated slurps of her cider.

"I *told* him to tune up during the mayor's boring set," she muttered.

"I liked that music," I protested, taking a tiny sidestep closer to Will.

"You *did*?" Caroline squawked. She pursed her lips and shot me a cynical squint. Her eyes swung from my red cheeks to Will. When I followed her glance, I saw that *he* was gazing at me.

And when I looked back at Caroline, I saw a quick succession of emotions flash across her round, oh-so-readable face—recognition, amusement, and a*maze*ment. Then she glanced at Sam and I saw one more emotion flash across her face—wistfulness.

Which was puzzling to me. Were Caroline and Sam already such a fusty, old couple that it made her nostalgic to look at shiny, new Will-and-me?

Before I had a moment to think about this, a swell of music jolted all thoughts from my head. Undertoad had launched into one of their edgy, throbbing anthems of angst. Most of Undertoad's songs were self-mocking meditations on being awkward, adolescent, and loveless. I realized now that Sam had probably written many of them while he was pining for Caroline.

She surely knew that too, because her twisty mouth softened as she watched Sam thrash at his guitar strings, his brow crunched up with the effort of singing:

"Then there was your voice

"Like a windup tin toy

"Like the sweetest nails on a chalkboard

"That I ever heard."

I threw back my head and laughed.

"I've heard Sam play this song a hundred times," I yelled in Caroline's ear over the peppery drumbeats. "How did we never realize it was about you?!"

Caroline gave a wan smile and shrugged.

"The guy knows how to make a romantic gesture, that's for sure," she yelled back at me. But instead of affectionate, her voice was hard, even a little bitter.

I'd been shimmying my hips, dancing to the music, but at that comment, I stopped.

"Caroline?" I said, turning toward her. "What's *wrong*?"

She shrugged again and waved me off.

"Nothing," she said. "I'm just being moody. At least that's what *Sam* says."

For the first time since they'd gotten together, Sam's name didn't lilt in her voice, like its own little song. Instead, it sounded off-key. And frankly, a little pissed off.

"C'mon," I said, hooking my arm through Caroline's. I began to pull her away. "Let's talk."

Even as I said it, I felt a pang at the prospect of leaving Will's side. My left arm felt a little cold after being pressed up against his right one.

But then Caroline shook her head and planted her feet.

"No," she said. "It's nothing. Besides, Sam'll unravel if he doesn't see me listening to the whole set. Prepping for this party was, like, all he did this week."

She glanced at Will's arm, which was making its way around my waist again, and her mouth got a little twisty. But she didn't say anything. She just returned her gaze to Sam and the band.

I craned my neck to try to meet her eyes, but Caroline was dancing vaguely, staring at the porch/stage. Had she detected my reluctance? That was the problem with friends who knew you as intimately as anyone in your family did. They could read your every gesture. It was a blessing and a curse.

I wondered if that was part of Will's appeal. His mystery. All the things I still *didn't* know about him—but wanted to find out.

Of course, I realized as I looked at Caroline's stony profile, you never knew *anybody* completely.

Not even yourself.

But at that moment, I was feeling anything but introspective. My world was simple. I was all about dancing on the smooth, flagstone patio in my bare feet. And feeling Undertoad's music thrum through my whole body. And hanging out with my boyfriend and my best friend.

Even the sight of my mom—absentmindedly hugging Kat to her waist as she chatted with Mayor Dunlap in the side yard—warmed me from the inside out tonight.

I closed my eyes and lifted my arms over my head as I danced, enjoying the small symphony of all these sensations.

Then I stumbled into Will. (Dancing with your eyes closed is not as easy as it looks.) He put his arm around my shoulders to steady me—and kept it there. I cuddled into the crook beneath his arm, feeling happily incredulous.

Was this really me? Was I half of a joined-at-the-hip couple?

Happy couples had always felt to me like the shoobees' glamorous vacation homes. They were all around me yet untouchable. But now there I was—on the inside of this mysterious phenomenon. Somehow it had been as easy as turning a doorknob.

Undertoad's set was six songs long. I could tell by Will's raised eyebrows and the intent way he was taking in the show that he was impressed by the music.

And when Sam brusquely introduced the final song by saying, "This is for Caroline," I could tell Will was impressed with *Sam*. I turned to Caroline to get her reaction and was surprised to see that she'd slipped away.

She must be at the front of the crowd, I thought with a smile.

Whatever tension was simmering between my friends, I was sure it would be smoothed over by Sam's dedication.

I melted back into Will for the last song. He moved me in front of him and wrapped his arms around me, compelling me to lean back against him. It felt as good as floating on my back in the ocean.

I could have stood that way for a *long* time, but too quickly Sam ground out the last chord. And then a voice in the crowd shouted out, "It's almost time, y'all!"

For fireworks of course. I glanced up at the sky, surprised to see that it had gone completely dark already. Beyond the shimmer of the white lights strung over the yard, the night looked like black satin.

"Whoops!" I gasped. I grabbed Will's hand (since it was still conveniently located on my shoulder). "We haven't gotten our ice cream yet!"

"I can't do it," Will mock groaned. "I'm so full."

"Will," I scoffed as I dragged him around the house to the ice cream case on the screened porch. "This is a Patrick party. You *can't* skip the ice cream."

My mom had gone simple this year and made a frothy but impossibly rich peach cinnamon custard. It was velvety, but with a sneaky, peachy punch. I reminded myself to compliment my mom on the flavor later. It was as elegant as Figgy Pudding was, well, *not*.

Once Will and I had loaded up two cups with ice cream, I ducked into the house and emerged with a beach blanket.

We hurried with all the other guests to the field behind

the house. People laughed as they tripped through the weedy yard.

We tiptoed around the pig pit, where orange-black embers still glowed in a bed of salt-and-pepper ash. Then we circled around the blueberry bushes. I grabbed a few early berries from one of them and plunked them on top of Will's ice cream.

"Blueberry and peach go perfectly together," I said.

Will grinned and took a big bite as I led him to a spot in the center of the field. All around us were the shadowy shapes of other couples cuddled up together, kids spinning under the stars, and the up-pointed feet of people who'd already flopped on their backs to watch the show. There was an electric murmur in the air.

I lowered myself to my knees on our blanket. My hand was on my ice cream spoon, but I didn't really feel like eating any more of it. For the first time that night, Will and I were invisible to all the other party guests. We could be together without all those eyes on us.

I could barely see Will's face in the darkness of the field. (That's what made it so perfect for fireworks-gazing.) I put my dessert down at the edge of the blanket and turned, just slightly, toward him.

He must have been waiting for this moment too, because suddenly I felt his palms—cool and slightly damp from his ice cream cup—on my cheeks. He leaned in and I closed my eyes. I couldn't wait to feel his lips on mine.

But then—I didn't. Confused and a little embarrassed, I

opened my eyes. Will was staring at me, looking serious. I felt a confused catch in my throat.

"Anna," he said, his voice a rumbly whisper. "This is the best night *ever.*"

I laughed, because of course I'd been thinking that ever since the first boiled peanut. Then Will silenced my laugh with an incredible, romantic kiss.

After a few minutes of kissing, things started to feel serious again. Will's hands warmed up on the bare skin above the back of my halter dress. He pulled me closer and closer to him. With each kiss, I felt more and more like I was melting into him, like I never wanted to stop.

I gently pushed Will away for a moment so I could catch my breath. And that was when, off in the direction of the beach, we heard a dull thud.

Then *everyone* was catching their breath, waiting, waiting for—

Boom!

Our group cheered as the first firecracker exploded over the water. It was far away from us, but still dazzling, a bright blue starburst tendrilling out in every direction.

Will gave me one more quick kiss before we settled onto our backs to watch. I turned on my side and rested my head on Will's upper arm. The soles of my bare feet just touched the tops of his.

I'd watched this exact same firework display from this exact spot my entire life. Every few years the Beach Club boosters added a few new dazzlers to the mix—twisty sizzlers, explosions in the shapes of hearts, or double pows from one rocket. Mostly, though, the show felt very familiar.

But watching it with Will made every firework feel new—louder and more vivid and definitely more exciting. I let the big bangs and colored lights envelop me. I succumbed to each one the way you melt into your favorite song played really, really loud.

The fireworks started coming faster and bigger. It crossed my mind, for a fleeting moment, that this show might feel piddly and small-town to Will. I'd seen Times Square on TV on New Year's Eve. I could only imagine how vast and sparkly the Fourth of July fireworks over Manhattan were.

But as the show got more intense, Will squeezed my arm. He even hooted along with some of the other party guests at some particularly big *pow*s. So I squashed the insecurity as easily as I would a slow-moving mosquito.

Will wasn't *in* New York. He was here with me. And he was making it clear that there was nowhere else he wanted to be. I was as confident of that as I was of the annual rise and fall of Figgy Pudding.

Until something happened that changed everything.

A few blankets in front of us, a cell phone bleeped, then flickered open in someone's shadowy hand. I blinked as I realized that the face reflected in the phone's silvery glow was Will's brother, Owen.

"Hey, baby!" he said. Clearly his girlfriend was calling. "Aw, I miss you, too. Happy Fourth of July. So you're with the whole crowd? Ash and Ethan too? And Josh. *And* Mo? I'm jealous! Although, I gotta say, this is quite the scene here. You should visit!"

He paused and chortled at something his girlfriend said.

"Well, you won't have to wait long," he said into the phone. "I'll be back in, what? Eight weeks? That's nothing! Oh, I think the finale's about to start. Better go, babe."

Another pause, then Owen said, "The fireworks? Naw, they're nothing like that. But they're cute!"

Clearly I'd been right. Our fireworks were "cute." Great.

Owen snapped the phone closed and settled back onto his elbows, probably letting the brief phone chat drift from his mind as easily as firecracker smoke dissipating into the breeze.

But I felt a chill wash over me, as startling and painful as an ice cream headache.

If Owen was heading back home in eight weeks, so was Will.

Of course, I'd always known this. Will was a summer guy; an out of towner, if not quite a shoobee. His Dune Island stop-watch had begun ticking the moment he'd arrived.

But somehow I'd forgotten this. Because in June, as the days are just starting to stretch themselves out and the tomato plants are still crisp-leafed and runty, the idea of September seems like just that. An idea, as remote and hazy as a dream.

But now we were just a week shy of mid-July. Suddenly the summer felt to me like one of those log flume rides at an amusement park. You skim along a pleasantly lazy channel, until you land on a conveyer belt inching you upward. With every crank of the belt you grow more breathless, more excited, and then—you thunder downward, and with a cold splash of water to the face, it's all over.

I felt myself stiffen. Just a moment ago I'd been so pleasantly aware of all the points where my body and Will's were joined. Our feet were tangled up, my knees touched the side of his leg, my arm was slung across his chest, and my cheek rested on his shoulder.

But now I was painfully conscious of all the points where we were separated. The night air—damp and coolly redolent of pollen and grass—seemed to whoosh between us, making unpleasant prickles on the backs of my legs and neck.

I continued to stare at the fireworks, but now I found myself focusing less on the sizzles and lights, and more on the clouds of gunpowder that lingered in the air afterward, black and acrid.

Like a little kid, I wished that the fireworks could go on forever; that this *summer* could go on forever.

Involuntarily, my fingers tightened on Will's soft T-shirt.

Will felt it and turned to me. And then we were kissing again, without hesitation, without a thought. Our kisses became urgent, with me squeezing Will's arm, him clasping me tightly around the small of my back. We weren't so much ignoring the fireworks as channeling them.

Only when the finale pummeled us with an endless stream of booms and pops did we drag ourselves from each other and watch the end of the show. We sat up and Will shifted behind me. He held me and rested his chin on my head as he cheered on the last of the show.

When it ended, there was a moment of silence. A hovering. An intake of breath. I found myself closing my eyes and wishing that we could all just remain suspended in this moment of happiness and satisfaction; in this moment when all was perfect.

But of course I was wishing for the impossible. In the next

instant everyone started hooting, pounding their hands together, and getting stiffly to their feet. They shook grass from their blankets and began picking their way across the meadow, back to the party.

Back to real life.

My ice cream, barely touched, had melted. Will suggested getting a fresh helping and I nodded numbly. I let him hook my fingertips in his and lead me around the blueberry bushes. This time it was Will who swiped some berries from the branches. As he handed a couple to me, one squished in my palm, a glistening, black-violet blotch.

"It's overripe," I observed dully. "Already."

Will gave me a small, confused smile. He opened his mouth as if he was about to say something, then reconsidered.

"You need a pick-me-up," he declared a moment later. "What do you think of an iced tea float with peach ice cream?"

Despite myself, I felt my eyebrows rise.

"That actually sounds pretty good," I said.

"See?" Will said. "Your crazy flavor combos are making an impression on me."

He stopped walking and pulled me into an enveloping, breathtaking hug.

"Your *everything*," Will murmured into the top of my head, "is making an impression on me."

Later, much later, Will and I ducked under Figgy Pudding to say good-bye. Owen and Ms. Dempsey had already started walking home. Will had brought his bike, so he'd told them he'd catch up to them in a few minutes.

We hid under a branch that was heavy with sticky-smelling figs. While Will put the cup of lemonade he'd been sipping on the ground, I leaned against the trunk, my back cushioned by the neon pink boa constrictor. Will kissed me good-bye, a delicious lemon and sugar kiss. Then we kissed again. And again and again.

It was I who pulled away first. I looked down at my hands, trying not to bite my lip in disappointment. The end of this evening somehow felt like the end of *everything.*

When I looked up at Will, though, it was clear that he wasn't thinking anything like this. He was only surfing the swells of those kisses, not to mention the crazy crowd, the weirdness of Figgy Pudding, and the exotic party food.

Will pulled something out of his back pocket—a handful of plastic spoons and a long twist tie that he must have found on a bag of paper plates at the food table. He grabbed his Styrofoam cup from the mulchy ground and slugged down the last of his lemonade.

And then he started poking the spoon handles through the Styrofoam, just below the lip of the cup.

"What are you doing?" I asked.

"Hold on," Will said. "This'll just take a minute."

He placed each spoon about an inch from the last, so their handles crisscrossed inside the cup and their bowls protruded outside of it. The spoon bowls all faced the same direction, reminding me of the curvy wings of a pinwheel.

Next Will knotted one end of the twist tie and poked it through the bottom of the cup. Finally he dangled the sad little sculpture in front of his mouth and blew.

It spun.

"It's the best I could do on short notice," Will said.

"That's a whirligig," I pointed out, laughing despite myself. "Are you *sure* you aren't Southern? You're, like, one step away from catching ghosts with a glass-bottle tree."

"A what?" Will said.

I waved off his question with a weary smile.

We crept around the tree until we found the perfect branch on which to hang Will's ornament. Then I watched him swing his leg over Zelig and roll down the dirt drive. The *tick-tick-tick-tick*s of his coasting bicycle gears were quickly drowned out by the whirring of the cicadas. A moment after that, Will was swallowed up by the night.

Every time I left the house for the next few days—until a raging thunderstorm put an end to Figgy Pudding for another year—I stopped by the branch where Will had perched his whirligig.

I would reach out with a fingertip and graze the plastic, wishing it was Will's hand that I was touching instead. I'd pause and close my eyes for a moment of languid sensation that existed only in my mind, in my memory.

And then I would remember that too soon, *all* I'd have left of Will were memories.

My hand would drop to my side, a dead weight. I'd stalk toward my bike with hunched shoulders and ride away fast. As I sped along I'd hope that my ragged breath would drown out all these thoughts about Will leaving. I tried to push them below the surface, because I knew that they could easily muck everything up, like a broken well silently spewing oil from the ocean floor.

But like an ugly oil spill, I feared my obsession about summer's end was going to be almost impossible to contain.

When I called Caroline on the fifth of July and told her to meet me at the beach, I told myself that I was doing it for *her*, because I knew she needed to talk.

The fact that I had an iced tea float hangover and was suddenly feeling very much like an about-to-be-ditched Allison Porchnik? Oh, that had *nothing* to do with it.

And that's how two girls in already-beginning-to-fade wraps—one blue and one orange—ended up scouring the aisle of Angelo's for their breakfast.

If we weren't already feeling bitter, our food choices were definitely going to get us there. Caroline grabbed a cellophane tube of shell-on sunflower seeds, the kind that taste like bark and lodge in your throat like salty moth wings. I went for beef jerky.

"It's like everlasting breakfast sausage," I tried to joke, even though my own crack made my throat close up.

Then Caroline chose vanilla wafers, which always made my mouth feel like it had been coated with a partially hydrogenated film. I got some of those cheese and cracker sets where the tiny tub of cheese is made out of wax or plastic or some combination of the two.

And finally, because this was breakfast, after all, we chose some minimuffins, but instead of getting blueberry or apple spice like two sane people might, we went with banana nut, which is universally known as the worst muffin flavor ever invented. (And yes, I *am* considering bran.)

It was a feel-bad brunch, and we dug into the plastic grocery sack before we even made it to the beach.

"So where's Will?" Caroline asked as Angelo's door swung shut behind us. She popped a sunflower seed into her mouth and chased it with a slurp of bottled iced tea.

"I don't know," I said, just a touch defensively.

Caroline gave me a sidelong glance as we crossed the parking lot and stepped onto the beach. Sand was sort of like truth serum to us. Caroline, Sam, and I had always had our most honest talks here.

"So it didn't go well last night?" Caroline asked as we walked down the beach.

"Um, actually." I sighed. "I'm pretty sure it was the best night of my life."

"Oh," Caroline said. She nodded as she took another sip of tea. "I can see why you're miserable."

"I'm *not* miserable," I said. I gnawed for a moment on my beef jerky, which was literally as tough as leather. When I couldn't get a bite off, I grabbed Caroline's iced tea instead and took a slurp.

"I'm just . . . pensive," I declared.

"You're overanalyzing," Caroline said, correcting me.

"I am not," I scoffed.

"Oh, yes you are!" Caroline said with a grin. "You're doing that thing where you imagine that you're a character in a Woody Allen movie."

I narrowed my eyes at my friend.

"You know," I said, "I think it is possible for someone to know a person *too* well."

"You love it," Caroline said.

And she was right. I sort of *did* love it. I think I'd forgotten for a while how much I needed Caroline to be my mirror in harsh light. I could always count on her to matter-of-factly point out my every blemish, literal and figurative—and love me just the same.

"Anyway, we're not here to talk about me," I said as we continued to tromp along. "What's going on with Sam?"

Caroline ducked her head quickly. She pretended to be fixated on tearing open the muffin bag so I wouldn't see her cheeks flush.

I knew not to press. Instead I walked ahead of her and chose a spot on the sand. I tossed my book and our bag of breakfast onto the ground, stretched out my wrap, and laid down on it, using one forearm to block out the sun.

"Why don't you get a pair of sunglasses ever?" Caroline asked as she sat next to me. There was a hint of annoyance in her voice.

"Too much to keep track of," I said without moving my hand. "I'd only lose them."

There was another long pause until Caroline said, "Sam told

me that before we got together, he used to dream about us having this perfect, romantic date."

"Really?" I said. I uncovered my eyes now and looked at her. "That's sweet, if . . . kind of girly."

"I know, right?" Caroline said. "I mean, a perfect date. What is that? A candlelit dinner with a violin player?"

"Can you imagine?" I said, trying not to cringe at the memory of my equally cheesy picnic with the champagne flutes under the Beach Club pool deck. "So what was the dream?"

"Oh, he's kind of vague about it," Caroline said. "It hasn't happened yet."

She glowered at the waves.

"He's probably off somewhere right now," she said, "plotting this evening of devastating romance instead of just being here with me. Being normal. Being fun."

"So Sam wanting to sweep you off your feet is a bad thing?" I asked.

"Noooo," Caroline said, sounding confused. "I guess I'm still getting used to the way things are now. I mean, you know how little things about Sam used to annoy me?"

"Like the way he consciously tries to work surfer terms into his vocabulary," I offered, "and loves raw onions and snorts when he laughs?"

"Oh, don't let me stop you," Caroline said.

"Hey, I'm just quoting *you*," I said. "I think all those things are endearing. Well, except the onions. Gross."

"That's the thing," Caroline said. "After we got together, that's how *I* felt. Suddenly I liked all these things about Sam that I *hadn't* liked before. Like it was his flaws that made me love him, in a weird way."

"That's so romantic." I sighed.

"Shut up," Caroline said, giving me a little swat on the arm.

I propped myself up on my elbows and looked at her.

"No, I'm serious," I said. "A perfect person is easy to love. But when somebody likes all your *im*perfections, well, that's when you know they really mean it."

"Well, try telling Sam that!" Caroline said. She grabbed a muffin from our breakfast bag but forgot to take a bite out of it. "I almost feel like now that we're together, he doesn't want me to see the real him. Only the dashing, romantic version of him. We never just hang out anymore, watching TV or sitting around on the beach being bored. Everything's a Date. That's why we ended up at the stupid putt putt golf place that night."

"Maybe he thinks since you're not just friends anymore," I said, searching for an explanation, "you shouldn't act like you did when you were?"

"Maybe," Caroline said. "Or maybe he was just friends with me so he could make me fall for him. Now that I have, he can spend his 'friend' time with *other* people, like the guys from Undertoad. Then when he feels like making out, or having someone to go to parties and dances with, he's got me. It's the perfect balance. For *him*."

Caroline's lip trembled just a little bit as she added, "But I miss being able to just bum around with my friend."

"I think Sam's just being careful," I said, trying to keep my voice optimistic. But deep down? I was as bewildered as

Caroline. "He doesn't want to mess things up. He wants you to make it for the long haul."

"Well, *that's* depressing on so many levels," Caroline said. "My God, Anna. We're sixteen. Who's thinking about the long haul?"

This made me bite my lip. I felt both bereft and ridiculous about *my* current angst.

On the other hand, I told myself, was it unreasonable to wish for more than eight weeks with Will? Eight weeks wasn't even a *little* haul.

Caroline finally noticed the squashed muffin in her hand. She began to pick the nuts out of it and throw them over her shoulder. A couple of seagulls immediately swooped down. They squawked and pecked at each other as they scrounged for the tiny bits of food.

I looked away from the bickering birds and squinted out at the waves. The sun hit the water at an angle that seemed to shoot the light directly into my eyes, making them almost hurt. *Everything* just felt too intense this morning—the sun, the taste of all this processed food, the stupid seagulls, Caroline's anguish. . . . Most of all, my feelings about Will were as raw as an exposed nerve.

My impulse, as always, was to jump to my feet and run for the ocean, for that head-clearing plunge into the cold murk.

I got to my feet.

"Come on," I said to Caroline.

Without hesitation she threw the rest of her muffin at the gulls and jumped up. Joylessly we sprinted toward the surf, high-stepped over the frothy shallow bit, and dove together under the first big wave. When she came up for air, Caroline's fine blond hair was plastered to her scalp, satin smooth.

We swam past the breakers until the waves softened into lazy undulations. The water was calm and sleepy this morning, as if it, too, was drained after the holiday.

Caroline and I faced each other. We let our legs go slack, planting our toes in the sand and fluttering our hands to keep our balance. Then we let the waves rock us from side to side. I felt a fish flick against my calf. I sank down until my chin rested on the water's surface.

Caroline gazed at me, her face calm now. We were both deep in thought.

"It's kind of scary being in love," I said after a while. "The stakes are high, you know?" I paused again. Then, even though I was sort of scared to hear Caroline's answer, I whispered, "What are you going to do?"

Caroline lifted her legs and rolled onto her back. She floated on the bobbing water and gazed up at the almost cloudless sky.

"Maybe Sam's right and I'm just being moody," she said. "Maybe I should just get over myself."

How many times had I heard Caroline say those words to me?

"Get over yourself," she'd say when I complained about Dune Island's dinkiness or mandatory pep rallies or the fact that I had to share a room with my sister. She'd gotten this saying from her track coach, who shouted it across the field approximately 150 times per practice.

It was, I realized now, the perfect motto for Caroline. She was a jock. She had complete faith in her own power, whether she was pushing for another ten laps or telling herself not to read too much into the changes in Sam.

So maybe I could get over myself too, I thought. Caroline bobbed about on the water's surface as if a sudden easing in her mind had made her body feather-light as well. *Maybe I could just* force *myself to think, 'Yay! Eight more weeks!' instead of 'Only eight more weeks.' You know, half full versus half empty.*

This was a tactic that would have worked like a charm for Caroline.

But deep down I knew I had a different interpretation of "half full." It was halfway to *gone.* My time with Will was draining away fast, and when it was over, all I'd be left with was a big, old empty.

That's what I was feeling, I realized. *Pre*-empty. And after the unadulterated fullness of the past few weeks, it was depressing indeed.

Will showed up at The Scoop the next night at exactly nine o'clock. I was working alone because it was my mom's book club night and my dad was home with the kids. Will gave me a casual wave over the heads of the customers who'd arrived just before him. Then he went over to one of the chalkboard tables in the kids section to wait for me.

By this time of year, the summer people knew as well as the locals that The Scoop closed at nine. So around 8:50, every ice cream addict on the island (or so it seemed) would rush their dinner checks or snatch their picnic blankets off the beach. Then, boisterous and giggly, they'd all pile into our shop. At this time of night, they tended to buy extravagant desserts. They wanted towering sundaes, chili-spiced chocolate shakes, or crepes filled with piped Nutella and hazelnut gelato.

They lingered in the booths, groaning over the ice creamy goodness.

They had all the time in the world.

Some nights this annoyed me to death. I wanted to shout at them, *Go away already! Don't you know that Gabriel Garcia Márquez is waiting at home for me, not to mention my lime-green bathtub?*

Other times I lingered along with them. I'd make myself what I called a sampler platter—tiny divots of my favorite ice creams lined up neatly in a banana split dish. Then I'd sit a booth or two away from the customers; close enough to eavesdrop without seeming to hover. I'd close my eyes while the ice cream melted on my tongue and feel the work-induced throbbing in my feet ebb.

But tonight, Will was here. Which meant I didn't want ice cream and I didn't want gossip—I wanted him. I wanted to scooch into a booth next to him and give him a flirty kiss hello. I wanted to make him taste my latest flavor (Root Beer Float), then cut my chore list in half so we could go for a walk on the beach.

I couldn't allow myself to do any of those things, though. Because everything that brought me closer to Will was also another step toward certain heartbreak.

Has Will not even considered this? I wondered as I dished up the last order.

From the way he was smiling at me, his face as open as a window, it didn't seem he had. Or maybe he just didn't care about what was going to happen eight short weeks from then.

I was hoping the last-minute customers would provide a buffer between us for a while, but as soon as I rang up the last order, they all drifted out to the boardwalk to perch around the extra-long picnic table out front.

I tossed my scoop into the sink and trudged to the door to flip the OPEN sign to CLOSED.

"Wow, you work hard here," Will said, still sitting at the chalkboard table. "Your love for ice cream must run way deep if you can still eat it after scooping all night."

"Well . . . ," I said, shrugging and giving him what was probably a pained smile.

I went to the little closet where we kept the cleaning supplies and grabbed a spray bottle of bleach water and a rag.

I didn't start with the tables farthest from the kids section just to avoid Will. I *always* started there. I shot him a couple of awkward smiles as I started spritzing and wiping down the tables.

Will just looked at me for a moment. He rolled a piece of green chalk between his thumb and forefinger, then said, "I called you yesterday."

"I know." I sighed. "I'm sorry. Caroline needed some girl time, and then I was so tired after being up so late the night before . . ."

I trailed off, not wanting to allude to the barbecue.

"I called you this morning, too," Will said.

I didn't know what to say to that one, so I just focused extra hard on my work, making careful, straight swipes across each tabletop with my rag.

Suddenly I heard a clatter from the supply closet. When I looked up, Will was emerging from it with a broom and dustpan.

"You don't have to do that," I said, my voice trembling a little.

Will just shrugged and started sweeping, following just behind me to catch the crumbs I was wiping off the tables. I skipped the chalkboard tables, because Kat and Benjie were in charge of those. They got upset if anybody destroyed the artwork before they got a chance to see it.

After that Will silently helped me put the lids on the ice cream tubs, set the lights on dim, and carry the final load of sticky spoons, bowls, and coffee mugs to the industrial dishwasher in the back.

But when I started updating the grocery list, Will finally said, "You're not really going to the store after you close up shop, are you?"

"No," I said wanly. "It's just, whoever closes is supposed to make a note of all the things we ran out of that day."

"I have a feeling you never, ever skip a day of school," Will said. He grinned and leaned against a stainless steel counter, crossing his legs at the ankle.

I didn't laugh or joke back like I was supposed to. I just nodded, confirming that, yes, I was a total rule-following nerd.

"I also have a feeling that you're avoiding me," Will said. Now he crossed his arms over his chest.

I could have denied it. I could have tap-danced my way out of it.

But already Will and I were beyond that. There was no option but to be honest with him.

So I nodded again.

"Okay, that's weird, because the Fourth of July?" Will said. "It was one of the best nights of my life."

"Mine too!" I burst out, finally looking up at him. It was only then that I realized I'd been avoiding his eyes ever since he'd arrived. Now that I allowed myself to look at him directly, I had to stifle a quiet gasp.

After not seeing him for a couple of days, Will looked so good I wanted to throw my arms around him. His hair was getting longer. It hung in his eyes, looking painfully cute. After all these days in the sun, he had a deep tan, which made his brown eyes look kind of sparkly. He was wearing another one of his T-shirts that hung just so off his broad shoulders. I wanted to touch it, to touch *him*.

But that, I thought to myself, would hurt.

In that moment of hesitation, it also occurred to me what *I* must look like after four straight hours of working. My hands smelled like bleach after cleaning the tables, and my hair was coming out of its sloppy bun. I could feel a few tendrils grazing my cheeks. I reached up nervously to smooth them behind my ears.

"Anna, stop," Will said, apparently reading my mind. "You're beautiful."

I slumped against the dishwasher so that Will and I faced each other from opposite sides of the kitchen.

"Don't say that," I whispered.

"Why *not?*" Will said. I could hear an edge in his voice, a kernel of exasperation.

"Because, this just keeps getting better," I said. I was gripping the counter above the dishwasher as if I needed its support to be able to say all these things. "That's only going to make it hurt more when you leave."

"Leave?" Will shook his head in confusion.

"Leave!" I said. I was the exasperated one now. "At the end of the summer, remember? When you go back to your kuh-nishes and the Brooklyn Bridge and . . ."

I trailed off when I remembered that Will didn't exactly have a life of glamour and happiness waiting for him back in New York. I waved a hand in front of my face as if it could erase what I'd just said.

"Just," I revised, "when you leave *here*."

"Oh." Will cocked his head to the side. "Huh."

"So you hadn't thought of that at all?" I said.

"I guess not," Will said. "I mean, yeah, I knew it was out there. August twenty-ninth. That's the date on our return plane tickets. But, Anna—that's ages away."

"It'll fly by," I said glumly. "It already has."

"So that's a reason to ruin the time we *do* have?" Will said.

"Who's ruining anything?" I said. I pushed myself away from the counter and stalked over to the tall shelving unit where we kept the paper products. I yanked down a stack of napkins and pushed my way through the swinging door into the ice cream parlor. After the bright lights of the kitchen, the shop felt dark and shadowy. I stumbled a bit as I headed to a table in the kids section and began to push napkins into the spring-loaded dispensers.

I could feel Will behind me, staring at the back of my head, but I didn't turn around.

"Just don't think about that," Will urged me. "Think about now. Think about the other night!"

"I don't know if I can do that," I grumbled.

"You probably never pull all-nighters because you forgot to study for a test, do you?" Will said.

I whipped around and glared at him. My eyes had adjusted to the dusky light and he looked annoyingly handsome.

"I guess I'm just not as cool as you," I said. "I can't just live in the present."

"Well, you don't really have a choice, do you?" Will said with maddening logic. "I mean today is today. You're *in* it, Anna. And you can be in it with me, say, walking to that dumb place down the boardwalk and getting some curly fries. Or you could just stay here and make that grocery list for a shopping trip that's not going to happen for a week."

I bit my lip and looked away from him. I just . . . I just needed a minute to think. I went to the table where Will had been sitting when he'd first come in that evening. I started to stuff a wad of napkins into the dispenser. But then a doodle on the chalkboard tabletop caught my eye.

It was a tree.

A big, messy, sprawling tree covered with familiar-looking five-pointed leaves—not to mention a pink bicycle, a bunch of pinwheels, and a snake twined around its trunk.

Also on Figgy Pudding's trunk? One of those old-timey hearts with initials inside: *AP* + *WC*.

"Aw . . . ," Will said as he saw me staring at the chalk drawing. "I'm an idiot. I'll just . . ."

He grabbed a napkin out of the dispenser and wadded it up, clearly intending to smudge out the heart, the whole thing.

"No!" I cried, grabbing his wrist before he could get near the drawing.

It was the first time we'd touched that night.

We looked at each other, wide-eyed. An instant later we were tangled up together, kissing so hard that I couldn't breathe. Clearly Will couldn't either because when we pulled apart, we both gasped. This made us laugh until we'd exhausted what little breath we had left. Then we were kissing some more, and giggling at the same time. It was kind of messy—but wonderfully so.

At some point during all the making out, I sat on the chalkboard table and wrapped my ankles around the back of Will's knees. Later we'd discover that my backside had smudged Will's drawing, ruining it completely.

"It was only gonna get erased tomorrow," Will said with another big chuckle.

At that moment it was easy for me to shrug it off too. It didn't matter that I couldn't save the drawing; stash it in my vanity drawer to keep forever. It had been a moment. One of countless wonderful moments I'd had—and would have—with Will.

That was, if I let myself have them.

As Will and I locked up The Scoop and headed giddily down the boardwalk together, I told myself that I could. I could handle being with Will now, even if I had to say good-bye to him later. It was worth it.

But did that mean I could forget about that looming good-bye? About August 29?

Not really. Not, in fact, for a minute.

After that, I didn't want to waste another minute of my time left with Will. But—we barely saw each other for an entire week. What thwarted us? The most unromantic obstacle you can imagine—the *weather.*

Every day Dune Island was pummeled by tropical thunderstorms. The rain, lightning, and thunder would start rolling in around ten o'clock. It would linger on and off through the day, like a grumpy guest constantly dozing off, then snorting himself awake right in the middle of your house. The storms held us hostage.

And during the brief windows between storms? The sun would come out baring fangs. The heat was wet and claustrophobic. Just breathing became a chore. You couldn't see all the spores and mold and motes floating through the air, but you knew they were there, and they made everyone feel cranky.

Steam rose off Highway 80.

The boardwalk developed a disgusting sliminess that never had a chance to dry out.

My bedsheets became so damp and sticky, I seriously considered sleeping in the bathtub. Figgy Pudding's decorations, of course, were ruined, and we pretty much had to forget about making waffle cones at The Scoop. They were too floppy to hold anything. My dad came up with the idea of passing out waffle cone rain checks and got a write-up in the *Dune Island Intelligencer* for it. Sophie was so embarrassed, she went into hiding for an entire day.

Me? I was sort of grateful for the diversion, even if it was an incredibly silly one. Because the rain had also seriously dampened my opportunities to be with Will.

We couldn't go anywhere outside because my parents wouldn't let me drive their car during the storms. And *I* wouldn't let either of us ride our bikes to see each other.

"Anna, you spend half your life in the ocean," Will said on the phone one dark, thunderous morning. He was trying to coax me into meeting him for coffee on the boardwalk. "You're not willing to get a little wet for me?"

"Please, you think it's the water I'm worried about?" I said. "It's the lightning."

"Oh, come on, nobody really gets struck by lightning, do they?"

"Are you near a computer right now?" I asked. Cradling my phone between my ear and shoulder, I headed to the kitchen and grabbed my dad's laptop. Within a few seconds I'd sent Will a link to an article about the hundreds of coastal Georgians sizzled by strikes every year.

"Oh my God!" Will said as he scanned the article on his end.

"Yup," I said. "Lightning strikes and tractor accidents—*very* common cause of death and disfigurement around here."

"Talk about Southern gothic," Will said.

I closed the laptop. It was too wet and noisy to go out to the screened porch, so I wandered into the living room. Kat and Benjie were sitting on the floor with bowls of Cheerios in their laps and a board game between them. My mom was curled up on the couch with some knitting. It felt like one of those boring national holidays where there's nothing to celebrate and nothing to do.

"Speaking of gothic," I said, settling into the lumpy chair near the window, "did you hear about the new horror movie that's out? Sounds amazing. I heard it turned a reviewer's hair white. Needless to say, he gave it a thumbs-down."

"Why am I not surprised that you're not the romantic-comedy type?" Will snorted.

"A movie!"

That was my mom. I glanced over at her. She'd dropped her knitting into her lap and she was grinning at me.

"That's the perfect thing to do today," she said. "We could go to the first matinee. Your dad doesn't need me at The Scoop until four."

"Movie, movie!" Kat and Benjie shrieked, which of course, summoned a *thump thump thump* to the staircase. Sophie poked her head over the banister.

"Are we going to the movies?" she asked. "Can I ask Emily?"

"Sure," Mom said, getting to her feet and smoothing her hair. "That's why we got the minivan. Anna, tell Will we can be at his house in twenty minutes. I'll go get the movie section."

"Um," I squeaked, "but I didn't . . . um, Mom?"

Over the phone I heard Owen's voice saying, "Wait a minute, are you going to a movie?"

And then a female voice called, "Take your brother. He's driving me crazy."

Before we knew it, Will and I were going on a date to a Cineplex in Savannah—with almost everyone in our families. I didn't know whether to laugh or cry.

But Will laughed—so I did too. In fact, Will seemed goofily charmed by the whole thing—scrunching into my mother's van, running through the rain to the theater, waiting in line at the concession stand while Kat and Benjie debated popcorn versus candy.

Then we all split up to go to different theaters. Will and I went to the horror flick, my mom and the kids picked something G-rated, and Sophie and Emily chose a chick flick. Owen was on the fence, but at the last minute, he said to the girls, "Ah, what the heck. I'll go with you."

"Seriously, Owen?" I squawked while Sophie and Emily dissolved into delighted giggles.

I looked at Will in surprise.

"Does your brother really like chick flicks?"

"Let me ask you something," Will said as Owen sauntered

toward the theater with the girls. "Who among us has the most snacks?"

Sophie and Emily had a giant tub of popcorn to share and a box of candy each, plus Cokes. I pointed at them.

"Not for long," Will said.

"Your brother is literally going to take candy from children?" I said.

"Shamelessly," Will said. "He's the best food-filcher you've ever seen."

I laughed as Will and I walked into our own theater. When the doors closed behind us, Will looked around with exaggerated paranoia.

"Are they all gone?" he asked. "Are we alone?"

"At last!" I said with mock drama.

He grabbed my hand. We hurried down the aisle, sank low into a couple of seats, and finally, *finally* kissed each other hello.

"This is so much better than coffee," Will murmured as the lights went dark and the previews started.

"Yeah, because there's candy." I cackled, rattling the box of overpriced gummy bears that I'd bought at the concession stand.

"Yeah," Will said sarcastically, before he started kissing me again. "That's exactly why. The candy."

I laughed. Then I forgot about all the family members in the building and snuggled up with Will. With the air-conditioning blasting, I actually felt chilly for the first time in ages, and Will's warm arm against mine felt good. Over the sinister music of the movie trailers, you could just barely hear the soft patter of the rain on the roof. It was the coziest sound.

Instead of clasping my hand, Will rested his arm on mine and traced the inside of my wrist with his thumb. For some reason, this made my upper lip tingle. And not in a bad way.

I was just resting my head on Will's shoulder and getting up the nerve to breathe something romantic into his ear when I heard someone tumble into the seat right behind us.

Will and I peered over our shoulders.

"Owen?!" Will said through gritted teeth.

"Dude, I couldn't take the chick flick," Owen said. "There was a shopping montage in the very first scene! Hey, did you guys get any popcorn?"

Will's thumb left my wrist.

My head left his shoulder.

And let's just say, after that, I didn't miss one minute of the movie. (But at least it *was* horrifically good.)

For the rest of the Monsoon—as Will and I came to call that rain-ruined week—we saw each other only during damp, snatched moments at The Scoop.

So at night, we talked on the phone. And talked and talked and talked.

"You were in my dream last night," Will said during one of our epic conversations. I was on the screened porch during a lull in the rain. I lay on the hammock at an angle with one big toe on the sandy floorboards, pushing the swing back and forth.

"Will, that is the cheesiest line," I said with a laugh.

"No, it's true," he said. "And believe me, it wasn't that romantic. We were in a supermarket; this *endless* grocery store.

We kept going up and down the aisles like we were searching for the exit, but there never was one. It was actually kind of boring."

"Okay, that doesn't seem good," I said with a frown.

"Well, I know I was happy to be with *you*," Will said. "I was just ready to get out of that stupid store."

"Hmm," I said. "What was in our cart? No melons or whoopie pies, I hope. Because that would just be too ridiculously Freudian."

"Or, from what you've told me, Woody Allenian," Will said, laughing.

Another late night, I lay on my bed with the phone between my ear and the pillow. I watched the raindrops spatter my skylight. They made me think of these little water balloons Caroline and I made one night when we were eight. She was sleeping over while our parents went out for dinner together, leaving us with a sitter. We filled about a hundred balloons and nested them in a box, like a giant, jiggly litter of baby animals. Then we waited on the balcony. We waited for *four hours*. Finally my parents came home and we pelted them with every balloon in our box, after which Caroline wasn't allowed to sleep over for a long, long time.

I told Will this story because I knew it would make him laugh.

And because that was what we did during these meandering conversations. We told each other our silly stories and ancient memories and random thoughts. They were our ways of revealing ourselves to each other, even if we didn't always realize it. Sometimes these talks felt more intense, more intimate, than kissing.

"So you were always scary stubborn," Will said about the four-hour wait with the balloons.

"Just like *you've* always had issues with crustaceans," I retorted. One of Will's silly stories had been about him crying when his parents boiled a batch of lobsters during a long-ago vacation in Maine.

"Yeah, I was scarred by the murder of my little friends," Will admitted. "I don't know what I was thinking asking you to go ghost-crabbing that night."

"Oh, *I* know what you were thinking!" I burst out with a laugh.

Will laughed too.

"Yeah, I guess I was," he said, speaking in a shorthand that we both understood. "I guess I was."

And then we got quiet for a moment. I listened to the distant creaking of Will's front-porch rocker. He could probably hear the soft *slap-slap-slap* of the rain on my skylight. And both of our minds swooped back to that night with the ghost crabs, the night of our first kiss.

"I wish I could see you right now," Will said, his voice low and a little husky.

I wanted to see him too. Desperately.

It was the desperation that made a small part of me *not* want to see Will too.

Mostly, being Will's girlfriend made me feel the same way I did after acing a test in school: a little light-headed, a little proud, and somehow utterly relaxed while also buzzing with excitement.

But given that Will was a boy, and not an English midterm, my emotions were more complicated than that.

The more I was with Will, even on the phone, the more I *wanted* to be with him. I was starting to feel like I could never get enough of him.

I'd be reading a novel, washing my face, or making Benjie a peanut butter and jelly sandwich and suddenly I'd remember a certain kiss. Or a moment when Will's fingertips had grazed the side of my neck. Or the feeling of his warm hand resting for a moment on top of my head before skimming down my hair. I'd literally relive the sensation, my eyes fluttering shut, my body giving a little shudder. My mind was like a luxurious landmine. At any unpredictable moment, I might be overwhelmed by a memory, by a feeling, by Will.

I loved being so consumed by Will. Adored it. But I kind of hated it too, because I felt like a huge part of myself had been wrested from my control. I mean, sometimes you just want to make a peanut butter sandwich without being overcome by your own passion, you know?

The fact of August 29 only made it all worse. That's what turned my desire for Will into desperation. I hated to hang up the phone each night, even after we'd talked so much we were dry-mouthed and half asleep.

I'd watch the weather radar online to try to pinpoint the one lightning-free hour when I could safely dash to Will's house for a fifteen-minute make-out session, then dash back without being electrocuted.

My ice cream–making skills were off. One batch was bitter

with too much vanilla. Another ice cream emerged from the churn as a masterpiece, one of the most subtly delicious flavors I'd ever invented. Only then did I realize that I'd forgotten to write down any of the ingredients I'd used and had no idea how to re-create it.

Every time I even glanced at a calendar, I had to fight off tears.

Basically, I felt completely out of control. And as Will had already figured out, I didn't like being out of control. Since *he* was both the cause and the cure for this feeling, however, I was flummoxed as to what to do about it.

When the rain sputtered out for the last time on Saturday afternoon and Sam hatched the idea for a double date, it seemed like the perfect way to reunite with Will. I could be with him all night, but with my friends there to diffuse the intensity, the *need*, I was feeling.

Maybe I'll get used to being with Will again and I'll get a grip, I'd told myself as I got ready. I carefully chose my favorite pair of holey jeans and a fluttery, cream-colored off-the-shoulder top. I dusted my face with shimmery powder and swept my hair into a loose topknot with a couple of chopsticks. I looked cool, breezy, and probably a little too wholesome for our destination—The Swamp.

"So this is the famous Swamp," Will said when we arrived. "If possible, it's even . . . swampier than I expected."

"The name don't lie, my friend," Sam said, clapping Will on the shoulder.

"Oh, please, the whole island's a swamp after all that rain," Caroline complained, grabbing a tea-stained cardboard menu off the bar and fanning herself with it. "You know it's bad when *my* hair is frizzing."

I would have laughed, but I was too high-strung. I felt about as vulnerable as an oyster in high season.

We picked a round table near the wall of screens that divided the dining room from the deck. Like the rest of The Swamp, the table looked like it was one hard wallop away from splintering into little pieces. It was fork gouged and wobbly, and its putty-colored paint was peeling. On the table was a roll of paper towels (no holder), a sticky jar of jalapeño vinegar, and about eight different kinds of hot sauce.

The Swamp walls were darkly paneled. Every surface that didn't hold a dart board was covered with artwork made by Arnold Eber Senior, who was the father of Arnold Eber Junior, who owned The Swamp. Mr. Eber Senior was an outsider artist who pretty much made the same thing over and over again—life-sized preachers cut out of old sheet metal and painted with metallic car enamel. The preachers wore candy-colored suits and had black pompadours, as well as voice balloons coming out of their mouths that said *You'll burn in hell, sinner!* in about fifty different ways.

"Isn't this a bar?" Will asked, glancing at the neon Pabst Blue Ribbon sign by the door. There were also foamy pitchers on just about every table except ours. "How can anybody take a sip of alcohol with those guys *staring* at them?"

"Well, *you* don't have to worry about that, sweetheart," said a high, scratchy voice above our heads. Our waitress had just tossed a bunch of neon-colored wristbands onto our table. Stamped on each band in blocky letters was the word UNDERAGE.

"Hi, Helen," Sam, Caroline, and I singsonged together.

"Put 'em on, kids," she said, sounding bored. She fluffed up her white-blond bangs with her frosty pink fingernails. No matter how tan and leathery Helen got in the face, she would always have the hair and nails of a teenager.

"Helen," Caroline protested, "we know you wouldn't serve us, any more than we would ask to be served. Don't make us wear the nerdy bracelets."

"Don't make me call your mother, little girl," Helen said, scowling. "Now put 'em on."

We put 'em on.

"Back in a minute for your orders," Helen said, swishing away in her very tight white jeans.

I watched Will take in the other Swamp customers. The Swamp attracted a very specific clientele, which didn't include people like my parents, my teachers, or any other professional types. This place was for fishermen and oil-rig guys, truckers, off-the-gridders, and curmudgeons. *And* high school kids, because it was the only bar on the island that would let us in—with our blazing wristbands, of course.

It was definitely a slice of the "real" Dune Island.

And once again I was noticing that only because I was looking at it through Will's eyes. Sam and Caroline were oblivious. They were fixated on the clouds of bugs swarming just outside the screening.

"Look at all those mosquitoes," Caroline said, pressing her nose to the screen. "They're as big as birds!"

"Yeah, you know you want it!" Sam called out to the mosquitoes, pressing his bare arm up to the screen. "But you can't have it, skeeters!"

"Don't you think you're tempting fate, teasing them like that?" Will asked with a laugh.

"Whatever, I like to live dangerously," Sam replied, grabbing Caroline around the waist and giving her a squeeze.

Caroline laughed, but it was a little forced. I reached across the table, plucked the menu out of her hand, and slid it over to Will.

"Ooh, they have boiled peanuts," Will said when he'd given the short menu a read. "My new favorite food."

He grinned at me, and I swooped back to us kissing on the wool blanket on the Fourth of July, the salty, briny taste of boiled peanuts still on his lips.

And then I *had* to look away so I didn't pounce on Will. I glanced at Caroline, whose lip was curled.

"Trust me, you don't want Swamp boiled peanuts," she told Will. "They smell like old-man sweat."

"Caroline!" I said. "Gross."

"Sorry, but they do. They do, don't they, Sam?" Caroline said.

"I like 'em," Sam said with a shrug. "But if they skeeve you out, babe, we'll skip 'em. And no crawfish."

"Wow," I said. "Sam forsaking crawfish?"

Caroline squirmed in her seat, and I started to get what she'd been talking about when we were at the beach. It was sweet of

Sam to be so considerate, but it was also so *different*. He wasn't acting like the happy-go-lucky, unapologetic crawdad-eater that Caroline had fallen for.

The truth was, I didn't really want to suck the head of a mud-bug in front of Will either, so I didn't make a bigger issue of it.

Which left us in awkward silence, until Helen stalked over with a bucket of jalapeño-studded hush puppies. She thunked it on the table along with four red plastic tumblers of sweet iced tea.

"Um, I didn't order any tea?" Will started to say, but Helen wasn't hearing it. She spun on the heel of her pink Keds sneaker and bustled away.

"Sorry about that," Sam said to Will. "Like I said, the name don't lie. I guess we're just used to, you know, the rudeness."

"And the dirt," I said with a grin.

"And the old-man sweat," Caroline chimed in, giggling.

"And don't even think about going in the men's room," Sam said.

"Will," I said, "we can just drink our tea and go back to the boardwalk if you want. I guess when you think about it, The Swamp *is* kind of gross."

"No way," Will said, folding his hands behind his head and leaning back in his chair. "I love this place!"

But as he said it, he was looking at me, as if he was saying, I love *you*.

It made my heart dance around in my chest, but it also made my neck go prickly and sweaty.

"Music," I announced. I held out my hand. "Who's got change?"

"I do," Will said, standing up to go with me to the jukebox by the front door.

"Great," I said just a little wanly.

The jukebox was not an antique and it wasn't charming. It was pure truck-stop-issue tackiness, with rainbow-colored lights skimming up and down the front and a digital CD selecter.

The songs ranged from new country to gospel to old country, along with a whole lot of Elvis. I'd always assumed that was the request of Mr. Eber Senior, who painted Elvis hair on every one of his tin preachers.

"It's two songs for a dollar," I told Will, flipping through the titles in the jukebox. "Fast or slow?"

"Slow," Will said, slipping his arm around my waist. I couldn't help myself, I leaned into him. Perhaps because I'd been trying to resist Will, pressing up against him seemed to feel twice as good as usual.

Still, I didn't meet Will's eyes as I made my choices. Only one of them was slow. The other was a swivelly Elvis number.

Only as we were walking back to the table did I remember that Elvis is famous for being so sexy, he'd made teenage girls scream and faint.

Maybe that wasn't *the best choice after all,* I thought, groaning to myself.

When we got back to our table, it was Sam who was hot and bothered—but not in a good way. He was standing up and glaring at Caroline, whose arms were crossed over her chest.

"What *is* it lately, Caroline?" Sam was saying. His face, usually as placid as water, was pale with confusion and anger. "I just want to have a nice night out with you and you're not in the mood? I haven't seen you all week!"

"Well, whose fault is that?" Caroline retorted.

"What, you think I control the weather?!" Sam said. "Well, if tonight isn't *convenient* for you, maybe you'd be happier if I just left."

Caroline shook her head and said, "No, I wouldn't. It's just . . . "

She trailed off and shrugged helplessly.

"Well . . ." Now it was Sam who was searching for words. He spotted me—Will and I had taken a few steps away from the table as if that would give Sam and Caroline some privacy—and gave me a beseeching look.

I gave him a sympathetic grimace, but the last thing I could do was chime in on a fight between my two best friends. Talk about a minefield.

"I need some air," Sam muttered.

"It's a screened porch," Caroline pointed out.

Sam took a deep, frustrated breath, then slammed through the screen door that led to the big deck. Shooting off one corner of the deck was a narrow bridge that led to another, small, circular deck. Sam kept it together while he wove around the crowded tables on the deck, but when he hit the bridge, he broke into a loopy run.

"He's going to see the gators," Caroline said, hanging her head. "Well, I guess this wasn't the dream date either."

"Caroline," I said. "Why don't I go talk to him?"

Caroline shrugged and nodded.

"Do you mind?" I asked Will.

I saw his shoulders deflate just a bit, but he waved me out. "Yeah, yeah," he said. "Go."

Now I felt torn between all *three* of the people I was with. But I headed outside after Sam. Before I hit the bridge, I stopped at the cart where the waitresses kept the water pitchers and grabbed a handful of dryer sheets out of a box. They were supposed to ward off mosquitoes if you didn't have any bug spray handy. I tucked one into my jeans pocket and one into a strap on my sandal. I took the other two out to Sam.

He was sitting at the edge of the deck, dangling his legs over the swamp. He dipped his hand into a plastic garbage can filled with fishy smelling pellets and tossed some to the alligators arrayed in the swamp beneath his feet. There were so many, they looked like a very uncomfortable area rug, all prehistoric crags and sleepy, reptilian eyeballs.

"Maybe you should pull your feet up," I said to Sam. "You don't want the gators to think they're a snack, too."

"Aw, these guys are so domesticated, they don't even remember that they're carnivores," Sam said sadly. He threw another handful of chow at the alligators, who growled and snapped at one another as they lunged for the little tidbits.

I sank down next to Sam and handed him some dryer sheets.

"Thanks," he said. "I forgot to get these. And Will was right. The mosquitoes are getting their revenge on me."

He slapped at a few of them as he tucked the dryer sheets into his pockets.

"Okay, so what is it?" he said, looking me in the eye. "How am I screwing things up with Caroline?"

"Why are you so sure you are?" I said.

"Aw, come on, Anna," Sam said, looking miserable. "I was bound to. I mean, I waited all that time to tell her how I felt because I was scared it would screw everything up. That *I* would screw everything up. Now I guess I went and did it, hard as I've tried not to."

"Sam," I said, "why *are* you? Trying so hard, I mean."

Sam looked at me like I was a little challenged.

"Anna! Because she's *Caroline*. She deserves it."

"Yeah, and you're *you*," I retorted. "Remember? The guy that Caroline fell for? Why do you feel like you have to be different from before, just because you guys are, you know . . ."

"Makin' hay?" Sam drawled with a mischievous grin.

"Oh, my God," I laughed. "You are so *country*."

Sam laughed too, briefly. But then he sobered up again.

"The thing is, things *are* different now," he said. "They can't not be. And if we can't make it work as a couple, that's it. Friendship's over. Maybe it'll ruin my friendship with you, too."

"It won't!" I said fiercely.

"Yeah, well, it's easy to say that now," Sam said sadly. He stared down at the rumbling gators. "I never should have told her."

"No!" I insisted. "You shouldn't regret going for it, Sam. It was so brave of you. Maybe that's what you need to be now that you're together."

"Brave?" Sam said, looking confused.

"Confident," I said. "You're worthy of Caroline. Don't forget it."

"Huh," Sam said, giving me a sheepish glance. This was pretty touchy-feely for us. I guess he was right about everything being different now. And not just with him and Caroline.

"Sounds like you're saying I just need to get over myself," Sam said.

"Yeah," I said. "Like Caroline always says." Now we grinned at each other. We had shorthand too, me and Sam.

After a thoughtful moment, I cocked my head.

"You know what else might be going on with Caroline?" I said. "I think she's mad at you because you've softened her up."

"Caroline?" Sam said. "Never."

"No, you have," I said. "She's gaga over you, and I think she doesn't like to feel that vulnerable."

"You guys are peas in a pod in that area," Sam said, flinging another handful of gator chow into the water.

"Um, what?" I said with a barky little laugh.

"Well, you're doing the same thing Caroline is," Sam said. "In a way. Anybody can see it, Anna. On the Fourth of July, you didn't know anybody was at that barbecue except Will. But now there's, like, this wall between you."

"Sam," I said, half outraged, half impressed. "Have you been watching chick flicks or something? You seem to know what you're talking about."

"I know *you*," Sam said. "I know you think too much. I know you like to hold this whole island at arm's length. And now you've found someone you *don't* want to hold at arm's length and it scares the hell out of you."

Whoa. It looked like Caroline wasn't the only one who could turn that mirror of truth on me.

"Sam," I said. It came out as something close to a moan. "I have less than seven weeks left with Will."

"Yeah, and . . . ?" Sam said.

"The harder I fall for him, the harder it's going to be when he leaves," I said, hating how needy that made me sound. "And *then* what do I do?"

"You do what you would have done anyway," Sam said. "You go to school. You make amazing ice cream. You crush Landon Smith's soul when he asks you to the junior prom and you turn him down. You just . . . deal."

"I deal," I said, rolling my eyes. "You make it sound so easy."

"It isn't, but you do it anyway," Sam stated with a shrug. He slapped at a mosquito on his leg.

"I don't think these dryer sheets really work," he said. "It's one of those urban myths."

I laughed.

Then we were quiet for another minute or two. We tossed nuggets to the alligators, zoning out to the swishing of their tails until we got to our feet and started back across the bridge. But before we reached the main deck, Sam stopped and turned to me.

"You know, *you're* brave too, Anna," he told me. "And strong. You can take it. Will leaving, I mean."

Suddenly I had that same choky feeling I got every time I glimpsed a calendar. It didn't exactly make me feel strong.

But Sam had been right about everything else. I *had* been

trying to push Will away to protect myself. And *that* was definitely weak.

So I decided to get over myself. For real this time. I pushed ahead of Sam and stalked right back into The Swamp. When I saw that Will was sitting alone at our table, I plunked down next to him. Then I planted a big kiss on his lips.

"Wow," he said. His smile was immediate and wide. "You smell like clean laundry. I *love* the smell of laundry."

This time, I didn't look away when he said it. Instead, I kissed him again.

"Now, none of *that*, children," Helen said as she skimmed by with steaming buckets of food dangling from both arms. Will and I broke apart, bright red, but grinning.

"So," Will said, raising his eyebrows at me, "good talk with Sam?"

I glanced around to make sure Helen wasn't looking. Then I gave Will one more kiss, sweet and lingering.

"Yeah," I said, gazing happily into his eyes. "Good talk."

The dinner invitation from Will's mom had been casual enough. It came a few days after our night at The Swamp, when I'd stopped by to pick up Will for a morning swim.

"We're going to get some fish for the grill tonight," Ms. Dempsey had said. "Why don't you join us?"

Since it happened to be my night off from The Scoop, I said yes without thinking twice about it.

But now that I was knocking on Will's cottage door at

six p.m., I felt a nervous thrill. Like our first kiss and our first fight, the first dinner with Will's family seemed like a sort of milestone. I gulped when Will swung the door open, his hair still wet from the shower. His T-shirt stuck to his skin in places where he hadn't dried off before throwing on his clothes.

He looked so irresistible, I wanted to throw my arms around him and bury my nose in his shampoo-scented neck. But we were in his doorway, with his mother bustling around the kitchen behind him. There was also the minor obstruction of all the things I was carrying.

"Anna?" Will said, grinning at me. "Are you in there?"

I plopped the rather large bunch of flowers I was holding into Will's arms.

"It's just a few hydrangeas," I said, fluffing up the pompoms of tiny blue-and-purple blooms. "I snipped them on my way out of the house. They're gonna start shriveling up in the heat soon anyway."

"A *few*?" Will said, pretending to stagger under the weight of the (not *that* huge, I swear) bouquet.

I followed Will into the kitchen. The big, open living/dining room was classic rental cottage. Everything was the color of ocean, sky, and sand. Every available surface was covered with sand dollars, starfish, driftwood seagull sculptures, and glossy wood plaques that said things like *Our memories of the ocean will linger on long after our footprints in the sand are gone.*

"Oh, Anna!" Ms. Dempsey said when she saw the hydrangeas. "Those are beautiful! Where did you get them?"

"Just, you know, from my front yard," I said.

Ms. Dempsey clapped a hand on her forehead.

"Of course, I remember noticing those amazing bushes at your house on the Fourth," she said. "You know, you live in New York long enough, you forget that flowers don't all come from the deli wrapped in plastic."

While Ms. Dempsey left in search of a flower vase, I plunked my other packages—a soft cooler and a grease-stained white paper sack—on the Formica counter. Will unzipped the cooler.

"Anna," he burst out. "There are *four* pints of ice cream in here!"

"Well, *I* can't exactly show up at a dinner party without ice cream, can I?" I said with a shrug.

"And what's that?!" Will asked, pointing at the paper bag.

"Um, just some fried pies," I said. "Well, a dozen. To go with the ice cream. What? Too much?"

Will wrapped his arms around me with that delighted/bewildered expression that I'd come to recognize.

"Yes," he said very softly, planting a sweet, smiley kiss on my lips. "Too much."

"You really are a Yankee," I whispered, grinning up at him. "This is nothing. Most people would have brought a casserole, too."

An instant after we parted, there was a shriek from the kitchen doorway.

I spun to stare at Ms. Dempsey, my heart flapping around my chest like an injured bird.

She just saw me kissing her son, I thought. *And now she's going to sit me down and give me a lecture about respect and boundaries, from which I will never recover.*

Ms. Dempsey's scream brought Owen running from the long, narrow hallway that led to the bedrooms. He was holding a book and wearing chunky black glasses that made him look like a nerdy hipster. I glanced at the book cover. David Foster Wallace. I raised my eyebrows, impressed, but Owen didn't notice. He was looking a little freaked-out.

"What happened?" he burst out.

"Are those . . . Hubley's fried pies?" Ms. Dempsey asked me breathlessly.

Hubley's logo—a grinning peach flashing a thumbs-up—was stamped in blurry purple ink on the side of the bag. Hubley's was a bare-bones bakery on Highway 80. They made cakes and cookies, but nobody paid any attention to those. You went to Hubley's for one thing and one thing only—half-moon-shaped, white-glazed fried pies.

"Those *are* Hubley's," I told Ms. Dempsey, the bird in my chest starting to calm down. "Have you had them?"

"Not for twenty years!" Ms. Dempsey sighed. She peeked into the bag and breathed in the pies' burned-sugar scent. "Mmmm. You won't believe this, but when I talk to my composition students about recalling sensual imagery, I use Hubley's fried pies as my example. I tell them about the glaze that piles up in the crimps of the crust and the almost-too-much nutmeg that makes your mouth tingle . . ."

Owen pulled off his glasses and rolled his eyes.

"Uh-oh," he said to Will. "Nostalgia alert."

"I just can't believe I forgot to make a pilgrimage to Hubley's myself," Ms. Dempsey said to us, shaking her head. "It's literally in my lesson plan."

"I got peach," I told her, "cherry, and sweet—"

"Sweet potato!" Ms. Dempsey interrupted, almost jumping for joy. Between that and the jeans and stylishly frayed T-shirt she was wearing, Ms. Dempsey looked about twenty years old. "That was the best one."

"Well, you can't leave Hubley's without the sweet potato pies," I said. "It's like a law."

"You know, I think that joint was actually in the guide book," Owen said, peeking into the bag.

"Anna, you are a sweetheart for bringing over all this stuff!" Ms. Dempsey said. "I'm going to eat big pile of them, even though it would give my yoga teacher back home a heart attack if she knew."

She took another whiff from the bag.

"Of course," she reconsidered, "they might not be as good as I remember."

She seemed to get a little pensive then, no doubt drifting into a memory.

"Mom," Owen piped up, "have one now. Call it an appetizer. I'll split it with you. We can save the rest for dessert."

Will crossed his arms over his chest and leaned against the counter, watching Owen break a pie in two and hand half to his mom. Will's face darkened, even looked a little sullen, and I remembered what he'd said about Owen's anti–Valentine's Day.

"I never would have thought of it."

But clearly he wished that he had.

My attention shifted to Ms. Dempsey when she took her first bite of the shiny glazed pie.

"Oh my God. It's exactly the same."

"So they were always that greasy?" I asked. "Even I can't eat too many of those in one sitting. And Will will tell you, I can *eat.*"

I shot Will a conspiratorial grin, but he seemed to have trouble returning it. That melancholy that I'd seen around his mouth and eyes when we'd first met—and which I'd barely detected since—was making his face seem long and pale.

Owen didn't seem to notice. He was too busy bonding with his mom over the revelation that was a Hubley's sweet potato pie.

"Yummm," he groaned. Then he glanced at his mom. "Maybe we should split another one?"

Ms. Dempsey giggled like a kid.

"Well, while they're fresh," she said, digging into the bag. "Anna, Will? Don't you want some?"

"I'm going to wait until after dinner and have it with the Bananas Foster ice cream I brought over," I said. Now I had a conspiratorial grin for *her.* Clearly Will had gotten his taste for salt from his dad.

The thought jolted me. Will's dad. Will had barely told me anything about him—yet even I could feel his absence here. It created a halo of sadness around even this goofily delicious little moment.

"Okay!" Ms. Dempsey announced, popping the last bit

of her pie into her mouth and dusting off her hands. "I'm quitting until after dinner. And I'm doing an hour of vinyasa tomorrow."

"Yeah, heard that before," Owen said, pretending to yawn. He wandered over to the fridge and started pulling out paper-wrapped packages of fish. "I'll man the fire."

Over his shoulder he added, "Hey, Will. As long as we're getting all nostalgic, you should show Anna *the room*."

"The room?" I said.

"It's my room," Ms. Dempsey said. She went to the counter, which was piled with salad ingredients and unshucked ears of corn. "It's the only one the owners didn't strip bare of all character, then stuff with seashells and driftwood."

"This place *is* a bit of a theme park, isn't it?" I had to admit, eyeing a scary-looking coral collection on top of the microwave.

"But they left one room in all its old, fugly glory," Owen said. "That's how *I* ended up with the master bedroom."

He pumped his fist in the air and hooted before he started ripping open the packets of fish.

"C'mon," Will said, lightly hooking my fingers with his. "I'll show you."

"Wait, I don't think I made the bed today!" Ms. Dempsey gasped. "Anna, what will you think of me?"

"You're on vacation," I told her. "You're not supposed to make the bed!"

"Will, I like this girl," Ms. Dempsey said as she tossed the lettuce into a salad spinner.

I felt giddy as Will led me down the hall. His step seemed

to lighten too. We were clearly approaching the cottage's star attraction.

"Whoa!" I exclaimed as we walked through the door. "I think I went blind for a second there."

There was a lot of wallpaper. Zigzaggy orange and brown, seventies-glorious wallpaper. And a big, yellow faux-fur rug. Clustered on one wall was a collection of framed needlepoints of owls, mushrooms, twiggy-looking girls in short A-line dresses, and other blasts from the past. The curtains had little orange pompoms dangling from the hems, and the disheveled bedspread was orange velvet.

"I know, right?" Will said. "It's like a shrine. I lie awake sometimes wondering why the owners kept the room this way."

"Why on earth?" I said.

"Anyway, my mom laughed for five minutes straight when she first saw it," Will said. "Which was definitely better than her bursting into tears. So we like The Room."

"And *Owen* got the master bedroom," I teased. "Did you guys fight for it or something?"

"Nah," Will said. He picked an ancient troll doll up off the low dresser and spun it between his two palms so its bright orange hair stood on end. "Soon he's going to be living in a cinder-block dorm with a roommate. I figured I'd throw him a bone."

"NYU, huh?" I said.

"The honors program," Will said, looking both proud and a little gloomy. "Full scholarship. You wouldn't know it to look at him, but Owen's kind of a genius. Someday he's gonna cure cancer or something."

"Right now it seems like he's trying to cure your mom," I said.

Will's mouth formed a grim line. For the first time I noticed that only one side of the queen-sized bed was unmade. The sheets and quilt were all over the place, and the bedside table was littered with books. The other side of the bed was still tucked, the nightstand bare.

"Do you miss your dad?" I asked Will quietly.

He shook his head angrily.

"Nope," he said. "I guess maybe I miss the past when, you know, everyone was together, but . . ."

"It must be a lot of pressure," I said. We both leaned against the edge of the dresser, our upper arms pressed together. Will was still fussing with that dumb troll. "Being the only one left with your mom after Owen leaves?"

"I guess," Will said, looking down.

"You know, you don't have to make up some ingenious scheme, or cure cancer, to cheer her up, right?" I said. "You just need to be *you*."

"Well . . ." Will gave me a heavy-lidded glance before returning his gaze to his mom's smashed pillow. "Thanks but it's not that simple."

"I know," I said. I leaned my head on his shoulder. "I know."

I guess this was another milestone—Will showing me how he really felt about what had happened to his family. I realized that the more Will and I revealed to each other about our quirks, our passions, and our wounds, the more complicated our relationship would become. We were getting more serious. The knowledge filled me with a surge of happiness . . . and a twinge of trepidation.

The rest of the month slipped by in a watercolor wash of swimming, snacking, strolling, and of course, kissing and talking, talking and kissing. As every day got hotter, we moved more slowly, like the lizards that dozed the days away under flat rocks.

Will took to showing up at my house early in the mornings to help me and Sophie fish prickly cucumbers off our vines and fill bulging grocery sacks with teardrop tomatoes. The tomatoes were ripening so fast now, we pretty much had to eat them as fast as we picked them.

Kat and Benjie were in charge of picking the blueberries, but Will and I helped them with the tall branches. We worked side by side, munching a piece of toast or a Belgian waffle with one hand while we gathered fistfuls of fruit with the other. We tossed the warm berries into a basket that rested on the ground between us, and somehow our picking rhythm always had us reaching down at the same time, our fingers grazing one another and our eyes meeting through the leafy branches.

By the time we finished picking, even though it was barely nine 'o clock, we'd be sweaty and spent. We'd stumble onto the screened porch, turn the ceiling fans to turboblast, and flop onto the hammock.

Or we'd coast our bikes to the beach and swim under the pier. Our laughter and chatter echoed in the dank cave of wooden planks and logs. When we couldn't take any more slimy seaweed twining around our ankles, we braced ourselves and swam back into the relentless sunshine.

We couldn't get enough shaved ice.

During all our lazy hours together, I memorized every detail of Will's face. The little crescent that appeared at the right corner of his mouth when he smiled, for instance, was deeper than the one on the left. Fanning from his eyes were white needles of untanned skin that had been sheltered from the sun by his squint. (Will didn't wear sunglasses either.) And he had just a hint of love handles around his muscled waist.

Someone else might call these flaws, but I liked these little detours on Will's body even more than the perfect parts of him. Maybe because they felt like my secrets, so obscure that nobody except Will's girlfriend could possibly notice them.

Will usually spent the afternoons with his mom and Owen while I worked, but just about every night, he came to The Scoop in time to flip the OPEN sign to CLOSED, then help me wash ice cream scoops, stuff napkin dispensers, and maybe even whip up a batch of custard to be churned the next day.

We often worked silently, side by side, intent on finishing as quickly as possible so we could get to the boardwalk or the beach; so we could just be together and talk—or not talk.

Sometimes it felt like our breathing slowed to match the waves.

The length and the sameness of the days were comforting to me. Each day felt endless, as if one just blended into the next. I couldn't have counted all the kisses, the embraces, the times we dozed off together on the hammock with iced tea glasses leaving sweaty rings on the floorboards beneath us.

I tried to lose track of the days of the week. I denied the fact that the sun was setting a few minutes earlier each day. I ignored anything that would mark time.

But there was one Dune Island milestone I *had* to show Will, even if it forced me to face the fact that July was coming to an end. And that was the hatching of the sea turtle eggs.

On the thirty-first, the Dune Island LISTSERV went crazy. That night, we were all assured, was going to be *the night*—birthday for hundreds of tiny loggerhead turtles.

When I told Will about this during that morning's meandering swim, he grinned.

"You mean the POTATOhead reign of terror is actually going to end?"

POTATO was the *really* bad acronym for the group called Protectors of Turtles and Their Offspring. In June the sea turtles had dug their nests in the dunes. Ever since, the turtles' protectors (or POTATOheads, as Will called them) had been camping out next to every nest.

The POTATOheads huddled in front of their little pup tents until around midnight, making sure no people stepped on the nests and no animals made off with the eggs. Then they grumpily went to sleep with their tent flaps open and their ears cocked for intruders.

They took their POTATO duties *very* seriously, and Will mocked them every chance he got.

"Will," I scolded him after the reign of terror crack. "You know loggerhead turtles are extremely endangered."

"I know, I know," Will said, lifting his shoulders from the water in a shrug. "I mean, it's great what these folks are doing. But do they have to be so *grim* about it? This one lady took my flashlight the other night and literally slammed it against a rock until it broke."

"Well, lights can confuse the baby turtles," I said. "If they're blinded by our cameras or flashlights, they can't find the horizon and crawl their way to the ocean."

"I'm just saying," Will said, "she could have just asked me to turn it off."

"Maybe the POTATOheads are just looking for a little excitement," I said. I dribbled a fistful of salt water on top of my head, which felt like it was sizzling in the sun. "In case you haven't noticed, Dune Island gets a little boring around this time of year."

Will dove under the surface, then came up with his arms around me. Water streamed down his face, but his eyes were wide open and smiling.

"No, I hadn't noticed," he said, before kissing me deeply. Which made me seriously consider just bagging the whole turtle-watching thing in favor of spending the evening making out.

But Will loved Dune Island rituals, and this one was the Dune-iest of them all.

When I was a kid, my family and I had tried to watch the turtles hatch many times. Every year the effort had been a bust. We'd stay until midnight, see not even a single hatchling, and then my parents would drag their sleepy kids home. It seemed the baby turtles always emerged right after we left. Or the very next night. But never for us.

To tell the truth, I expected that to happen again this year. But I decided not to tell Will and squelch his anticipation.

That night after sunset, Will and I joined a few dozen turtle-watchers at a rarely used beach entrance off Highway 80. A narrow, creaky bridge vaulted us over the dune grass into the turtles' protected area. Waiting at the end of the gangplank (at least, that's what it felt like) was a POTATOhead.

And not just any POTATOhead. It was Ms. Humphreys, who'd been my seventh-grade science teacher. Ms. Humphreys could make any middle-school kid's insides shrivel up with a single glare. She was terrifyingly tall with a long, fuzzy steel-gray braid and a hawkish nose. She was the only teacher who'd *ever* given me detention.

Will grabbed my hand and squeezed.

"That's the one who broke my flashlight," he said. "The brute strength on that woman. It's formidable!"

I tried not to snort.

I gave her a shy glance and suddenly realized that her hooked nose was less birdlike than it was turtleish. Her eyes had a reptilian coldness about them as well.

Well, now I know where the passion comes from, I thought, then immediately bit my lip and squeezed Will's hand to keep from laughing.

Ms. Humphreys glared at us, her small, dark eyes glittering in the moonlight.

"No talking," she ordered our group in a loud, hissing whisper. "You could scare the offspring. No cameras, flash or no flash. No flash*lights*. No trash. No food. You may drink beverages, but no alcohol. Note the orange flags marking the placement of the nests."

Ms. Humphreys pointed with a knobby finger at dull orange flags attached to thin metal rods. They demarcated a wide swath of sand.

"Stay outside those flags!" Ms. Humphreys threatened. "Lastly, be patient, people. It's likely that the offspring have already hatched and are, as we stand here, digging their way out of their nests. They may emerge tonight, but they may not. It's their business, not ours."

Ms. Humphreys stepped aside.

But we were all too intimidated to do anything but gape at her. The only sound was the distant roar of the waves and the nervous rustling of everyone's Windbreakers. Until Ms. Humphreys finally growled, "I said no talking, yet now you are making me use my *voice* to tell you to *move it, people*?"

We all jumped, then hurried down the steps, fanning out on both sides of the large, flag-marked area. In the dunes behind us, several nests were surrounded by bright orange posts and *lots* of threatening signage.

Everybody went to stake out a spot along the line of flags. Some people paced the sand excitedly. Others sank gingerly onto blankets, sitting ramrod straight. Will and I hadn't brought a blanket so we simply plunked down in the sand and cuddled up together.

Then we all stared at the nests, willing the little hatchlings to come out and start creeping toward the sea. The waiting sand almost seemed to glow in the moonlight.

But of course, nothing happened.

"I think we might be here for a loooong time," I breathed into Will's ear.

"With absolutely nothing to do," Will said. "Except . . ."

Well, I thought as Will leaned in to kiss me, *I guess we're going to spend the evening making out after all.*

The almost-full moon was a good notch higher when Will and I came up for air. Shyly, I glanced at the silhouettes around us, wondering if anyone had noticed what Will and I had been up to.

But most people seemed absorbed in their own little worlds. The individuals stared needily at the turtle nests. The couples whispered or maybe did a little making out themselves. I was relieved to realize that it was hard to tell what anybody looked like or what they were doing.

It was a strange feeling, being here to experience this profound moment with, but *not* with, all these people. The anonymity of them somehow made me feel closer to Will, the one I *could* see. And touch. And taste . . .

With that thought I was ready to resume the kissing, but Will was distracted. He was staring at the moon over the ocean. In its glow he looked a little nervous, his lips pressed together, his jaw tight.

"Will?" I whispered. I touched his shoulder and felt a lurch of nerves myself.

Don't, I pleaded in my head. *Don't say anything to mess this up.*

I'd been doing a pretty good job of living in the lazy, luxurious present with Will. Basically I was in big, fat denial—and loving it the way I loved an endless morning in the ocean or a giant bowl of ice cream.

But I knew my ability to maintain this willful state of delight was precarious. So I'd been trying to keep things between me and Will breezy and blissful. No heavy conversations. No allusions to our future (or lack thereof). I just wanted to *be.* With him.

But now I was sure Will was working up the courage to say something. And it didn't seem like it was going to be breezy.

Will got to his feet and searched for something in his pocket. Whatever it was seemed to be caught. After a brief struggle he finally extricated it, turning his pocket inside out as he did.

I stood up too as Will quickly stuffed his pocket back inside his pants. He was wearing, I realized, the same roughed-up khakis that he'd had on the first night I'd seen him at the bonfire. I found myself staring down at his pant legs. For some reason I didn't want to lift my eyes and look at him.

But finally he whispered, "Anna," and I had to.

He still looked nervous, but also happy. And a little sheepish.

"I got you something," he whispered, thrusting the thing that he'd pulled from his pocket at me.

"Like, a present?" I whispered back. I don't know what I'd expected, but it *hadn't* been a present. The idea of Will and me giving each other gifts had never occurred to me. Maybe because I knew we'd never have a Christmas together. And Will's birthday was in May, while mine was in October.

"Yeah, like a present," Will said.

I could barely see what Will was holding out toward me. Only when I took it could I tell that it was a square velvet sack, about the size of my palm, with something round inside.

I stared at Will.

"It's no big deal," Will started to say, forgetting to whisper. A chorus of *shush*es pelted us from all sides and Will ducked his head.

"It's just something I saw in one of those little boutiques on the boardwalk," he whispered very, very quietly, "and it made me think of you."

I continued to stare at him like a turtle in a flashlight beam.

Will's gaze dropped to his feet and he shook his head, muttering to himself. I had a feeling this moment was not going at all how he'd wanted it to.

I opened the cinched top of the little velvet bag and pulled out a bracelet—a silver bangle that was somehow both chunky and delicate. It was shaped like a flat ribbon with three half twists in it. It immediately made me think of a high diver gracefully turning through the air before skimming into the water.

"It's a Möbius strip," Will explained, still whispering. "It's kind of an optical illusion."

Will put my fingertip on one thin edge of the silver ribbon, then guided it around the twisty circle. The metal felt slick and cool. As my finger traveled along the edge of the bangle, Will kept turning it and turning it.

"See, it only has one side and one edge," Will whispered.

"You can follow along it forever and it never ends. Cool, huh?"

"I . . . love it," I whispered. I slipped the bangle onto my wrist, enjoying the weight of it. Then I put a hand on each of Will's shoulders, stood on my tiptoes so that we were almost eye to eye, and repeated myself. "I love it."

Will kissed me softly. When we sat back in the sand, we didn't talk or kiss. We just gazed toward the loggerhead nests. I think Will was a bit drained. Maybe he'd been nervous all night about giving me the gift.

As for me, I was stunned.

Suddenly everything felt different. Solid. As solid as this pretty band of silver.

I wrapped my hand around the bracelet. It was a memento of Will, one that I *could* keep in my vanity drawer forever if I didn't intend to wear it every day. But I very much *did* intend to wear it every day. It immediately felt like a part of me.

Like Will was a part of me.

And *that* was heavy indeed. It made me feel ecstatic and shaky all at once.

But before I could even begin to process it, I heard a gasp.

Somebody on the other side of the orange flags stood up. She began bouncing on her toes and pointing urgently toward the dunes.

We all scrambled to our feet and stared into the dune grass, which seemed to be jostling and rustling. Collectively, we held our breath. Literally. I could *feel* the people around me inhale and then stop. Frozen. Waiting.

And then—there they were. At first I just saw one or two little black discs creep out of the grass. They were tinier than I'd expected, maybe the size of my thumb.

As these first hatchlings started inching their way forward, a sudden flood of them followed. They almost looked like a wave of ants spilling out of a mound but, of course, a lot cuter. There were *hundreds* of them. The turtles' legs moved stiffly and rhythmically. They began to parade with surprising swiftness toward the water.

I clapped my hand over my mouth (and clocked my chin with my new bangle) to smother a cheer.

I could tell other people were having trouble containing their excitement too. Will perhaps most of all. He threw his arm around my shoulders and jumped up and down.

"This is the most amazing thing I've ever seen," he hissed, trying to be quiet.

A few of the hatchlings seemed to be confused and headed toward the orange flags instead of the sea. A turtle watcher leaned over the barrier and gently nudged them in the right direction with his fingertips.

But most of the little turtles knew exactly where to go. Their flat, winglike legs churned so hard they almost hopped down the sand.

Tears sprang to my eyes. I wanted to cheer for the little turtles, but since I couldn't, I just clasped my hands beneath my chin and grinned as I watched them.

I think every person on that beach—maybe even Ms. Humphreys, too—was feeling one simple emotion at that moment: joy.

The turtles started to reach the water. The breakers crashed into them, sending them tumbling backward and skidding sideways. Most of them immediately regained their bearings and kept on creeping.

And then the waves began to sweep them out to sea.

"They're making it!" I said to Will, pointing at the disappearing turtles.

Will was grinning back at me when I heard the first squawk.

Seagulls.

The sound was familiar. I heard gulls every day at the beach. Or rather, I *didn't* hear them. They were just white noise, like the waves and the soft whoosh of the breeze. I never gave them a thought.

But these gulls hovering over the beach—their wings arched out to the sides and their bills aimed downward—weren't wallflowers anymore. They were predators. Greedy, *mean* sea rats, getting ready to strike.

"Oh no," I muttered. Then the first seagull made its dive.

It must have been the easiest hunt of their lives. Each gull swooped down, plucked up a turtle, then flapped away, squawking in triumph.

People started making noise.

Men took off their T-shirts and flapped them in the air, trying to slap the birds away, but the gulls just dodged them and flew to the middle of the turtle pack. The only way to get at them would be to hop the orange flags and risk crushing the turtles under our feet.

I wanted to scream as I watched one gull snatch up a

hatchling by its leg. The rest of its body dangled, limp, from the gull's hooked beak.

I found myself looking back at Ms. Humphreys, who still stood at the foot of the bridge. Her back was straight. She seemed stoic. In fact it looked like she was gazing at the surf, not at the diving seabirds. She was focusing on the hatchlings that got away, rather than the ones that died.

Maybe this was why Ms. Humphreys was so harsh. Every summer she guarded those little eggs with all the viciousness of a mama bear (since mama turtles obviously weren't the most protective types) only to see scads of them gobbled up before they'd even had a chance to begin their journeys.

And as anybody who's gone to school on Dune Island knows, the carnage doesn't end on the beach. Big, toothy fish, crabs, and countless other predators nab more of the hatchlings once they hit the water. Only a tiny fraction of the turtles survive.

Those who do could live for decades. Still, as I watched the gulls feast, the odds against the sea turtles seemed devastating.

I started shaking.

The bangle bracelet suddenly felt intrusive and unfamiliar around my left wrist. I wrapped my right hand around it, squeezing it until it pressed into my skin, probably leaving a mark.

I started crying.

No, I sobbed. In big, loud, embarrassing heaves.

I turned and stumbled away from the hatchling run, heading north. I wanted to put my fingers in my ears to block out the horrible squawks of the gulls, but that seemed even more childish than running away.

So I just ran until all I could hear were the waves and, a moment later, the huffing and puffing of Will running after me.

Immediately he wrapped his arms around me. He held me while I gasped and sniffled.

But I didn't melt into him the way I usually did. I couldn't.

"I'm sorry, I'm sorry," Will said. "But think of how many of the turtles made it to the water. They *made* it, Anna. And it was awesome."

This only made me stiffen more.

Will pulled back and looked at me in confusion.

"Anna?"

"What!" I blurted. Then I cringed. I'd sounded so impatient, even hostile.

"Sorry," I muttered.

Oh great, now I sounded sulky.

"Is this . . . ?" Will began. "Are you . . . ?"

He searched for the right thing to say, because he clearly had no idea what was wrong with me. I wasn't sure I knew myself. All I knew was I was suddenly hurting so much, my body almost ached with it.

I spun away from Will to face the ocean. I imagined turtles paddling their way through the dark shallows right in front of me. I could picture their tiny bodies buffeted by the water, but doggedly swimming along. Evolution had wired them for this. But it hadn't taught them how quickly, and brutally, everything could end for them.

This thought made me start crying *again*.

"Oh, Anna," Will moaned. "Stop. Please stop."

I shook my head angrily.

"I am *not* a crier," I declared.

I heard Will stifle a laugh. I should have laughed too. It had been a ridiculous thing to say under the circumstances.

But instead I whirled around and glared at him. It was dark on the beach, and my tears were blurring my vision, but Will *still* looked beautiful to me.

I wanted to look at him forever. But since I couldn't do that, suddenly I didn't want to look at him at all.

Or perhaps, ever again.

Every once in a while, my sisters and brother and I spend an obsessive day building a sand fort. We pack and smooth the sand until it looks as sturdy as cement. By day's end, part of me fantasizes that *this* fort will somehow last. It always seems impossible that something so strong, so solid, can just be washed away by the tide in less than an hour.

I realized now that I'd done same thing with Will. I'd built a happy little fortress of denial around us, filling it with blueberry picking, ice cream, and kisses. I'd convinced myself that August 29 would never *really* arrive.

But of course it would.

And when I forced myself to finally acknowledge this, it hurt like a sudden, startling muscle cramp. Like a flash of heat.

And who wouldn't try to protect themselves from that, right?

"Will," I said, shaking my head slowly and for too long. "I can't do this."

"We won't go back," Will agreed, glancing over his shoulder

at the loggerhead run. "Let's just go get some coffee or something. And we can talk."

"No!" I said. "I'm saying I can't do *this*. Us."

Will looked at me incredulously. And then his face shifted, subtly, to stone.

"If *I* can do this," he asked in a low almost-growl, "why can't you?"

"You don't know how badly it's going to hurt when you leave," I said. "Do you even care?"

"It'll hurt me, too," Will said. "Believe me."

"But the difference between you and me is"—I clutched at my middle with both hands, the way you do when you have a bad stomachache—"it's hurting me *now*."

"I don't get it," Will said. I saw his eyes flicker to the shiny bangle on my wrist. "Anna, I'm having the most amazing summer—because of you."

"And then your summer *ends*," I flung back, "and you go back to New York, to your old life where there's not a glimmer of me. But me? I'm still gonna be here bumping into you, the memory of you, *everywhere I go*."

"I know that," Will said. He took a step closer to me. "And it's not fair. But, Anna, we talked about this already. Why ruin what we have now just because we can't have it later?"

"Because that *does* ruin it for me," I said, backing away from Will.

"Well, if you ask me, *you're* ruining it," Will said. He crossed his arms over his chest and glared.

"You're a shoobee, Will," I said.

It was the first time I'd said that word to him, though certainly by then he'd probably heard it around the island. He probably also knew it wasn't complimentary. I saw shock register on his face, but I couldn't stop myself.

"You leave at the end of the summer," I said. "Maybe you go home and tell your guy friends about the townie you had a fling with. The one who couldn't pronounce 'knish.' The one who couldn't keep it casual like *you* could."

Will just shook his head in disbelief.

"Why are you doing this?" he asked.

"Because we're not the same, Will," I said. "That's why you don't understand how I'm feeling. And that's—"

I gasped, on the verge of tears again.

"And that's why we shouldn't be together," I declared.

Will stared at me.

And then he closed his mouth so hard, I could hear his teeth click. He shook his head angrily.

"You know," he said, "I get it now. You hate Valentine's Day and you love Independence Day."

"What does *that* mean?" I sputtered.

"You don't want to be with *anyone*, Anna," Will said. "Even me. Maybe *especially* me. Maybe you've just been looking for a way out."

Will stopped and swallowed. He stared at the ground, breathing hard. I stood there, my hands fisted at my sides, waiting for him to speak. I was still crackling with indignation but I also felt confused. *How* had this fight happened? It felt like it had come out of nowhere. And I couldn't make it stop.

When Will looked up again, his eyes were defeated.

"Well," he said quietly, "you got it. You got your way out."

He turned abruptly and stalked away with swift, sure strides.

As I watched him go in stunned silence, it occurred to me that Will was walking without stumbling. He had spent his first two months on the island struggling to get his bearings in the sand, always sinking in too deep or losing his balance in a hole. But now he was skimming over the beach like a local.

Like me.

Not that it changed the reality. He *wasn't* a local. And *I* was stuck here on Dune Island.

And that was that.

I watched Will until he was swallowed up by the darkness. Even if I had wanted to call out to him, I don't think I could have. My throat felt so choked, I was surprised I could breathe.

Will had gone back to taking my breath away.

This thought made me laugh. A dry, humorless laugh.

And then, instinctively, I turned to the ocean. I stared at the waves and cried—for a *long* time.

When I couldn't cry any more, I sat at the very edge of the surf and gazed at the water some more. Only the roar of the surf, pushing, pulling, and thrashing, could drown out my thoughts about Will. About everything.

At some point I jolted out of this trance and looked around, blinking. The moon had shifted in the sky. The turtle watchers had gone home. I was all alone.

And that's exactly how I felt—alone, which was perhaps even more shocking than what had happened between me and

Will. Never in my life had I felt lonely at the beach. Even on a weekday in winter when *nobody* was around, the sea and sand had always felt like a haven. Like home.

And now, I didn't want to be here.

Which meant I'd lost more than Will—I'd lost a part of myself.

And the part that remained was already roiling with regret.

August

My mom always says August in south Georgia is like February in Wisconsin. The weather is so beastly and unrelenting, it's like a cruel joke.

The ice cream is always runny, no matter how long it hibernates in the deep freeze. Our back field turns brown and crackly, littered with grasshopper husks and lost blueberries, as dry and hard as pebbles. The cicadas sound tired, their chirps thin and grating. Or maybe they're just drowned out by the grind of the air-conditioning units, which blast constantly, or so it always seems.

In August we all retreat indoors. We can't even stand the screened porch, where the ceiling fans just waft hot air at you, which is about as refreshing as being under a hair dryer.

My parents spend the month puttering (when they're not at The Scoop). My dad does the taxes on the dining room table and my mom pulls out her to-do list. Then she grabs any kid within reach and assigns him or her random, awful tasks like scrubbing the bathroom grout with an electric toothbrush or spray painting all the chipped air-conditioning vents.

Every year Sophie and I have to choose between two evils—mom and her chore chart or the furnace blast that was the world outside.

This August, I decided, I would stay in.

I wandered around the house for the first couple of days, clutching Judy Blume books under my arm. In chick flicks, brokenhearted women always seem to devour pints and pints of ice cream. That, of course, was normal behavior for me so I devoured Judy Blume instead.

I kept telling myself that, yes, I felt lonely and awful now. But if I'd let the relationship go on longer—and get that much more serious—the ending would only have been worse.

I was doing the right thing, I insisted in my head. I was looking out for myself.

I was being a realist.

I was being the strong one.

And did any of these things I told myself help? Not even a little bit.

By the end of day three (or was it four?), I couldn't stand my own wallowing any more. If I couldn't get happy, I decided, at least I could get distracted. So, I went to my mom, who was decked out in rubber gloves, scouring something in the kitchen sink. Dinner was over, Sophie was working with my dad at The Scoop, and Benjie and Kat were running around the backyard with dryer sheets hanging out of their pockets, snatching fireflies out of the air.

"Okay, what have you got for me?" I asked my mom, going over to the bulletin board where she'd tacked her to-do list. She'd been jotting on the long sheet of yellow legal paper for months.

The list was a little crinkled, with a tea stain on the corner and about four different colors of ink. I skimmed through it. I spotted *sand and stain porch table* and *organize photos, past 2 yrs.* I shuddered.

But if I read one more page of *Deenie,* I was going to throw myself off my bedroom balcony, so I stood my ground.

My mom turned around and leaned back against the sink.

"Oh, honey," she said. "You don't have to do anything. I know . . ."

I watched her face as she paused and searched her parental database for the proper words.

". . . I know you're going through a hard time right now."

Tears sprang to my eyes. I was grateful that neither of my parents had pried into what had happened the other night. They'd gotten the gist—that Will was no longer in the picture. And though I'd spied them exchanging lots of meaningful glances and gestures, they hadn't interrogated me about it. Even Sophie had been sympathetic in her own way. She'd offered to do my laundry, adding, "I'll even iron stuff so you don't have to look all wrinkled, the way you usually do."

The problem was, all this familial sensitivity hammered home how wretched my situation was. Which only made me feel more pathetic. It had gotten so bad that I had to fight off tears every time my mother even *looked* at me.

I hadn't been lying when I'd told Will that I wasn't a crier. I hated crying, especially in front of people. It was humiliating and soul baring and just . . . messy. So the fact that I was now a blubbering mess was making me *really* cranky.

I guess that was why, in response to my mother's completely

nice comment, I snarled, "*Mom*, could you please just be *normal* and give me one of the dumb chores already?"

Acting like such a jerk, of course, made me feel even worse. And trust me, *that* was a feat.

I don't *think* Mom was getting revenge for my smart mouth when she gave me shower curtain duty, but I couldn't be sure.

In case you're wondering, shower curtain duty means taking down the vinyl curtains from all three of our claw-foot tubs (and remember, a free-standing bathtub requires *two* shower curtains), laying them out flat, scrubbing off all the black mildew and pink mold that's accumulated at the seams, then hanging them back up.

It was a yucky, tedious, *hard* job and it suited me perfectly.

I was actually a little hopeful, as I unhooked the curtains from my parents' tub on the second floor, that the tedium would help me. Sam had once confided to me that he'd done some meditating after his parents' divorce and that it had really helped him just wash all the churning thoughts from his mind, even if it was only for the twenty minutes a day that he was able to sit still and focus.

What was more meditative, I thought, than scouring a giant sheet of funky plastic, inch by inch?

I got some soapy rags and headed outside, laying the curtains out on the patio.

I knelt before the yucky bottom edge of the curtain, took a deep, cleansing breath, and started to scrub.

Fifteen minutes later, I was ready to go back to my Judy

Blumes. If I'd done any meditating at all it had gone like this:

Okay, breathe in, breathe out. Focus on the task at hand and only the task at hand. . . .

Ugh, not only is this mold disgusting, it's not coming off. Why can't we just buy new shower curtains when they get all funky like this?

Okay, that's not very green. Something tells me meditators frown on disposable culture.

Maybe some bleach will help.

(Five minutes later.)

Okay, breathe in, breathe out, breathe—agh! Bleach is searing lungs!

(Suddenly, bleach smell reminds me of cleaning Scoop tables with Will.)

Don't think about Will, think about scrubbing. It's like a metaphor. I cleanse the curtain, I cleanse my mind of unwanted thoughts. Like thoughts about the last kiss I had with Will. I think I could still sort of taste it—until breathing in this bleach probably killed some of my taste buds!

Whatever, just breathe, darnit. Breathe in, breathe out—

Hey! I wonder if you could put these things in the washing machine!

And that pretty much was the end of my meditation—and my help with the to-do list. (For the record, the washing machine didn't work so well, either.)

So now on top of feeling tragic about Will and guilty about sassing my mom, I also felt like a failure at both my hideous chore *and* my meditation.

I climbed up to the screened porch and slumped onto the swing. Through the open front door, I could hear my mom rallying Kat and Benji for a bath.

"Hey, where are the shower curtains?!" Kat asked cheerfully, making me feel like even more of a loser. The air on the porch felt like warm, soggy wool on my skin and my hands smelled of bleach. Yet after a few minutes, the cricket chirps and the *creak, creak, creak* of the swing's chains began to make me feel a little less wretched.

I glanced through the window into the kitchen. The room was quiet, empty, and lit only by the small light over the stove. I'd always loved our kitchen at this time of night, when the cooking smells from dinner still hovered in the air but the counters and appliances were shiny clean, like blank canvases, lying in wait for inspiration.

Of course, tonight I had none. I hadn't had a vision, or a taste, for any ice cream for days. Which just . . . sucked. Usually I could *always* find comfort in ice cream. I loved zoning out to the I-could-do-it-in-my-sleep process of making the custard—heating the milk, tempering the egg yolks, whisking the cream. Then coming up with a new flavor always felt a little bit like magic; like having a muse whisper in my ear.

Now the muse was so very absent that I was worried it would never come back. I would live the rest of my days in this radio silence, never again to come up with a Pineapple Ginger Ale or Buttertoe.

Just as an exercise, I consciously tried to think of some new flavor. Something, anything, that I'd never heard of before. I actually squeezed my eyes shut and pressed my fingertips to my temples, but—nope. Nothing.

I was starting to feel a little panicky when I remembered something. I had a notebook—just a cheap, pocket-size one from the drugstore—in which I'd once jotted ice cream ideas for future reference. I'd started the list last summer, but when I'd gotten better at creating flavors on the fly, I'd forgotten all about it.

Where was it?

I dashed upstairs to my room and searched my dresser drawers, peeked into purses and tote bags, and even looked under the bed. I'd almost lost hope when I thought to look in the dusty old jewelry box on top of my dresser. Since I had almost no jewelry to speak of, I often tossed other random items inside.

I creaked open the wooden box and there, among some Mardi Gras beads and barrettes, was the notebook. I sighed with relief. My present self was clearly hopeless, but the past one just might come through.

I flipped through the pages hungrily; looking for an idea that made me feel zingy inside.

Once again, nothing. I simply felt tired and so lonely that I physically ached. And bitter. Oh, was I bitter.

But that was one reason I'd always loved making ice cream. It was such a sweet, simple antidote—if a temporary one—to all of life's bitterness. It was a little vacation that lasted until you popped the last bite of your sugar cone into your mouth.

After losing Will, I was finding it hard to care about much of anything, but deep down I knew I still cared about this. I didn't want to lose this.

So I decided to choose a recipe at random. I closed the notebook and reopened it, landing on a page with the heading *Greek Holiday*. The title, I remembered vaguely, had been inspired by an Audrey Hepburn movie my mom had rented.

I skimmed the ingredients: *honey, orange zest, a little almond oil, maybe some crushed pistachios.*

If I wasn't exactly moved, I wasn't repelled either. I might have even been a tiny bit intrigued. It wasn't a bad idea, if I could pull it off. We had all the ingredients. I could make up the custard now, chill it overnight, and churn it up tomorrow.

With nothing else to do (believe me, *nothing*), I went downstairs to start separating the eggs.

By the next day, I'd really settled into my new routine. Open eyes around ten, lie in bed staring through skylight until the sun rises high enough to blind me, then roll reluctantly out of bed for a day of reading and weeping.

The wrench in this day's plan, though, was Caroline. She arrived at nine, hauled me out of bed, and stuck a slice of toast in my hand. Then she barely gave me a chance to brush my teeth before she brutally kidnapped me.

When I stumbled outside with her, I blinked at the stuff piled in a trailer attached to Caroline's bike. In addition to a metal tackle box, a plastic cooler, and a bulging backpack, I saw . . .

"What are those?" I said, my voice full of apprehension.

"Fishing poles," Caroline said with a grin. "My dad's and my brother's."

"We don't fish," I pointed out dully.

"We do now," Caroline said with a grin. "I hear it's meditative."

I shook my head.

"Oh, no," I protested. "I tried meditating yesterday and almost asphyxiated from all the bleach."

"Okay, I'm not going to even ask you to explain that one," Caroline said. She fetched Allison Porchnik from beneath the screened porch and wheeled her over. "Hop on."

Within a few minutes we were sitting at the very end of the pier that jutted off the North Peninsula. I had to admit, after being such a shut-in, hovering out there over the gently lapping waves was blissful, even in the sweltering August heat.

I closed my eyes to soak in the sun for a moment while Caroline began unloading all her equipment.

"What are we going to use to catch these alleged fish?" I asked. "Did you dig for worms or something?"

"Oh my God, Anna. I don't even *eat* fish and I know that saltwater fish don't like worms," Caroline blustered. "They eat *other* fish."

She flipped open the cooler to reveal a plastic bag filled with raw fish chunks.

"Ugh," I said, putting a hand on my stomach. Caroline looked a little green too, but her stubbornness beat out her many food aversions.

"Come on," she said. "We're doing this."

We actually started laughing as we picked up the disgusting

fish chunks and awkwardly threaded them onto the hooks.

"How is it that we're expert ghost crabbers and clam diggers," I asked, "but we've never been fishing?"

Caroline shrugged and grinned as we got to our feet to clumsily cast our lines into the ocean.

I sat back down and propped my fishing pole on the rail of the pier.

"Okay, what do we do now?" I asked.

"I guess we just sit here and wait for a nibble," Caroline said. "Pretty lousy excuse for a sport, huh? *That's* why we've never been fishing."

"Mmm," I said. Now that we were past the giddy novelty of this expedition, I was quickly swinging back to my previous state—tragic and dreary. I drew my knees up beneath my chin, wrapping my arms around my shins. I sighed a shaky, on-the-verge-of-tears sigh.

"It's seriously annoying how much I've cried in the past few days," I complained. "I mean, I'm not—"

"—a crier. I know," Caroline finished for me. "But sometimes you've just got to cry until you're done."

That did it. I buried my face in my knees and wept. Caroline's sympathetic hand on my back only made me cry harder.

"If I'd known how awful it would be to say good-bye to him," I sobbed, "I never would have gone out with him in the first place."

"No, no," Caroline insisted softly. "You won't always feel that way. You know that saying, 'Tis better to have loved and lost . . .'"

I wiped my nose on the back of my hand and wailed, "I always thought that saying was a load of crap."

Caroline gave a quick snort before slapping a hand over her mouth.

"It's not funny," I said, looking at her through what felt like a river of tears. "You're lucky you never have to know what this feels like—"

Suddenly I stopped my soggy rant. I wasn't the only one with boy troubles, I remembered. I hadn't even asked Caroline what had been happening with Sam lately.

Between sniffles and hiccups, I said, "So are things still weird with you guys?"

Caroline allowed a small smile.

"Actually, the other night," she said, "we had our first good, meaty talk in ages. Maybe because we were just sitting on the beach eating huge, sloppy, sno-cones instead of doing the whole Dinner at Eight thing."

"That's good," I said, nodding as I blew my nose in my orange wrap.

Caroline smiled a little wider, then fiddled with the handle of her fishing pole.

"Sam finally came out and told me how much pressure he's been feeling to make this relationship perfect," she said. "So I told *him* that perfect is not only an illusion, it's just no damn fun."

"Good answer." I actually laughed a little. "So . . . what now?"

"I don't know," Caroline said. "I guess we just wait and see. I'm hoping this is sort of like growing out a short haircut. You know if you can just stick it out, you'll be rewarded with long, lustrous locks. Or you could freak out and chop it all off. I'm trying for the long and pretty hair."

"Somehow I actually understood that metaphor," I said. I smiled, if wanly, rubbed the last bit of moisture out of my eyes, then grabbed my sports bottle and held it out toward Caroline.

"Here's to long, lustrous locks," I said.

She grinned and bumped her sports bottle against mine, making a plastic *thunk*. We both took big swigs of iced tea.

Zzzzzzzzzzz.

I looked around.

"What's that sound?" I wondered.

ZZZZZZZZZZ!

Caroline gasped, jumped to her feet, and pointed at my pole.

"Fish!" she shrieked.

"Oh my God!" I cried. I'd forgotten all about our propped-up poles. Whatever it was at the end of my line was pulling so hard, it was threatening to take the pole with it. I grabbed it just in time and scrambled to my feet.

"What do I do?" I yelled.

"Turn the handle thingie!" Caroline said. She was gasping with laughter now. "Reel it in."

I started to crank the handle backward. The fish was really tugging.

"It's big!" I cried. "Help me hold this pole. I'm freaking out here."

Caroline grabbed the pole and I reeled. I reeled and reeled and reeled, but the fish didn't seem to be coming any closer. I peered into the water and didn't see a thing.

"You want some help with that? You're about two reels away from breaking your line."

Caroline and I peeked over our shoulders.

"Sam!" Caroline squeaked.

"Sam," I huffed. "Take this thing, please!"

Somehow, Caroline and I maneuvered the pole into Sam's hands. With some mysterious rhythm, he began pulling at the pole, letting the line zing out, then reeling it back in. At the same time, he chatted with us as if this was the most normal situation in the world.

"Hey, baby," he said to Caroline. "So is this spontaneous enough for you? It doesn't get any less formal than this, am I right?"

Caroline grinned and gave Sam a kiss on the cheek.

"You're right," she said.

They didn't make a big deal out of the fact that, instead of orchestrating some big date night, Sam had moseyed down to the beach just like old times. That he seemed more comfortable in his skin than he had in a long time. And that Caroline was looking at him the way she had when they'd first gotten together.

I think maybe they got over themselves, I told myself.

Sam finally pulled a thrashing, foot-long fish out of the water.

"Redfish!" he announced, exchanging a gleeful smile with Caroline. "Good one!"

I felt myself choke up again, this time from sentimentality. A dull glow of happiness for my friends was bumping up against my own shadowy sadness.

Perhaps it had made a small dent.

But despite Sam and Caroline's sweet efforts, the emptiness I felt in the wake of Will remained.

When I got home, I quickly retreated to my new normal—me brooding on the screened porch while my brother and sister played a noisy prebedtime game of hide-and-seek upstairs.

My parents had given me several nights off from work, but I decided that I would head back the next day. Even if the idea of being out among people (read, *couples*) kind of made me want to walk straight into a riptide, anything would be better than another night stewing alone at home.

Of course, I still had *this* night to get through. A few *ping-ping-ping*s of rain on the porch's tin roof, along with a distant rumble of thunder, were encouraging. A big ol' storm would suit my mood.

The rain's gentle patter quickly became an onslaught.

I got off the porch swing and pressed myself against the screen to catch a whiff of it. The rain smelled dark and acrid as it steamed up the clay and gravel in our driveway. In a few more minutes, I knew, it would start smelling green, as the parched trees and grasses began soaking up the water and coming back to life. When everything had been completely saturated, the night would smell blue. Clean. Renewed.

I wanted to enjoy it. Or *anything* for that matter. But I felt as flat as a pancake.

When I decided to go ahead and freeze the ice cream I'd mixed the night before, it was only because it would kill a half hour. I found myself wondering if the rest of the summer was going to be like this—incrementally trying to fill the Will-free hours.

I went back inside and got the Greek Holiday mix out of the fridge, then pulled the ice cream churn from the pantry. But just as I was plugging it in—*zap!*

The power went out.

I heard a screech from my siblings upstairs, followed by my mother laughing to calm their nerves. Then there was that eerie silence that happens only during a power-out. No humming appliances, no thrumming air conditioner, no ticking oven timer, no nothing.

"Seriously?" I sighed.

It seemed a perfect excuse to just give up and go to bed.

Instead, I glared stubbornly at the plastic container of luscious-looking custard. Then I went back to the pantry. I grabbed the flashlight from the hook on the door, then dug our manual ice cream churn, along with a box of rock salt, out of a dusty corner.

After all, why snuggle up in my nice comfy bed when I could engage in the self-flagellation that was *hand churning* ice cream?

I pulled some ice out of the dark freezer, then brought the whole business outside. I set up the churn on the front steps, where I could get a prime view of the rain from under the eaves.

Then I started cranking.

I almost didn't notice that I'd started crying again. I suppose that was my new normal too. Through my tears I watched the rain puddle in the dirt and splash my outstretched feet. It made

Figgy Pudding's tired leaves do little shimmies; made them shine like they had on the Fourth of Jul—

I closed my eyes, leaned my forehead on my knees, and stopped cranking.

Now I'd gone and done it.

I'd gone back to *that* night.

So many of my dates with Will had seemed charmed, even the completely dorky ones like that putt putt golf outing.

But the Fourth of July had been more than charmed. It had been magic.

That was the night I'd fallen in love with Will.

I'd realized this—that I loved Will—a while ago, but I'd never put it so bluntly into words, even in my own mind.

But now, as I stared at the fig tree and remembered the way we'd leaned against its trunk, kissing and kissing and never wanting the night to end, suddenly the words were there.

I almost said them out loud: *I am in love with Will Cooper.*

Caroline had been right. There'd been no earth-shaking sign of it. No before and after. It was just a feeling that suffused my entire body, the way a hot bath warms you from the inside out on a chilly night.

"What did I *do*?" I murmured. "Why did I let him go?"

I'd told myself so many times since that horrible night of the turtle hatching that I'd done the smart thing, pushing Will away before he could leave me. That I was taking care of myself.

But if that was true, why was I so *broken*? So pathetic?

My tears were angry now. I stamped my foot on the rain-slick steps, spattering myself with water and sand. I went back to cranking the stupid ice cream. I wanted to crank until I got blisters on my palms.

In truth, I wanted to scream my frustration out into the rain, but I knew that would only bring my mother running down the stairs to see what was wrong. So instead I cranked harder, almost glad to feel tender welts begin to rise up at the base of my fingers. As I cranked, I stared out at Figgy Pudding, awash in blissful, painful memory.

And that's when everything stopped—the scenes running through my head, my hand on the ice cream churn, and I'm pretty sure, for an instant, my heartbeat.

Because just beyond the fig tree, at the end of the driveway, a figure had appeared—on a chunky red bike named Zelig.

Will rode toward me, his hair rain-plastered, his T-shirt drenched, and his face looking both hopeful and tortured. His eyes looked about as puffy as mine felt.

I don't remember running down the stairs to the driveway. In hindsight, I'm surprised I didn't fall on the slippery steps and break an ankle.

But somehow, in an instant, there I was. With Will. Rain pelted down on me, soaking me almost immediately. I barely noticed it, much less cared.

Will stumbled off his bike and let it fall to the ground without bothering to kickstand it. Then he stood before me, his arms hanging limp at his sides.

For a long moment we just stared at each other. Looking at his face, I felt like I was getting my first bite of food after starving for days.

"I missed you," Will said. His voice sounded raspy and he was still breathing hard from his bike ride.

I couldn't talk at all, so I just nodded hard.

I reached out to touch his arm, then pulled my hand back again. I'd just been telling myself that I'd been right to end things with Will. Completely miserable, but right.

So now I didn't know what to do.

Will, however, seemed to have arrived with a plan.

"Anna, I've thought and thought about this," he said. "And being apart now *isn't* better than seeing this through the summer. Because *this* is a breakup."

Hearing Will use that term—"breakup"—made tears spring to my eyes again. Over the past few days, I hadn't ever used that expression because it had seemed so melodramatic and ugly.

But Will was right. Melodramatic and ugly was exactly what this was.

"If we stayed together," Will said, "we would have to say good-bye at the end of the summer, yes. But we'd be saying good-bye to something amazing, Anna. Something happy.

"But this?"

Will held his hands out, his palms turned upward.

"This feels awful."

"You're right," I said through the lump in my throat. "Terrible."

"And do you know why?" Will said.

I shook my head, confused.

"Because, Anna . . ."

I saw a flicker of fear in Will's eyes. He looked downward for a moment, the same way he had the other night after the turtle watch. He was considering his next words very carefully.

When he looked up, he took a swift step toward me. He put a hand on each of my cheeks and gently lifted my face so that we were gazing into each other's eyes.

"I love you," he said. He almost yelled it. "And I know that sounds crazy. That's what you say at the beginning of something, not when it's almost reached its end. But—I don't care. I just want to be with you. Maybe it'll only be for these next few weeks. Maybe it'll be forever. We can't know what'll happen, Anna. All I know is *I love you* and . . . we should be together. We just have to be together. We *need* to be together."

I began to sob. I lifted my hands and put them over Will's, which were still cupping my face. His skin was warm beneath the chill of the rain.

And then I was kissing Will; crying and kissing him all at the same time. He wrapped his arms around me and lifted me off the ground. All the hurt and confusion and regret of the past few days flowed off us along with the rain.

When we pulled apart, I turned my face toward the sky, gasping as cold droplets landed in my eyes and mouth and even my ears.

Then, suddenly, my crying turned into laughter. Incredulous, grateful laughter.

I was getting a second chance.

Will was right. Being with him now was worth braving the uncertain future.

This was worth it.

I blinked the rain away, gripped Will by the shoulders, and said, "I love you, too, Will."

Will grabbed me again, so hard it took my breath away, and buried his face in my neck. I felt his shoulders shake for just a moment before his lips were on mine again.

And these kisses weren't about cleansing away our hurt, or healing the rift between us. They were simply, and happily, about sealing the deal—Will and I were together again, for however long we had.

Like Will had said, that *was* an amazing and happy thing. I was finally and absolutely certain of it.

I just *knew.*

I wanted to do so many things with Will before he left. I wanted to walk through all twenty-four of Savannah's historic squares. I wanted to go back to The Swamp, play nothing but slow songs on the jukebox, and dance to them. I was going to teach Will how to eat crawdads, head sucking and all. I was going to invite him to family dinners and private picnics. Or maybe we'd just skip some meals altogether and proceed directly to making out (plus ice cream).

I could have made a to-do list as long as this one on my mom's tattered legal pad.

But I also wanted to do *nothing* with Will. I wanted our last days together to be luxurious, lazy, and most of all, long. I wished I could spend an entire day just drinking in his face, his salty, shampooey scent, the way he looked in those khakis, the way he looked at me. I wanted to memorize all of it, somehow store it away.

The morning after he'd shown up at my house in the rain, I had an idea for a memory to give Will—a part of the island I knew he hadn't seen yet. I wanted him to see it now—with me. And I wasn't going to let the chance slip by, even if it meant waking up at six a.m.

Out of politeness, I waited until six fifteen to call him.

"Hello?" he rasped, his voice cutely sleep clogged.

"Hi," I said. "It's me."

How I loved being able to say nothing more than that and know that it had probably made Will smile, even if he wasn't a morning person. (And he definitely wasn't.)

"You know not *all* of us have skylights above our beds waking us at dawn, right?" Will joked.

He was definitely smiling.

"Oh, I've been awake since before dawn," I said. "Look out your window."

From where I was standing—which happened to be on the deck of Will's cottage—I saw the slats of his window blinds wink open and shut.

Two minutes later, he burst through the door in a frayed green T-shirt, gray cotton shorts, and bare feet. His eyes were still puffy with sleep and his rained-on hair was going every which way, but he was grinning.

When he closed the door behind him and took me in—I was wearing a faded blue sundress dappled with white flowers, my also-rained-on hair ringleting down my back—his smile faded to something more reverent. He all but ran across the deck and wrapped his arms around me. Without a word, he kissed me—a long, hungry, amazing kiss.

A minty one.

"You stopped to brush your teeth before you came out," I noted, a hint of teasing in my voice. "Confident, aren't you?"

"I had a feeling I might get a kiss," Will admitted, his smile sly.

"Just one?" I asked.

It was an invitation and he took it. I have no idea how long we stood there kissing and holding each other tightly. I think both of us were still trying to get our brains around this new reality—that we got to be together again. We could kiss and touch and hold each other to our hearts' content.

At least for another few weeks.

When we finally broke apart, I handed Will the coffee I'd brought for him, lots of milk, no sugar. Then I picked up the canvas bag I'd brought and started down the bridge that led over the dune grass to the beach.

"I want to show you something," I told Will.

"Am I going to need shoes?"

I pointed at my flip-flops, which I'd kicked off the moment I'd arrived. "Do you have to ask?"

Will gave a little laugh, took a big slurp of coffee, then caught up to me so he could grab my hand.

When we reached the beach, I turned right.

"Wait a minute," Will said. "We're going south? Where you might actually be forced to commingle with shoobees?"

"Shut up," I said, veering into him. "I happen to have a new-found respect for shoobees. And besides, nobody's going to be there this early."

"Why are *we* going to be there this early?" Will broached.

"You'll see," I said.

We walked down to the lip of the shore where the sand was slanty but nicely packed for a long walk. I pulled a sports bottle of sweet tea out of my bag, and Will and I walked for a few minutes, silent other than our occasional slurps of caffeine. I watched Will's bare feet make shimmery dents in the wet sand. I drank in his presence, his warm, dry hand in mine, his matted hair breezing off his forehead, his beautiful shoulder just at my eye level.

I pulled him to a stop. I couldn't help it. I *had* to kiss him again before we walked on.

The next time we stopped, it was Will's fault.

"You're so pretty," he said, sounding a bit awestruck. "Can I just look at you for a minute?"

Suffice it to say, it took us a while to get to the spot I'd been aiming for. But finally we were there, a round patch of sand that jutted out into the ocean. Everyone called it the Knee, because as soon as you passed it, the island curved west, making it look a little like a bent leg.

I led Will out to cusp of the Knee and stopped. I pulled my wrap out of my bag and spread it on the sand for us to sit on.

"Wow, this thing has seen better days," Will said as we settled onto the faded orange fabric. He skimmed his fingers over a frayed, unraveling edge and poked his thumb through a sizable hole.

"Yeah, it was a good wrap," I said. "I'll be chucking it soon."

I ran my hand along the rough, wrinkled wrap until it landed on Will's hand.

"Actually, maybe this one I'll save," I said. "I can pull it out one day and remember . . ."

I didn't need to finish my sentence; list all the things I wanted to remember. There were too many anyway.

Will leaned over to kiss me, and we kept on kissing until his stomach growled loudly.

I pulled away, laughing, and reached for my bag.

"How are you hungry when you're usually asleep this time of day?" I wondered. I took out a container of biscuits with honey butter and another of sliced peaches, watermelon chunks, plums, berries . . . summer fruits that would be good for only a short while longer.

I couldn't help thinking that everything was on a countdown now, from the fruit to my wrap to Will. I was no longer letting this fact defeat me, but it still made me feel a tiny bit tragic—and glad that I'd started this, the first of our last days together, early.

I leaned my head on Will's shoulder while he munched the breakfast I'd brought. Both of us gazed out at the water until Will suddenly straightened up, pointing toward the horizon.

"Is that . . . ?" he said. "Anna, *look*."

Even before I spotted them, I knew what Will was seeing. Dolphins. Perhaps fifty of them in a tightly packed school. They leaped out of the water in rhythmic, silvery arcs, racing back and forth in a pattern that clearly made perfect sense to them, even if it was a mystery to me.

"This is fantastic," Will gasped. "I knew there were dolphins here. Owen said he saw them one day when I wasn't around. I always kind of kept an eye out for them, but never saw them myself."

"Well, the Knee at seven a.m. is kind of a sure thing," I said. "They're almost always here, having breakfast. They leap to corral the fish. Something about the water pattern out there brings 'em in droves, I guess."

Will shook his head in amazement and gave me a quick kiss.

"Thanks for the wake-up call," he whispered, before returning his gaze to the school of dolphins.

I watched with him. Dolphins had factored into my childhood fantasies almost as much as mermaids. Those leaps through the air looked so joyful. I didn't want to believe my parents when they told me dolphins leaped for practical reasons, to spot the fish or perhaps shake off barnacles.

Instead I told myself that they were reveling in their freedom, their strength, their ability to swim forever and never stop.

Now it occurred to me, though, that the dolphins never strayed very far. They came back to the Knee every morning, like clockwork. Who knew, maybe they liked their glimpses of people pointing at them excitedly.

Or maybe the dolphins just liked Dune Island itself. At the moment—and not only because it was full of wonders to show Will—I was in love with it, too.

* * *

A couple of nights later, I introduced Will to the Crash Pad behind Caroline's house. Sam was there too. The four of us sprawled on the enormous trampoline and counted stars through the halo of bushy crape myrtle branches.

In Savannah, I'd noticed, the crape myrtles were trimmed into orderly little shrubs—tasteful gateways to elegant mansions. Apparently, that was how those trees were *supposed* to look.

But Caroline lived in a lemon-yellow house as sprawling and janky as my own. The patio furniture was kelly green, there were planters filled with bright, plastic flowers, and the crape myrtles were wild and leggy. The trees were garish and overgrown, just like so much on this crazy, lush island. Being here with Will made me see it all with new eyes, as had happened so many times that summer.

Sam and Caroline seemed shiny and new too, or at least more comfortable with the blurry line between friendship and more-than-friendship. They teased each other, but bookended their jibes with kisses. They spoke in shorthand and private jokes.

From what each of them had told me, they were still adjusting to being SamAndCaroline. Maybe they always would be. (I was starting to get the sense that shifts and adjustments were a constant of couplehood.) But instead of freaking them out, their blips almost seemed to bring them closer together.

"I think I'm getting the hang of it," Caroline told me on the trampoline while the boys were in the house making us all smoothies. "I just kind of fold the maddening parts of being with Sam in with all the good stuff. You know, for better, for worse."

"Wait a minute," I blurted. I'd been lying on my back, but now I sat up. "That's what you say at *a wedding*, Caroline. Is there something you want to tell me?"

"God, no!" Caroline said with a laugh. But to tell the truth, she didn't sound *that* freaked out by the W-word. "I'm just saying, when you commit, you commit to the whole package, that's all. Even if it's not necessarily forever, you know?"

Sam and Will emerged from the house, each carrying two frosty glasses filled with something orange and delicious-looking. They'd even fished around Caroline's kitchen and found some paper umbrellas, no doubt a relic from one of the family's famous luaus.

Will saw me look over at him and grinned. He clinked his two glasses together and lifted one of them in my direction, as if sending me a toast.

I grinned and gave him a little wave, jangling the silver Möbius bracelet on my wrist.

I always thought romance novels were being ridiculous when they used phrases like "Her heart swelled." But being there with my best friends and Will, all of us so full-up with love that it was a wonder we could even think about food, I think I definitely felt some extra *thump-thump*s going on inside me.

With a bit of difficulty I tore my eyes from Will and looked at Caroline.

"Yeah," I replied. I could hear the gratitude and happiness in my own voice. "Yeah, I know."

The smoothies cooled us off a bit, but they also somehow made us more hungry. Lately, I'd been of two minds about food. I was either completely uninterested—*why eat when you can kiss?* Or I was ravenous and everything I ate tasted way more delicious than usual.

Tonight, I was in the latter camp. I wanted to get a shrimp po' boy and lick the remoulade from my fingers. I wanted a slaw dog with extra mustard. I wanted curly fries.

I didn't have to ask anyone twice. We all headed to Crabby's Crab Shack and emerged as they were closing up shop, clutching our overfull stomachs and smelling like deep-fried fish.

Caroline tested the air like she was feeling a piece of fabric, rubbing it between her fingertips.

"Is it possible that it's hotter now than when we went in that place?" she asked.

"Sno-cone?" Will proposed, pointing at the crowd milling in front of The Scoop a block down the boardwalk.

"You know I never go there on my night off," I said, shaking my head firmly. "Especially during the rush. They'll rope me in so fast . . ."

"I'd help," Will said, slipping his arm around my waist.

I knew he would, too. He'd gone back to coming to The Scoop each night at closing time, grinning at me as he flipped the OPEN sign. He'd wipe tables while I squeegeed the windows.

Or we'd stand side by side at the sink in the back, Will rinsing dishes and me loading them into the industrial washer. I'd nudge him with my hip or let my hand linger on his while he passed me scoops and sundae glasses. Then we almost always had to pause for kissing. One night, we just blew off the chores and raided the ice cream case, fixing ourselves a towering sundae for two and kissing between bites.

I'd always thought these post-closing chores were dowdy and domestic, especially when I saw my parents doing them together. But with Will, they were kind of sexy.

Of course, not when we were surrounded by my family and a bunch of customers, so I put my foot down.

"Y'all say hi to my folks," I said to Will, Sam, and Caroline, waving them toward The Scoop. "I'll wait for you out here."

Then I whispered loudly to Caroline, "Just don't let Will scoop any ice cream. The guy makes the most lopsided cones I've ever seen."

"Oh, nice," Will said, stalking toward me slowly with mock menace on his face.

"Uh-oh!" I giggled at Sam and Caroline. "I made it mad."

Will stiffened his fingers into claws and lunged at me.

"Aaaah!" I shrieked. I darted to one of the short staircases leading from the boardwalk to the beach, skipped down it, and started running.

Will laughed as he chased me toward the water. He didn't catch me until I'd hit the surf and turned to run along it, away from the boardwalk. He grabbed me around the waist and spun me around until I cried out, "Stop! I just ate!"

Will put me down and we clutched each other for a moment to keep from falling down in a dizzy, sweaty sprawl. I could feel the muscles in his chest move beneath the soft cotton of his shirt. His arms circled around the small of my back.

And since we were holding each other anyway . . .

Only after we'd been kissing for a good two or three minutes did I suddenly gasp, "Oh, no! I forgot about Sam and Caroline."

Completely mortified, I peeked over Will's shoulder to see if they were watching us from the boardwalk, and possibly sticking their fingers down their throats.

It would serve them right, I thought with a sly smile. *They nauseated me all spring with their kissy-kissy ways.*

As I searched the boardwalk for Caroline's pale ponytail and Sam's slouchy lope, my cell phone rang. I dug it out of my purse.

"Put it on speaker," Caroline said when I answered it.

"Where are you?" I yelled at the phone after I hit the speaker button.

"We're watching your dad shave ice," Caroline said. "You put the bug in our ears."

I covered the mouthpiece and whispered to Will, "I don't think they saw the PDA."

"And don't worry," Caroline added with a cackle. "I won't tell your dad about the hanky panky I just saw on the beach."

"Guess they did," Will said with a shrug.

When you're from New York City, I think you're much less mortified by people seeing your business. Nobody stays home in their tiny apartments, Will had told me, so people do all *kinds* of things right out in the open. Or at least in the backs of taxis.

Speaking of, Will was . . . peeling off his shirt? Then he hopped around on one leg while he pulled off one of his shoes.

"Uh, *what* are you doing?" I asked.

"O*h*-kay, on that note," Caroline said, "good ni-ight."

"No, Caroline!" I screeched. "It's not what it sounds like—"

Click.

Will grinned, took off his other shoe, then unbuckled his belt.

"Okay, really," I said, getting a little nervous. I glanced over my shoulder to make sure nobody *else* was watching us from the boardwalk. "What *are* you doing?"

"Don't worry," Will said, tossing his belt on the sand next to his shoes. "This is as far as I go."

Holding up his khakis with one hand, he started to walk into the water.

"Will." I laughed. "No! I love those khakis."

"A little water's not going to hurt 'em," Will called over his shoulder. "Now, are you coming in or not?"

Had we been on the North Peninsula, I wouldn't have thought twice about following Will into the water in my cutoffs and tank top. But we were a shell's throw from the boardwalk, which was teeming with post-dinner people—both tourists I didn't know and school friends that I did.

I bit my lip. Letting other people see me cavort in the waves with my boyfriend felt kind of like going out in public with my underwear on outside my clothes. On the other hand, skulking around with Will felt even more wrong. If our breakup had taught me anything, it was to embrace the scary. You missed out on too much otherwise.

So with only one more furtive glance to see if we were surrounded (we weren't, but we certainly weren't alone either), I kicked off my flip-flops, carefully slipped my silver bangle inside one of Will's sneakers, and splashed into the water.

As I waded toward Will, he ducked underneath the surface. When he came up, he flicked his hair off his forehead and whooped.

"Oh, that feels *good*!" he said. "What am I gonna do when I don't have an ocean outside my door every day?"

"I can't tell you," I said as I swam toward him, skimming easily over the lazy nighttime waves. "I've never had that experience."

"Man, I can't imagine this being my everyday world," Will said. He shifted onto his back and blinked up at the stars. "It doesn't seem real."

"Right back at ya," I said. "New York is *my* idea of a vacation. A frantic, crazy, sensory-overloaded version of it, anyway. I mean, you ride in elevators and shoot through underground tunnels every day. Do you know how weird that is?"

Will went upright and looked over at me.

"Sometimes it feels like we're from two different countries." His voice wobbled a bit as he said it.

I swam closer still, until my hands were on his bare chest.

"At least we don't speak two different languages," I said softly.

"Oh, no," Will said, one side of his mouth rising a bit, "*y'all* don't think so?"

"Watch it," I growled, "or I'll feed you to the ghost crabs."

"Hey, that's what I can be for Halloween in my building this year," Will said, snapping his wet fingers. "The kids'll be *terrified*. Or really confused. I don't think anyone in New York knows what a ghost crab is."

I grimaced. Halloween? With its Indian corn and pumpkins and nip in the air? Now *that* was surreal. I could barely imagine it.

"At Halloween, it'll have been two months," I whispered.

I didn't have to say *two months we'll have been apart*. Will knew what I meant. He sank deeper into the water, resting his chin on its surface and looking up into my eyes.

"What'll it be like, do you think?" he wondered. "Two months isn't very long."

"It'll feel long," I said. Now my voice was wobbly. "But maybe after that, it will feel less so."

I wondered if *that* would be even worse.

Will pulled me into a sad, salty kiss.

"Forget the ocean," he said. "What am I going to do when I don't have *you* every day?"

I was going to cry. If I didn't kiss Will right then, I was going to cry. So I did kiss him—with a heat and urgency that felt different from before.

We were heading into the end and we both knew it. It was time to weather the bitter and embrace the sweet and suck the marrow out of all the time we had left.

* * *

A couple of nights later, it was Will who had a plan.

"Guess what we're doing tomorrow?" he said as we cleaned up at The Scoop. "I signed us up for something."

I cocked my head.

"You signed us up . . ."

I paused and pondered what was going on on the island the next day. Then I gasped.

"You did not!" I said, slapping at Will with my bleachy rag.

"I did," Will said. "We're entered in that sand castle competition you told me about."

"Will," I sputtered. "People take that competition very seriously. They, like, *train* for it. My sister's been practicing with her girlfriends for months. They're making a re-creation of the Sydney Opera House."

Will snorted.

"You're kidding, right?" he said. "Anna, I don't want to dis your sister, but she doesn't seem like the Sydney Opera House type. Have you guys been to Australia?"

"Oh, please," I said. "We haven't even been to California. But the Sydney Opera House is a big favorite with the sand castle competition. Someone does one almost every year. That and Hogwarts."

Will's eyes went wide and he put a hand on top of his head.

"Oh, man," he said with a laugh. "I didn't know. You'd think for something this hard-core, they would have had an entrance fee or something to keep out the dilettantes. I just went to the chamber of commerce and put our names on a clipboard."

"Oh, well," I said, waving him off. "It's all just for fun."

Then I narrowed my eyes and added, "Grueling, cutthroat, *punishing* fun."

"This is *not* good," Will said. "But wouldn't it be lame to be a no-show? Especially since we got slot number six in the line-up. I think that's pretty close to the main action."

I shook my head in confusion.

"Wait a minute," I said. "When did you sign us up for this thing?"

"Um, I guess it was in July," Will said. Suddenly, he looked a little sheepish. "July fifth, as a matter of fact."

I put a finger to my chin.

"I get it now," I said. "That's why you showed up at my house in the rain. You need a partner for the sand castle competition. You just *had* to get that blue ribbon, didn't you?"

"What can I say," Will said, leaning rakishly on his broom. "I'm a sportsman above all else."

I spritzed my bleachy water in his direction. But after wiping a few more tables, I stopped and turned to him.

"How did you know we'd even be together now?" I asked softly. "When you signed us up in July?"

Will shrugged.

"It just seemed impossible that we wouldn't be," he said.

He walked toward me, trailing the broom behind him.

"Call it a leap of faith," he said, alighting before me and planting a soft kiss on my lips.

I wrapped my arms around his shoulders.

"So you had faith in me?" I asked, half flirting, half serious.

"I had faith in *us*," Will said. "Still do."

Will's broom clattered to the floor as I kissed him. And that was all the talking we did for a long while.

"Will?" I asked the next morning, "have you built a sand castle? Like . . . ever?"

"Well . . . " Will pondered this question as he mucked about our little lot on the South Beach, piling sand, smoothing it, and piling it again.

"I remember one summer when I was a kid," he said, "we went to Long Island and my mom taught us how to make drip castles. You know, where you fill your fist with super-wet sand and just drip-drip-drip it until you have these pointy towers."

I gasped. I would have covered Will's mouth if my hand hadn't been breaded with sand.

"Whatever you do," I said in a low voice, "don't mention drip castles around these folks. It's the sign of a complete amateur."

"I *am* a complete amateur," Will declared without a hint of embarrassment.

I sighed and glanced at the banner hanging directly over our heads. It read FOURTEENTH ANNUAL DUNE ISLAND SAND CASTLE COMPETITION!

I cast shifty looks at the castle builders stationed on either side of us. They, of course, were well into their architectural feats. It was only ten in the morning and I already saw some flying buttresses and six-foot-tall turrets.

If I'd been really brave, I would have walked the whole gauntlet of sandy construction sites to check out the competition. We were placed in a straight line that extended for about half a mile. The castle builders seemed to fit three different profiles.

First there were the gray-haired curmudgeons who'd been doing this forever and worked alone (or perhaps with a couple of cowed grandkids as assistants). They grumbled and growled through their castle building, working as intently as scientists trying to cure cancer.

Then there were the teams, like my sister Sophie's team of six fourteen-year-old girls. They gave themselves cute titles and usually functioned as both competitors and cheerleaders. Whenever things got too quiet along the assembly line, they'd start jumping around in their bikinis, hooting and shouting things like, "Team Patty Cake *rocks*!"

Finally, there was the pathetic minority—tourists who'd joined as a lark and had *no* idea what they were getting into.

Somehow—after a lifetime of looking down my nose at summer people—there I was in the last category. I was a dismal dabbler. No better than a shoobee.

But I loved Will, and he'd made this sweet gesture for me, so I was embracing the humiliation. I'd instructed myself to smile (and smile *big*) when Dune Island High kids strolled by and snickered. I'd agreed when Sophie had begged me to deny that I knew her, much less shared a bedroom and DNA with her.

And I wore sunglasses and a big floppy hat along with my shorts and bikini top.

When Caroline and Sam had stopped by our construction

site a half hour earlier, Caroline had given my wardrobe selection a skeptical squint.

"What?" I said defensively as I adjusted my enormous hat. "It's for UVA protection!"

"Uh-huh," Caroline said. Then she gave my bare brown torso a pointed look. I had the sort of honey-colored complexion that never burned. By this time of the year, my whole body was always as brown as an almond. Between that and the thick layer of SPF 50 I was wearing today, I didn't *really* have to worry about burning.

Caroline shook her head and gave me an indulgent smile. Then she gripped me by my upper arms and looked me straight in the sunglasses.

"Anna," she said, "I love you. I support you. But we can't be seen hanging around with . . . this."

She gestured at the crude beginnings of our castle.

"So we'll see you after you're done, okay?" she said gently.

I nodded somberly.

"I understand," I said. "It's too late for me. Go save yourself."

Then we both laughed so hard that we fell to our knees in the sand, crushing a good portion of the moat around the castle.

"All right, all right," Sam said, helping Caroline to her feet and pointing her toward the lighthouse at the southern end of the island. Every year the chamber of commerce set up a carnival in the lighthouse parking lot to coincide with the sand castle competition. I could already see the distant swing ride, roller coaster, and carousel flinging people about.

"We're getting breakfast, then going to the carnival," Sam said. "See you there?"

"If we make it out alive," I called dramatically, whereupon Will pretended to give me a swat.

"You better curb the attitude, *Allison,*" he said with a grin.

I laughed and smiled at the little laser-printed sign that had been planted in front of our building site. It read STARDUST MEMORIES, BY LEONARD ZELIG AND ALLISON PORCHNIK.

About *that,* I had no objections whatsoever.

Once Caroline and Sam had left, though, and Will and I had gotten to work in earnest, I did have a few complaints. A lot of them, actually. I'd always known sand castle building was hard, but not *this* hard.

"Why couldn't this be an ice cream competition?" I grumbled as I slapped sand around with little plan or purpose.

"Anna, don't take this the wrong way," Will said, "but I'm not the only amateur here."

"I know." I sighed. My experience making sand forts with my siblings had given me exactly *no* edge in this contest. So far all Will and I had done was dig our foundation and assembled a very tall mound of sand, ready for carving.

But since our castle was supposed to be a tall, skinny triangle, our curvy hill was of little use to us.

"Are you *sure* people are going to recognize this building?" I asked Will, peering at the already damp and runny photo printout he'd brought to the beach. "I mean, it's cool, but *I've* never heard of the Flatiron."

"It's the third most famous building in New York," Will said with a shrug. "I guess we could have done the Chrysler Building or the Empire State, but I figured those would be trickier."

"Ya *think*?" I said sarcastically.

I began rifling through our box of tools, which mostly consisted of spatulas and spreaders, buckets and shovels, plastic cutlery and a large spray bottle of sea water. I pulled out a long, floppy cake-frosting knife and tried to shave a section of sand off our mound to make one of the long, flat walls of the Flatiron.

The wall promptly caved in on itself, shedding a big chunk of sand that plopped right onto my foot.

"Okay, it might be time to think about forfeiting," I said, trying not to break out into funeral giggles, which is what Caroline and I call it whenever we laugh at completely inappropriate times. "Or at least taking a swim break."

"No, we can do this!" Will ordered. I could hear a laugh in his voice too. If not for the super-serious builders to the right and left of us, I think we would have kicked our castle attempt down that very minute and gone off for a sno-cone.

But even Will knew that giving up on the sand castle competition would invoke mockery at best, righteous scorn at worst. So . . . we stayed. Will grabbed our spray bottle and started moistening the collapsed wall of the castle.

"We let it get too dry," he said. "If we keep it wet enough, we can keep the shape together, then carve in all these details."

Will pointed at the curvy windows, crown molding, and elaborately decorated bricks of the building in our photo.

"And then we'll be done," Will said, "and we can go do something else. *Anything* else."

"That's all the motivation I need," I said, squelching the last of my giggles. "Let's go."

We got quiet as we heaped our wet sand into a passable Flatiron shape, then got busy with forks, knives, toothpicks, and our ever-present spray bottle. Before long, we'd started carving all the building's beautiful details out of our giant, skinny triangle.

"I still can't imagine," I said as we worked, "growing up with a building like this right down the road. Hundreds of 'em."

Will chuckled.

"'Down the road,'" he said. "That's something you don't hear too many New Yorkers say."

"Oh, God," I groaned. "I'm a bumpkin."

"Bumpkins don't make ice cream flavors like Greek Holiday," Will said, making me hide my face with my hat brim so I could blush proudly. "Anyway, I like it. 'Down the road.'"

"Okay, enough of that," I admonished, returning my focus to the tricky columns at the curved point of the building.

"You're right, though," Will said. "Living in New York is amazing. I take it for granted sometimes, but then something always happens to make me remember that there's no other place like it."

"I want to go back some day," I said. "I always have."

It went without saying that now I had even more reason to want to go back to New York. But I *didn't* say it.

Just like we didn't talk about whether Will and his family might come back to Dune Island the following summer.

We'd silently agreed not to make our last days together all about clinging to fantasies about the future. We didn't propose spending school vacations together or applying to all the same colleges. Because those things might never materialize and we knew it.

It felt better just to be honest. Just to *be*.

Even if now we were being seriously bad sand castlers.

I did allow myself to ask Will one question as I started shaping window frames with a popsicle stick.

"Do you think you'll go to college in New York like Owen?"

"I used to be sure I would," Will said. "But after being away from the city this summer—I mean *really* away—and loving it so much, I wonder if I wouldn't want to do the same thing for college. Maybe go somewhere that's completely different."

"That's exactly what I want to do," I said. "I'm definitely leaving Dune Island, probably the South, too."

Usually when I talked about graduating from high school and leaving (and I've been known to talk about that a *lot*) I felt restless and itchy, defiant and even a tiny bit bitter. Those emotions were so familiar, they'd worn a groove into my life; a permanent sound track that I'd considered unalterable.

But as I told Will my plan, those familiar emotions weren't there.

Which wasn't to say I'd suddenly become a born-again Dune Islander. But now when I pictured myself leaving, I imagined myself as an adventurer, rather than a rebel.

Small towns, as everyone knows, don't like to lose their young people, so I'd always thought of it as a triumph/scandal when someone graduated from Dune Island High, then seemed to disappear forever to the nebulous Up North.

I used to wonder if I'd be one of those disappearing acts, except for brief visits home for holidays and special occasions. But after this summer, I was starting to think that that wasn't how it was going to go for me. Now I pictured my future self—the one who might or might not dart down subway steps with a chic handbag under her arm—coming home often. I saw my sweet, chaotic house as a haven in the world, instead of a shelter that was holding me back from it.

Maybe, like Will's mom, I'd bring my own family back to Dune Island someday and spend a summer exploring all my old haunts.

I didn't know if Will would be a part of that future, but I *did* know that he was partly responsible for my new vision of it. Just like Will, I'd taken my home for granted. And *he'd* been the something that had made me remember there was no other place like it. He'd made me realize that having the ocean outside my door was a gift, not a given.

He'd made me want to leave Dune Island—but not flee it.

After four hours of packing and carving, our Flatiron Building wasn't great. It wasn't even good. But it was finished.

"All that work!" Will huffed as he gave our castle a final spritz of water to make sure everything set. "And it's just going to be washed away by the tide tonight."

"You do know that those other folks probably put twice as much time into their castles, don't you?" I said. I'd just used a trowel to smooth Fifth Avenue out in front of our building.

"Yeah, but it only looks like they put in thrice as much time,"

Will scoffed. It took me a moment to process what he'd just said and then I laughed—wearily, but still.

I tossed my floppy hat and sunglasses into the toolbox along with all our other makeshift tools. Then we stashed the box behind our castle and I took a deep breath.

"Well," I said to Will with a wry smile, "let's go congratulate the winners."

"Now where's the optimistic Anna that I know and love?" Will asked, wrapping his arm around my sweaty, sandy waist and giving me a squeeze.

I turned to him with wide eyes.

"Do you even *know* me?" I blurted.

"Um, Anna," Will said, "I was being sarcastic."

"Oh," I said. We stumbled down the beach gaping at one unspeakably brilliant sand castle after another, including Sophie's opera house, which was huge and elegant.

I shook my head to clear it.

"I think all the manual labor—not to mention our impending disgrace—has left me a little impaired," I said.

"I've got something for that," Will said, pointing to the carnival.

"Oh yeah, the carnival," I said sleepily. "I'd almost forgotten."

"I think you forgot something else," Will said. "It's not *us* who are going to come in last place in the competition. It's Allison Porchnik and Zelig!"

I *had* forgotten that. I grinned at Will.

"Our poor bicycles," I said. "They must be horrified that we roped them into this *crazy* scheme."

"You're right!" Will cried. "I was a fool, Allison. It won't happen again."

I stopped clowning then.

Of *course* it wouldn't happen again.

Every time Will or I inadvertently said something like that, it shut us up quick. Then we had to glance away from each other and swallow hard until the moment passed.

"I'll make it up to you with cotton candy," Will whispered in my ear before planting a sweet kiss on my cheek.

"You better," I said. "*And* frozen lemonade."

With that, we forgot about sand castles entirely and went to the carnival.

We found Caroline and Sam quickly after we arrived and dragged them to all the rides—the bumper cars, the small roller coaster, and the spinning teacups.

My favorite ride was the giant wheel of swings that simply spun us around in long, lazy loops. We weren't whipped about or turned upside down. We just made swoop after swoop around a giant ring with flashing lights and chimey organ music. The swings made me feel windblown and free after my very grounded morning of castle building.

When our feet touched the ground after the swings came slowly to a stop, I clapped my hands like a little kid and cried, "Let's go again!"

So we did.

We ended up skipping the cotton candy in favor of corn dogs and blooming onions, which we ate while we played the silly carnival games.

Will and I both failed to lob Ping-Pong balls into a row of glass milk jugs, so we moved on to the contraption where you tried to ring a bell by pounding a pedestal with a giant hammer. A roly-poly guy was manning the game in front of a table piled with stuffed animals and plastic prizes. Among them, I recognized the hot pink boa constrictor that had been twined around Figgy Pudding on the Fourth of July.

I touched the garish plush lightly and pointed it out to Will. "Do you remember that?" I asked.

"I'll never forget that," he whispered in my ear. "I'll never forget a bit of that night."

I leaned into him. Who knew if that was true. Who knew if that was even possible. But I wanted to believe, as much as Will did, that all these days and nights together *would* stay with us, etched like a tattoo into our memories.

Sam broke into our bubble by offering the heavy hammer to Will.

"Naw, you go first," Will said. "I'll watch your technique."

"Watch and learn, buddy," Sam said with a grin. He planted his feet and swung the hammer. It hit the end of the pedestal, which seesawed to send a little metal disc zinging up a cord toward the bell. The disc hovered for a moment *just* below the bell, then plummeted back down.

"Awww," Sam groaned.

Then it was Will's turn. He flexed his muscles at me, waggling his eyebrows.

"Sah-woon!" I joked in a high-pitched girly voice. Of course,

I *was* actually admiring the way Will's arms looked as he hoisted the hammer—all sinew and muscle and smooth, tan skin.

Will pretended to spit on his palms, then swung. Once again the metal disc seemed to slow down just before it hit the bell. But it *did* hit it.

Or rather, it just barely tapped it, making the weakest ding in the history of bells.

"Sorry!" the carnie yelled. "Try again!"

"Aw, that counted!" Sam yelled with a grin. "C'mon, dude. Throw the guy a bone. Or at least these giant sunglasses."

Sam plucked a pair of preposterous lime-green glasses off the table and put them on.

"Nope!" the carnie said, pulling the prize off Sam's face and shooing us away. "Move it along, kids."

"I was robbed," Will complained. "I guess you think me less of a man now, Anna?"

Caroline hooked her arm through mine and whispered in my ear, "Can you imagine being here with boys who actually *cared* about winning these things?"

"Yes, I can," I said with a shudder.

I grabbed Will's hand with my free one and squeezed it hard. I loved how different he was from so many competitive-about-everything guys.

I loved how much fun he was having at this dinky carnival and how much fun *I* was having because I was here with him.

I supposed I was just giddily in love. It was as simple as that.

Or so it felt right then, when Will was still so solidly here.

How many times had I wished I could freeze a moment with Will and just live in it, luxuriate in it, forever? It was a silly wish, but I couldn't help making it over and over. I wrapped my arm around Will's waist as we left the midway, feeling grateful for the wish, even if I couldn't have the actual phenomenon.

Very soon after that, the moment really did have to end because I had to go to work. The Scoop was always slammed on the day of the sand castle competition.

"I'll come by later," Will promised me. "After I have dinner with my mom and Owen and, of course, go to the sand castle judging."

"You're going?!" I laughed. "What, the big hammer thing didn't bruise your ego enough?"

"That thing was rigged," Will said, flexing his biceps at me again.

I laughed and because of all the people milling around us, gave him a quick kiss on the lips. But I wished it could have been much, much longer.

Later that night, Will marched into The Scoop, dodged around the swarm of people peering into the ice cream cases, and slapped a muddy brown ribbon onto the counter.

"Our prize!" he announced proudly.

I stared at the rosette-free ribbon. In small gold letters it said PARTICIPANT.

"Participant!" I sputtered. "Not even honorable mention?"

"Would you rather it say 'last place'?" Will asked.

"Good point," I said with a laugh. I started to take the ribbon but Will snatched it away.

"I'm keeping this for posterity," he said. "It's much cooler than my childhood baseball trophies."

I thought of the little keepsake drawer in my bathroom and wondered if Will had one of his own.

Then suddenly my mind zipped into a distant future in which I was poking around in my vanity drawer for a walk down memory lane. I pictured myself pulling out the toothpick I'd saved from my first date with Will. I wondered if it would make me get dreamy and smiley, or if I'd be all tragic soul-searching.

Where will I be then? I wondered. Who *will I be?*

Not that I had time to get philosophical. I had a long queue of hot, sandy customers clamoring for something cold. So I shook myself out of my daydream and smiled at Will. Adopting my best aren't-you-a-pathetic-little-puppy voice, I said, "It's a *great* ribbon, honey. Now what I can I get you? The Greek Holiday's going quick."

"Mmm," Will said. "How about Pineapple Ginger Ale."

Oh, great. That only made more memories wash over me. I looked away from Will. If he added anything else to this bitter-sweet brew of mine, I was going to have to retreat to the cooler, where I could become a puddle in private.

Instead, I was jolted out of my brooding by the high-pitched whoops of a gaggle of girls coming into The Scoop. When I turned, I saw that one of them was my sister, waving a red ribbon over her head. Her friends surrounded her, pumping their French-manicured fists in the air and shimmying their hips.

"Se-cond place!" they chanted. "Se-cond place!"

"Sweetie!" cried my mom, who was working the cash register. She waved at Sophie. "That's wonderful!"

As a fellow castle builder, I finally understood *just* how wonderful second place was. A simple thumbs-up wouldn't do. I handed my ice cream scoop to my mom and scooted around the counter. Then I gave my sister a big hug.

"Congratulations!" I exclaimed. "We saw your opera house. It really was amazing."

From behind me, Will added, "It was awesome, Sophie."

"Thanks!" Sophie said. She glanced down at my arms, which were still wrapped around her, and gave me a look that meant, *You're weird*.

But she quickly followed it up with a sweet smile.

"I saw your castle too," she said. "It was . . . well, it was nice? Um, what was it?"

"The Flatiron Building," Will piped up. "It's the third most famous . . ."

Will trailed off as Sophie's teammates began chanting again and my sister, as always, got sucked into the center of her social circle.

Through the crush of girls, I gave Will a *don't sweat it* smile.

He returned it with a smile I'd learned to recognize. The one that meant *I'm crazy about you*.

Me too, I thought with a deep, shuddery breath. *Me too.*

Then I went back behind the counter to make Sophie a Diet Coke float with chocolate chip ice cream, and scoop up some Pineapple Ginger Ale for Will. His favorite.

The next thing I knew, I was waking up and it was August 28.

It was a day when all I wanted was routine. I wanted to go with Will for a lazy swim and a long, luxurious bike ride. I wanted to go to work and have him show up at nine like he always did.

But there was nothing routine about this day. Instead, there would be Will returning Zelig to the bike shop and packing and cleaning the cottage and having his last Dune Island moments with his family.

And me there for all of it, my heart threatening to explode.

In the morning, I went to Will's house. When I got there, his T-shirts were in a neat stack on the bed. I *loved* Will's T-shirts, so soft and worn and perfect-fitting.

When Will left the bedroom to help his mom with something in the kitchen, I sat down next to the T-shirt stack and gave it a little pat.

Then I laid my cheek down on it. The shirt on top—a light blue tee with a faded navy crew neck—was as soft as always. But without Will's torso inside of it, it didn't move me at all.

In fact, it made me feel unspeakably empty.

"Anna?"

I bolted upright to see Will standing in the doorway, trying not to laugh.

"Shut up!" I said. "Hey, at least I wasn't *smelling* your shirts. They always do that in the movies, have you noticed?"

"I know," Will said shaking his head. "Cheesy."

"So do you want to say good-bye to The Room?" Will said, pointing across the hall to his mother's orange-and-brown lair.

"Eh, that's okay," I said. "I'll say good-bye to your mom and Owen, though."

They were eating breakfast on the deck. As we walked through the tchotchke-clogged living room to the back door, I felt a wave of grief wash over me. This house, with a suitcase by the door and another splayed out on the dining room table, already felt stale and empty. Lifeless. Will-less.

Out on the deck, Owen took a break from a massive bowl of cereal to give me a bear hug.

"Hell of a summer," he said, shooting Will a not very Owen-ish look of concern. "Anna, I will think of you every time I see a ghost crab."

"I think I've just been insulted," I said with a laugh.

"Definitely not," Owen said, giving me his usual devilish grin. "Definitely not."

Ms. Dempsey's good-bye hug was more fragile. When we looked at each other, both our lower lips were trembling.

"Oh, Anna," she said, her voice filled with lots of things—sympathy and worry, but also joy and maybe a vicarious twinge.

"Are you glad you came back?" I asked her. "Was the summer what you hoped for?"

"I think I'll need to ponder that for a while before I know," Ms. Dempsey said. "But you know what? I think so.

"And it was *lovely* knowing you, my girl," she added, her smile looking more mommish now. "Now, you guys go on. Have a good day."

She gave my hand a quick squeeze.

I wondered for the first time if Ms. Dempsey knew exactly what I was going through; if she'd fallen for a boy on Dune Island, too, long, long ago.

If I'd had more time maybe I would have asked her. But there was so little time left. And Allison and Zelig had one last ride in them.

"Are you ready?" Will asked.

I nodded eagerly, and with a last little wave to Will's family, I followed him down the steps to the road.

We rode up and down Highway 80. We swooped back and forth across the highway, passing each other at the road's center line. It was a habit we'd developed during our many bike rides that summer, in which the destination had mattered so little that half the time, we'd just given up on it and kept pedaling.

We'd become experts at that center-of-the-road crisscross, even high-fiving sometimes as we passed each other. But today we were clearly off our game. At one point, we came so close to each other, we almost crashed. Will skidded to the side of the road and had to jump off his bike to avoid falling. He took a few stumbling steps, then stopped himself with his hands to keep from face planting into the gravel.

We looked at each other and shook our heads at our own patheticness.

I motioned northward with my head.

"Let's go, huh?"

Will nodded, picked up his bike, and we headed to the North Peninsula.

Our beach.

I was happy to see that it looked as deserted as ever when we got there, maybe even more desolate than usual with its sun-fried dune grasses and the CLOSED sign on Angelo's door. (Angelo always took his vacation between the tourists' departure and Labor Day.)

I unfurled my desiccated wrap from around Allison's handlebars and dropped it on the sand near the water. I quickly peeled off my shorts and tank top. Underneath I was wearing my blue flower-print two-piece, because it was my favorite—and I knew it was Will's favorite too.

We were silent as we waded out past the breakers. Then, once we were up to our necks in the water, we circled each other, our faces somber. Will swallowed hard. Then *I* swallowed hard.

But just as I thought we'd both buckle under the weight of all these *lasts*—last bike ride, last swim, last date—Will lifted his feet and swam splashily toward me. And I remembered—in the water, you're weightless.

So I floated too. And then we were floating together, kissing and kissing, our arms and legs tangled up, hanks of my long, wet hair sticking to Will's bare shoulders. I didn't quite know where he began and I ended. I was only aware of his lips on my lips, on my neck, on my shoulders, his hands skimming over my body, memorizing it, while I did the same.

I love you, I love you.

We said it over and over again.

I felt a quick flutter of my old desire—to just duck beneath the waves, do my mermaid kick, and head out to sea. This time I wanted to take Will with me.

But instead, I looked at the sun, which was already going slanty in the sky, and told Will that it was time to go.

We'd floated a good bit away from our shoes and clothes, and the walk back to them gave our swollen lips a chance to start returning to normal.

We rode back to the boardwalk together, but I headed for home before Will went to return Zelig to the bike rental shop. For some reason, *that* was a "last" I couldn't bear to watch.

While Will had a last Dune Island supper with his mom and Owen, I took a long bath to get ready for our date that night. As I combed out my hair and put on makeup at the vanity, I opened my little keepsake drawer, dug beneath the note paper and the sea glass, and found that little plastic toothpick from the Dune Island Beach Club.

It was hard to imagine how guarded and clueless and terrified I'd been on our first date; hard to fathom the fact that I hadn't *always* known Will, and loved him, the way I did now.

It was even harder to believe that I'd known him for less than three months.

The fact that after tomorrow I might never see him again was the most difficult to envision. I didn't want to, anyway. Like Will always said—there'd be time for that later.

Instead, I slipped on my silver bangle and a swishy,

long-skirted white sundress and headed out the door, feeling the same flutter of comfortable excitement I always felt when I left for a date with Will.

And I went right on feeling fluttery and excited until Will and I sat down for dinner that night. We'd decided to go to Fiddlehead, one of Dune Island's fancier restaurants. (Will had promised to eat light with his family.) We sat at a low-lit, imposing table, complete with burning candle, basket of artisanal bread, and massive, leather-bound menus.

The place was beautiful.

The menu was impressive, too, all iced platters of raw oysters, high-grade steaks, and buttery pastas. The ambiance was pure, manufactured romance.

It was also purely *wrong*. For us.

"I feel like I have to whisper in here," Will whispered, leaning across the table.

"I feel like I should be wearing a corset," I responded.

I threw my head back, looked at the bronze-painted, pressed-tin tiles on the ceiling, and felt miserable.

And I didn't want to feel miserable tonight. We didn't have *time* for that. So suddenly I stood up. I grabbed my purse from the back of my chair and rifled through it, pulling out a ten-dollar bill. I tossed it on the table.

"What are you doing?" Will sputtered.

"That's for the bread and the waters and a tip for the server," I said, grinning at Will. "You've already eaten with your mom and Owen anyway, and I'm not hungry. Let's go!"

Will got to his feet so fast, he almost tipped his chair over.

We gritted our teeth to keep from guffawing into the ambiance, then dashed out the door.

We made a quick, surreptitious stop at The Scoop for a soft cooler with a long strap, an ice pack, and a couple of pints of ice cream.

And then, holding hands, we headed south.

"Where are we going?" Will said as we walked down the sandy sidewalk that led from the boardwalk toward the lighthouse.

"I can't believe I never got around to taking you here," I said. "I'm just glad it's a clear night."

"Where?" Will almost yelled.

"You'll see," I said. "We're almost there."

Before we reached the lighthouse parking lot, we veered left onto a gravel road, which culminated after about a quarter mile at . . .

"The water tower?" Will said, peering up at the giant, oblong tank on top of a crisscrossing network of steel stilts. "Seriously?"

"Oh yeah," I said. "It's great during the day, but it's magic at night." We walked around the tower until we reached its ladder. I kicked off my sandals, slung the long handle of the ice cream cooler across my chest, and started climbing.

"You're not afraid of heights, are you?" I thought to ask when I was halfway up the ladder.

"I'm a New Yorker!" Will scoffed.

"There *are* a few tall buildings there, aren't there?" I laughed.

We crab-walked up the curved side of the water tower until we were in the center of the tank, which was spacious and fairly flat.

Then we sat with our backs to the lighthouse and the ocean. We gazed out at the skinny, bent-leg shape that was Dune Island. In the moonlight, the swamp grasses undulating in the breeze looked almost mystical, like a fluttering golden cloth. The swamp pools were like tiny islands themselves, black shapes stretching out toward the mainland, looking like a work of abstract art.

"See what I meant about the shapes in the pools?" I said to Will. "They're better than clouds."

"Huh," Will said, squinting at the landscape. "All I see are a whole lot of Jesuses!"

I burst out laughing and threw myself at Will, hitting him so hard that he fell backward. He laughed too, and coughed a bit when he hit the tank.

We lay there for a moment, with my top half laying on his, looking into each other's eyes. And then we were kissing, our bodies pressed together as close as we could get them. But after a moment, the sobs that I'd held in so valiantly all day broke free. I buried my face in Will's shoulder and cried so hard, I could barely speak. He stroked my hair, held me tightly, and didn't try to quiet me.

"I can't do this," I cried.

It was the same thing I'd said to him the night we broke up. Then I didn't think I'd had the strength to be with Will.

Now I didn't think I could be *without* him.

But I had to.

The thought threatened to set off another bout of tears, but instead I turned to Will and put my hands on his shoulders. I looked into his eyes, which were drawn downward by a new sadness now, and got pragmatic.

My curfew was at eleven. I had ninety minutes left with Will. And I didn't want to waste them.

I swiped the tears off my cheeks. Then I peered over Will's shoulder at the swamp and said, "I actually do see a shape. I think it's a canoe."

Will nodded slowly. He understood what I was doing. So he looked too.

"Um, I see a turtle over there," he said, pointing at a round patch.

"Oh, please," I scoffed, "turtles are the easiest ones to spot. Hey, do you see that trombone?"

"Seriously? A trombone?" Will laughed. "Now you're just being ridiculous."

"I know," I said, snuggling into him, my arms wrapped around his waist.

"I can picture you at your school in New York," I said. "I'm seeing a blazer with a crest and a striped tie."

"Sorry to disappoint you," Will said, "but we don't even wear uniforms."

After a pause, Will said, "I wonder if I'll be different now. At school. At life. You know, after you."

I squeezed Will a little harder and thought of my own life before this summer. I'd held so much, and so many, at a distance lest they prevent me from breaking away from Dune Island. Would *I* be different?

I hoped so, at least in some ways.

I looked into Will's eyes again.

In a good way, I thought before I closed my eyes and kissed him.

When it was too dark to see anything but Will's watch, which said ten forty-five, we carefully climbed back to earth.

"We forgot to the eat the ice cream," Will said, pointing at the cooler hanging from my shoulder.

"I know," I said. I handed it to him. "Take it home with you. For your mom and Owen. Maybe they're still awake."

We held each other for a long, long beat. Our kisses felt endless, but also way too brief. Tears streamed from my eyes, but I managed not to sob for this moment.

Finally, Will cleared his throat.

"I think I need to walk home by myself," he said. "I don't want to say good-bye with suitcases and boxes and stuff all around us."

Our eyes were open during our last kiss. Will's lips were so soft, so delicious. His eyelashes fluttered with the pain he was feeling and I felt them brush my own. I pulled away and smoothed his hair back from his face so I could look at him, really look at him, one last time.

Will kissed my forehead, softly and sweetly and so, so sadly. Then we drew away from each other, our arms outstretched and our fingers touching until we finally pulled them apart.

I watched Will walk away until I couldn't see him anymore.

Then I went home myself, crying until I literally couldn't anymore.

That feeling, of having no tears left, somehow felt even worse than all the crying. I felt dry. Passionless.

I wondered if I'd ever feel passionate about anything again.

After every date with Will, I'd fallen into a deep, heavy, happy sleep.

After this one, of course, I couldn't sleep at all. I don't think I even *tried*. I just lay on my back under my skylight, staring through the clear night sky at the stars.

At two a.m. I got out of bed without even really deciding to. Suddenly I was just up and slipping into a pair of cutoffs and a tank-top. As I tiptoed across the room, carrying my flip-flops, I stared at my sister in her bed, willing her to stay asleep. Then I slipped out of our room.

My parents slept with a machine that piped the sound of waves and gulls into their room, as if they didn't get enough ocean sounds living on an island. So it was easy to tiptoe my way out of the house without them hearing. I didn't feel even a twinge of guilt. I was certain I wasn't doing anything wrong.

As I pedaled down Highway 80, I also didn't worry about how I was going to rouse Will from his bed. I think somehow I knew he wouldn't be in it.

Sure enough, when I arrived at his stretch of beach, there he was. He was gazing out at the waves with his hands dug deep into the pockets of his khakis, his bare feet scuffing at the sand.

He didn't even seem surprised when I came up behind him and touched his shoulder. He simply wrapped his arms around me and buried his face in my neck. We stood there, swaying slightly in the wind coming off the waves, breathing each other in.

We walked along the beach for a long time. And when we were tired of walking, we lay down, Will's arms around me, my head on his chest.

There was nothing left to say. We just lay entwined on the sand, listening to each other's heartbeats during the pauses between waves.

We fell asleep like that, and didn't wake until the sun began to rise. We sat up to watch it, all flaming, pink-orange shimmers and golden beams. I rested between Will's legs, leaning back against his chest. He clasped his arms around my shoulders, holding me close.

Just as the sun broke free from the horizon, Will spoke. His voice was gravelly.

"I don't know what's going to happen with us, Anna," he said. "But I'm always going to love you. *That* I know."

I knew it too—that I would always love Will, even if I never saw him again.

I knew it as I walked him back to the rickety bridge that led to his cottage.

I knew it as we luxuriated in one final, delicious kiss and as we said good-bye for real this time. In a few hours, Will would go back to that foreign country of subways and elevators and I would remain in this lush habitat where it never snowed and you could hear the sizzle of the surf everywhere you went.

As I pedaled my bike slowly home, I realized one more thing. I didn't have to wonder if I'd ever be passionate or happy again. I *was* happy, even as I tasted tears on my lips, along with Will's last kiss; even though part of me dreaded this day, my first without Will.

I was happy because I knew I'd never forget Will. Even if parts of this summer faded from my memory over time, even if Will's face grew vague in my mind, I'd never forget what it had felt like to be with him for a few short months. What it had been like to be sixteen and in love for the first time.

I wouldn't forget *that*—not ever.

Many thanks to . . .

Emilia Rhodes, for giving me quite the summer.

Micol Ostow, for being a lovely yenta.

Sonya McEvoy, Katherine Moore, Laurel Snyder, Melanie Regnier, and Alissa Fasman, wonderful friends who pitched in with playdates.

Morelli's Gourmet Ice Cream & Desserts and King of Pops in Atlanta, for the ice cream inspiration.

Our beloved granny nanny, Bunny Lenhard, who did too many above and beyonds to list.

Mira and Tali, who bounced through this crazy summer with so much cheer and charm.

And Paul, who kept me going with tremendous support, lots of housework, and most of all, inspiration for a love story.

Michelle Dalton is the pen name for Elizabeth Lenhard, who is the author of more than fifty books for kids and teens. They include the Chicks with Sticks trilogy and *Our Song* (in the Flirt series). Elizabeth lives in Decatur, Georgia, with her husband and two daughters, who are finally old enough to read some of her books. (Just not the "kissing ones.")

The *New York Times* Bestseller

FAMILY SECRETS. UNEXPECTED ROMANCE.
THRILLING ADVENTURE.

EBOOK EDITION ALSO AVAILABLE

SIMON PULSE
simonandschuster.com/teen